A CROW NAMED
Torment

SILAS A. BISCHOFF

MORBID
TASTE
PUBLISHING

Editing by Catherine Dunn of Stardust Book Services
Cover Art and Illustrations by Hernán Conde de Boeck

Hardcover ISBN: 978-3-9826509-0-6
Trade Paperback ISBN: 978-3-9826509-1-3
eBook ISBN: 978-3-9826509-2-0

First Edition, 2024

Published by Morbid Taste Publishing
Tonhallenstraße 21
47051 Duisburg
GERMANY
www.morbidtastepublishing.com

To Jed, Mike, Rob and Dyrk from the Wizards, Warriors & Words podcast for inspiring and motivating me long after they had already pulled the plug on their show.

'A symbol of spite and sin, yet playfully innocent and truly empathetic. Both clumsy and the embodiment of elegance and wit. With its driven and contradictory nature, the crow suffers more than any other beast, save the human ape itself, from the human condition.'

—Ogden Flynt, *Spirits between Earth and Sky*, Vol. 1

Chapter 1

A DROP OF BLOOD

IT HAD NO name or hopes or great ambitions, but it had dark wings and a dark purpose. It carried insidious whispers from the Baroness of Quelm, who constantly plotted murder and deceit and sowed discord among her many enemies. It carried them in a little capsule tied to its little talons, and it was eager to fulfil its duty, for each capsule delivered promised a reward of red and shiny meat, dripping with blood, and perhaps a pair of eyeballs if it was lucky.

Above, through the attentive little beads it had for eyes, it caught sight of the flaming thread that stretched from the sun to the heart of the city. The crow remembered a dream it once had in its cage, and it let out a vigorous caw. In that dream, it had followed the burning band on high, along which had scurried swarms of the tiny long-tailed morsels that were usually found on hot stones and in rocky crevices. It had hunted them, and at the end of the fiery band it had found the Crow All-Mother, sublime and black as the night. She who had cast her fledgling kin into this wicked world and abandoned them, as all mothers must. She who was no creature's prey, who roamed free where play and food and wonderful treasures abounded. It envied her.

Below, it saw the One City glide past – a labyrinthine sprawl of buildings stacked upon buildings piled upon more buildings, connected by a cobweb of footbridges and ladders and ropes and filled with the many strange things of men. It was all the crow knew of the earth. Even if it let its black-feathered wings carry it so high above the clouds that its little head became all dizzy, it would not see the end of this city. The sprawl stretched far beyond the horizon. It was a mountain of man-made structures, the peak of which disappeared behind an ever-brewing storm from whence the sun's burning band erupted.

The crow didn't give any of this much thought, however. It was a perfectly normal crow. It thought of the wind in its feathers, of juicy red meat and pretty little else. At the moment it was thinking of a nice little breather from this long flight, and it had its eye on a shiny brass dome on top of an exceptionally high-rising human dwelling.

As it approached the tall structure, an open segment appeared in the dome, and from its shadowed interior shone a gleam of glass that piqued the crow's curiosity.

Flying in for a landing, it discovered the glass to be a convex disc set into the outer end of a long metal cylinder, and it perched comfortably on the lower edge of the frame. This was a good elevated resting place. The circular glass, roughly the same size as the crow, was interesting and shiny and made satisfying *clink* noises when the crow pecked at it.

Peering around the edge of the frame into the murky interior of the dome, the crow noticed a human male standing bent over the opposite end of the cylinder. This human was clutching a thick woollen cloak by the collar and had his eye pressed to the end of a small tube.

'By all the immortals,' the man muttered, tapping the side of the instrument, 'what's wrong with this cursed thing?'

Hearing the human speak, an idea flashed through the crow's mind – one of many that had been imprinted upon it as a fledgling. This place was called the Tower of Undreamed Truths – a sequence of sounds that, if uttered by the baroness's crow master, would convey the utmost urgency to bring hither a capsule like the one on its leg. The prospect of the reward of succulent carrion this would bring – and the memory of the pain that would follow failure – drew an excited caw from its throat.

The human looked up with a discontented expression.

A human's attention always gave the crow ambivalent feelings. It cawed again, looking at him askance – a plea for the human to reveal his intentions.

'Pesky critter,' he muttered, raising a hand. 'Off the lens with you.'

But then the man stopped. His gaze wandered briefly to where the glass was aimed: the lightning-ravaged maelstrom of clouds swirling around the city's summit. The man and the crow looked at each other, the former's eyes alight with inspiration, the latter's with suspicion … and two fates were sealed at that moment.

Tilting its head, the crow watched the human approach cautiously along the side of the long cylinder. It was not supposed to interact with any human except the crow master and the recipient of its capsule. This particular specimen, however, was holding a peculiar shiny thing. The crow was very fond of shiny things. The human, threatening though he seemed, had just taken the thing out of his coat and was now presenting it to the crow. Primal instincts compelled the crow to marvel at the shiny thing, and the shiny thing in turn compelled the crow to freeze, binding it with shimmering, mesmerising shapes of reflected light.

~

IT CAWED AND croaked and clawed and pecked at the metal bars. It rattled the cage with angry flaps of its wings, proclaiming its plight with all the force it could muster. But no one but an observant black cat could hear its lamentations – which did nothing to alleviate the crow's distress. The hungry-eyed predator sat upright on a ledge above the crackling fireplace, its pricked ears twitching at every squawk.

The human had tricked the crow, had grabbed it with his squishy, naked man-talons. The fleshy appendages of humans were meant to fiddle with the crow's capsules, perhaps, or put food in its beak, but not to wrap themselves around its body and carry it away, tugging uncomfortably at its feathers. It became increasingly clear that making a racket wasn't helping, so the crow reluctantly calmed down, settling for the occasional indignant croak as it surveyed its new surroundings, looking for a way out.

This human nest was filled with human things stranger than any human things the crow had ever encountered. Many-coloured lights emanated from many-shaped vessels containing curious liquids and powders. Complex and confusing smells wafted through the room – smells that were nothing like the icy smell of the sky, or the enticing smell of meat, or the comforting smell of its murder up high in the crowery of Castle Quelm. Then, of course, there was the disquieting, musky presence of that cat, the crow's natural enemy.

The feline foe stood up on all fours, arching its back, black fur bristling as it groaned with relish. The beast's mouth opened wide enough to fit the crow's head in entirely, and the teeth it exposed seemed capable enough of breaking its neck with ease. The crow shook uneasily. With a graceful leap and silent, pinpoint steps the cat started to make its way through the clutter, along the delicate shiny instruments and the stacks of strange thin sheets of animal skin upon which humans painted symbols. The cat traversed this chaotic territory like a ghost, snaking tracklessly around the objects on its way to the crow's cage.

Coming to a halt before the grate, the cat sat down and eyed the crow intently. The crow eyed back, its hooked beak twitching to the side as it turned its right eye on the cat, inspecting the tiny quivers of its whiskers.

The cat's eyes widened at the rapid movement. A hunter's urge. The crow's heart raced in anticipation of violence. But, surprisingly, the cat suppressed its predatory instinct and instead raised a paw, pressing it against a symbol-painted sheet that, unlike the others, was attached to the wall. Its paw rested next to a row of squiggly lines of ink that meant nothing to the crow whatsoever. Then it turned its gaze on the crow, looking at it like humans so often did when they were spouting their human words and expected the crow to understand.

When the crow did not react, the cat lowered its paw and let out a disappointed mewl. It behaved altogether not very cat-like, thought the crow.

A sudden noise drew the crow's attention to the opposite end of the room.

'You hear how they call you the *stormgazer*?' said a chubby human female in a simple blue robe as the crow's captor pushed her gently through the open door.

'What of it? It aptly describes what I do – even has a nice ring to it.'

The woman walked two paces into the room, looking around with a crease above her eyes. In her hand she carried a small obsidian dish sealed with a lid.

'They are mocking you.'

Unsettlingly, the cat appeared to be listening to this human babbling with amused interest, and its yellow eyes shone with unexpected comprehension. The beast's gaze wandered back and forth between the obsidian dish and the crow. *Does it understand?* the crow wondered, which was about the limit of what its corvid mind allowed it to wonder.

The man came in after the woman and closed the door. He wore a patterned garment the shade of crushed berries and a tight-fitting black leather cap that accentuated the hawkishly haggard lines of his face.

'Someone ought to tell them, then,' he replied, 'how bad they are at mocking. Before they go and make fools of themselves.'

'They also say you are insufferably arrogant.'

'Well' – the man walked up to the cage, his thin lips curled upward – 'I never said I was perfect.' He held up a finger, moved it slowly from side to side, and observed closely how the crow's eye followed. 'Just a great deal smarter than everyone else.' Then he turned around and held out his open palm. 'Now be good and hand it over.'

The woman hesitated. 'I can't keep doing stuff like this for you.'

'But of course you can. Unless you are no longer in need of my elixir?'

The ridge above her eyes darkened as she placed the obsidian dish in the man's hand. 'I should never have taken it.'

'Indeed. But we're all the wiser *after* the experiment, aren't we?'

The crow sensed a tense energy in the room, the woman burdened by an unseen weight and the male exerting dominance. A smell of trepidation lingered in the air.

'You are a sick man.'

She pointed at a row of five stakes on little pedestals lined up on a wooden board on the wall, each bearing a young human male's well-conserved severed head. 'Like, what is this disgusting travesty, for instance?'

'Don't be rude. They were talented musicians. Called themselves the Five Gilded Pipers, I believe.' The man took a peek under the obsidian lid. 'This seems in perfect order. You're dismissed, Sister Catalina.'

He waved his hand and shooed the woman out of his study, and she seemed eager enough to leave, still exuding a scent of distress. Just after she had opened the door and passed the threshold, the man snapped his fingers and the door slammed shut of its own accord.

Then he spun around with elation. 'And now to you, my new avian apprentice.'

The crow tilted its head. As a messenger crow it knew it was being spoken to, but few of the words spoken bore any meaning to it.

The man placed the obsidian dish on the table, next to the cage, and lifted the lid. A subtle, raw and appetising smell rose from its contents, catching the crow's interest. It hadn't fed in quite a while.

'Would you be so kind as to bring me the tweezers, Vladimir?'

In the crow's experience, it and its kin were far better at deciphering human speech than any other kind of animal, but this cat seemed an extraordinary exception. It looked up at the philosopher and mimicked that head-bobbing gesture humans tended to use, then it proceeded to fetch a small oblong piece of metal from a rack on the far end of the table in its mouth and place it in its master's open hand.

'Thank you, dear. You remember this, don't you, Vladimir?'

The cat bobbed its head again, touched the obsidian bowl with a paw, then proceeded to touch its neck.

'Precisely.'

And thus the human carefully extracted a small scrap of meat from the bowl, pinching it gently with the tweezers. Blood dripped from it. It looked delicious and fresh, as if it had been alive mere moments ago. He carefully cradled it up to the cage wall, one hand cupped underneath to catch the little droplets of blood.

'Go ahead, little fellow. Indulge.'

The crow perked up in suspicion. Being fed was the last thing it had expected. It let out a stifled, drawn-out croak. This was a piece of brain, human at that – one of the crow's favourite snacks.

'It won't kill you,' purred the man in a soothing sing-song voice. 'Probably.'

Unlike the cat, the crow was not so unnaturally gifted with self-control, so it bowed to its ravenous appetite. The jet-black beak shot through the bars and snatched the bloody meat like a pair of tweezers of its own. Then, with an upward swing, it devoured the moist and tender meal. It tasted almost too fresh, as if it had picked it right out of a living human's skull.

'It is alive, you know,' said the man. 'As long as it is marinating in fresh human blood it even grows, ever so slowly.'

The crow turned its head, watchful for any more meat that might come its way.

'If you don't cut it regularly, there might even be a chance it will regrow into a fully formed vampire again. But don't worry … it won't continue to grow inside you.'

He made a commanding gesture and the cat set off on swift paws to retrieve a black leather bundle from one of the shelves.

'It will do something far more wondrous.'

Cringing in sudden, unexpected pain and confusion, the crow cried out and flapped its wings frantically. The world collapsed in on itself as its mind was torn to shreds and reassembled. A dark seed sprouted somewhere deep within it, black tendrils reaching out. It was a black hunger, insatiable and old beyond comprehension. The blackness rose to devour the crow, and only dimly could it see the cat put down the little bundle before its captor.

'Yes. Fight, little fellow.' The human gleamed with anticipation. 'I shall need your spirit to arise from this struggle victorious … and stronger than before.'

As the crow fell over in the cage, squirming, twitching, screaming, the man unfurled the black leather and exposed a silver syringe filled with a viscous, dark-red liquid.

'One ingredient is still missing, though.'

And so he opened the cage, put one hand around the helpless, writhing crow, put the tip of the syringe at its neck with the other, and gingerly injected a small dose of the liquid.

'One that I shan't disclose. We wouldn't want you carrying around such dangerous secrets once you have recovered, would we?'

The cage was closed again and the crow lay in it, breathing heavily, unable to move. The cat named Vladimir circled the cage, staring at the crow closely and with great fascination. Meanwhile, his human master rewrapped the bundle and stowed it on the shelf.

Voices started to whisper in the crow's head. Images formed, ideas, entire worlds of sensation, of memory, of desire and despair. It hurt so much, but it began to contain the blackness, drowning it out until it retreated to some deep, dark pit inside her. One voice whispered of secret knowledge and the power it held, of exploiting the weak and taking control. Another whisper, softer and fainter, urged the crow to be careful, comforted it and lamented the pain it was in.

'*Wrahk …*' squawked the crow.

'Yes?' asked the man, turning back to the cage, a triumphant spark in his eyes.

'*Wrahk … wrahk have you … done to me?*'

'Hah!' Phileander punched the air above his head in exhilaration. 'You intuitively grasped within seconds how to utilise your unique vocal apparatus to bring forth *speech*. I have to note that down.'

Hastily, he grabbed a quill, splattered ink across the table as he dipped it into the vial, and scribbled several rows of symbols on one of his rectangular leaves. 'Parchment', it was called, the crow realised. It realised a great many things. More than its tiny head could take. It felt like it would soon burst.

'It hurts,' croaked the crow. 'Make it stop.'

'I will not,' responded Phileander simply, still scribbling. 'You will adapt. Vladimir did, and his mind was not half as complex as yours to begin with.'

Vladimir gave off a scandalised meow.

'*Was*, Vladimir; I said *was*.'

The cat put its paw against a rather precariously positioned bottle near the edge of the table and sent Phileander a threatening glare.

'Threats? Your pride exceeds even mine, and that is an unlikely feat indeed,' he grumbled. 'All right. I value your company and your keen skills as an assistant. There. Happy now?'

With a contemptuous parting glance, Vladimir withdrew the paw, turned around and retreated to his resting place above the fireplace.

'I must be careful. I fear I might be hatching my own doom with you two.' Phileander chuckled. 'So what shall I call you?' The crow's captor looked at her in thought.

'Torment,' croaked the crow.

'What?'

'Call me … Torment.'

〜

DAYS CAME AND went, as did secrets, lessons and lengthy conversations, all in that cage in Phileander's study. Days became weeks and the crow became … something else. Torment had named herself for her state of mind. There were actually two minds at war, maybe three. It was hard to tell them apart in the fray. A terrifying, hungry and scornful presence raged within her. It wanted to dig her beak deep into human flesh, to drench her feathers in blood, to feed, devour, destroy. The other minds had imprisoned this thing deep inside her. They were whispering to her, feeding her knowledge that a crow's brain was not made to contain. They vied for her attention.

'*There is power in blood.*'

'*We must be loved by him. Live for him.*'

'*Maggots. Prey. Tools at our disposal, all of them.*'

'*Beware. Beware of the others.*'

'Shed your filthy meat and rise.'

'What have you done, my love?'

But her brain had undergone a radical transformation of late and was still in the process of doing so, painfully, while Phileander himself did his own part to help Torment sort it all out.

He was a philosopher of the Order of Undreamed Truths, where he apparently studied the esoteric fields of astronomy, meteorology and 'ill-researched phenomena', the latter of which he liked to point out were 'known to lesser minds as *magic*'. Readily he would tell her of his thoughts and work, meandering deep into manifold mysteries. He had also taught her the letters, so she could now communicate with Vladimir, who could not speak and instead pointed his paws at words written on a piece of parchment nailed to the wall.

Vladimir wasn't so bad, especially since Torment was safe behind these metal bars, but also because he seemed genuinely glad to have a companion in woe in Phileander's captivity. How exactly Vladimir was a captive, however, Torment did not yet understand, because he certainly seemed free enough to roam the tower as he pleased.

'Torment, my dear,' crooned Phileander one sun-drenched morning, 'do you, by any chance, know what's in here?'

He was devoting himself to his all-morning letter-writing when suddenly he held up the little sealed capsule that had been tied to Torment's talons until what now seemed a lifetime ago. The philosopher entertained a considerable amount of correspondence with a considerable number of people. Almost as many as the baroness. Torment wondered whether he also sent them by crow, and if so, why he had felt it necessary to capture her.

'Why don't you just read it?'

'Because it makes for easier extortion,' said Phileander, 'if its seal is still intact. So tell me, what's in there?'

'A letter from my former mistress.'

'Thank you ever so kindly, little genius,' sneered the philosopher.

11

'What does it say?'

'I could not read back then.'

'I'm well aware, but you might remember words that were being said. Words which you now understand.'

Torment thought for a second. She could indeed recall entire conversations that, as a common bird, had been nothing more than curious noise. It was a peculiarity of the way corvids remembered sounds, she had realised. She also pondered whether it might benefit her to lie. She had found that lying and deception came quite naturally to her, although she was not sure why. At any rate, she saw no reason to do so now, so she spoke truthfully.

'I've heard her speak of treason.'

Phileander sighed. 'She does that with every second sentence. At least in my experience.'

'You know the baroness?'

'She commissioned me once.' He chuckled. 'You see, there is a strange door deep in the bowels of her keep that she requested me to study.' Torment saw memories light up the philosopher's eyes, and in the movement of the corners of his mouth she recognised his desire to share them. She learned a lot from observation. 'It appears to lead to a space much larger than the room's exterior should allow. It is far older than the baroness herself or her family records, so she has no clue where it leads or who built it. She has thrown half a kingdom's worth of traitors in there and then some, but nothing ever gets out. At least, nothing has so far. And the baroness is very anxious it stays that way.' The philosopher grinned in reminiscence. 'And now she is much less anxious and I am much richer.'

'And where does it lead?'

'Nary a clue, Torment dear. Some inscrutable yonder realm, perhaps?' He tapped his temples. 'A common misconception that there should be only one *Yonderrealm*, filled with demons and spirits. Indeed, I suspect we visit other worlds whenever we embark on a dream.'

Torment did not share any 'common misconceptions', as the myths of men were as new to her as most other things she knew. She had, however, become attentive to logical inaccuracies.

'If that door was so inscrutable, master,' she asked, 'how did you get richer and the baroness less anxious?'

'Ah, you clever thing. I must admit that this impossible door withstood my studies quite acrimoniously.' Phileander sighed. 'Every word in my report was made up.'

'So you're a fraud?'

Phileander's face contorted into an outraged grimace. 'If I can help a fool to suffer her deserved fate sooner rather than agonise through a futile, careworn existence, and in the process secure funds for my research that will elevate humanity to soaring heights of enlightenment, then I see it as my duty as a scholar to do so.'

'Your pride gets you yakking,' Torment felt compelled to point out. 'It does not suit you.'

Phileander scoffed. 'My pride suits me quite well. The yakking … not so much. Since when did you get so cheeky?'

'Since I have the vocabulary for it.'

'Well, you're welcome for that,' Phileander huffed. Then, suddenly, he looked at her in a most unwonted way. His aloofness gave way and he rubbed a palm over his heart, a look of pained longing welling up in his eyes.

'What is it, master?' asked Torment, as a part of her reciprocated his longing, very much against her will or comprehension.

'You … just reminded me of someone there. Someone who was very dear to …' His gaze lost itself in Torment's eyes. Torment, in turn, found herself wanting hands to touch him with. It was quite an unnerving sensation. A near inaudible whisper arose from a part of her that had always had hands and was rather confused at this tiny body with feathers and a beak and eyes pointing sideways instead of forward.

SILAS A. BISCHOFF

Phileander quickly regained his composure and cleared his throat. 'Anyway' – he waved the capsule at her once again – 'can you at least tell me who this was headed for?'

'I was to deliver it to the Temple of Lilith,' Torment replied, more than happy to bury and forget this unpleasant interlude, 'where a child of the Covenant was to receive it.'

'Huh. The temple of the red goddess.' Phileander's thoughts seemed to trail off, little gears starting to turn behind his eyes. This was, Torment had learned, when he was searching the crevices of his mind for means to exploit new information to his advantage. 'What does the baroness know of the Covenant?'

'That they have a captive. A vampire of old.'

The philosopher's eyes widened with sudden enthusiasm. 'By all the demons yonder, why didn't you lead with that?'

'I didn't know its significance,' she answered truthfully, as all knowledge was still equally new to her, be it about vampires or commerce or what latrines were for. Judging by his reaction, she wondered if this was information it would indeed have been wise to withhold. Then again, nearly every decision caused her the gravest of headaches since Phileander's painful procedure. Where primal instinct had once governed her every move, now an uncharted universe of aspiration and principle unfolded, Torment thrown blind into the thick of it.

'Didn't know its significance,' Phileander repeated, shaking his head.

With a generous sweep of his arm, he cleared away the clutter on his desk, broke open the capsule's seal and unfurled the letter contained in it. He stood up to do so and bent low over the tabletop, almost pressing his long nose against the parchment.

'It is of tremendous, life-changing, fateful, possibly cataclysmic significance,' he muttered absently. 'A consummate, conscious vampire ... a *true* vampire,' he murmured as he read on. 'Are they completely mad?'

14

'You fed me part of a vampire, didn't you?'

'Of course I did,' replied the philosopher, barely paying attention. He was pulling out books now, dusty old tomes which he slammed on the table, hastily flipping open dog-eared pages and tracing lines with his fingers as he whispered to himself before turning back to the letter.

Torment fluttered onto the raised perch in her cage, hoping to catch a glimpse of the letter's contents. 'Am I turning into one?' she croaked.

Despite having just implied that vampires were so dangerous that it was imprudent to deal with one, Phileander's eyes were alight with cunning schemes and ill intentions, and entirely riveted on the letter and his books. 'Don't be ridiculous.' He waved her off. 'You have a shadow of one in you, perhaps. At any rate, it would consume you, not turn you.'

'I can feel it. It is wrath and hunger and pain.'

'It will fade,' he said, not in a consoling way but as a simple statement of fact, 'and only the transmutation it has caused will remain.'

'What are vampires, exactly?'

'The former masters of the Earth, if legend is to be believed. Before the sun was set ablaze by the first Lords and Ladies of the Courtly Beacon, and when the Earth was still shrouded in the cold dark of the cosmos, they were said to have roamed and ruled the lands for millennia, while humans hid in caves and forests like animals. We were their prey. Now they are practically extinct.'

It was often like this. Torment asked questions and Phileander answered. It was a mutually rewarding relationship. Torment was very curious and Phileander was very fond of his own voice. Sometimes Torment suspected the philosopher might have caught her for that sole purpose – to have an excuse to be constantly explaining something, wallowing in the company of a less literate audience gratifying his abounding vanity. But that was not too likely, for she had come to understand that Phileander rarely undertook anything that did not further a coolly calculated and efficient end.

'What is my purpose, master?' asked Torment, desperate to find some sense in what was happening to her.

'Aren't you full of questions today, my feathered friend?' he said, a smile on his lips. The philosopher disengaged himself from the baroness's letter and his books, turning to the crow in her cage. 'Do you consider me your friend, Torment?'

An unbidden impulse called him 'father', a whisper in her head whimpered 'lover', while a cold hand gripped her heart that cried out 'master'. Torment pondered on this for a moment, on relationships, on how they seemed to define a person … and how without these haunting voices, Torment seemed not to be a person at all.

'Captor, teacher, friend,' she answered, a bitter edge to her voice. 'There is no difference when there is no choice, is there?'

Phileander regarded her thoughtfully. 'Fair enough.'

He gently picked up Torment's cage and carried it to the windowsill. As he did so, a rush of pleasure comforted her and she closed her eyes, taking a deep breath, relishing the sensation of fresh wind and warm tendrils of sunlight caressing her feathers. When she opened her eyes again, a familiar and liberating vista unfolded before her – a city that never ends. Only that this time she understood many of the things below that had been meaningless shapes before. Shingles to keep out the rain, chimneys for the fireplaces, bridges for the merchants' carts. As a mere crow she had not distinguished between poorer or richer districts of the city, yet now she found it glaring how the tower was embedded in a neighbourhood of luxurious interconnected castles – fertile ground for Phileander's schemes. It was beautiful. For a brief moment, it felt as though she had just to spread her wings and soar into the boundless sky – a delightful dream of freedom.

'Do you intend to torture me?' Torment croaked.

'I'm not needlessly cruel, my dear. I intend to use you, nothing more.' He pointed at the centre of the One City, up in the direction of

16

its peak that wound skyward to shadow and lightning until it vanished in the eternal storm. 'Do you see this atmospheric phenomenon?'

'It is hard to miss, master.'

He shot her an admonishing glance. 'Count yourself lucky your intended purpose might require you to keep your tongue, Torment.' He raised his finger even higher, along the bright, burning band that erupted from behind the roiling storm and arched across the light-blue sky, growing thinner and thinner until it connected with the white-hot corona of the sun. 'This is called the "sunthread" and it is said to erupt from the Courtly Beacon.' Now he pointed at the spire of intertwining towers at the city's heart that sought to pierce the heavens. 'It is the origin of both the One City and human civilisation on Earth. This incessant storm, legend has it, is the wound it has ripped into the sky.' He faced Torment with terrifying determination in his eyes. 'It is the greatest power in this world – it lights up the sun itself for all we know – and I want to possess it. They call me the "stormgazer", but you will help me become the storm *tamer*. You will fly into the Ever-storm for me, be my eyes and ears, and serve as a relay for any manner of manipulation I intend to apply to this phenomenon.'

Torment gulped. 'Will I die in the process?'

Phileander looked at her gently and said, 'Almost certainly.'

He stuck a finger through the bars and stroked the crow's neck. The melancholy smile on his face seemed sincere.

'Take solace, Torment, in the knowledge that you will have served a greater purpose.'

'Thus it is my theory that within the Yonderrealm must lie a land where spirits go to dream.'

—Ogden Flynt, *Spirits beyond Earth and Sky* (unfinished manuscript)

Chapter 2

A SPELL OF BONDAGE

THIS TROUBLESOME NEWS Phileander had burdened her with challenged all of Torment's newly acquired prowess of intellect. To ponder her mortality … She understood almost instantly that this lay at the heart and centre of every higher mind's deliberations. To ponder mortality. What to do with the time you were given. But was it not unfair she should be given so little, just after she had been endowed with the gift to make something of it? And trapped in a cage, no less. She had lived in a cage all her life before, yet she had roamed the skies nearly every day. Phileander had not released her since he had put her in this iron prison, and Torment's urge to spread her wings had become painful. It was understandable, of course, as she had every reason to simply flee at the first opportunity. But then, so she would when he finally sent her out to fly into the Everstorm. There had to be more to this, but she lacked the pieces to figure it out, so all she could do to calm her nerves was pace up and down the perch in her cage.

Yet her new wits also gave her other ways of reprieve to explore – ones she had never known before. To outsmart an opponent in a battle of prediction and careful planning, for instance, or the laying of complex traps.

'Knight to C3,' Torment crowed.

Vladimir, sitting on the desk next to her cage, tail swishing in concentration, bowed forward to push a white marble piece across the board laid out before him. As so often before, Torment had asked the philosopher to put it there before he had gone out on an errand. Vladimir seemed to enjoy this new distraction as much as her, despite his pitiful lack of skill, and they had been playing every day now for almost a week.

Rain pattered soothingly against the closed shutters and the study was bathed in mellow candlelight, the gruesome grotesquerie on its shelves graciously hidden in shadow. Torment could almost forget the horrible fate ahead of her. Almost.

Vlad pushed his queen to D6. Always bringing her out early, the impatient fool. Torment puffed out her feathers in anticipation of yet another easy win. In all except the first match she had beaten him, every single time, even though she had just learned the rules and he had read books on it since before her transformation, when her greatest cognitive achievement had still been counting past four. And every time she won, Vlad would bring her a dead mouse to peck apart in her cage. It felt good to be using what little freedom she had to feed herself. Of course, Phileander fed her diligently, as had the baroness's crow master, and back in her old life she had always looked forward to feeding time. Now ... it just felt humiliating.

'Bishop to B5,' she croaked.

Vlad tilted his head and scrunched up his muzzle. He sat like that for a short while until he gave a loud *meow* and tossed over his king. Raising his paw to the sheet of letters, infuriated, he spelled out, 'Damn you.'

'I'm damned already, but thanks,' she cawed, fluttering up to her perch. 'You owe me carrion, crony.'

He jumped off the desk to go hunting just as Phileander opened the door. 'Ah, defeated once again, Vladimir?' he said as he hung up his dripping coat. Vlad hissed and scampered past him into the hallway, tail erect.

The philosopher chuckled. There was something familiar to his coming home like this. One of the voices in her head reacted to it with a whisper just below the threshold of intelligibility. A wistful whisper. One that sounded hurt and despairing and affectionate. It disgusted Torment, for she despised this voice that made it so needlessly hard to hate this awful man.

'Good that your game is finished,' said Phileander. 'I have business with you, my dear. In fact, we're almost late.' He patted down the pockets of his waistcoat. 'Where is it? Ah, yes.' Then he reached into his coat pocket, muttering, 'That hysterical woman, always needy for more elixir, holding me up.' He retrieved a shiny crow's capsule, walked over to his desk and placed it in a little velvet bag full of capsules that Torment knew he would bring to the tower's crowery later that day. 'And now I have to spend personal funds again to purchase ingredients.' He sighed. 'Torment, would you be so kind as to remind Vladimir that I tasked him with spying on the botanists two floors down? I suspect they're withholding some hidden stash of mandrake root from me.'

Torment was fixated on that shiny capsule. It would probably hold a letter containing information on the composition of that elixir Sister Catalina depended upon. It was … something of value.

'Torment?' Phileander admonished.

'Yes, master?'

'Distracted again? Still those voices in your head? I need you sharp, you understand?'

'Yes. You said we were almost late for some business?'

'Right.' A grin crawled over his face, the kind that gave Torment the shivers. 'I need you to learn something.' The philosopher approached her cage and, for the first time in many weeks, opened it. 'Follow me.'

Torment's mind raced. This was her chance – perhaps the only one she would get. But it was raining and the shutters were closed. There was no way out. She would have to wait for the right moment, then.

She hopped out onto the desk, feeling the rough wood under her talons. What utter relief it was just to stretch and spread her wings. Torment let out a satisfied caw.

'Chop chop,' said Phileander, marching briskly into the hallway, out of the room that since her new birth had been the whole of Torment's world.

She fluttered after him, following closely, only landing occasionally on a bust or the stucco frame of a painting. There were enough junctions and side corridors that she should have been able to lose the old man. But she followed, as he had bid her. It was an instinct. Of course, with all her new capacity for rational thought, she was still beholden to instinct. It was easy to forget that when you were left alone with your rational mind and little reason for your instincts to ever kick in. It was probably wiser not to rush it anyway. Torment did not know this maze of corridors, lined with murals and carvings, filled with chattering humans, often leading into dead ends, whereas Phileander was at home in it. And then there was her curiosity. Both a strength and a weakness, she realised.

Through all the stale and dusty human scents, a rich, familiar one caught Torment's attention. A bird smell. A kin smell. It came from an elderly man who was just passing Phileander, exchanging a nod with him. Torment recognised the look the man cast her. A look to cow a crow. This must be the tower's crow master.

She wanted to ask the philosopher something, but she understood instinctively he wouldn't want her to talk loudly in front of others. Not unbidden, at least. And it seemed Phileander understood instinctively that she wanted to talk to him. He held out his arm and – as though this was rehearsed – she fluttered over to hold on to it with her talons.

'If the tower has a crowery,' she asked in a low voice, 'why did you feel a need to capture me?'

'It was you who gave me the idea in the first place – how you sat there on my telescope' – he looked down at her with something like admiration in his eyes, and Torment hated herself for feeling a twinge of pride – 'a figure of perfect corvid grace, black and lustrous, with your curious eyes and that beak against the Everstorm behind you. I found it only fitting you should be the one to receive this honour.'

The honour of being slaughtered for his greater purpose. Whatever that meant.

Torment tried to memorise the tower's layout, but traversing human structures was confusing. There were always doors blocking the view, and you never saw the whole thing from above. It was annoyingly twisted and confined. But she recognised some patterns. The youngest humans tended to wander the corridors in droves, chattering among themselves, carrying books, and they all wore the same kind of midnight blue robes. Then there was the fact that almost everyone greeted Phileander, while not everyone greeted everyone else. And in greeting her master, Torment noted, they looked at him as Sister Catalina had. They said things like, 'Care to join us for a drink in the Thrice-Woven Curse tonight?' but they meant, 'I have not forgotten you hold leverage over me; please let me know when I can be of service.'

At the foot of a winding staircase, they came across a small group of philosophers who were busy trying to hang a very large painting on a wall that was already hung with a great number of them. 'In Memory of our Brothers and Sisters' was engraved on a bronze plaque above them. The paintings were all portraits, she recognised, and this one was fresh. Torment could still smell the oil in the colours. She felt Phileander's arm tense beneath her feet and fluttered onto a nearby statue as a precaution.

'What are you doing?' Phileander snapped.

The group of young men and women flinched. 'This— this is Brother Gustav. He died twenty years ago, and with all his achievements, and in light of the anniversary of his—'

'Achievements?' spat Phileander. He was fuming. 'He was executed, you bumbling fool. For treachery. We do not commemorate traitors.'

Torment did not exactly regard the old hypocrite as a champion of integrity and faithfulness. At least, not as it concerned his own actions. But the way the philosopher glared at that painting, there might be something else at play. Torment could indeed envision him as someone who would hold a grudge for twenty years or more over the merest slight. The portrait showed a young, freckled man with curly hair, grinning in a way that came from the heart. Exactly the kind of man Torment thought Phileander might hate just for that grin.

Once Phileander had finished giving the young philosophers a good hiding – almost literally – they fled into one of the side corridors with the painting wrapped in a cloth and their heads between their shoulders.

From there, the two of them went on through a large double door into a great hall tiled entirely in black marble slabs the size of several men. The space was dozens of feet high, with two rows of mighty columns lining a path to an enormous front gate of carved wood lined with silver and gold leaves and ornate patterns. Above the gate was flaunted a gilded symbol; myriad interlocking multi-pointed stars – the mark of the Order of Undreamed Truths. A fountain adorned the centre of the hall, crowned by a statue of a hoofed figure, hands outstretched in invitation, a different head facing in each direction: an owl, a fox, a raven and a monkey.

Various groups of philosophers and visitors clad in foreign attire were scattered, many sitting around coffee tables in the corners, all in hushed conversation. There were some with turbans, some with many ornaments and charms and small carvings of bone – Torment knew those to be members of the mysterious and feared Merchant's Guild – and many others in the oft-ludicrous pomp of the highborn families from the districts of the Three Baronies. The latter were the ones Torment was most familiar with from her former life. They were the kind of people she had carried orders to assassinate across the districts on behalf of the baroness.

A loud scraping resounded and crisp air blew in, carrying with it the many scents of the city after rainfall and of sweet, sweeping freedom. Torment had just landed on the edge of an ornamental relief lining one of the columns, halfway between the front gate and Phileander, and all that now lay between her and escape were but two seconds of straight flight. There was only her and this widening gap of violet dusk and a view of distant spires.

And there was Phileander, pulling her gaze, grinning at her in that insidious way of his, gesturing to an unoccupied seating area at the edge of the hall. Her wings were already splayed, her feathers puffed out … and she took off and … took a turn and landed on the back of one of the upholstered armchairs he had gestured towards.

She heard the scraping and the echoing slam of the gate and the moment of opportunity was gone.

Why? Why had she done his bidding? Torment remembered the baroness's crow master. She could not remember a time without the compulsion to satisfy a master. Why? And why did this grand new intellect allow her to question her compulsions but not overcome them? How unfair. How cruel. She cawed in frustration.

'Calm down, Torment,' said Phileander as he sat down in one of the chairs. 'I need you to stay there and listen in silence.'

'Why?' she croaked huskily.

'Because you will learn something. Now hush.'

Briefly, so very briefly, Torment pictured what it would feel like to peck out his eyes, to dig her beak deep into his skull, to eat from his brain, claw open his arteries, let it flow, the sweet red blood, delicious—

Something yanked her back from that image and she was left nauseated, swaying on the back of the chair, staring into Phileander's eyes. Terrible Phileander. Beautiful Phileander.

Master.

Torment heard the gate open again, felt the mocking wind, the scornful scents. She couldn't even try to take off this time, could not take her eyes off Phileander.

The philosopher stood up as two other humans approached – a spindly woman with a pearl-blue gown hung with sapphires and silver all over and a blond tower of hair atop her powdered face that challenged even the loftiest works of architecture, and her rather inconspicuous servant.

'My lady,' crooned Phileander, taking her hand with a bow and a kiss.

'Yes, yes,' she breathed with what Torment thought to be half a dramatic act of consternation, half the real thing, 'enough of the pleasantries. I am so terribly, *terribly* distraught, Master Philosopher.'

'So I see,' he said with a compassion equally acted, if less dramatically.

This woman was far truer to the typical noblewoman than the Baroness of Quelm, Torment understood. She remembered her former mistress mainly in her night robes, with a raven's nest of dishevelled black hair and screaming at the top of her voice for the execution of the latest servant she was suspecting of treason.

'Please,' said Phileander, 'sit, Lady Lidelle.' And after all humans were seated: 'I understand you seek to commission my aid in a mystery.'

'Yes, yes, indeed, quite the mystery. Terrible, *terrible* mystery.' She clasped her hands in front of her chest. Her servant kept mimicking her gestures and facial expressions. 'It is about my daughter Adelaide. Do you know my daughter Adelaide?'

'Why would I know your daughter Adelaide?' A hint of annoyance shone through. 'When … I am just a humble philosopher rarely invited to the grand balls she would attend.' He quickly saved himself.

'Oh, *have attended*, Master Phileander – past tense.'

'Conditional perfect, actually.'

'What?' She hand-fanned herself, at pains to pass as close to fainting.

'Never mind – go on.'

'Yes, yes. So, a most strange and terrible ailment has befallen her. She—' The woman kept glancing at Torment, and she could smell that her presence made this human uneasy. 'Pray, Master Philosopher' – some of her act fell and she let her irritation show – 'is it really quite necessary to have this thing sitting around here? Doesn't it, I don't know, have letters to deliver?'

'Oh,' Phileander purred, clearly relishing Lady Lidelle's discomfort, 'Torment here is not a messenger crow. She is my assistant. My … familiar, if you will.'

'Familiar?' She looked aghast. 'Like the Wayward Witch's beasts?'

'Well, that's only a figure of superstition, so more like a … sorcerer's familiar, I suppose.'

'Torment … what a ghastly name. You're—' A hint of fear in her scent. 'You're just a philosopher, though, aren't you?'

'One who researches the more esoteric aspects of the world, so rest assured I know some things you would be inclined to describe as sorcery. Now please' – his patience was waning – 'what is Adelaide's ailment?'

'Oh, woe is me, she has fallen into an inexplicable slumber and will not stir, not from smelling salts, not from tickling, not from – immortals forgive – slaps to her fragile little porcelain face.'

Phileander nodded knowingly. 'Yet her breathing is strong and normal,' he asserted, 'and sometimes she moves her eyes under her lids as though she dreams. Correct?'

'Yes, yes, Master Phileander – why, that is perfectly correct. Do you know what ails her?'

'I have a hunch.'

The front gate opened once again, and this time Torment noticed very distinctly that Phileander caught her eye as it did and smiled as she stood transfixed, listening to what he had to say.

'I assume your daughter fell into that mysterious sleep about three days ago?'

'Yes, yes, she did.' She sighed in relief. 'Why, you know so much already, surely you must know a cure.'

Again, the gate fell shut and Torment cursed herself for being so distracted. None of this human babbling was important. Torment began to gather her resolve so that next time the gate opened – she swore – she would soar from this chair.

'I don't believe a cure is what Adelaide needs.' Phileander leaned forward, elbows on his knees, fingers interlaced under his chin. 'I don't think she is ill at all. I fear she is lost.'

A horrified intake of air. 'Lost? Dying? Irrecoverable?'

'No, I meant *she got lost somewhere.*'

'Where? In her dreams?'

'In a manner of speaking. What happened to Adelaide, I have come to discover a while ago, happens to a different young girl someplace in the One City once every hundred and forty days or so.'

'Oh, what a terrible, *terrible* affair. Poor things.'

'Certainly.' He made a dismissive gesture. 'But intriguing nonetheless. Have you heard of the final years of a man called *Ogden Flynt?*'

'I don't squander my time studying the fate of the rabble, Master Phileander.'

'No, of course not. He was …' The front gate opened once again and Torment spread her wings. '… and appointed adviser to King Suli-

28

man …' Torment stood there, straining, legs bent, trying to take her eyes off Phileander. '… and as a plague doctor, he gave false advice that cost the lives of hundreds of thousands.' She could not … could not … *could not* … *fly away*. 'Flynt became obsessed with the notion of vengeful spirits of the dead, and as a scholar of the highest order felt he should research a method of meditation that would project his mind into the Yonderrealm, so he might seek out and appease those spirits.' The gate slammed shut and Phileander ended his monologue, winking at Torment. 'Flynt's death after weeks of nightmare-ridden, uninterrupted sleep was ultimately very similar to the fate of those poor girls and, of course, Adelaide.'

Torment's head hurt dreadfully.

'I know how to acquire a rare transcript of Flynt's original records on his experiments. I will start my investigation there.'

The rest of the humans' conversation was more businesslike, with Phileander negotiating a fee and giving instructions on how to keep the girl's health up as best as possible, while he would search for a possible remedy. Torment tried to listen, but she felt utterly drained. Her breaths came short and her beak hung low.

She hardly noticed when the gate opened for Lady Lidelle's departure.

'How nicely you sat there and waited.' Phileander stood up and straightened his waistcoat. 'And for being such a good girl, you shall be rewarded. I think I might have potted eyeballs stashed somewhere.'

On the way back up to the study, Torment remained quiet for a while. Then she asked, 'What did you want me to learn, master? Something about the Yonderrealm? About getting lost in dreams?'

'I think you understand perfectly well what I wanted you to learn. Say, Torment, why is it you call me *master*?'

'I had a master once.' Torment settled on Phileander's arm again. 'The crow master. You're like him, in a way, but also you're nothing like him. It confuses me. He bound me with … punishment and reward.'

Phileander looked down at her. He had put on his teacher's expression. 'In theory, you could have left Castle Quelm easily and be one of many wild crows in the city.'

'I understand that now, but back then, before my transformation ...' She could picture the crow master, looming and merciless, and at once felt a part of her – a tiny remnant of her former self – that was afraid of how she had failed him by not returning to the castle. 'I was always convinced, in my bones and feathers, that the crow master's punishment would find me wherever I went. It was like ...'

'Conditioning.' Phileander finished her sentence.

The meaning of this word sprung to her mind from the vast new ocean of knowledge it contained, and it made her shiver. 'Yes, master. Is that what you've done to me?'

'Oh, no, Torment. Nothing quite so crude.'

'What, then?'

'Simply know this ...' He opened the door to his study and Torment flew over to land on the desk, while he sat down in his chair. 'It would be a waste of time and energy to rifle around in my books and records, or anywhere in this tower, to find out what truly transpired when I made you or what it entails. It's all in here' – he tapped his temples with a smug smile – 'and nowhere else. I don't even have to do much to avoid some pesky old grimoire or other cropping up.' Phileander leaned back and crossed his hands behind his head. 'After all, there are whole organisations operating across the One City dedicated to the eradication of such dangerous texts. Like the Order of the Scarlet Knight, for instance, or the Inquisitors of Grahm.'

A soft pitter-patter drew Phileander's attention. Vladimir was coming back with a dead mouse in his muzzle.

Torment seized the opportunity and snatched the sparkling capsule from the velvet bag – the capsule holding the list of ingredients for Sister Catalina's elixir. She hid it inside her beak.

Phileander stood up, stretched and yawned. 'I think it would be best if you withdrew to your cage now, my dear.'

Torment did as her master bid.

'*Survival is a curious, contradictory motivator. It is the reason for loyalty and love as much as it is the reason for betrayal and cruelty. Most spirits inhabit fleeting forms that they are desperate to keep intact. Thus love and betrayal are every spirit's daily bread, down to even the lowliest of beasts.*'

—Ogden Flynt, *Spirits between Earth and Sky*, Vol. 1

Chapter 3

A PEEK OF WONDER

*H*AIR OF NEWBORN, *plucked with malice. Three.*
Heartstrings of rabid dog, acquired any which way. One.
Essence of desire to hang oneself, denied and enfleuraged in goat fat. Ample amounts.
Oil of lavender. Two vials.
Cinnamon.
Mandrake root. Two and a half ounces.

Torment had memorised these ingredients, then destroyed the note by eating it whole. The halves of the opened capsule she had hidden underneath her wings until Phileander had placed her cage on the windowsill, leaving her to gaze at the night sky, as was their custom when he retired for the night. Then she had flung them out into the city's depths to cover her tracks.

It dawned on her that the nature of her predicament required the counsel of a philosopher of the tower to unravel. One other than Phileander. Seeing as Catalina was the person most closely involved in what he had done to Torment, she seemed the most obvious choice of ally. Tonight, if all went to plan, she would meet with her.

Torment could not roam the tower as freely as Vladimir, so she had employed his help. It was dangerous for him to go against their master, of course, and unlike her, Vlad was not scheduled for any deadly experiments in the foreseeable future – but he understood this to be merely a matter of time, so he had come around eventually.

If the All-Mother willed it, he had already delivered Torment's note to Catalina and would soon pluck the key to the study from a dozing Phileander. The cat had spelled out with painstaking paw-pointing how the philosopher often fell into wine-induced slumber in his reading room, with Vladimir on his lap. Then Vlad would bring the key to Catalina, while all Torment could do was wait, listening to the wind whistling around the towers and bridges, smelling a world rich with prey and curious things she could not have, and bathing in the light of stars.

It was she who had asked the philosopher to leave the cage on the windowsill whenever possible, so she may familiarise herself with the force that would one day end her life … should she not solve this puzzle in time. Torment's gaze into the sky was truly a gaze into the cryptic curves of fate. Cruel, loathsome fate. She liked the night sky best, when the sunthread was reduced to the thinnest filament of light vanishing at the horizon, outshone by both the stars and the skyroad. In one of his monologues, Phileander had explained how those light-grey patches that were scattered like stones across the sky were actually giant rocks floating through space. Remnants of a once greater whole, shattered, torn apart by cosmic forces … to what end?

A greater purpose …

What *did* she have to die for? Phileander's purpose could not be all that noble. Torment had conversed much less with the philosopher of late and much more with herself. She made a point of ignoring the strange voices in her head. In fact, she did her best to silence them. She longed to listen to her own thoughts. The power of language, she had found, went far beyond communication. Language was a conveyer of meaning, perhaps the very engine of meaning itself. And the hum of this engine, she realised, was the silent soliloquy of self-reflection. Every day and night on that same perch, in that same cage, in that same room, she tried to find herself.

Torment heard someone tapping, gently rapping at the study door. Then silence. Then the turning of a key. She recognised the scent before the woman entered.

'Ah, splendid,' Torment crowed. 'So our little scheme was successful.'

Sister Catalina was not a tall woman. Few of the tower's inhabitants could be described as physically impressive specimens of the human species – as compared to the baroness's soldiers, for instance – but among them Catalina would have to be classified as about the least intimidating. She was pudgy, pony-tailed and wearing the robes of a mere student. Or an acolyte. That was what Torment had deduced the blue garments must mean.

'Hello,' the woman muttered, practically petrified in the doorway. 'What … are you?'

'Never seen a crow?'

'None that could talk.'

'How could you tell just from looking at them?'

Catalina stayed silent for a moment, then said, 'Are you messing with me, Phileander?' She glanced around, peering into the shadows of the room. 'Or testing me?'

'I'm not Phileander. My name is Torment.'

The woman seemed unconvinced. Still she sought signs of a trap.

'Look, human, I was more of a regular crow before – limited speech capacity and all – until recently, when you brought Phileander a bowl of vampire brain.'

Catalina winced at the mention. Hesitantly inching closer to Torment's cage, she scrutinised her from under a furrowed brow.

'I do remember seeing you then.'

Torment tilted her head to the side to have an eye facing the human. 'We don't have much time,' she croaked, 'before Vlad has to return the key to the old bugger.'

'Vladimir? The cat? Is he too …'

The human didn't appear to intend to finish her question. 'Yes,' said Torment eventually. 'Lacks vocal cords, though.'

Catalina stood there for a moment, wringing her hands, processing, then she took a deep breath. 'All right, Torment. What is it you wanted to talk about?'

Torment squawked, satisfied step one of her first undertaking of a social nature had been accomplished. 'Righty-o. I hope I'm not overtaxing you, seeing as you're still learning.' Torment twitched her head to indicate the woman's robe. 'But here goes nothing: Phileander fed me part of that brain you brought, and then he injected me with something, and then I was dastardly unwell, and then … I changed. It has its perks.' She wiggled her head. 'I'm really clever now, for instance. But the downsides are truly disproportionately unpleasant.' Torment turned her other eye to face the Everstorm – a boiling blackness swallowing the stars, flickering with purple flares. 'Phileander is bent on sending me to my doom for research purposes, and apparently he has some kind of psychic control over me.'

With every word Torment said, the unease in Catalina's scent increased. Her expression was appalled, maybe terrified, perhaps pitying. Torment could not yet read her well.

'As for you,' Torment crowed, 'I know the recipe for that elixir you so direly require. Not all of it, but ingredients and quantities – enough for you to figure out the rest if you're trained in alchemy.'

Surprise entered Catalina's expression.

'If you want this information,' said Torment, 'you'd better tell me everything you know about this vampire brain ritual. Help me get rid of Phileander, and I'll help you do the same.'

Sister Catalina gave a humourless chuckle. 'Blackmail,' she said, slowly shaking her head. 'Figures. The old creep would surround himself with kindred spirits.'

Torment felt offended, but now was a time for diplomacy. 'I'm sorry,' she croaked, puffing herself up. 'I'm not proud of it, but it's a matter of life and death for me.'

'So it is for me,' Catalina said. Torment was quite confused at this human's apparent disapproval. 'Were you aware that you could have asked for my help without dangling this … this leverage over me? I would have given it freely.'

'No, human, I was not aware,' Torment cawed, irritated, 'so clearly gaining leverage over you was the safer bet. What is it you want from me? Would you like it better had I *not* procured a solution to your dilemma?'

Catalina scoffed. 'It won't do me any good anyway, will it? I can't help you, so … I suppose you have no reason to help me either.' She cast a look of disappointment at the crow. 'And just so you know, I'm a fully fledged sister of the Order of Undreamed Truths. I wear these robes by choice, because I will never stop learning.'

Torment thought this human had quite the audacity, meeting her with *disappointment* when the two of them hardly even knew each other.

'Whatever,' she cawed. 'I'm sure you're not entirely useless. Open this cage for me, will you?'

Catalina's look grew more reserved, her lips pursed. She proceeded to open the cage, so apparently she was going along with the deal, but

Torment sensed she had not been too successful at making a friend.

When the cage was open and there were no bars separating her from the vast night beyond, Torment found she could not find it within herself to fly into it. It was not unexpected but painful nonetheless. She did not exhaust herself like before, for she knew it with absolute certainty now. She could not fly out of this open window. Her mind forbade it just before the decision could manifest as action. She was bound. Cursed.

Rearing up, beak raised to those taunting stars, she squawked and cawed her anguish over the roofs.

'Tell me,' she screamed, fluttering, 'what do you know, human? About the ritual, the brain, vampires, anything – what?'

'Nothing,' Catalina whispered. 'I know nothing about any of it.'

Torment folded her wings. She lowered her head and levelled a glinting stare at the woman.

'Doesn't look good for your recipe, then,' she crowed. 'Anything? Anything of use to me?'

The woman seemed to be straining her mind, desperate for her own salvation. But she only shook her head.

Torment was pecking at straws. 'I heard something about meditating into the Yonderrealm, leaving one's earthly body behind. Do you know about that?'

Catalina stared at Torment through narrowed eyes. 'You really do suit that man, Torment, did you know that?' She crossed her arms. 'I know nothing so powerful as that. I only know the Yonderrealm is no place you'd want to stay in, in case that was your idea. It drives its inhabitants mad, shatters their minds for the shards to turn to soil from which the monsters grow that haunt our nightmares.'

'Still sounds like an improvement to me,' Torment said. Nothing. This had all been for nothing. Torment shrank into herself and let her beak droop low.

But then an idea flashed in Catalina's eyes. 'One thing comes to mind that comes close, though.'

'What?' Torment lifted her head just an inch. 'What is it?'

'I don't think I could teach it to you in the short time we have.' She sighed. 'I never really managed to master it myself, and I've been trying for over a year.'

'Tell me.'

'All right. I actually picked this technique up from Phileander. It's a form of ... *inward gaze* that lets you wander around the palace of your own mind – explore it like an actual place.' The tiniest curl of a commiserating smile appeared at the corner of her mouth. 'It won't free you, but it could grant you a certain kind of relief. A mind at peace can find the most serene places in there, and the further you manage to stray from your *Hall of the Conscious Mind*, the more time flows differently.'

Torment's interest was piqued. This sounded exactly like the sort of thing she needed. 'Different how?'

'You can spend what feels like days drifting through wonderful memories, and some say they found true happiness in meeting their hopes and dreams in their mind's Hall of Reverence, all while only hours are passing in the waking world.' Catalina's gaze turned urgent. 'But it's dangerous too. It's said your spirit can die in your mind palace, fall prey to your demons, leaving your body an empty shell – or worse, possessed.'

'Never mind the danger. I want it,' Torment croaked. 'I have a death sentence anyway. I want to learn it. Tell me how and I'll give you your recipe.'

It was the thing Torment craved second most desperately, right after an escape from the tower: to explore the depths of her new mind, to find her true self, her true purpose beyond the abasement of being a sacrifice for that madman's delusions of grandeur. And who knew, maybe this would allow her to better understand the nature of Phileander's grip as well.

Catalina peered over her shoulder through the ajar door. Then she nodded.

'All right. I can give you some instructions to get you started. First, close your eyes, sit comfortably and relax.'

Torment settled in the corner of her cage, her eyes half lidded as she listened intently.

'Imagine yourself at the place from which you gaze upon the world. It's a personal place. I can't describe it to you; you have to picture it exactly as it is for you.'

Torment imagined her cage at first, but that did not feel right. The study … the window. That was it. She gazed upon the world through the window, stuck in a cage that was stuck in a room that was stuck in a tower. Her home, forced upon her, was a cage in a cage in a cage. She pictured metal bars lining Phileander's study instead of walls, a room hung in an endless space of ever larger metal bars encasing each other, an infinity of nested cages dangling in a void.

'Do you have an image?' asked Catalina.

'It's beginning to form. What now?'

'Now comes the step that may take you years to master. It requires an intimate understanding of that space, the room your conscious spirit resides in. Where do you imagine yourself in it?'

'I am on a windowsill, looking out into the night.'

'Now listen. Next you have to *take a step back*. Not with your legs. Not the ones on your physical body, anyway. You have to—'

Torment took a step back. Not in her cage – not the real one. She stepped back from the window in the room in her head that was both a cage and something very similar to Phileander's study. There was a scribbling sound coming from somewhere beside her.

'Got it,' she cawed. 'What now?'

'What?' Catalina sounded bewildered.

'I'm in that room. It's not a room, really, more like an oversized cage furnished with bookshelves and a desk, but all built in a way that makes it more convenient for crows to use.'

Torment took a stroll around this room, marvelling at the space beyond the metal bars all around, where there were only ever larger cages
to be seen surrounding the one she was in. A surreal forest of grey
stems faded beyond the reach of the candlelight. There was a candle
on the desk, emanating a soothing tallow smell, earthy and rancid and
raw. The furniture was all crow-sized. The bookshelves had volumes
on them that had little rings on their spines, so she could easily tug at
them with her beak. Her desk did not have a chair but a perch, like the
one in her cage, mounted on a pedestal and just the right size for her
feet. A crow's feather danced over a piece of parchment, writing down
every single thing that Torment thought, right as she thought it.

'You mean you're imagining walking around in there?'

'I think so,' she croaked, 'but it feels … pretty real.'

'Move your wings.'

Torment spread her wings and stretched. She did it in the imaginary room. She had no idea whether her real wings were moving along.
She knew she must still be sitting in her cage, but she had lost all sense
of that body. This was her body now. The impossible giant cage felt
uncannily corporeal, if somewhat … flimsy, filled with odours beyond
the candle smell like that of a crowery, of droppings and homely crow
scent but mingling with the aromas of ink and paper and fresh carrion that lay on a silver tray in the corner. She was a little hungry, she
noticed. Her feathers caught a breeze wafting in through the window.

'You're not moving your wings yet,' said Catalina.

'I'm stretching. At least it feels like I am.'

'You're not.'

Torment startled as she saw the giant chubby face of Catalina appear outside her window, blocking out the night sky and peering into
her mind cage.

'What are you doing there?' croaked Torment.

The window was kind of just … hovering there, with its masonry sill and frame not connected to any walls, showing through it what her real eyes must be seeing. Torment stuck her head in between the bars to peek behind the window, but she only saw the dream-like cage walls that surrounded everything.

'Examining you,' said the giant face. 'What do you see?'

'Your face in my window. It seems to be a kind of … portal or something.'

'Window? Portal?' Catalina's expression turned into one of astonishment. 'So you *did* manage to do it. On your first try.'

'Do what?'

'Step back from the window to the waking world and into your Hall of the Conscious Mind.'

'So that's what this is?'

The giant face outside nodded, thoughtful and concerned. 'It shouldn't have come so easily to you.'

'I'm not exactly your everyday crow,' Torment crowed. 'There's some freaky alchemy involved after all. Irregularities are to be expected. What now?'

'Do you see an opening somewhere? A door?'

Torment saw that where the door to the study would be, in here there was a cage door made of metal bars. Its hook-shaped latch, however, lay on the inside, easily accessible to her beak.

'Yes.'

'Open it.'

'But it just leads into nothingness. Or … a larger cage, I suppose. Nowhere meaningful.' Also, the bars were far enough apart she could have flown through them anyway, though there didn't seem much point in that.

'Just do it,' said the face in front of her window.

So Torment flicked the hook up with her beak and the door swung open, creaking, and the crack forming where it spread showed not the infinity of cages as seen through the metal bars but a bright blue sky and puffy white clouds. Daylight flooded her Hall of the Conscious Mind.

'It's—' Torment was confounded by the strange effect. 'It's beautiful.'

It should not make sense that the opening of this door led anywhere else but the space between the gratings. Like the window, the effect was akin to a hole in the fabric of space itself, lined by the silvery frame of the study-cage's door, and through it beckoned all the scents of all her past and a boundless, glorious sky.

'You can always return,' explained Catalina, 'and seat your spirit back onto that windowsill in your Hall of the Conscious Mind to return to your body and to wakefulness. So if you want … explore.'

Torment did not need to be told twice. She took off with abandon and launched herself through that door into a picturesque cloudscape living entirely in her mind.

'Each spirit carries within itself a world unto its own.'
—Ogden Flynt, *Spirits between Earth and Sky*, Vol. 2

Chapter 4

A PINCH OF
KNOWLEDGE

HIGH ABOVE THE One City, above the Tower of Undreamed Truths, above Castle Quelm, far from people and cats and cares, Torment glided on currents of familiar and comforting scents. She drew wide circles, the wind in her feathers as it should be, and heard a voice from the strange doorway that hung in the air nearby.

'This is your *Nexus of Association*,' Catalina said. Her voice seemed somewhat distant now, a little distorted, deeper and slower.

The door was identical in shape to the cage door in the strange room she had come from, her Hall of the Conscious Mind, which could still be seen through it. But it was hard to make out anything inside, as it was so much murkier than this wonderful midday sky. When she turned on wide wings to look at the back of this floating door, however, it seemed to vanish altogether.

'I might not be free,' she squawked loudly, 'but I sure feel like it.'

Torment spun past the portal in a wild spiral, catching herself to slice through the cool air in a perfect curve. She erupted in a gleeful cackle.

'You're mumbling too quietly, Torment,' the voice said. 'This far from your window to wakefulness, I fear I won't be able to understand what you're saying. Wherever you are now, there should be pathways of association leading you to other parts of your mind palace.'

The winds. They flowed quite chaotically, unnaturally so, like many different streams of scents winding downward to the carpet of tiny buildings below. Torment latched on to one of those currents, one that smelled of home and kin.

'Most of these should lead into your Halls of Meeemooooryyyyy, wheeeeeere …' Uncannily, Catalina's voice dropped deeper and slower and fainter as Torment descended, until it died away.

And as Torment rode that stream, the city fell towards her. It was not as deep a drop as it had seemed. The buildings were much smaller than their real counterparts. Crow-sized. The one her kin-scented current carried her to was a replica of the very vertical Castle Quelm. It was clinging like an insect to a heap of old walls and bridges, jutting up from the bulk of the city with its central tower and digging deep into it below, down a shaft formed by the dwellings of the baroness's subjects. Her vassals' mansions at the top, tenants and serfs below, then peasants and riffraff and the dank, sordid pits where all the killers and cutthroats gathered whom she so eagerly employed.

The airflow, Torment realised, was directed into an entrance to the crowery, high up in the main tower, flanked by scat-covered gargoyles. The perpetrators of that soiling sat on the wingtips and guttering,

46

squawking loudly in unison with the noise coming from the entrance. Another smell escaped the miniature castle, a human one, skin and sweat and bad teeth … that of the crow master. Torment had no desire to explore this particular aspect of her memory and descended a little further.

Landing on a gabled roof, she considered entering the castle through a lower-level window. But Phileander's story about that mysterious door came to her, which allegedly led All-Mother-knows-where and had devoured the baroness's enemies by the thousands. On the other hand, she had never been down in the castle and had never seen that door. If this was just her memory of Castle Quelm, would it even contain that door? Would she find only empty corridors behind those windows? Or would she find everything she had ever *imagined* down there in the castle proper? That thought did not encourage her to venture inside either.

She looked around, sniffing out more of those wind currents. They connected various buildings she knew, gardens she had loved to linger in, digging up lush earthworms and inhaling the scents of roses and lilacs and rich black soil. Other croweries, where her capsules would be untied from her talons and where she would drink and perhaps spend the night if a storm raged. They were not located relative to each other the same way they were in the One City, she realised. It appeared to Torment that these places were actually arranged chronologically in relation to when she had made her first memories of them.

If these were her memories, why was this all so alien to her? Back in her cage Torment felt trapped, but in here she felt lost and overwhelmed. And lonely. A sudden fear struck her that she might not get back again, that the doorway in the sky might have vanished and left her stranded in a place where there was nothing but the fading echoes of the pitiful life of a bird she didn't even know anymore. Who was that crow that had made all these memories? A dreadfully simple creature she would never want to be again. Yet, at the same time, being what she was now seemed infinitely worse.

This whole idea began to scare her, and she took off and flew up again. She found she could trace the wind currents backwards, pushing against the stream and away from the scents of her past. In fact, she found there was a current leading her to the scent of her present day, towards Vladimir's feline musk and the amalgam of alchemistic ingredients stored on Phileander's shelves. As she followed it, Torment saw below her that this current led to a particularly tall building that resembled the Tower of Undreamed Truths, complete with a brass dome and a telescope sticking out. She remembered her fateful first encounter with Phileander and shuddered. The tower was a miniature of the real thing, like everything here, but among her other memories it was the largest looming.

Torment steered well clear of it. She made out a fine strand branching off from the air current and rising upwards. Its scent contained a strong hint of Sister Catalina's slightly buttery body odour. She followed it with haste, picturing all manner of dire scenarios of what Phileander might do if he were to burst in on their conspiratorial meeting.

Rising higher and higher, Torment did indeed spot the open doorway above her as she had left it. A low droning sound emanated from it, and as she drew closer, the sound grew clearer and louder. It was a voice.

'… diiiiiiiffeeeeer froooom peeersoon to person.'

By the time Torment, after a final thrust of her wings, slid gently down a cushion of air into her shadowy Hall of the Conscious Mind, the voice had returned to a normal timbre and was once again recognisable as Catalina's. Her oversized pug face was still peering through the window, and she didn't look particularly worried, so apparently Phileander hadn't burst into his study in the meantime. That was a relief.

As her eyes adjusted to the languid candlelight, Torment fluttered onto the perch in front of her desk and watched the dancing quill spell out the words she crowed as she crowed them. 'What did you just say "differs from person to person"?'

'The layout of one's Halls of Memory,' answered Catalina.

'And before that?'

'I said that there should be pathways guiding you.'

Torment remembered Catalina saying that. She also remembered that she had started that sentence about the Halls of Memory just before Torment had dropped out of earshot. While she had been flying around exploring, Catalina had uttered barely a handful of words and not even noticed she was gone. Time flowing differently.

Torment fluttered onto the windowsill, leaned her head through the opening towards Catalina's rosy button nose, and immediately found herself stumbling forward on unsteady feet in her cage in Phileander's study. Catalina pulled her face back from the open cage door and folded her arms.

'Back already?'

Torment's body felt heavier than it should. But perhaps it was her spirit self that had felt lighter. There was a pressure surrounding her that she realised had always been there, but she had only become aware of it now, after spending a short time without it.

'How long was I out?' she croaked, looking around the study and out into the night until she got her bearings.

Catalina shrugged. 'Not at all, really. You seemed pretty lucid until you started mumbling for a second or two.'

'And then?'

'Then nothing. Then you asked me what I said. Then it's now.'

'Seconds turned minutes,' Torment mused, looking out at the Everstorm brewing in the distance. 'That time slowing thing could come in handy. Time is exactly what I lack.'

'Well, you seem to be a natural at this,' Catalina said as she took a quill from Phileander's desk and searched for a blank piece of parchment.

'What are you doing?' Torment flicked her head from side to side. 'Phileander might notice someone was going through his stuff.'

'He won't notice a single piece of parchment missing. I only want to note down the ingredients and quantities you memorised.'

'But I'm not done with you yet,' Torment crowed.

The woman put the quill down and took a deep breath. She turned back to Torment and regarded her long and earnestly until something like a subtle smile of pity crept onto her face.

'Of course you would think and act like him,' she said. 'I don't blame you. He's the only example you've known since your transformation.'

Torment leapt onto the bar that was the threshold of her cage and flapped wildly. That barrier in her mind, Phileander's irresistible will, held her back as she squawked, 'I'm nothing like Phileander. I hate the man, you hear me? Hate!'

'I don't doubt it. And you believe I could not possibly still want to help you after you have given me what I need.'

'Wrong,' she croaked. 'I just don't *know* if you will, and since I'm desperate, I'd rather *secure* your cooperation.'

'Why should I even believe you know the ingredients?'

'Because you're desperate too. And when I ask you to meet with me again, you will come, and you will prepare a serum that will tell you whether I'm lying or not.'

Sister Catalina stared at her and said nothing. Perhaps she was thinking about how to produce such a serum or where to obtain it. Torment knew that it existed, since the Baroness of Quelm had had ample demand for it, but nothing more. Then Torment thought she might also be thinking about where to tell Torment to stick it, and she was afraid she might have squandered her one slim chance of seizing an advantage over her master.

'Isn't that right, Sister?' she crowed anxiously.

Catalina's face was a rigid mask of pursed lips from which Torment could read neither pity nor anger nor betrayal. It seemed that her newfound ability to read Phileander was not so easily transferred to other humans, and it unnerved Torment.

'Yes,' said Catalina then. 'I will come. And I will bring a vial of Nasum Perfidiae.'

'Splendid.'

And so that was settled.

~

AFTER THAT, TORMENT and Catalina met at every opportunity, which meant about every other night, and she owed Vladimir a whole host of favours for the risks he was taking on her behalf. At their second meeting, Catalina had indeed claimed to have ingested a vial of a serum that allowed her to detect lies and had asked Torment to repeat to her that she knew the ingredients of Phileander's elixir. Torment had done so, and Catalina had nodded, and she had wondered ever since whether the woman had been bluffing. But Catalina seemed too honest a soul to even attempt such a thing.

Yet there she was, meeting with Torment in secret, betraying their mutual abuser. Much of their time was spent teaching Torment the theory necessary to explore her mind palace safely. Torment was very diligent in this regard. Only a fool would ignore a safe source of intelligence before plunging into an unknown and potentially hazardous environment.

Torment learned that each sentient spirit had their own mind palace and that this world she entered whenever she *took a step back* was hers and hers alone. Catalina likened it to the house her spirit lived in, complete with its own layout and idiosyncrasies, secret passages and hiding places, and stashes of unexpected possessions. Torment had never had a house, let alone a *palace*, only ever a cramped, shit-filled pen or cage. There were various theories as to where mind palaces were situated, metaphysically. The simplest one was that they existed inside the actual heads of their owners, as suggested by the fact that the window to the waking world gave the impression of looking through one's pupils from the inside of the eyes. But Catalina dismissed this idea as common naivety, explaining that the most accepted theory among the more astute and learned thinkers – such as herself – was that mind palaces existed on the border between our world and that of the spirits: the border between the *Hither-* and the *Yonderrealm*.

She had also taught Torment a method of meditation that essentially reversed the mind palace's relationship to the passage of time in the waking world. It was a technique to be used when waiting for something, to make time pass more quickly. Torment, however, had no interest in *shortening* her experience between now and her demise in the Everstorm. So that session was an hour wasted.

Their relationship was cool and businesslike, with Catalina smiling dutifully at Torment's jibes and proving to be a productive teacher. Occasionally, an unexpected flash of warmth would meet Torment from the red-cheeked woman, quickly smothered and withdrawn into an awkward silence that all but screamed out what was always lodged between them, ruling out any chance of true friendship: the recipe for her elixir and Torment's withholding of it.

In those moments, a strange and uncomfortable feeling would flare up in Torment's chest. It took her a while to put a name to it, and she was still not sure if she could. Guilt? Remorse? Perhaps the most likely was a wistful disappointment that circumstances had denied her the opportunity to find a friend in this otherwise warm-hearted human. For it truly would have been foolish to give up her only assurance of Catalina's help.

There was one consideration, however, that almost made her risk giving up her leverage. Once Catalina had obtained the recipe and regained her independence from Phileander, she might just agree to murder the man. After all, she ought to have vindictive feelings towards him. But if anyone was the opposite of a killer, it was Catalina, and Torment wasn't even certain that killing her master actually led to her liberation. Perhaps she would be forever tied to this cage, with no one to release her from Phileander's last unspoken commands. Or maybe Torment would just die along with him, or revert to a dim-witted bird who understood little beyond counting to four or how to open a nut with a rock in two hours. Without knowing the details of that ritual he had performed on her and Vladimir, nothing was certain.

In between their secret meetings, Phileander was busy with his research on the curious case of Adelaide Lidelle, and his desk was often laden with heavy tomes on topics remarkably close to the metaphysical deliberations that also occupied Torment as she reflected on her sessions with Catalina – namely, the nature of what really distinguished the worlds of spirits from those of the flesh and the elements.

'It surprises me, master,' she crowed one such noon, when Phileander was having his lunch in his study, hunched over a yellowed volume by the dead scholar Ogden Flynt, 'that you would take such great interest in the fate of a young girl you don't even know.'

'What?' He looked up, irritated. 'Ah, yes. Well, young Adelaide's fate is unfortunately sealed, actually. She will die, and I fear I have neither the time nor the interest to prevent it. But delay it I will.' He took a bite of his roast, a sip of wine and a deep, much-satisfied breath. 'After all, this opportunity for practical experimentation with the late Ogden Flynt's more controversial ideas, at no risk to myself at that, is a preciously rare one. Lady Lidelle's request was truly immortals-sent.'

Torment had not honestly believed in any compassionate motives behind Phileander's fervour, but to suggest it was a good way to get him talking, lest she get the wrong idea that he was some fanciful, fatuous romantic.

'What are those ideas?'

'Oh, you don't need to trouble your feathered little head with that, my dear. They are of a highly abstract cosmological nature, and despite your sharp wit, I fear you lack the necessary academic groundwork.'

'I might surprise you, master. And you wouldn't be so absorbed in this had it nothing to do with your plans for the Everstorm, in which I am involved as well. Try me.'

Phileander chuckled and rubbed his chin between thumb and forefinger as he eyed Torment. 'Oh, why not, you inquisitive little devil.'

He took up his fork and began rearranging the food on his plate to serve as a demonstration. The roast went to one side, the mash to another, with that russet sauce that smelled so appetisingly of butter and berries sloshing underneath.

'Where we are now, the two of us,' he said, 'in this room, this tower, this city and all that is around it, including the air and the sun and the stars beyond, is a world that scholars of cosmology call the Hitherrealm.' He tapped the roast with his fork. 'It is the rigid realm of corporeal things, governed by inexorable laws of nature.'

Then he began to swirl the fork around in the cream-coloured lump of mash. 'And almost everyone agrees that there is also a realm of spirits and ideas woven from a more ephemeral substance, commonly referred to as the Yonderrealm.'

Finally, gesturing vaguely towards the pool of sauce, he added, 'Some also fantasise about a third realm, forming a sort of triptych with the others, if you will, that houses the spirits of their dear departed, naming it the *Netherrealm*. Bogus mysticism, in my book, utterly unfounded and rooted wholly in fear of the finality of our mortal lot.'

'Trivia, master. Cut to the interesting part about dreams and travelling and how it all relates to that storm.' It annoyed Torment that she had to stare at that food she was not allowed to eat.

'Patience, my dear.' Phileander winked, but with a warning glint in his eyes that told her to watch her tongue. 'What old Ogden Flynt believed – and I am inclined to agree with him – is that the common view of the Yonderrealm is overly simplistic.' He began to break his mash into separate dollops. 'It is far more reasonable to believe that there is a rich, possibly infinite variety of realities out there. To think that there is only "here" and "elsewhere" is simply part of the human bias to overestimate the significance of one's own position in the grander scheme of existence.'

He continued to join these dollops together until his mash was unaesthetically splattered across his plate. 'In fact, since we do understand there to be elusive yet indisputable connections between our realm of things and the realms of spirits, it is to be assumed that all these realities are intricately interconnected.'

At this point, Torment had to admit that this lecture was indeed beginning to go a bit over her head. All she really wanted to know was how it all related to her mind palace, so that she could assess the possibility of using it as a means of escape, but she couldn't very well ask Phileander that outright. He would not take kindly to her learning things behind his back, and it would certainly not bode well for Catalina either.

'So, what about the sleeping girl, then?' Torment asked.

'Well, this is where it gets interesting and where I can assure you we're nearing the conclusion.' To complete the utter mess he had made of his delicately garnished plate, Phileander smeared traces of his mash on the cut edge of his roast – or rather, his Hitherrealm. 'What Flynt hypothesised is that we peer into such realms whenever we dream. Imagine a veil that appears opaque when viewed from a distance' – he took his silk napkin and held it up – 'but becomes transparent when your face comes close enough to touch the fabric.' The philosopher let his fork touch the silk from the side opposite Torment's cage, so that she could see its silver tips shining through the delicate weave. 'This is – according to his hypothesis and simplified for your benefit – what our spirits do when we dream. They touch the veil of a yonder realm, glimpse what lies beyond, while their imprints shine through on the other side. All without ever penetrating.' He plunged the fork through the napkin so that the points pierced it, tearing the fine silk sheet. 'Unless you learn to apply the appropriate type of force, that is.'

Torment remembered Catalina's remark about mind palaces lying on the border between the Hither- and the Yonderrealm. Was entering her mind palace step one in leaving this world altogether? According to Catalina, Phileander had already mastered everything there was to master about mind palaces. If he still had to chase theories and conduct experiments on this, it was not likely Torment would get very far in her short time. And also, with her own mind palace already making her as anxious as it did, she did not want to imagine what it was like to get lost in a realm of alien spirits and demons. No, she would concentrate on trying to find the root of Phileander's control over her in her mind palace. That was a daunting enough task as it was.

'That's all very fascinating, master,' said Torment, 'but it seems to me, when I think of Adelaide, that it's all not really good for anything other than getting lost in some weird alien dimension while one's body withers away.'

'Hence the importance of this research opportunity.' Phileander started to eat again, then wrinkled his nose at the mess he had made on his plate and settled for the wine. 'Moreover, I believe the power of the Courtly Beacon to extend far beyond the boundaries of the Hitherrealm, possibly across all realities, but so far my reach has proved too limited to give that aspect of my project the attention it deserves. I have the means to contact the odd spirit, but they are strange and fickle creatures.' He wiped a drop of wine from the corner of his mouth and sulked as he realised he had ruined his napkin as well. 'Anyway, I think I have indulged your curiosity enough for the day. There is much work to be done. Please refrain from distracting me again.'

So she was condemned again to sit in her cage for hours on end, watching him drudge away at his books and calculations. She did get the opportunity for a brief game of chess with Vladimir around dinnertime, but Phileander quickly grew tired of her teasing comments on his bad moves and Vlad's infuriated howls whenever she took out one of his rooks or thwarted one of his futile attempts at a gambit or mate, and he sent Vladimir off to clean out the mice in one of his stashes of alchemical materials.

But such days of hard work were also usually the days at the end of which Phileander retired to his reading room to relax and drift off into inebriated slumber. And thus they were the days when Torment had her nightly sessions with Catalina. And Torment felt ready to advance further into her mind palace tonight, or at least saw no reason to put it off any longer.

'LET'S GO THROUGH this again,' crowed Torment, scratching at the cage floor like a nervous fledgling before its first flight. 'Right now my spirit is in my Hall of the Conscious Mind, where it usually resides whenever I'm awake and where I will find myself as soon as I step back from consciousness. It's like the master bedroom of my spirit house.'

Catalina nodded and shrugged at the same time. 'Well, I've always equated mine with an entrance hall, but whatever metaphor works for you.' She rocked back and forth on Phileander's desk chair, clutching an old book on mind palaces in her hand, which she had looked at from time to time whenever Torment had asked more in-depth questions.

'Beyond that place lies my Nexus of Association, which for me is a big blue sky with lots of different air currents that carry scents I associate with different memories. This is what I have to stick to in order not to get lost.'

'Yes. For me, it's a network of streets and thoroughfares and I use the architecture and signage for orientation. But the pathways do not only lead to memories.'

'Right – there are also storages of knowledge. Which reminds me,' she croaked proudly, 'to tell you that I managed to come up with a pattern to organise mine. I built a couple nests on the roofs, different ones for different categories, in which I collect enlightening curiosities. And shiny things. There's one on mind palaces too.'

'On the roofs?'

'Yes, my Halls of Memory. They're these buildings, like the One City, only smaller.' Torment realised she was gesticulating with her wings again, which Vlad said looked like she was having a seizure, so she suppressed it. 'Like I see them from above, you know? Crow-sized. I've found that even when I'm conscious, I can access my knowledge much more reliably since I set that up.'

Catalina nodded absently. 'Good.' She took a deep breath and looked at Torment with tired eyes. 'So what's up today?'

Torment croaked gruffly. Wasn't all this a small price to pay for her freedom? Catalina could muster a little more enthusiasm, she thought. 'You mentioned that place where people can find their hopes and dreams. What was it called again?'

'The Hall of Reverence. It's a bit controversial.' She tapped the cover of the book. 'Some claim to have found theirs and transcended to some higher state of mind or something, but to be honest, they all sound a bit kooky. I've never found mine, if it exists, so I can't really help you with that.'

'That's all?'

'Yes, Torment. I have told you everything I know. When are you ever going to honour your side of the bargain?'

'Yes, yes,' snapped Torment. 'Time to get rid of that pesky bird in its stupid cage.'

She was all puffed up again. Why did this get under her feathers so much? It had been clear from the start that Catalina was after her recipe first and foremost. And Torment ... what was she after? Just information? This partnership didn't have to be so cold. Why did Catalina not simply do what Torment wanted *nicely*? After all, Torment managed it most of the time with Phileander, too. That woman was making it unnecessarily difficult for both of them.

'When I return from this expedition sane and happy,' crowed Torment sullenly, 'you shall have your cursed recipe. There. Satisfied?'

'How am I responsible for your *sanity* and *happiness* now?'

'You are the one who equipped me for this. Any last advice?'

'Well' – she scratched her head – 'none that I didn't give you already. Don't try to tamper with your memories. That's the sort of stuff that has ripple effects, collapsing whole sections of your Halls of Memory. At worst it can make people go mad or turn them into drooling halfwits. In general, just don't break anything. Watch out for your inner demons, et cetera, et cetera.'

'Right. The usual drill.' Torment shook herself and settled on the floor of her cage. 'Then just wait here for me and your All-Mother-forsaken recipe.'

And so Torment took a step back once again.

'Do not speak of vampires. That is all I shall ever write about them, in spite of all that I know, most of which I wish to forget.'
　　—Ogden Flynt, *Spirits between Earth and Sky*, Vol. 2

Chapter 5

A TOUCH OF MADNESS

TONIGHT'S GOAL WAS to find her Hall of Reverence, or any other place that might hold her innermost secrets. As always, Torment's Nexus of Association was a perfect shade of blue, dotted with perfectly fluffy clouds. After a few circles over her Halls of Memory, the endless landscape of miniature human structures, familiarising herself once again with the way the scents on the wind currents related to her life's recollections, she noticed a certain pattern that had struck her before. There seemed to be a place that sucked in all the air, that drew all the currents towards it, and to which all paths must inevitably lead.

The Tower of Undreamed Truths.

It was the tallest of all the buildings in her Halls of Memory, which was certainly not the case in the real world. Which reminded Torment that her mind palace's version of the One City was rather flat, lacking the mountainous mass of structures that usually darkened half a hemisphere and culminated in the Everstorm. In place of those storm-clad spires, the Tower of Undreamed Truths loomed. Of all the places Torment could think of to begin her search, this one certainly gave the impression that it might hold a haunting secret or two.

'Bird's gotta do what a bird's gotta do,' she murmured with a fluttering heart and set off on windswept wings.

The scents that led her to the tower reminded Torment of Phileander, his alchemical experiments, the odour of his skin and the silks he wore, and a subtle, crackling hint of ozone. The closer she got, the more she felt a tingling and an energy in the air that made her feathers bristle.

There was, of course, only one way in: through the open segment of the brass dome from which the telescope was aimed at the clouds.

As Torment plucked up her courage and plunged into the shadowy interior, the charged air became almost painful, and a roar of thunder sent her sprawling. She skidded across a cold, hard floor and came to a halt. The room was lit by constant purple flashes in the walls. And the walls swirled, a barrier of black clouds enveloping a circular room tiled with black marble slabs. Only the crack through which the telescope rose showed a band of reassuring blue.

Torment picked herself up and shook herself. Feathers rose and were quickly ripped from the air by the storm. Something hung from a chain over the centre of the room, swinging like a pendulum. A huge scalpel was attached to it, the kind Phileander used at his dissecting table. And below the pendulum, a dark figure was pinned to the floor. Torment could faintly hear its wailing through the roar of the wind. A human woman's voice, pained and panicked.

She hopped closer, tentative, dazed. The Everstorm, Phileander, the secrets that bound her … she had to find them – no, she had to fly away. She dared not look. Whose was that voice? Advance, flee – Torment's thoughts tumbled, torn from her, leaving only primal curiosity and fear.

It was a black-feathered figure, a crow, its wings spread and nailed to the ground. But it had no beak. Instead it had a human face, female, pale-skinned, vaguely familiar but unknown to Torment. It repelled her, uncanny, that featherless oval where a beak should be, oddly too small, oddly too flat for the bird's body it adorned. Most of the figure's screams were unintelligible, but Torment thought she could make out the words 'my love' among them, as well as anguished cries for help and mercy.

As one of her eyes peered down at the bird-woman, Torment's other faced the pendulum. Was it swinging lower than before? Almost imperceptibly – a difference in height. The blade seemed to descend upon the trapped figure at an agonisingly slow pace.

Torment shuddered. There was nothing to learn here. Only death.

And she soared up through the opening, back into the bright blue sky. Should she return to her body now? Time flowed differently in the mind palace. Catalina could have waited only a minute or less, but Torment was afraid of taking unnecessary risks. Well, that was not entirely honest. She was simply afraid of the contents of her mind. She was afraid to look beyond the surface, into the nooks and crannies and shadows. If what she had just encountered was what her mind was like, she was not prepared to dig any deeper. Shame washed over her. Not a crow, not a human, and a mind that felt not like her own but like a prison or a torture chamber. And she was too timid to explore it.

Torment pushed herself up and up towards the clouds and could already make out the tiny dark speck that was the floating doorway to her Hall of the Conscious Mind. Catalina had suffered long enough at the whims of that black-feathered little freak in a cage in Phileander's study. Torment would give her the list of ingredients and end this …

well, torment.

Something caught her eye – a golden glint in one of the clouds. The sun was peeking out from behind it, and the sunthread seemed to break right through its soft white surface before stretching far out to the horizon. Torment knew by now, from the knowledge that had been implanted in her, that the sun and the sunthread were unreachably far from Earth. Much further than any cloud, certainly. But she hadn't known that for most of her life, and it was common for crows to chase the sun or dream of walking along the sunthread. After all, it was the bridge to the realm of the All-Mother. Mere superstition, Torment had since realised with regret.

But in her mind palace, the cold facts of the outside world need not apply. Torment circled around the hovering door to her consciousness, pondering, torn back and forth. Even if her exploration took hours upon hours, in the waking world only minutes would pass. Surely Catalina would be wise enough to leave Phileander's study in time on her own. And a golden sparkle in the clouds seemed a pleasant enough oddity for her curiosity to outweigh her fears.

So Torment rose higher, touched the clouds, dived into them, wetting her feathers, and broke through on the other side.

What she found was something she had never seen in her conscious life. She had expected bulbous white cloud plains beneath a perfect blue expanse. And perhaps that was what she would have found in the waking world. But in her mind palace, the tops of the clouds were green as grass. Green fields, gently rolling, a memory not her own. Torment felt a great connection, reaching far out and far back, beyond her mind palace and her tiny crow life. This was a memory of all crowkind. This was what the Earth had once looked like, perhaps still looked like far, far away. It was the most beautiful thing, the most fragrant and comforting place, greater than anything she could have consciously imagined.

Torment landed on the grass, and she was delighted to see and smell that it was in a perpetual state of morning dew. The soil beneath was soft and rich in worms. And there, in the distance, the sunthread did indeed break through one of the clouds, a golden band, and though tiny from where she stood, Torment saw all the scrumptious little lizards scurrying across it like ants. It looked like a solid bridge cast of actual gold, smooth and with rounded edges, rising from the ground and continuing in a slight curve into a distance too far to make out. Was there also a version of the Crow All-Mother waiting for her at the end? Should she go and find out now?

But something was wrong. A smell cut through the grassy serenity, an old smell, a fear smell, a smell of blood and ominous tidings. The scent of the all-predator to whom all things are prey, crow and human alike, even the greatest beasts of the earth. Torment trembled. This was not knowledge. This was instinct. It was something ingrained in her spirit, as it was in all – lingering, dormant, ever beneath the surface.

Yet Torment found herself bounding towards it. Unsettling whispers accompanied the scent. She followed it through this tranquil scenery, which now felt strangely like a trap. She followed it because there was also a beckoning song – the softest hum, promising comfort and cradling arms. Why Torment craved the comfort of cradling arms was beyond her. Crows did not have arms. Yet she felt it, was desperate for it, deprived of it.

It was not rational. Torment noticed this and tried to buck up and stay alert. She was no longer a simple crow who lived to eat, sleep, shit and carry capsules, enslaved by compulsions she could not understand. She was … well, that was an ongoing question, but she was definitely not a simple crow. Torment had no doubt that she had found her Hall of Reverence. The name made sense now. Everything about this place defied her measured and calculated nature. Nothing here seemed to be about reason. It was all about rapture, the good and the bad.

There was a hole in the ground not far from where the huge golden band touched the ground. It was a black tear in the grass, and from it came the oppressive smell, the whispering and the soothing hum. It was a woman humming, and it sounded like a lullaby. Torment fluttered to the edge, curious, impatient, feeling a foreboding and a sadness, her tiny heart pounding anxiously against her chest. Was that her real heart? Or just the imaginary heart of her spirit self? This whole mind palace thing was really doing a number on her already-confused sense of self.

The hole went deep, deeper than the cloud she was standing on should be thick, and it was pitch black. She heard something down there – not just the whispers and the hummed lullaby but the rattling of chains. Something was shuffling around deep down in that abyss, faint echoes lost in the black void. The lullaby drew her in. She was already leaning further over the edge than she had intended to, and – Torment slipped.

She was a bird, of course. Falling from great heights was nothing to be afraid of.

But the things she saw as she fluttered frantically to rise again, mere flashes … those, she was afraid of. A pale face under a black sun, feral and intelligent and old as time. A drop in an ocean of blood, erupting in a bright red flower. *Drip, drip*, like the chimes of a bell, blood trickling. The scents of copper and death and freshly torn flesh. They washed over her like a wave. The breath of a carnivore. A world of delicious pain, writhing, pulsing, growing, ensnaring her like tendrils of flayed muscle. She could not move her wings, could not scream, could do nothing but plummet like a droplet into an ocean of blood.

Until something yanked her back up.

'Naughty, naughty, my dear.' She heard Phileander's voice.

Was that him in his study waking her? No. He was hauling her through her mind palace on a chain. This did not seem like the real

Phileander. Perhaps it was her mind's version of him. At least Torment hoped it was. And she hoped that this was not somehow worse.

'Let me go,' she cawed, feeling her petrification ebb away. Cobblestones scraped painfully against her back, twisting her tail feathers.

'Naughty crow,' she heard the voice snark. 'You should not go there, not be in here. You should not wander. Might go astray.'

She had been pulled out of the blackness but not back onto that cloud, she realised. A stench of sewage and decay pervaded. Walls passed her left and right, and between the gables of houses she could see a cloudy sky. They were all crow-sized houses. There was a fuzziness and lightness to everything that told her she was still in her mind palace. This was below the roofs of her Halls of Memory, down in the streets. Had she fallen too far? She felt a cold metal ring jerking at her left foot and a chain clanking as she was dragged.

Torment squirmed and flapped and bent forward to peck at the ring. After three pecks it snapped, fell off and she came to a halt.

Whoever had dragged her fled, cackling. She saw only black feathers falling in its wake. Why had it spoken in Phileander's voice? Was it her mind's representation of his spell on her? If so, why should it have black feathers? Why should it share her corvid features?

Torment scrambled to her feet. She really should leave this treacherous place now, and swiftly. What had that dark hole been? Catalina hadn't told her about anything like it. It seemed to contain an aspect of the vampire whose brain she had fed on. But why would it lure her in with the sound of a human humming a lullaby? A predatory tactic, perhaps, but why it would work on her, a crow, was beyond her.

She felt a tugging at her limbs, a disgusting pinching feeling on her skin, like threads that had been pricked right through with a sewing needle and tied around her bones. Her whole body was lifted up by these threads. Now that Torment began to look around in a panic she even saw them, thin black filaments reaching upward, plucking at her, pulling her forward in a jerky mockery of a wing-flapping gait.

'Come, naughty.' She heard that voice again. And another cackle.

It came from the roofs. She looked up to see who was holding her strings, but before she could really see the shadowy figure hobbling along the edge of the roof, a thread connected to her beak twisted her gaze away.

'What – *wrahk* – what are you?'

'Master, little one. Keep you safe. Keep it chained. Keep you in line.'

She tried to bite through the threads, but her beak was jerked away every time. All that Torment's struggling achieved was to hurt her where those strings went through her skin. Finally, she surrendered to the grotesque dance it forced her to perform, relaxed and let the puppeteer on the roof drag her on.

'Why?' moaned a voice from below her feet.

Torment tried to look down as best her strings would allow. The cobbles were as humans must be seeing them. Not the massive blocks of stone her own size she was used to but a pattern of bug-sized pebbles stretching across a walkway merely a few wingspans wide. And just below her feet, a cast-iron manhole led to a lower level of the city. Spotty, maggot-eaten fingers grasped the grating, and from the darkness a face peered up at her, bloodless and desperate.

'Why, you accursed crow? Why did I have to die?'

'What do I know?' muttered Torment, jittery, her heart racing. 'What are you doing in my mind palace?' But the strings tugged her further down the street, jerking her this way and that.

'You did this!' wailed another face. It was human. If man or woman, young or old, the rot of death had taken that away from it. Now it was just the face of a rotted soul. 'You sent the word. Might as well have struck the blow.'

'I don't know what you're talking about,' Torment croaked, still being made to hop on. She only wanted to take off now, to go back and be good and never return to this dreadful place.

Half-rotted arms groped at her feet as the strings kept plucking at her, trapping her in this hapless, moronic dance. Bony fingers
scratched, reached through the gutters from ridges down below, a chorus of accusing laments rasping through putrid throats.

'Oh, wings of doom, messenger, murderer,' they screamed, and
their sickly sweet breath, carrion breath, could almost have been appetising, but it sickened her to the core. It burnt her. An acid breath. 'You
bring death, crow. Only death.'

Among them she recognised the face of Lord Sulbai, who had
wronged her former mistress, humiliated her at a ball and conspired
against her. Or so Torment had overheard many nights ago, long before she could have made sense of the words. These were the many
souls in whose demise she had been complicit, she realised. The bodies
in her basement.

Arriving at a square, the strings finally pulled her up and away from
the streets and the dreadful lamentations of the dead, away from her
sins, away from her shame. Her wings ached where the strings tore at
them with sudden movements to make them flap, rending the skin beneath her feathers bloody. Torment tried to look up, but with the way
the strings were tearing at her, her vision was too shaky to make out
the figure pulling them. She thought she could hear its cackle again,
see it shed black feathers as it hoisted her into the sky, but that was all.

The ones she helped murder. Those poor rotten souls. She had not
given them a single thought with this new mind of hers. The things
she had done for her mistress … she had only been a crow. Surely she
could not be to blame? She hadn't known or understood. She had only
been the messenger. And the message had been death.

That puppeteer who was pulling her up … it was saving her. That
was what Torment thought as they rose. Whatever the thing was –
Phileander, his spell, or something else – terrified her, but it was saving
her from something more terrifying yet. And as she did her best to
synchronise the beating of her wings with the pulling of the strings, to

make her ascent faster and less painful, the strings appeared to gradually dissolve. Torment did not stop, pushing higher, away from the stench of death, away from her shame and the harmful deeds of the past. Dark wings with a dark purpose must harbour a dark soul, surely. The city fell away beneath her, and Torment had learned nothing of her purpose. She had only seen what purpose she could serve for others – *had* served for others. To bring suffering. To serve her master. To die.

The doorway in the sky sped towards her and Torment rushed through without hesitation. She had seen enough of her mind for this night and all the nights to come. Her mind was not a place of comfort, at least not beneath the surface. That much she had learned.

Several tomes lay on her desk in her Hall of the Conscious Mind. The dancing quill had written down her insights, her every thought of the night, composing a library of madness to be stored in some nest on a rooftop she would steer well clear of.

Torment flew through the window at full speed, rushing into the night and back into a world where her nightmares were just that – bad dreams.

She opened her eyes. The weight of her body hit her, the uncompromising pressure of real air on her real feathers, the many nuances of scent and sound mingling chaotically. This was a world that did not care one bit about what was on her mind. It felt freeing. The mind was meant to be contained and life was meant to be lived in the open. Torment felt that now, felt that the contents of her mind alone could never sustain her. If it had ever been an option to simply spend as much time as possible down there, to extend the time she had before her sacrifice, she ruled it out now.

The night had progressed and grown darker, the sunthread thinner but a spider's thread by now, and Catalina was nowhere to be seen. Torment found Vladimir curled up on the mantelpiece, one eye open, watching her almost accusingly. At the desk, Phileander was slumped in his chair, one boot on one knee, his chin resting in the palm of his hand. He was awake. He was watching her.

'Master?' Torment crowed softly.

'Do you seek your purpose, Torment?' he asked. He had been sitting there for a while, she noticed. Was he aware of what she had done?

'I know my purpose,' she croaked. She felt tired.

'You do not. You are mine. My little crow. You serve your purpose, you don't *know* it. Don't ever presume otherwise.'

Phileander's eyes were sharp and hazy all at once. She was afraid of him. How could one long for the affection of another yet be so afraid of him? Why should fate have gifted her with the ability to seek love, only for her to seek it in the eyes of her killer? Why must her expanded mind come with such pain and such terrible confusion?

TORMENT HAD NOT visited her mind palace since. She had felt the desire, especially when she was peering into the night and the urge to spread her wings became unbearable. But she wasn't ready yet. 'A mind at peace,' Sister Catalina had mentioned. That was not her. To think her first thought had been to name herself 'Torment'. To toil and taste wisdom and agonise over what it meant to exist and then die … that could not have been the whole of her purpose.

Her sleep had also suffered from the experience. Every night she would wake from a nightmare, flapping and squawking. But not all her dreams were about being a crow. She had nightmares of being a little human boy, sitting on a pavement, hungry and cold, ignored by the faceless masses. In another, a recurring one, she sat at a long dinner table opposite Phileander, who said the most disgustingly sweet things to her, smiling in a way that his face should never have been able to smile, and when she looked down she saw herself in the body of a woman in a beautiful white summer dress. Then there was the one that was comforting at first, where she was cradled in a warm place, like an egg but softer, listening to the hum of the lullaby she had heard in her Hall of Reverence. But then the shell that held her was cut open and searing air entered her lungs, and a hand ripped her from her cradle by the feet, and the last thing she saw before she awoke was Phileander's vacant stare as he slit her throat.

She had dreamed before, even as a simple crow. Phileander had told her of dreams being glimpses of the Yonderrealm. She rather believed that her dreams were glimpses into her mind palace. Not an exploration of her own, as she had done that night, but rather a curated experience. In dreams, a guide from her subconscious would shove her beak into the most horrible thoughts and images and everything bad her existence had ever wrought, while at the same time cruelly pointing out her hopes and heart's desires. Had she had a mind palace before? A very simple one, consisting of nothing but memories of pecking at stuff that sounded nice, finding shiny things and eating?

A greater purpose ... utterly meaningless to a common crow, but now it meant everything to her, if not the same as it did to Phileander. Yet for all its importance, Torment's greater purpose proved frustratingly elusive. As a crow, her purpose had been simple: to survive, to feed, to please the crow master. But now? Her will to live – which she undoubtedly still possessed – had grown beyond the mere fear of death. Death had become an intimidating uncertainty, another riddle not to be faced unprepared. Now, of course, that uncertainty loomed uncomfortably close, and another question intruded.

What, by the All-Mother's tail feathers, was wrong with Phileander?

Torment's increased sentience was a fairly recent development, of course, but even ordinary crows had their own, simpler versions of compassion, conscience and decency. As her mind had evolved, so had her understanding of such philosophical concepts, and it was not lost on her how pathologically lacking Phileander was in all these respects.

One night, when the philosopher was out for red wine and a meeting at the Thrice-Woven Curse – apparently the name of a lodging and dining establishment – Torment asked Vladimir about their captor's sociopathic tendencies.

The cat looked up from his half-slumber, blinked twice, and began to make his way in a leisurely manner towards the cage and the communication parchment on the wall beside it. On arrival, he was briefly halted by a sudden instinct to lick his forelegs clean, but then he raised his paw and began to spell something on the parchment.

Torment read along as the black feline pointed.

'He ... killed ... his ... love ...'

Torment tilted her head after Vladimir had finished. It was a bird's gesture that she could not break the habit of, but she skilfully incorporated it into her gestural accompaniment of human speech.

'*He killed his love?* What is that supposed to mean?'

Vladimir pondered for a moment, then started pointing again.

'Do ... you ... know ... how ... trapped ... question mark,' Torment read along. 'No, I don't. I was going to ask you that too. I know that this thing' – she gave the cage bars a loud clang with her beak – 'is not the half of it. And I've seen some things in my mind palace. How does he command our minds?'

Vladimir ran his claws through his whiskers while he surveyed the communication parchment before finally giving off a frustrated sigh. Then he spelled out the words 'long story'.

'Well' – Torment looked at the large parchment with all its letters and the occasional spelled-out word, then back at the cat – 'that's unfortunate.'

As Vladimir mulled over a solution, his gaze wandered from the parchment around the room, finally settling on one of Phileander's bookshelves – the one with the ritual codices and grimoires. A mischievous gleam flashed from behind the black slits in his eyes. 'Always wanted to do this,' they revealed, with no need whatsoever to spell out the words. He dashed off and in two effortless, lightning-fast leaps scaled the rise to the topmost shelf.

He strolled along the spines of the books, studying their titles.

'You're not going to peck around with magic, are you?' Torment croaked with grave concern.

It seemed as though Vladimir had found what he was looking for. He tugged at an especially meaty volume bearing the conspicuous caption *Liber Esoterica Somniorum*.

'Oh, great. You are.'

It tipped over the edge of the shelf, tumbled down and slammed onto the floor with a hearty *thud*. A flower of dust blossomed from its impact, instantly disintegrating and swirling off into the room. At its root remained the tome, poised dramatically on the age-old granite slabs and beckoning bad news.

From the title she could gather it had something to do with sleep or dreams. Phileander's recent work on the case of poor lost Adelaide Lidelle must have given that daredevil some stupid ideas.

Torment fluttered nervously and started walking up and down the perch in her cage. 'Just because you can form full sentences doesn't mean you should dabble with the forbidden forces of the universe, you know? It's dicey enough when *he* does it, and – ethical flaws aside – he *knows* his "ill-researched phenomena".'

But Vladimir had already dropped elegantly to the floor and heaved open the book with his nose. He sat in front of it, leafing through the pages, while his tail swung to and fro in a steady cadence, just like when he lay in wait for the sparrows that occasionally strayed onto the windowsill.

'Cat nibbles a nugget of vampire noggin and thinks he's a sorcerer … This is a bad idea, crony. No matter how many cranium crumbs you chomped, how many mind morsels you munched' – her nerves got her rambling like that sometimes – 'how many thinker tidbits you tasted, how—'

Without looking up, Vladimir presented Torment with the shiny black beans on the underside of his left paw.

'Did you just *shush* me, you shaggy back-alley stray?' She could not refrain from an indignant, utterly bird-like and inarticulate crow.

The cat seemed determined to carry out his demented plan. Torment tried to reason with Vladimir, even apologising for her undignified outburst earlier, but to no avail. Eventually she resigned herself to watching him anxiously from the top of her cage. As soon as Phileander returned, Torment noted inwardly, she would insist on adjusting the conditions of her confinement. If that raving tomcat was allowed to roam the tower, surely the philosopher could arrange something similar for her. After all, she couldn't just fly away, and Phileander was obviously aware of that. She did not like her inability to intervene in such situations one bit. Her life was precious now, even if she still had to find out why, and death loomed close enough. If she could at least check if Vladimir was following the instructions properly … whatever he was doing.

Vladimir was visibly struggling with his lack of hands, but it was impressive what he had already achieved without them. He had heaped a variety of the philosopher's rarer ingredients into a mortar and was now grinding around the sturdy pestle with nothing but his tiny muzzle. There were toadstool spores gathered from the crumbling hollows of ancient trees, spider legs delicately harvested from the cobwebbed corners of forgotten caves, and eye of newt plucked under a blood-red sky. If Torment had followed Vlad's actions correctly, there was even a tuft of Phileander's own hair in there, which, strangely enough, the madman kept in a labelled vial.

'I think you just lost an iguana eyeball there, chef.'

Vladimir forced a long, gurgling meow past the pestle, and he didn't have to command speech for Torment to understand that he was cursing.

'If it turns out you want me to eat what you're concocting there, which I'm beginning to suspect, you could at least leave the scant bits of yummy stuff in. Meaning eyeballs.'

In all his recklessness, Vladimir did exhibit commendable diligence in procedure, returning to the book again and again, making sure everything was in order. Maybe that cat was far more resourceful than Torment had given him credit for. Even if he was terrible at chess. After all, he wasn't doing this just to ruffle some feathers. He was doing it for her, to convey crucial information about the nature of their shared captivity. Now that she reflected on it, to have instinctively labelled Vladimir as this barely sentient troublemaker who was good for nothing more than a bit of comforting company reminded Torment so much of Phileander that it downright shamed her.

'Please forgive my cranky attitude, Vlad,' she said. 'I'm not used to this, you know. Being stuck in here and having this … new perspective on the world. If I could just fly out there with this new mind of mine, oh bird.'

Vladimir dropped the pestle and meowed.

'It must be even harder for you. You might get around more, but having been injected with that intelligence and then not being able to articulate it …' Torment regarded him thoughtfully. 'You have a cage of your own, Vladimir. I see that now.'

He paused for a moment and answered her gaze. Torment could practically see the cat pulling all his non-verbal registers to tell her with just his eyes, 'Thanks. Much appreciated.'

Then he returned to the task at paw, which apparently involved digging into a generous mouthful of that brown sludge he had just created, chewing on it with unconcealed disgust, his muzzle all scrunched up, and then fighting really hard to gulp it all down without retching.

'Looks fun.' She was just glad she didn't have to eat it after all, whatever its effect was supposed to be.

Vladimir took another portion of it in his mouth, jumped onto the table and walked up to Torment's cage. He stuck his snout through the bars and spat the mush onto her cage floor. After that, he gave her a prompting nod.

'Crikey. Me too?'

Vladimir nodded again.

'What does it do?' she asked hesitantly.

He pointed: 'Dreams.'

'What? You want us to take a nap?'

Impatiently, he pointed: 'Eat. Exclamation mark.'

'Calm down, crony,' Torment replied, fluttering down to the cage floor. She eyed the pungent paste reluctantly.

Suddenly, Vladimir swayed, staggering sideways. His eyes flickered wildly, turning inward as he fell onto his side and, with a final sigh, fell asleep on the spot. Then he just lay there, his breathing shallow and his eyes moving rapidly behind the lids.

In dire discomfort, Torment looked back and forth between the sorcerous slime and the unconscious cat.

'Taking flight on a wing and a prayer,' she crowed to herself. Then she took a deep breath and ate it all up, scraping every bit of it off the cage floor with her beak. It was pretty much as disgusting as it looked.

It took a moment to kick in. But when it did, it did so with a bang. From a place so deep within her consciousness she never knew it had been there burst an explosion of memories and dreams and colours and scents. A whole world grew from nothing at the centre of her skull, an embryo of experiences and hopes, transforming in time-lapse into a foetus of heartaches and struggles.

There was a young human boy being beaten; a stolen loaf of bread; an acrid smell of herbs; a kitten alone in the dark; a puddle of blood and a mountain of bones; fresh prey in the streets and a choir of moans; things and beings of all shapes and forms that laughed and chattered and reeked; day, night, pain, snow; an eggshell made of milk. And behind a range of mountains raced the stars across the sky, and the Earth spun round and round without the sunthread passing by. A huge black sphere shot up, rose higher, erupting soon in red-hot flame; a mother, father, filthy liar; a newborn life, a knife and *shame*.

This foetus grew to fill her up, spirit, body and mind. She became it and it became her. Torment settled in this new body. Black feathers, black feet, black soul. It was just like her old one, just … lighter.

She was the dream of a crow in a land of dreams, most of which were not her own.

'It is a tenet of Talmaaran philosophy that the mere fact that we can imagine a world in our minds, alive with spirits of its own, is all the proof we need that we ourselves are but imaginations of a spirit even greater than ourselves. I am inclined to agree.'

—Ogden Flynt, *Spirits between Earth and Sky*, Vol. 2

Chapter 6

A TASTE OF DEATH

S HE STOOD ON the shingled roof of a human dwelling that stretched endlessly in two directions. It rose on one side of a wide cobblestone overpass, below which there were more houses, and on the street were smaller buildings still, with smaller bridges spanning between them. Thus this nested pattern went deeper and deeper, to houses small as ants and bridges thin as threads. Above her head, similar stone bridges stretched across a clear sky, overlapping each other and growing larger the farther away they were. The most distant ones faded into the azure hue, celestial colossi half occluded by clouds, not unlike the rings of Saturn. Structures taller than mountains towered at the fringes of her vision, shrouding the horizon in a cloak of grey blocks and arches that dissolved into an ill-defined nimbus of all-encompassing human architecture.

It reminded Torment of her mind palace but deconstructed somehow, merged with other ingredients … fuzzy at the edges.

Beside her sat Vladimir, sniffing fresh air that bore subtle hints of steaming human foods, whiffs of chimney smoke and the acrid odour of pigeon droppings, and his ears twitched at the gentle hum of a million muffled voices behind bricks and wood and the fabric of dreams.

'Did you see all this crazy stuff before you got here too?' Torment asked as she stretched her wings and ran her beak through these new feathers.

The cat nodded.

The visions reminded her of that unpleasant episode in her mind palace when she had fallen down that shaft. Torment pattered around on the roof impatiently, trying to continue the conversation, but she just couldn't resist the overpowering urge.

She took a wing-flapping run-up and rose into the air. Her heart rejoiced as her wings caught the wind and tamed it into a cushion that carried her. She drew a few circles and ribbons and suddenly let herself drop along the brick wall like a stone, fast as an arrow, several whole yards below that bridge, before catching herself and riding a playful current.

Just as in her mind palace, she noticed, the quality of it was not exactly the same as in the real world. It was … softer, somehow. As for candidates for that *greater purpose* she was looking for, to fly freely was surely a high contender. But ultimately it was just a fleeting satisfaction and a tiny part of the answer at best.

She sought out a surging gust to soar up again and lower herself onto the shingles next to Vladimir, cawing with delight.

'Sorry, this was just too long overdue. Where were we?'

The cat put a paw to his temple, mimicking a headache and an eye-rolling display of confusion.

'Ah, right. The crazy stuff. So, what did it mean? You knew this would happen?'

Vladimir made a gesture that was as close to a shrug as a quadruped could muster. Then he started strutting along the edge of the roof, occasionally bending his head over the precipice and sniffing the air below.

Torment hopped and fluttered after him, high on a rush of contentment.

'Thanks for this, crony. To fly, to be free like this ... it means everything to me. And with you around, I feel much safer than in my mind palace too.'

'We're in a shared dream state, birdie,' the cat grumbled, 'but sure, you're free.'

Torment stopped in her tracks and let out a caw of surprise.

Vladimir looked back over his shoulder. 'What?'

'You speak.'

Vlad's eyes widened. 'Scratch me,' he said, 'you're right. This is gonna be easier than I thought.'

'If you didn't know you'd be able to speak, how did you expect all this to be of any help in telling me your "long story"?'

'I was going to *show* you instead. We share this dream with Phileander too.' He let his eyes wander over this strange mirror version of the One City that his tincture had cast them into. 'In a way.'

'So he's in here with us?'

'Not like we are. I think.'

'How, then?'

He meowed irritably and shook his head. 'I didn't really have the time to become an expert on *dream magic*, did I?'

Torment tilted her head. 'I suppose not. Hence my initial trepidation at this reckless venture.'

A low growl escaped Vladimir's throat. 'So you wanna stay in that cage forever?'

'It would hardly be forever. That's kind of the problem.'

Abashed, the cat averted his eyes, claws raking across the shingles.

Torment looked off into the sky, wondering about the clouds above, about whether the Crow All-Mother might be out there somewhere, collecting her kin's departed spirits. It was no deliberation her mind had been capable of before her transformation. Now she wasn't so sure she still counted as kin. What was she, then? Torment felt she might be inching closer to her *higher purpose* here, but she could not get a clear grasp of it. Nor of what place they were in. It wasn't her mind palace. But it wasn't that far off either. Phileander's lecture about the many yonder worlds came to mind.

'I won't give up without trying, though,' she said firmly. 'I will earn Phileander's trust, be a good companion, feather my nest in that tower, and whenever he gets talkative … I'll peck his brain for secrets.'

'Lately I've seen more silent brooding on your part than secret-pecking.'

'You're one to talk.'

'No, I'm not, actually,' the cat replied sourly. 'Silent brooding is literally all I've got.'

'Oh, right.' Now it was Torment's turn to scuff her talons sheepishly. 'Sorry.'

'Forget it. Anyway, in coaxing out his secrets' – he jovially tapped an outstretched claw against her beak – 'I got one up on you. A secret tough as sinews, birdie.'

'You could just *tell* me now.'

'Wouldn't do it justice,' he said tartly. 'Lack of oratory experience.'

'Would be a tad anticlimactic too, after all this effort,' she quipped. 'Show it, then.'

'Would if I knew where to lead us.'

Torment watched the cat glower around, overwhelmed, for a bit longer before she took off, sorted out the scents on the air and flew over the edge, down onto a windowsill a few feet below the roof. A wooden shutter screened the inside of the house.

'What are you doing?' yelled Vladimir, sticking his head over the edge above her.

'Leading us,' she replied before she began pushing her beak between the shutters. Very carefully, his eyes reflecting the deep descent to the city's bowels, the cat dropped onto the bricks beside her.

Prying open the window, Torment revealed a cosy wood-panelled reading room. Warm, musty air poured out at them. Inside, bookshelves lined the walls, a half-burned-out fireplace lay at the far end, and in front of it stood a burgundy wingback chair with its back facing the window.

A slight acceleration of Vladimir's tail swivels told Torment she'd led them to the right place. He turned to her, asking, 'How did you know this would be here?'

Torment returned his gaze in that oblique way of hers. 'It's just how dreams work. Or mind palaces, for that matter. You tumble around haphazardly, following your nose, and wind up somewhere meaningful. I followed Phileander's scent.' She leaned in to see her dark, elongated profile reflected in his yellow eyes. 'Don't you have dreams, Vladimir?'

The cat endured her scrutiny for a few seconds, then glanced sideways sullenly. 'Sometimes. They were much simpler before my transformation. Just … running away from bigger strays or hunting things.'

'Curious,' she remarked. 'I've had dreams like this all my life. Dreams about ideas, about memories, about the All-Mother. All crows do.' Torment was not sure why she had exaggerated like that. A sudden haughty impulse. 'Though since Phileander's injection they did … intensify.'

'Well, congratulations, birdie,' he hissed. 'Wanna get back to business?'

'Sure,' she said, straightening up. 'Caw the shots, crony. What are

SILAS A. BISCHOFF

we looking at?'

Vladimir was still sniffing the air with an expression of distrust. 'The outside of this building doesn't look the part right now, but this room actually lies in the Tower of Undreamed Truths. It's where I snatch his keys every other night. His reading room.'

He leapt down onto the shiny, well-trodden planks and stalked in the direction of the armchair, soft paw taps resounding in the room's heavy, creaky silence.

Torment followed with two dust-raising wing beats, gliding towards an ornate orrery that stood atop a sideboard. She settled on the outermost golden ring of Jupiter's numerous lunar orbits.

From her new position, she could see a still figure immersed in the cushioned seat, silhouetted by the orange glow emanating from a four-armed candelabra. The profile was unmistakable, and not even Torment could dismiss how much the philosopher's nose was reminiscent of the beak of a carrion bird. Since Catalina's remarks, she had grown somewhat sensitive to reminders of similarities between her and Phileander. On the side table, next to the candle holder, rested a tray with a chalice and decanter filled with dark red wine.

'Why isn't he moving?' she wondered aloud.

Vladimir rubbed his head against the edge of the armchair as he circled it, surveying this seemingly suspended moment in time.

Now that Torment saw it, the candlelight did not flicker and the sparks from the fireplace hung motionless above the logs. Even the gleaming grains of dust hovering in a golden sun ray by the window stood perfectly still.

Coming to a halt in front of the frozen philosopher, Vladimir just sat down and waited awkwardly.

'That's what you wanted to show me?' Torment crowed. 'I do know what he looks like, you see.'

'No, smart-ass,' he snapped. 'Something he told me while I lay on his lap in here.'

86

Reflecting on the memories she had flown past in her mind palace, led by trails of association, Torment had an idea. She had not explored too many of them, but she had gained some insight into the often strangely figurative logic of it all.

'You might have to complete the picture, I believe.'

Vlad exchanged a glance with Torment, who nodded at him reassuringly. Then he jumped onto Phileander's lap. After plodding around a bit to find the right position, he curled up into a furry bundle.

And sure enough, like clockwork, the scene set into motion.

In the blink of an eye, a rumble rolled through clouds that gathered in front of a suddenly setting sun. A chill gust slammed the shutters, tossed about the flames and embers, and Phileander came to life.

'Ah, Vladimir,' he rasped, as if mid conversation. 'I remember it distinctly. It was a bleak winter's night like this.'

The philosopher's gaze was distant, his cheeks uncharacteristically rosy, and there was a slight slur to his voice. Flames – now crackling and hissing briskly – danced in his glassy eyes, and shadows flitted across his face like the ghosts of winters past.

'I've never told anyone this, but you're not one to babble, are you, Vladimir?' Phileander grinned absently as he took a deep swig. 'Elisaveta … not of particularly good stock, but she used to bring something out in me that I never …'

He trailed off into a silence that harboured a melancholy nostalgia.

'She was my first and only love, you know,' Phileander whispered.

And Torment squawked and fluttered up in fright when suddenly the orrery's golden rings lost all their substance under her claws, as did the wooden sideboard underneath. Dissolving into flowing dream fabric, the contents of the room now collected in a swirl in front of the armchair. The dream dust reshaped itself into the form of a scrawny human woman. Raven-black lengths of hair framed her prominent cheekbones and draped in waves over her shoulders. Her thin white robe lay loosely over a bulging belly. Clearly she carried a human hatchling inside her.

Torment circled in agitation and searched for something to hold on to. There was nothing around them but this murky void in which the chair and the woman faced each other. For want of a better option, Torment settled atop the headrest, directly behind the philosopher's shaved scalp.

'She had an acute intellect as well as a strong spirit,' he went on, 'both of which I admired far more than her beauty. A beauty so radiant, most of those simpletons that so crowd the One City could not for the life of them see past it – certainly not her halfwit of a father.'

The woman brushed a lock of hair out of her eyes and cast Phileander an endearing, impish smirk. The philosopher smiled back, and in his half profile Torment glimpsed a vulnerability eerily unbecoming the jaded man she knew. She was certain that what they saw here was the exact image of what his mind's eye had shown him that very night in his reading room. Moreover, in a way that made her feathers stand on end, Torment found this woman to be strangely familiar. Had she seen her face in her mind palace?

'Hence she was the only suitable candidate to conceive my child.' His smile lingered a moment, then turned bittersweet. 'And I the only suitable man to even attempt the deed I did – which had not been done in centuries. Oh, had she only known, Vladimir' – he gazed bleakly into the fire – 'but even the keenest of minds will never know of my plans more than I divulge.'

'And divulge them you do, you clueless ape,' Torment croaked with glee.

'*Shh,*' hissed Vlad, while the philosopher frowned in irritation, as though something had distracted him.

Then he got up from his chair, throwing Vladimir onto the featureless black floor, and once again everything around them disintegrated, including the armchair this time, much to Torment's chagrin. She held herself aloft where her foothold had once again betrayed her, while

Vlad scampered away across an invisible floor, bowing into a lurking position below the hovering crow.

The dream dust gathered once more, manifesting a shiny silver table in front of the philosopher, and on it the pregnant woman, naked now and drowsy.

'There, there,' Phileander murmured, apparently more to himself than the woman. The remaining dust enveloped him in the shape of a white apron, from which he pulled a vial that he uncorked and waved under Elisaveta's nose. He gently stroked her cheek until her body went limp and her breathing shallow.

Cautiously, Torment landed on a patch of the elusive blackness below, right next to the cat. 'Did he do that too when he was telling you this in the reading room,' she croaked sceptically, 'like some deranged pantomime act?'

'No,' Vlad whispered without taking his eyes off the proceedings. 'It wasn't half so vivid the first time round.'

The woman lay entirely unconscious now, and from a non-existent tray somewhere to his right, the philosopher retrieved a scalpel that materialised in his hand just as he grasped it. With a deep breath and one last pained look at her face, he whispered, 'Goodbye, my love.' Then he carefully placed the blade against her lower abdomen and set about his bloody work.

For one whose daily business it was to pick apart carcasses with her bare beak, and one who liked to amuse himself by torturing small rodents to death, the two of them were quite uncomfortable at the sight they witnessed. Spellbound, they watched as the woman's abdominal skin was removed, layer by layer. Something smouldered right at the centre of Torment's torn soul, only recently kindled and barely more than a spark. It was the part of her that understood, as the purest of facts, like knowing that up was up and down was down, that what she saw was *wrong*.

Elisaveta, ashen and still asleep, released a low, inhuman moan as her blood-smeared hatchling was pulled from her womb by its knobbly feet. The dripping umbilical cord hung dangling into the gaping cavity that had been her belly.

'It was then, Vladimir,' the philosopher prattled on, 'that I started to understand I was sacrificing far more than my lover and child.'

He sounded as though he was still slouched in that armchair, tongue loosened by wine. At the same time he stood there, tense and focused as he slit the throat of his own prenatal offspring over a silver bowl, bleeding it like a lamb for the slaughter. Afterwards, he placed the frail, underdeveloped body back into its mother's womb and watched the woman's face until all life had ebbed away from it.

Nauseatingly, an appetite rose in Torment at the overwhelming metallic scent of blood. She fought it down, disgusted at herself.

When it was finally over, a sliver of life had left Phileander as well, and his shoulders hung lower than before.

'I had sacrificed my ability to love ever again,' he whispered, 'and all for the *greater good.*'

There was something about the way he emphasised those last two words – not remorse but a bitter reassurance. Meanwhile, with black liquid from a flask he likewise appeared to seize out of nowhere, he diluted the blood with gentle sways. He proceeded to draw it up with a certain silver syringe that Torment remembered all too well, harvesting his vile elixir.

'This makes it even more precious, you see,' the philosopher said reverently, 'for I will never be able to create a second dose, because besides being untainted by birth and returned to the cradle of the womb, the child must also have been conceived with *love.*'

'Dear me,' Torment crowed. She and Vladimir sat silent, gazing aghast at a past Phileander who now examined the syringe against an indiscernible light.

'But what does this have to do with how we're trapped?' she continued after several moments. 'I get the "he killed his love" part now, and how he's so screwed up in the head, but you said—'

'Oh, but it is so obvious,' Phileander chimed in, looking directly at her now, 'is it not, Torment? My blood runs through your veins.' The darkest of smiles crawled up the corners of his mouth, resurrecting the version of him that Torment knew. 'This most rare and powerful potion not only protects you from the vampire, it also made you my *homunculus.*' He let go of the syringe and it immaterialised, along with his apron, the table and everything else but him. They were alone with their tormentor in an empty darkness without end. 'It lets me in; it gives me the reins to your spirit, should it ever be in need of reining in. And from the looks of it, it is – for the both of you.'

With these last words, he turned his attention to Vladimir, who knew nothing better to respond than 'Oh, shit.'

The philosopher crossed the distance between them without taking a single step; space simply seemed to contract, too fast to react, until he towered directly over them. They sprang up to flee, but his long-limbed hands had already seized them by their necks.

But the crow and the cat slid right through his fingers as if they were but clouds. Phileander's arms drifted apart, left in the wake of Torment's take-off. He regarded his body as it began to blow away into the darkness, becoming yet another wisp of dream stuff.

'You shall be granted a slight delay to your punishment, it seems.' His cold voice slowly faded along with his form as he spoke. 'And after I've made my way back to the tower, I shall pluck you up from where you lie, while you find that returning to your bodies from this is not as easy as …'

The rest became inaudible, but they had heard enough. Besides, they were too busy fighting the sudden force that now pulled at them from the void. They tumbled and shrieked and mewled and were tossed onto a cold cobblestone street, a heavy door slamming shut in front of them.

~

THE TWO COMPANIONS in woe found themselves in the streets again, several levels deeper in this fractal reinterpretation of the One City. Vladimir scrambled to his feet while Torment shook the stinking slime of a muddy puddle out of her feathers. But their respite was short-lived, as they also found themselves in the midst of a stampede of hurried human feet – leather boots, clacking wooden heels, fine buckled shoes, a vagrant's dirty foot rags, all stomping past them, over them, nearly on them a couple of times.

The crow and the cat zigzagged across the road, swearing and frantically searching the rushing tides of human traffic. Torment repeatedly tried to take off and rise above the crowd, but the forest of swinging limbs was simply too dense.

Her four-legged companion, on the other hand, appeared to be far more competent at navigating this terrain. Was it a part of his own mind palace, perhaps, bleeding into whatever *this* was? Vladimir was already a few paces ahead, poised for a beeline towards a shady side alley that was invitingly clear of people.

When he had an opening in front of him, however, instead of making a run for it, he turned his head looking for Torment. Something was terribly awry about his face, though she could not pinpoint it exactly. A strange distortion of her field of vision left her reeling in confusion.

Vladimir's eyes locked onto her as she hobbled after him, her plumage mud-encrusted, while swaying boots brushed her, kicked her around, stepped on her tail feathers.

'Torment,' he shouted over the din, 'come over here and hold on to my— *whoa*, what happened to your face?'

'Later,' she gasped. 'Escape first.' And she was relieved when he turned to face that side alley again, averting the gaze of his distractingly deformed visage. Slowly but surely she adjusted to this strange new way of seeing, which focused on what lay before her and hid what lay to the sides.

'Hold on to me,' Vlad yelled, ready to dash.

Torment heaved herself onto his back with an exhausted, ungainly flap of her wings and dug her claws into his fur. As she tried to hold on to the thick coat on his neck with her beak, she made a disconcerting discovery: her beak was gone.

But Vlad darted off as soon as she'd landed on him, his hind legs propelling them forward with unpredicted velocity. All Torment could do was press her chest and wings flat against the cat's body, holding on with her talons and letting the feline's superior flexors, thighs and motor reflexes do their work. He pounced this way and that, changing direction with a speed that felt downright physically implausible.

Moments later, they were launched through a curtain of shadow into the safety of that back alley he'd spotted, and the noise from the street grew dull and faint in an instant.

Finally a moment of reprieve. People rushed past them only a beak's length away yet seemed as distant as rain beyond a window. Torment slid off Vlad's back and took a much-anticipated breather, lying down and fluffed up like a plump old pigeon.

'And you've been *living* down on the city streets?' she asked incredulously. She found the floor of her mind palace not half as stressful, and that was populated by a horde of resentful corpses.

'It's not nearly as bad as this in the real— no, really, I can't put off the topic of *your face* any longer.'

She glanced up, once again shuddering at the sight of Vladimir's chalky human features looking back at her from the front of his coal-black cat's head. It had thick, dark eyebrows and a strong nose, rugged stubble, and the human hairline merged into his silky fur. The ears sat a little too high for the face and had human lobes but black-fleeced, pointed ends. He was eerily reminiscent of the copperplate print of a *sphinx* she'd seen in one of Phileander's books.

'Having already lamentably noted the loss of my beak,' she said, in a voice that she noticed to be far softer sounding than usual and far less croaky, 'I assume I am also wearing a human face now.' There was a flash in her mind's eye of a figure nailed to the ground, its doom descending upon it.

'Also?' Vlad hastily scanned his face with his paws. 'Immortals help me, I hope I don't look like Phileander.'

'Not quite.'

There was a subtle resemblance, but he didn't have to hear that. The eyes were still Vladimir's, yellow irises, slitted pupils and all. He also still had feral fangs among his human teeth, which he found out with a sigh of relief as he plucked at them with an extended claw.

He then pointed it at Torment, saying, 'Cos yours damn well looks like that Elisaveta woman.'

She puckered her lips in thought and at the same time was amazed at how normal it felt all of a sudden to have lips at all, not to mention a habit of puckering them.

'Having heard what we've just heard—'

'And seen,' Vlad pointed out.

'And seen, I would argue that besides the best of cronies, we are possibly also … siblings, in a sense. Thanks to that abominable elixir.'

'As much as I'd like to expand on the topic of our relationship, I'm afraid we have a more pressing issue. What are we going to do about Phileander?'

'You mean,' Torment intoned reprovingly, 'what are we going to do about the fact that in your efforts to demonstrate just how murderous and unpredictable he is, you also trapped us in some kind of dream dimension and made him incredibly mad?'

Vladimir's man-face glowered at her. 'Yes.'

94

'Let's see.' Torment put a wing against her chin in a gesture that would probably have made more sense had she had fingers. 'That hideous homunculus ritual seems to be what permits him that weird mind control over us. A useful piece of information. Also, he seems to be limited to spying on us for now, at least from his current location at the inn of the Thrice-Woven Curse.'

She got up and started to pace from side to side. She took care to step over the tufts of miniature towers jutting out of the gutter, connected by miniature bridges on which throngs of miniature people went about their bustling business.

'Also, this is clearly more than just a regular dream you've thrown us into. I suspect this place might be allowing the three of us access to each other's mind palaces to a degree. Or maybe it just mashed them all together? Anyway, I'm not yet sure how much we can consciously control that.' A moment of rumination, then she stopped, pointing her wing at Vladimir. 'Conclusively, if we want to turn this excursion to our advantage, my monkey-faced comrade, we need to do three things.'

Vlad still glowered. 'If that was supposed to be an expression of affection, birdie, it sounded a bit condescending.'

'One,' Torment continued unapologetically, 'we need to pry a little more into Phileander's ugly head to learn how to break his spell, preferably without giving up its obvious upsides, like our new brainpower. Two, we need to learn how to break *your* spell before Phileander gets hold of our unconscious bodies. And three, we need to make him forget this little adventure of ours ever happened.'

After finishing her conclusion, Torment's gaze wandered anxiously from Vlad's new face to the dark alley behind him. A number of looming, lurking figures emerged from ink-black shadows. 'And four—'

'Three seems plenty, actually,' Vlad said dryly.

The figures approached, silently stalking, muzzles twitching – a band of hungry stray cats on the prowl. In the nested scale of this dream city, they seemed to originate from a level higher up, as even the smallest towered over Torment and Vladimir as though they were common house mice.

Sniffing the air, Vladimir whirled around, only now picking up the scent of his oversized conspecifics.

'And four,' Torment whispered, 'these guys don't look like they're here for tea and biscuits.'

Her companion began to back away, and for a moment Torment saw in him a kitten, intimidated and forlorn, and in his face a boy, thrust coldly into a world of dangerous men.

'They sure don't,' he growled, while an orange beast bent down in front of him, wagging a raised tail that tore the shingles off neighbouring roofs in playful hunting lust.

Vladimir seemed to recognise that specimen and quivered, looking haunted in its shadow. They must have spilled over from his mind palace, from some violent memory … past demons of his. Torment was still unsure whether their lives were in actual danger – whether this was really just a dream or if the same rules applied that Catalina had warned her about – but when the orange beast lashed out and Vlad's blood spattered onto the pavement, her survival instinct kicked in anyway.

She rose two beats up in the air to swoop down on the attacker, beak first.

Torment noticed her error only when her soft little nose had already squashed painfully and ineffectively against the orange cat's skull. Dazed, she fluttered along the alleyway, only narrowly escaping the flailing claws of the yowling, gargantuan strays.

Vladimir was cornered now, surrounded by opponents whose paws he evaded only thanks to his diminutive size and sheer dumb luck. Blood dripped from a deep cut that ran from his forehead to his chin.

Torment attempted a few more aerial forays, but, beakless as she was, they amounted to little more than minor distractions.

'Flee, Torment,' yipped Vlad.

96

'No, you'll—'

'These bullies did me in before in other nightmares – I'll live!'

'But this is no regular nightm—'

A slamming paw cut Torment short, hurling her hard against a brick wall.

Warm, unpleasant-smelling breath wafted around her as a fanged maw descended to finish her, but a black shadow leapt in between them. Vladimir had hooked his claws into the cat's delicate nose and was holding on desperately as the beast shook its head in a rage.

A darkness stirred in Torment, a presence waking to the scent of fresh blood. It whispered bone-chilling promises, but Torment swiftly shut it down. She had glimpsed that darkness once before. Still concussed, she floundered upward, bouncing off the alley walls and leaving a trail of feathers. She flew and flew until she broke free of that gloomy gorge of houses.

The cats expelled the strangest of noises, warped wails and hisses that at times were eerily reminiscent of human screams of agony but at others of the cries of children in their cribs. Torment heard them fading as she rose, pushing herself higher and higher above the streets, beat by beat. Some of those howls must have been Vladimir's, fighting for his life, but, looking back, Torment could not make him out in the frenzy. She just remembered the glistening red gash across his milk-white face and those streaks of blood on the rugged cobbled ground.

Had she betrayed him? Had she left him for dead in a realm of dreams, never to awaken? Like poor little Adelaide? Catalina had warned her of dying in the mind palace. Every beat of her wings carried Torment farther from the ambush where her only friend did battle, backed against a wall. Roofs and roads and bridges fell away from under her as she pushed skyward into a world of giants. Meanwhile, the shame of cowardice gnawed at her soul and pulled her gaze down to what was now no more than a blur where her imagination showed her the most terrible things being done to Vladimir's tattered, bloodied body.

Torment was too preoccupied to notice the protrusion poking out of a castle wall up ahead, crowned by a grim pair of gargoyles. Her inelegant manoeuvre to avoid slamming straight into the wing of one of the stone sentinels sent her staggering through an arched aperture in the masonry.

With a clatter, she made a crash landing on a tabletop, incapacitated by her human eyes that took an unreasonably long time to adjust to the dim lighting. But she remembered those gargoyles well, for they had guided her homebound approach many a night, and even before the murky image of Castle Quelm's crowery took shape before her eyes, she recognised the familiar smells of excrement, straw and murder.

'I hear the dead when I sleep. I hear them when I close my eyes. I hear them now, as I write, and with their whispers, they accuse me. What shames me most is my inability to answer. Yet I firmly believe that this is only a matter of technique.'

—Ogden Flynt, *Spirits beyond Earth and Sky* (unfinished manuscript)

Chapter 7

A Ray of Sunshine

THE CONTOURS SHARPENED to reveal iron cages swaying slowly on creaking chains, behind them cold stone walls, and the rotting straw beneath clotted with bird droppings. Whenever one of her hundred black-feathered fellows stirred, there was an oh-so-gentle rattle. They surrounded Torment, hanging all around and overhead, suspended metal prisons wherein the members of her murder cocked their heads to display long black beaks and cast critical black eyes upon her.

Under their gaze, Torment became awkwardly aware that her face showed neither anymore – at least not in her current form. She'd once been one of them, the crow master's pets, penned in walls and cages and doing the bidding of men. Phileander had not truly imprisoned her, she realised, but merely consigned her from one cell to another.

Torment stood up, stretched her wings and took a look around her. Capsules to hold a messenger crow's cargo were scattered on the table, as well as chains ending in shackles small enough to close around skinny little legs, and a long metal fork to administer punishment and reward through iron bars.

A single echoing caw from up above startled Torment. She looked up but couldn't recognise who had crowed it. White beams from narrow skylights dazzled her, casting the flustered flock in their cages like a play of shadows. Another caw came from her left. Was it a warning? A sign of distress? She could not read it. She sniffed the air to make out the odours of oils and dander on their skin and feathers, to tell the birds apart, but neither could she read that. All Torment could hear and smell were … animals.

Caw!

Torment looked down her bird's body that seemed but a disguise now, a cruel lie. And at the end of her left leg, puzzlingly, now clung a metal ring connected to a chain that led to the edge of the table.

Caw – caw!

The rattling picked up and the crowing gained vigour. Soon a clamour of caws arose and the chain on Torment's leg tensed. She followed it with her eyes, over the table's edge, link by link, across dirt-stained slabs of granite, toward the door and, standing before it, the baroness's brutish master of crows.

His underlings saluted him at the top of their lungs, the strident song of a hundred crows reverberating through the circular hall and – *snap* – falling silent at a flick of his finger.

He bore the banner colour of the corvids, black leather from glove to boot. In his other hand he held the end of Torment's chain, and he started to pull.

Torment tripped. The crows watched silently.

'No,' Torment yelled, pulling against it. 'This isn't right!'

But it was no good. She was weak and small, and he was big and strong. Inches at a time, she slid across the table, leaving long scratch marks.

'I'm not here and you're not there,' she railed. 'None of this is real.'

She fluttered up and clutched the bars of one of the hanging cages. Her grip was firm, but the crow master's pull was relentless. He drew Torment in, closer and closer, along with the cage she held on to so desperately.

As the cage tilted on its chain, the captive within let out an offended squawk. It grabbed hold of one of the bars for balance. Its head twitched one way and then the other as it eyed Torment indecisively through the bars.

Torment met its gaze while she clung on. She should have picked up on *something*, some hint based on body language or scent, but she had no clue as to what went on in this crow's head. She had unlearned it.

'Friend?' she whispered, while the tug on her claws started to hurt.

Once more the crow jerked its head, holding its inscrutable stare for a second … then it pecked at Torment's foot.

She cried out in pain. 'Why?'

'*Caw!*' came the answer, and the crow kept hacking and pricking and chipping away at Torment's grip.

Below, the crow master was wrapping the chain around his hand – once, twice – then he yanked. At the same time the beak hit Torment hard and her grasp was released.

With a flutter, she fell, calling, 'Traitor.'

'*Traitor,*' answered the crow.

'*Traitor, traitor,*' echoed the rest of them, '*traitor!*' A cacophony of denouncing croaks.

She was no longer one of them.

Torment hit the ground and was hauled over the stone. On the crow master's face looking down at her, stern edges like rock etchings drew sharp shadows that harboured the grave of any grace he might have had as a youth.

'What do you want with me?' cried Torment.

The crow master continued pulling impassively.

'*Traitor,*' croaked a straggling crow before silence fell once more.

Not crow, not human … Was she anyone but the patched-together scraps of the souls of others? A wraith, a bad copy, an unperson? A *homunculus.*

With one final, painful jerk, the crow master pulled her to the toe of his boots. She lay curled up and quivering in his shadow.

'You've gone rogue,' he snarled down at her. 'Conditionin's all buggered. You're no good for nobody like that.'

Torment squirmed on the frigid floor to get away from him. 'I'm not … I've grown, I've changed. If you let me go, I-I'm …' Part of her wondered why she bothered trying to argue with him. There was no mercy to be had here.

The crow master drew a knife from his belt, blade glinting in a stray ray of sunlight.

'No,' Torment yelped. 'You can't discard me like some spoiled fowl. I-I'm no man's possession.'

The crow master's mouth twitched in amusement. 'Oh,' he said, and his features melted. His eyes and mouth rearranged themselves, his nose thinning and elongating, until the grinning grimace of Phileander leered down at her. 'Is that so, Torment?'

Then she remembered what all of this was.

'Y-you're not Phileander,' she said, hoping it was true. 'You're just my— my fear of him. This comes all from my mind, my insecurities, my own nightmares … like those cats came from Vladimir's.'

'Or am I the part of him he has injected you with? Or am I a demon from the Yonderrealm, donning this face to torment you?' He gave one of her master's terrible grins. 'Oh, Torment, you're such a clever little thing. But it doesn't matter.' The crow master's body squatted down. It was slightly too bulky for the philosopher's narrow face. He held the chain tight and brushed the icy steel along her featherless cheek. The gentle caress of death. 'I have a knife, and you are trapped, and I will kill you.'

Surrendering, she recalled, was often the surest way to wake from a nightmare, but all instincts told her this might not hold true for this particular dream. It all felt at least as real as wandering her mind palace. This felt much as though she was in it right now, or some version of it blown out of proportion by the alchemical drug Vlad had fed her. This, she might not wake from at all. She tried to argue further or to plead, but no more words would escape her trembling lips, with her throat and chest alike constricted by the pressure from her racing heart.

A squeaking leather glove fastened around her body, and the knife's edge settled on her neck.

Trickle, trickle drips the blood, from steel, from tooth, from claw.

A rupture tore through Torment's soul, and her dream came to a halt. The world became a feather floating gently on a breeze, taking its own sweet time to descend. And she heard a whisper from within, a dark voice, eons old and hungry.

Let me take care of this.

Every fibre of her being screamed 'No!' Her riven soul itself resisted, and something that guarded its darkest depths reared up. But this was survival.

Trickle, trickle sings the blood; it hails the night eternal.

And survival was paramount. She wouldn't bite the dust now just because of Vladimir's stupid dream trip mush. She wouldn't surrender … not to death, anyway.

Let me …

Torment let it.

And a power surged through her – such an incredible, all-consuming power as she had never imagined. There was an endless well of it. Her feathers fell. Her bones reformed. And then her hand closed around the crow master's wrist. With the other, she clutched his throat.

Panic welled up in the philosopher's eyes. He drove the knife deep into Torment's throat with his free hand. It severed skin, tendons, arteries and trachea, causing the most exquisite pain, but as swiftly as the steel sliced through her flesh, the rising darkness in her mended it again.

She rose up on her strange flat human feet and lifted the lumbering man up with her. He weighed nothing. While she held him at the end of her outstretched arm, his boots dangling in the air, she looked down her tall and unfamiliar form. Sporadic black feathers still sprouted from her skin, but otherwise she was naked, smooth and pale. Except for that collar of bright red blood that ran down from where the knife had cut her, forming a rivulet between her breasts, trickling along the curve of her ribs and belly and seeping into a plume of black feathers that crowned her crotch.

Bright red blood. She was so hungry. A pounding drum drowned out all other sounds. A steady beat of tantalising convulsions. *Rich, lush blood.* She felt it pulsing in waves from the crow master's chest, felt it with the tingling skin of her fingers digging deep into his neck. It was rushing through her arm and into her head. *Oh, what sweet debauchery it shall be again.*

Like smouldering paper, a blackness burned through Torment's vision. It encroached from the edges, a ravenous haze, until the world was gone.

And babies shall be taken from their cribs and they shall be eaten, and the wails of their mothers and fathers shall echo through frozen ruins under a blackened sun.

Torment retreated into the same dark pit inside her from whence she had just released this *thing* that now took over. She watched it only through a thin rift in the darkness, like the tiniest crack in her eggshell – a flare of red heat and depraved desire that would never be quenched. The ravaging dance of skin, bone and fangs. And as she watched, layer after layer of her very essence simply faded away.

And when their wails have been silenced, we shall reclaim the wastes of our earth, and we shall forever war for dominion and sow them with sweet red blood, and we shall become one with the land.

All that defined it had been stripped from the little crow by a tidal wave of darkness. Now it wandered through the void, trying to shut out this abysmal, primal voice. The little crow was hiding from something, it remembered. It should not be here. This was a prison for … something gravely dangerous. The void was cold and lightless, and the crow was so alone and so afraid, and at every step it lost a memory until it did not even know its name anymore. Time had lost all meaning while the crow drifted aimlessly.

'Hello, little one,' a soft voice called out to it.

The crow turned to see a slender, black-haired woman in a loose white dress standing over it amid a soothing glow. It had seen her before, remembered the crow, and something that had happened to this woman pained the little bird greatly.

'Who … who are you?' it croaked.

The woman bent down and let it climb onto her hand. Her skin was warm and pleasant.

'I'm a friend, little one,' she answered. 'Until now I've been hiding from a monster that was trapped in here with me, but then it was unleashed and escaped, and you came.'

'Trapped? Unleashed? What is this place?'

'Oh, you may call it the depths of your despair, if you're so melodramatically inclined, but really this is no place at all.' Her eyes revealed pity and a deep-rooted pain, yet her voice had a comforting cheer. 'You've given your body over to the monster, and this is the corner of your mind you chose to crawl back into.'

The crow shuddered, glimpsing a flashing image of a black-feathered woman, eyes aflame with fury, bathed in blood. Then it pondered for a moment. 'If we are inside my mind, then what are *you* doing here?'

'Just like the monster, I am a part of you.'

'A part of me? I've lost so many parts of me,' said the crow. 'I've lost … my name.'

Its human friend straightened up and held the little crow directly in front of her face with both hands. She seemed to radiate from the inside.

'No, Torment, you haven't.' The woman smiled at the crow. 'You're still here, though you've made a dangerous decision that puts your very soul at risk. But I don't blame you. That was quite the pickle you got yourself into in that crowery.'

'I don't remember it. Can you help me get back?'

She gave the crow a motherly kiss on the beak. 'Let's see what I can do, little one.'

The woman closed her eyes and began humming a tune, a consoling melody, a lullaby for a child that never was. Her radiance increased and its white-hot light washed it all away, blinding the crow.

And the world came crashing down on Torment. Her head hurt as if it had been split open, and she remembered very little of what had just transpired. But then it all came back to her – Phileander, Vladimir, the dream potion, the ritual … the crow master's knife.

She stood in her former home in Castle Quelm, still alienated from the sensation of inhabiting this new human-shaped vessel, and in her hand she held the lacerated body of a crow that had once been one of her siblings. Its cage still swung before her, the bars bent open with bare hands, and she felt something rubbery in her mouth. Torment spat it out. It was a violet lump of muscle, a tiny heart. Her whole face was wet and dripping. The air reeked of death and the taste of iron lingered on her tongue. All around her lay the corpses of crows and the scattered, mangled remains of what had once been the crow master. Her sallow skin was almost entirely covered with warm blood. It was oozing down her fingers.

Torment felt sick and dizzy and she stumbled toward the door, slipping on scattered gore and almost falling down a stairwell into chilling twilight. Everything was spinning, and she could hear nothing but this high-pitched whirring, while dreary corridors passed her by. She left red handprints on grey stone where she groped her way along the walls. This tottering body seemed so unsteady, its heavy head so far above the ground, bobbing on a lanky neck, and its naked, blood-smeared skin so utterly exposed to the cold castle air.

Left, left, right, left, down a flight of stairs. It all looked the same – blank walls, empty halls, a dismal maze.

Finally, there was another door, a lone portal at the end of a hallway. She just had to get out, she thought, to get somewhere without walls, somewhere that didn't leave a sour taste in her mouth and a knot in her stomach.

The door stood ajar, and behind it might have been lurking escape or hope or unspeakable terrors.

'There is a strange door deep in the bowels of her keep.' Phileander's voice rang from her memory. 'She has thrown half a kingdom's worth of traitors in there, but nothing ever gets out – at least, nothing has so far.'

With cold and sticky hands, Torment pushed open the portal and walked out into the great unknown.

THIS DELICATE HUMAN skin blistered so easily under the searing rays beating down upon her. The sweat pasting her hair of black feathers to her forehead had long ago turned to a salty crust as dry as her aching throat. Her feet were worn bare by fine sand, ensnaring her clumsy human feet and making her stumble, sending Torment falling forward rather than walking.

We could have fed more, drunk more, ripped more.

Torment had done her very best to suppress that sordid voice. It seemed to have grown weary of her disregard of it after a while, but every now and then it returned with unhelpful notions such as this, and every time, her guts contracted. It sent her wistful memories of the bodies of plump, healthy crows, still huddled, frightened, in their cages, ready to be feasted upon.

'None of those crows were real, you stupid thing,' groaned Torment, her voice a strange intruder in a silent, desolate expanse. The flippant tone was unlikely to fool her unwanted companion. Her heart soon burst with horror, but she was sick and tired of victimhood. 'They were dream crows and you're a dream vampire.'

But I am not, little crow. And this place is more real than you know.

Torment had had enough of the mind games, the toil and struggle, this onslaught of paradoxical obstacles. Not too long ago all she had strived for was a slab of meat in reward for good service. Now she was graced with this profound insight into the world that, frankly, had so far done little more than help her realise that slabs of meat were merely a simple source of sustenance and her prior life was all but meaningless degradation. Instead it had endowed her with a vague desire for something greater – something likely to be as unattainable as it was indefinable.

Her journey into her own mind had turned out more traumatising and confusing than helpful in her quest for purpose. Then this journey into a land of dreams had rekindled her hopes, but now Torment traversed a vast desert in a human body, her head replaying that nightmare in the crowery over and over again, and she could not for the life of her discern the purpose of that.

It seemed an eternity ago that Vladimir had prepared this ludicrous tincture as a foolhardy prank, merely to show her a secret. And now they were lost, reaping dire consequences.

110

'What you ask of nature,' she remembered Phileander lecturing once, 'always comes at a price, my dear. It matters not if you chop a log, grow a crop or cast a spell. There is no shortcut, no loophole, no tit without a tat.'

Apparently she and Vlad were bloody fools who had swung the pendulum too far and got knocked over the edge on the backswing. *She* should have been the one outside the cage reading that grimoire, she ruminated. She'd have read the fine print. Torment wasn't even sure if she was still alive or if her body back in the waking world had already been disposed of, her severed spirit lost in this realm forever. For all she knew, she might already have been trapped in here for days. This sun, fixed high up and never setting, made it hard to track time. The philosopher should long have had his chance to return to the tower and exact his vengeance.

At the thought of him, Torment saw her master next to her, walking slowly on shimmering, undulating tiles floating above the desert floor. His pace was creeping, like resin oozing from bark, and he was half translucent. The philosopher didn't look much taller than her, dressed in his velvet going-out frock, and a pensive apprehension creased his face the same as the harsh, hot sand creased hers. She had no inkling whether she was catching a glimpse of the real Phileander on his way back from the inn or just some figment of her fevered brain.

Above this mirage an enormous sun burned brightly, and the strangest thing about it was … no sunthread extended out of it towards a tower in a storm. Nothing man-made was visible whatsoever, and that was definitely a first, even when it came to dreams. There was only an endless sea of dunes and scorching, arid winds under cloudless skies and a seriousness with which this nature treated her that was unbecoming of a dream. The heat felt real. The thirst felt real. And for better or for worse, this feather-spotted, sunburnt body of a human female felt real.

Just as I *am real. Your defensiveness, your doubts, your dread, they are …*

delicious. But you can make use of me. As you did before. Let me take over and survive.

'Sweet offer,' Torment snapped, a twinge of nausea belying her nonchalance, 'but there isn't anyone around for you to exercise your singular blood-crazed talents on. Or do you intend to rip apart the sun and eat its heart?'

I am not a senseless slayer. I am the original hunter, apex of the cosmic food chain. All of creation has been my hunting ground since the dawn of time.

'Apex hunter, huh?' sighed Torment in a bout of bravado. 'I stand corrected, then. You've got all kinds of nuance.'

Torment felt the beast in her release a growl of wounded pride.

'All right, you bloody parasite. Convince me.'

You have been a hunter too. Remember, how did you hunt, crow?

She recalled the threads of scent she had chased, tiniest movements detected from on high, rousing a predator's thrill. 'With my senses,' she murmured. How she missed her corvid senses. This beast might be on to something after all. What Torment lacked right here and now was a destination she could see, hear or smell. She lacked a most basic tool of survival. Indeed, the heightened senses of a mythical predator from the dawn of time sounded a great deal more helpful than the crude human devices to which she was left at the moment.

But to release the beast again … 'It would consume you' – she remembered Phileander's voice – 'not turn you.' Torment still wasn't sure how she had made it back from the darkness the first time.

He was not wrong. I would devour you whole. But only if you are weak. Are you weak, crow?

'I don't know,' answered Torment. 'All I know is that you abused me back there. Whatever you did, it was foul and wrong, and I'm terrified to let you loose again.'

Right now, the beast was locked away safely in that pit inside her and guarded well. But she had an unbearable thirst and a headache and a piercing pain where her lips and palms had cracked open like dried-out earth. Torment wasn't sure she would last much longer. Could spirits die? Why, by the All-Mother, had she never thought to ask Catalina or Phileander *that* question before setting off on spiritual expeditions?

Weak. Cowardly. Your death will be well deserved.

'Tell you what,' she said, as a flutter of defiance rose in her chest. She made a decision. 'I also know that I'm curious and ready to fight tooth and beak.'

Yes, little crow. Yes … and I shall savour it.

Torment closed her eyes, took a deep breath, and her muscles tensed in readiness. Once more, she tried to enter the palace of her mind.

Her Hall of the Conscious Mind was gone. Or at least it was not where it used to be. Or maybe it was just that she didn't reside in it at the moment? Torment tried to take that step back in her mind, back from the window, but she only felt her human feet stumble through the sand. It hadn't occurred to her before that her relationship to her mind palace might be entirely different in this world. Whatever 'this world' was.

Torment still felt it, felt that there was a world within her, harbouring both those meadows over the clouds as well as the bodies in her basement. She felt it stronger than she had when she had first come here. From emerging on that endless roof through escaping Phileander and those giant cats and finally the crow master, it had felt as though her mind palace had been seeping out of her, changing the world around her. Now, it seemed, her inner world was contained again. Something had changed when she had passed through that door in the depths of the castle that had led her into this desert and then disappeared on her.

That deep, dark pit inside her she still felt as well. Torment might not know how to go there, in a literal sense, but she sensed it pulling at her spirit. She felt it twisting her insides. Torment understood that giving in to the hunger emanating from it, the hunger she had been repressing since opening her eyes again in the crowery, was how she brought the vampire to the surface. It was an instinctive kind of knowledge. Torment wished she had some kind of instructions for this, because trying to control a vampire trapped in one's brain did not seem like an act conducive to amateurs.

But the thing practically threw itself at her – wild, starving, pulling at its chains. She tried to loosen its bonds ever so slightly, to restrain the rage and hunger. It felt much like trying to take off into a violent storm from the safety of the castle. Her pulse quickened and Torment was strained to the point of bursting as the darkness ascended to her consciousness. Then *it* opened her eyes.

Torment felt the beast recoil from the sun. She had expected her blisters to heal, like her cut throat had healed in the crowery, but the rays seemed to hurt twofold and the brightness blind her even more.

This made it easy, at least, to keep the beast restrained. Torment was still in control of her body. Yet the thing remained close enough to the surface to make a difference, and she noticed the amplification of her senses distinctly. When she shaded her eyes with her hands, she saw single grains of sand at a dizzying distance and a reddish shimmer betraying minute variations in the temperature and density of the air. And the smells, all kinds of them – bodily fluids of the tiniest insects crawling through the sands, the imprints of faraway lands on the wind, cinnamon, mildew and ash. She felt vibrations of hearts beating half a world away.

And she caught the scent of trees and wildflowers – and two humans … not at all very far away.

Following that earthen thread of scent, she soon saw a forest, all but a green smudge at first. 'Forest' was also a vast overstatement. 'Coppice' was more like it, or 'grove'. All of these were mere theoretical constructs for Torment, of course. As a creature of the One City, she had never seen either of those things. But then again, the same held true for a desert.

She could smell the dew on the leaves, the sap on the bark, the oils in the fur of small animals. She sensed fresh water, moisture for her dry throat. Her step gained vigour, her spirit lifted and a seed of hope gained ground against cynical desperation.

I crave not water, I crave rich, red bl—

'Oh, sod off,' said Torment and trotted on.

But the beast defied her. It bucked every step, crawling forth from shadow into the foreground of her mind, despite the pain this inflicted on both of them. Her skin began to sizzle in the sun.

'Stop this!'

That place over there will get you nowhere, little crow. We will keep searching.

'There is no *we*, you rotten worm.' Torment leaned into her stride as if against a mighty storm, balling her hands into fists, bent on asserting herself. If ever there was a time to test the boundaries of this thing's possessive power, it was now.

Inaccurate. There is no you. You're but an aberration that exists by my grace alone. Turn away now.

Jaw clenched, body braced, Torment took the next step … and the next. That spot of green in the distance unravelled slowly into the silhouettes of trees … then blades of grass. She even heard the murmur of a brook. And she felt the beast inside her quiver.

'Wait – are you … afraid?'

The beast stayed silent.

But its growing reluctance the nearer she got to those trees was all the answer Torment needed. Now more than ever, she was determined to reach that grove. Her skin boiling, Torment drew herself up to full height, inhaling deeply against a tightened chest – and turned her widened eyes directly on the sun.

The darkness in her screamed, shrinking back to its pit like a beaten dog.

Torment quickly averted her gaze again. Her agonised optic nerves already bled spasms of distorted, stabbing light. She covered her face, gasping with exhaustion and cautious relief. The vampire had withdrawn, yet still a lingering echo of its self-healing power seemed to repair some of the damage to her eyes. At the same time, the burning sensation on her skin subsided, though much of it remained ruined and sore.

With inward vigilance, Torment continued on her way. The beast was locked away, her mind was calm and the copse ahead beckoned with a whiff of sweet refuge. An irrepressible laugh bubbled out of her as her seed of hope began to grow into a little sapling. She kicked tirelessly against the yielding sand – and in the distance she spotted a figure.

Hurrying onward, she recognised it as the upright shape of a human in red robes leaving the grove to step out across the dunes. Several strides later, Torment made out a woman's form in the dress, with skin as black as Torment's feathers. Horns were growing from the woman's skull, coiled like a ram's, and her eyes glowed green as she caught sight of Torment.

Torment shouted and waved at her. She was still many yards away. The woman paused only briefly, and although Torment's vampiric senses were waning, she saw clearly that the horned woman smiled at her.

But then the woman turned and walked on, and before Torment could reach her, the wind had worn her away, her horns, body and dress carried off on a breeze like the sand until there was nothing left of her.

'Curse this dream nonsense,' Torment gasped, dragging herself the last few paces up to the tree line.

This otherwise undistinguished spot in the middle of the desert, roughly twice the size of Phileander's study, was overgrown with birch, beech and oak trees that did not fit even remotely into this environment. Underneath their rustling crowns there were ferns, mossy branches and stones, wet leaves, and even a red squirrel that looked at

Torment curiously for a moment before disappearing into the under-growth. A concert of rustling and burrowing emanated from the place, pulsating like the breath of a single complex organism.

There were gardens up in the higher levels of the One City, and Torment had sampled quite a few of them on her messenger flights, but never before had she witnessed such writhing fungal glory, such unhinged natural growth, or smelled such a harmonious amalgamation of the heady scents of life, death and decay. It suffused the damp air that flowed at her between the twisted trunks. Neither, in all likelihood, had Phileander ever witnessed such a thing … nor Vladimir. From so deep inside the One City as the Philosophers' Tower, no wingless crea-ture could ever hope to make it to the outskirts and back again within a mortal lifespan.

So where *did* this forest come from? Up until that door in the baroness's castle, everything had made a convoluted kind of sense – the warped reconstruction of the city, the philosopher's memory, their past trauma confronting them, inner demons wanting out. But this … this hadn't sprung from any dream of theirs.

'Will you be standin' there gawking forever?' rang out a grouchy voice from the glade.

'Many myths persist about the world yonder and its demons. Lies "Yonder" between Earth and Sky? I like to think it does, and thus a great many spirits that ought to be mentioned in this text remain regrettably in the dark. Yet one true thing might be said about them: they suffer pain just like spirits hither, and seek to rid themselves of it.'

—Ogden Flynt, *Spirits between Earth and Sky*, Vol. 2

Chapter 8

A BIT OF PRACTICE

TORMENT BRUSHED ASIDE branches and vines and entered a small clearing. In the centre of this patch of shrubbery and greenery, in the middle of an almost perfect circle of mushrooms, sat an old crone, cross-legged with her eyes closed. Her matted hair of copper and snow was adorned with pinecones and tree bark, and she wore a simple garment with motley patches.

'Hello?' said Torment warily.

'Well, at least you have manners,' rumbled the crone, morosely lifting one eye.

A fresh breeze played around Torment's bare skin, soothing her burns like balm. The smell of sap was everywhere, bees were buzzing nearby – and indeed, a stream ran through this grove, but where it came from and where it went remained a mystery.

'What is this strange place?' asked Torment, pacing the clearing, caressing the burly bark of the twisted trees in awe. Their canopies cast dancing flecks of shadow across the ground.

'You'll have to be more specific there,' said the woman. 'This strange forest? This strange desert? This strange world within a world?'

Torment stopped and turned to face the crone. Tiny shrews peered timidly from behind her robes and sparrows from her tangled hair. 'I'll take an answer to any of those,' Torment said, 'if you have them.'

'How very cheeky of you.' The crone opened both her eyes now and surveyed Torment from top to bottom. 'And who are you to be callin' me forest *strange*, anyway? Blood-encrusted, naked lass with feathers for hair who wanders alone in the desert … you're plenty strange, you are.'

'*Your* forest? So you have an answer to one of those questions, at least.'

The hag's reply was a resounding laugh, strong as an oak and rough as its bark, and the grove seemed to laugh along with her, leaves rustling like the faintest cackle.

'I can give you the whole set if you like, but it won't do you much good, mind you, cos things are just what they are.' She spread her arms. 'This strange place is a forest, which lies in a desert, which lies in a world that is wrapped in another world, which tumbles through a big, bad mess of worlds that've gone to the dogs, and outside that … well, state of things was all topsy-turvy there too, last time I checked.' She scratched her chin and pursed her lips. 'I could go on, but it'd be pure guesswork from here on, so it would.'

Torment crossed her arms and raised an eyebrow. 'But you're certain about those first four layers of reality?'

'Pretty much so.' The hag withstood Torment's sceptical stare for a while until she shrugged her shoulders apologetically. 'What can I say, lass? I've been around.'

With each new curtain that opened, revealing new cogs in this engine of madness, Torment felt more ignorant. This crone was quite unlike the shifting puppets who had populated the earlier parts of this dream world – or her mind palace, for that matter. Those, Torment was certain, had been conjured up by her, Vlad's or Phileander's subconscious. They had seemed symbols rather than spirits of their own. This one seemed like a proper person in the flesh, albeit one talking gibberish.

'So,' the old woman said, 'who are you and what are you doin', stumbling into my private meeting place?'

'You're not here for me?'

She raised a brow. 'Wee bit self-centered, are we?'

'Uhm ...' Torment rubbed the delicate feathery fuzz of her eyebrows. 'Where I was before, I ... everything, everyone came from ... my mind, my life, my memories. Certainly no one thought I was intruding or asked who I was. I'm ... I'm lost.'

'I see.' Her face crumpled into a comforting wrinkled smile. 'You took the long way round, you poor fool. Includin' a nasty encounter with your repressed griefs, no doubt.' She gestured invitingly to a comfy-looking clover patch in front of her.

Torment stepped into the clearing and sat down opposite the woman. It felt awkward, with those long human legs getting in the way and shamrocks tickling her in funny places.

'I thought I was in a dream,' she murmured, 'but now I'm not so sure anymore.'

'Dream, no dream.' The crone flailed her arms about. 'Blarney. Balderdash. Hogwash, all of it.' To Torment's bewilderment, the crone pressed her gnarly finger up against Torment's nose. 'You're *here*, that's what matters.'

'But *here* is no real place at all, is it?'

'Is this real, is that real,' she aped. 'Poppycock. Stop spinning in circles already. Wars have been fought over what's real and what's not. Whole feckin' worlds have been burned to cinders, and all of it for naught, I tell you.'

Torment wrinkled her nose. She did not appreciate being made a fool of, but the old woman had a point. She had very important things to do, and Torment was getting herself bogged down in a maze of metaphysical confusion. She had to be practical: find a way back to Vlad, a way back to her body and a way to deal with Phileander. But before Torment could trust this stranger to help her, she needed to understand who and what exactly she was.

'Why and how are you here?' Torment asked. 'And why did you say this was *your* forest?'

'Finally you're getting closer to questions that might actually help you.' The crone tightened her posture and settled her hands on her bony knees. 'I'm a traveller and I left my body in the world I came from, much as I reckon is the case with yourself.' With a sweeping gesture, she indicated their surroundings. 'This is *my* forest because I made it. It resembles my meditation grove in the other world, from where I set off to this one.'

'You can simply *make* a forest?'

'I can manifest nearly anything I fancy.' She nodded toward the forest floor between them, where suddenly a green plaid picnic blanket appeared out of nowhere, richly set with nuts, berries, bread and apples, and a cup full of fresh water. 'This world is more ... *malleable* than the one we came from.'

Torment grabbed the cup and drank up the water greedily, spilling some of it from the corners of her mouth.

'It submits readily to the spirits that dwell here,' the crone continued, 'or those who are just passin' through, like us.' She picked up one of the hazelnuts and threw it over to the squirrel that was just poking its head out of the bushes again. 'But most are far too tethered to their daft expectations of how the world *should* behave to make proper use of this nifty feature, so they are.'

Torment took a deep breath and looked around. This place gave her a deep sense of longing. 'Where I come from there are no forests.'

'Well, statistically speakin', it was pretty much inevitable that you were gonna come from the One City, so I'm not surprised.'

She knew the One City. So when she had said 'the world we come from', what she had probably meant was the Hitherrealm. Torment made a mental note of this. She had been asking herself what a stranger was doing in her dream, but perhaps she should be asking herself whether at some point she might have passed over into the Yonderrealm … like Adelaide Lidelle.

'Your forest lies outside the One City?' Torment asked while clumsily trying human feeding. Only now did she realise how famished she was.

'Until the day that Moloch of stone and smoke grows to swallow it,' answered the crone, 'which will be my cue to move on again.' She hummed a mournful note. 'Fleein' the outskirts to the coast until one day I'll be pinned between city and sea.'

'And you could return to your real body right now? Just like that?'

The woman frowned as if Torment had said something very foolish. 'I have retained a link to the world we both came from, aye.'

'Can you teach me to do the same?'

'If you have a few centuries to spare for the training, maybe. Though I'm a shite teacher, mind you. And if you travelled here by different means than I, it won't do you no good.'

'I travelled here by means of some alchemical concoction …' A chill ran down her spine as Torment thought of her body lying in that cage. 'And I don't think I have any time at all.'

Torment looked up at the sky, which she no longer had wings to rise into, which she might never rise into again, which wasn't even *her* sky to begin with. Her little sapling of hope began to wilt in a shadow of uncertainty. A strange pressure built up in her eyes … until they shed droplets of bitter relief. An odd experience, she found, but one that inexplicably helped her to cope with the suspicion that she might be trapped here forever.

'Or maybe I have all the time in the world,' Torment whispered, 'but lost everything else. I've been here far too long already. A day, perhaps, or two. Eventually the body I left behind will be found and killed or wither and die.'

The old woman threw her head back in peals of laughter. It was very unexpected. On second thoughts, it also struck her as rather cruel, but Torment's experiences with Phileander did not provide the best reference for what was socially appropriate human behaviour, as Catalina had kindly pointed out so often.

Noting Torment's hurt, the crone coughed apologetically and put on a reassuring expression. 'Keep your tears, lass. Hardly half an hour will have passed back home.'

Torment glowered at her questioningly but her hope perked up again.

'Time flows differently here,' the woman explained. 'I just concluded the equivalent of a three-day sit-down with an old friend and I'll be back home in time for dinner.'

Torment let this information sink in. Half an hour in the Hitherrealm was well over a day in whatever this was. That was an even larger difference in the passage of time than between her mind palace and the waking world. Torment assessed what this implied for her situation; judging from past experience, for a meeting in the Thrice-Woven Curse, Phileander usually set out about two hours beforehand. He was not one to waste time either, so two hours would be just about the actual time the way there took him. Of those two hours that he'd need, one and a half were still left. That meant she and Vlad had at least three more days in this world before he would get to their bodies, probably closer to five. Her sapling of hope perked up once more, even grew some leaves.

'Your old friend,' Torment asked, wiping her eyes, 'was she the woman in red?'

The crone unceremoniously pulled a bottle out of thin air. 'You met Lilith?' she asked conversationally. The bottle bore a label ornamented with gold letters and contained an amber liquid.

'She smiled at me,' said Torment, whose curiosity stirred at the mention of a name she had heard before. Right before Phileander had captured her, she had been carrying the baroness's message for the Temple of Lilith. 'The red goddess,' Phileander had called her, worshipped by a cult called *the Covenant*.

'That's good.' The crone winked at her. 'Lilith is a mighty judge of character, so she is.' Then she uncorked the bottle and poured both herself and Torment a cup. 'Reckoned our chat might take a while, and you look like you need it.'

Torment sniffed the liquid sceptically. 'There wasn't much in the way of conversation for her to judge me by.' The drink had a pungent, boggy odour that reminded her of charred oak and leather but also faintly of honey and dried berries. It was clearly some kind of liquor. Torment had never ingested alcohol before, so she took a very cautious sip.

Her face contorted instantly, and the tangy taste of peat was eclipsed by a burning sensation in her throat as she gulped the stuff down. However, a lightness immediately rushed to her head that was most welcome indeed.

'So, this Lilith,' Torment asked, still chewing on the unaccustomed aftertaste, 'is she the Lilith from the Covenant's temple in the One City?'

The crone drained her cup in one draught and went to pour herself a refill. 'Honestly, lass, I've lost track of all the cults and religions that've been cropping up around her over the centuries.' She waved her hand dismissively. 'In some sects she's a goddess of enlightenment, in others the Great Destroyer, Mistress of Demons, and in some of 'em she's got her own fingers in the pie, the little minx. Lilith's a busy old witch.'

For a while, Torment stared thoughtfully at the golden-brown liquid in her cup, which caught the light very beautifully. She contemplated a leap of faith. The woman before her was clearly no ordinary human. She was a powerful sorceress at least, perhaps even one of the ancient beings the humans called *immortals*. And this Lilith she was friends with might just be the one that temple was dedicated to, in which a 'true vampire of old' was being held captive – which apparently was a big deal, according to Phileander. Surely this Lilith could help Torment get rid of a teeny tiny thought vampire trapped in her little crow brain. But perhaps they might also capture her to perform even more ghastly experiments than the philosopher had in mind. Torment had only her not-quite-as-*mighty* judgement to rely on. The crone seemed nice. And, of course, Torment was curious.

'I don't have centuries to spare, unfortunately,' Torment said, her mind made up, 'but if your admittedly somewhat squishy maths checks out, I should have a day to spare to learn what you can teach me. And I have it on good account that I'm a quick learner.'

'I know nothin' about you, lass,' said the sorceress with scrutinising eyes, 'so answer me one question in return.' Her expression took on a more serious tone. 'When you close your eyes, what do you see?'

This had all the hallmarks of a test, thought Torment. She closed her eyes.

What she saw was a darkness streaked with pulsing purple veins, a black sun rising, and evil eyes that smouldered red. The beast was still so close below the surface. A quickened pulse, nausea, fear.

That, Torment thought, had all the hallmarks of failing the test.

'Meadows,' she lied. 'A sea of green swaying in the wind. They may not really look like that, but that's what meadows look like in my head.' And to crown it all, an appeal to the old woman's ideals, as far as Torment understood them. 'A world without the One City. A world that breathes.'

She opened her eyes again. That wistful mask slid so easily onto her face, despite the anxiety throbbing in her chest, her horror but a wailing echo from a well-concealed corner of her mind.

A wide and wrinkled grin spread across the sorceress's face. 'Well, my grove back home's well protected and dinner can wait for an hour or two. Looks like you're in for a fast-track apprenticeship with this auld biddy.'

'Great.' Torment downed her cup, which was rough but sent a blissful shiver down her spine nonetheless. 'It's agreed, then.' She held out her hand to the sorceress, as she knew that humans did it. 'I go by the name of Torment, by the way, and I am, in fact, a bird.'

~

'A BIRD, YOU say?' The sorceress raised an eyebrow. 'Mighty odd, so you are. Anyway, you may call me Violet. Although city-dwellers like yourself know me better as the Wayward Witch these days.'

She looked expectantly at Torment, who could only shrug and shake her head.

'Let's see, then.' Violet scratched her head and squinted at the trees in thought, then looked back at Torment. 'West of the One City I'm known as Old Wolf-Mother.'

Torment shook her head again.

'Well, maybe it's good you haven't heard of me. The raider lords of the northern plains call me the Marshblood Mare and other, much less flatterin' names. But they've good reason to consider me a scourge.' She shrugged, then winked at Torment. 'But Violet's me oldest name, that I like best, that friends know me by.'

All those people and places meant little to Torment, of course, but it was good to hear that there was more to the world than the One

City's tiresome immensity of timber and stone.

'I'd love to introduce myself in return and spend time chatting,' said Torment, 'but I fear my friend might be in grave danger, if he isn't lost already.' She leaned forward urgently. 'He's a … cat. Last time I saw him he was being attacked. Can you help him somehow?'

Judging by the creases on Violet's brow, all this talk of cats and birds was more confusing to the old witch than Torment had anticipated.

'I'm afraid you'll have to start at the beginning, lass,' said Violet.

Torment bit her lip. She thought of what to say, and the darkness in her closed a cold hand around her heart.

'We are,' she began, combating a big lump in her throat, 'we are s-souls r-remade.'

Careful, little crow …

It was only the faintest chilling whisper in her head. Torment wanted nothing but for Violet to help rid her of the beast.

'We are …'

The cold grip tightened.

We are one.

'We are …'

We are but a wicked beast in that witch's eyes. An enemy for her to smite. To tell her of me would mean your end.

The vampire was right. Shame coursed through Torment. Violet was an agent of life, that much was certain. The thing inside her, on the other hand, was its very antithesis. And Torment herself … at best she was just a bird, insignificant in the grander scheme of things, a tiny sacrifice to slay the fiend that hid inside her. At worst she was a harbinger of doom, accomplice to murderers. Torment relented. The vampire had to remain a secret.

'A man named Phileander made us … the way we are,' she said. 'I can't … I can't say any more about it.' She took a deep breath. 'Suffice it to say that he is a cruel man who keeps us in chains. Me, the crow, and my friend, the cat.'

Violet put her haggard hand on Torment's. 'It's all right, dear. Whatever you dare confide will suffice.'

So Torment confided everything she could, from Vladimir to the dream tincture to Phileander's chilling discovery of their intrusion into his memories. When Torment got to the point where she and Vladimir had been forcibly parted, Violet summoned a small, short-beaked bird from the bushes, with white-and-russet feathers. It sat on her finger and she whispered to it, then it flew off through the canopy at her behest.

'I've never seen its kind,' said Torment wonderingly.

'It's called a *breacán*, or brambling,' answered the witch, 'and you wouldn't. They don't fancy the city much. This one was my dear friend Fringilla. I just sent her to fetch your friend.'

'You think he's still alive?'

'I think he might be lost, just like yourself.' With a wave of her hand, the picnic deck vanished. 'And he'll be meeting naught but trouble in the dream wilds.' She picked up a small twig and eyed it sullenly. When she shook it, it quickly elongated into a gnarled staff with a knotty growth at the tip. 'Without a proper guide, that is.' She pulled herself up by the staff and straightened her back. Her joints cracked like nutshells under a rock. 'If he's out there, Fringilla will find him. And now your teachin' shall begin, young crow.'

As Torment scrambled to her feet, the old witch kept twirling the staff in front of her, and just like that, sheets of fabric began to wrap themselves around Torment's skin. Once she stood, her legs were encased in soft buckskin breeches, her feet in black boots, and a white linen lace-up shirt covered her torso. Torment had always found the idea of clothing decidedly silly, but this felt very cosy – not unlike her protective black plumage.

Violet coughed. 'As much as I enjoy a congregation of bare-naked women in a moonlit glen,' she explained, 'it's also mighty clichéd, and

I like to steer clear of that.'

'What does "moonlit" mean?'

Violet raised her staff and said, 'This.'

The glow of the sun faded, revealing a star-speckled night sky behind the branches, and in it, the sun was replaced by a large white disc covered in a fine grey pattern. It mesmerised Torment, bathing the clearing in mellow twilight. Something inside her, a glint deep at the bottom of her being, older than herself or the spirits that possessed her, remembered that celestial orb with an ancestral yearning. As if all her life it had actually been strange *not* to see it up there at night.

'What is it?' Torment breathed.

'It's called the moon, this grand old lump of rock. Shame me and my friends had to blow it up.' The witch kept looking up in reminiscence for a moment. 'Now you lot call what's left of it the "skyroad", I believe. Anyway.' She turned back to Torment. 'Long before your time. Long before anyone's time, I reckon.'

Torment merely continued to gaze around, open-mouthed, as everything was shrouded in night yet softly luminous. And she kept swinging her legs, kicking stones or hopping on the spot to familiarise herself with the glorious, invincible feeling of wearing boots.

Violet began drawing circles in the earth before her with her staff. 'So, the dream wilds ...' She finished her raking of the earth by drawing a wide circle around the many smaller circles. 'They are all the places *in between* our dreams. They are the stage on which dreams play out. The dream wilds are part of a much wider network of entire worlds unto themselves, with their own rules, their own inhabitants, you followin'?'

Torment nodded, trying not to get distracted by her new clothes again. 'Yes, they are part of the Yonderrealm.' She had expected as much.

Violet scoffed. 'An eejit name, if you ask me, but aye. But there is no—'

'No single Yonderrealm.' Torment blurted out. 'I've heard of the idea.'

'In a way, there was once,' Violet said, squinting as though she was trying to remember something she had long since forgotten. 'You have to understand, what you call the Yonderrealm is older than our world. Strictly speaking, our world—'

'Where I'm from, our world is called the Hitherrealm.'

'You lot and your daft feckin' names.'

'I didn't choose it.'

'Anyway, the *Hitherrealm*' – she said it like pulling a worm out of an apple – 'is actually a part of what you call the *Yonderrealm*, which is where all your lot's names and preconceived notions fall apart.'

'Oh, I don't have any preconceived notions. But' – Torment pointed to the earth circles on the ground – 'what are those blotches supposed to be?'

'Lots o'little worlds within a bigger world, obviously. I said I'm a shite teacher, didn't I?' Very pointedly, she picked one of the circles and traced it a few more times so that its edge was twice as thick as the others. 'Anyway, the *Hitherrealm* was deliberately built very long ago, long before any of your kind started croppin' up—'

'Crows, you mean?'

'Would you please just stop interruptin'? No, not crows. Where was I? Ah, yes. The Hitherrealm, with its hard shell and its strict rules, was built as a kind of sanctuary, because, quite frankly, existin' in any of the other worlds is a shite experience for the most part. It's all very unstable, and there's a leanin' for the maddest and most deplorable spirits to end up becoming, well, essentially tyrant gods.'

'So spirits can suffer?'

'Of course. You're a spirit. Have you never suffered?'

'Well, I'm a spirit now, but—'

'Nonsense.' Violet gave her a knock on the head with her staff. (*'Ouch!'*) 'You've always been a spirit. In the Hitherrealm, you may have to don a meatsuit to gad about, which is part of the security measures built into that world, but otherwise you're no less spirit-y than any spirits from elsewhere.'

Torment rubbed the spot where the staff hit her, but also looked at everything around her with new eyes. She went around the edge of the grove again, touching the trees. She tried to make out any aspect of feeling their texture with the tips of her fingers that didn't seem real. It felt different, in a hard-to-describe way – more poignant, like a manifestation of the sheer idea of rough bark under skin – yet it felt utterly and wonderfully real.

'Can spirits die too?'

'Oh, yes. Harm come to your spirit,' said Violet gravely, 'should trouble you more than cuts and bruises and broken bones. The death of a soul leaves not a corpse to feed the earth, it leaves a monster.'

Torment withdrew her hands in an irrational fear that she might prick her skin on some poisonous thorn. At least she had her answer now. A monster ... Torment saw Phileander as one, but she suspected Violet had meant it more literally. The vampire was certainly monstrous. Was that what dead souls became eventually?

'What did you mean,' Torment asked, 'when you said *tyrant gods*?'

'I told you how this world is more malleable than ours. Just imagine living in a world where those most resilient are those who don't even know what *vulnerability* is, where those most likely to succeed at anything are those who never doubt themselves, where delusions are power. Imagine a world where an iron rule of fear and dogma can only be defied by utter madness. Am I paintin' a clear enough picture here?'

'Well, it's a picture. Clear ... I don't know.'

'Oh, you whippersnappers always take the luxury of a world of well-behaved matter and predictable rules for granted. It was wrought at great pains, your "Hitherrealm", believe me.'

'How? What is it, exactly?' She was looking around for a low-hanging branch to climb onto and sit, elevated as a crow would sit. 'And how do you know all this?'

132

The old woman followed her activities with mild annoyance. 'Well, the architects of our world are long gone, along with their craft. All that I know is that what you call the Hitherrealm is' – she waved her twig-like arms – 'well, like a bubble of *stabilised* reality in a big, messy foam of *raw* reality. Or something. And the dream wilds' – she vaguely indicated their surroundings – 'are a part of that foam clinging to the edge of the bubble. Here is where spirits from our world dip their toes in when they dream. They don't really travel here, though, like you and I have. Dreamers are more like ... ghost images, creating fleeting pocket realms in which their dreams take shape.'

While she climbed onto a branch, Torment thought that much of this sounded very much like Ogden Flynt's theories that Phileander had told her about. Somehow, it gave Torment a great satisfaction that she had cut the old man to the chase in breaking through into the Yonderrealm. Although that credit probably belonged to Vladimir. Or happenstance. She also recalled the mirage of Phileander she had seen in the desert. Could that have been him, daydreaming on his way back to the tower?

'This makes me wonder,' Torment mused. She was sitting on a thick, low-hanging birch branch now, dangling her feet. 'There is this place inside my mind, I actually go there sometimes ...'

'Go on,' said Violet, leaning on her staff.

'I call it my *mind palace*,' Torment continued. 'In it I can wander through memories and hidden parts of me. I do it for ... self-searching purposes.' She jumped up to perch on the branch. 'I still feel its presence, but I can't go there the usual way. So I wonder, might my mind palace be an actual place somewhere out here?'

Violet set to reply, but Torment let out a shriek as she lost her footing and plopped to the forest floor. 'You're one fidgety woman, aren't you?' the witch remarked with a frown.

'Sorry,' muttered Torment as she sprang up and dusted off her new clothes.

'You're on the right track, though, you rampant crow-child.' Violet rapped the thick end of her staff loudly against Torment's head. 'Inside that thick skull resides a whole universe, so it does.' Then she waved her staff around and a flock of crows fluttered from Torment's feathered mop of hair, cawing as they swooped away among the trees and soon dissolved into puffs of black feathers. 'And as your spirit's interwoven with this place, so your mindscape may leak into it.'

Again, Torment put her hand on her still-throbbing head. 'So …' She started connecting dots, forming a strategy. 'Interwoven, you say … leaking …' Grasping her chin between thumb and forefinger, she said, 'Phileander, the old crook, is most definitely interwoven with this place – through Vlad's dream potion. And the very means by which he transformed us, according to his own words, connect him to me and Vladimir.' Torment raised her finger into the air for her final bit of reasoning. 'And we are all immersed in this world claw, beak and feather.' She flicked the air triumphantly, another human gesture from somewhere in her subconscious. 'He even told me he communicates with spirits sometimes. If anyone's mind palace would wind up somewhere in the dream wilds, it's his. I just need to find it. Or … *manifest* a way there or something.'

Violet nodded. 'Solid notion, that is.'

Torment narrowed her eyes in further contemplation and looked up at that pale, round shape in the sky, that 'moon'. Nothing about this felt *solid* to her yet, she had to admit. 'We have to find it, Vlad and I.'

'What then?'

'Then we break in and steal all the secrets we need,' she said uncertainly.

'And after that?' Violet pressed on.

'Then we wake up.'

'How?'

'By …' Torment's thoughts raced and tumbled and she grew increasingly annoyed. 'We, uhm … how did you say you did it?'

'I said I retained a link to my body in the Hitherrealm.'

'But what does that mean – a *link*?'

'In my case?' The old witch shrugged. 'Something you won't be able to replicate, lass. There are other kinds of connections that could work, though. Think.'

'Ugh!' groaned Torment in frustration. She raised her hands and looked around frantically, as if ideas or answers might just fly past her to be fetched from the air. But there were only bees, mosquitoes and one particularly iridescent dragonfly. 'I … I really like my body? I can really … vividly picture myself waking up in it, wings and all?'

'Wishin' for a true connection is not quite the same as havin' one.' Violet sounded slightly disappointed as she rose from her leaning posture. 'A widespread human fallacy, that. Makes 'em make up fanciful hogwash and kill each other for no proper reason.'

Before Torment could ask her what might be a *proper* reason to kill one another, the witch waved her staff and out of nothing, a door appeared before them.

'Open it,' said Violet brusquely, 'and enter your mind palace.'

Torment looked at her, perplexed. 'Just like that?'

The crone tapped Torment's head again. 'Less crowin' around, more doin' what I tell you.'

With a throbbing head, Torment pulled the iron ring on the door and swung it open.

An open doorframe stood in the middle of the grove leading nowhere. No portal, no anything. Just three useless nailed-together posts of timber.

Torment shrugged. 'I don't think—'

'Less thinkin' too,' snapped Violet and slammed the door shut. 'Do it again.'

'But the door doesn't—'

'Hogwash!' Violet hit her with the staff again. Torment was starting to regret her decision. 'Open it.'

'Much has been speculated about the immortals who live among us. It is true that each and every one of them possesses powers beyond the abilities of mortal spirits, and that they are as knowledgeable and old as they are few. Yet each and every one of them has long since gone mad, and there is a desolate air about them. I have always thought of them as symbols rather than spirits; warnings against meddling with the divine and reminders of the value of mortality.'

—Ogden Flynt, *Spirits between Earth and Sky*, Vol. 1

Chapter 9

A GLIMMER OF HOPE

IT FELT LIKE it had been hours of just opening and closing that door and getting hit on the head with Violet's staff. Repeatedly, the old crone had asked Torment, 'What do you have to do to enter your mind palace?' and Torment would yell, 'I don't know!' and open that door to no avail. At some point, Torment had begun to simply make up answers just to satisfy her teacher.

'You have to hop three times on your right leg,' Torment said, did that, then opened the door.

Nothing.

'You have to … knock a little rhythm on the door.' And so she did – opened it.

Still nothing.

Torment had expected Violet to get mad at her for not taking this seriously, but oddly enough, she seemed pleased. As if this was progress. She would almost have preferred the witch to get mad at her. She had been lying to her, after all, hiding the vampire from her. What if it all blew up as soon as she got that door to work? What if that vampire marched out of there and slaughtered the both of them?

'You have to kick the door real hard,' Torment panted, exhausted from all the leg-hopping and door-slamming, 'and then you have to hit your teacher on *her* head with a lump of wood for once.'

Violet pulled a piqued face. 'I don't think so, Torment.'

'Well, then …' Torment was running out of silly ideas. She remembered the first time she had entered her mind palace. 'You need to … to *take a step back.*' Then she turned her back to the door and grasped for the iron ring.

For some reason, her heart was pounding, and a rush of anticipation went through her. Was it because she couldn't see what would happen? But why should that excite her when nothing had happened a hundred times before? Perhaps, Torment thought, it was because this time she believed, just a little bit, that she might actually be right. After all, this was close to the correct method to enter her mind palace from the Hitherrealm.

Torment yanked at the ring and felt a slight gust of chill air on her neck. She held her breath, took a step back—

And fell.

She tipped over and tumbled, and all around her the world turned a bright, gentle blue. *No wings!* Torment thought in a panic. She only had hands and arms, and they *hurt.* A sharp pain tore at her muscles. And only then did Torment realise she was holding on to Violet's staff, which the old witch had stuck out to her through a doorway that hovered in the sky.

It looked much like the doorway between her Hall of the Conscious Mind and her mind palace proper, only this time it was connected to Violet's grove. Below her, much further down than she remembered, Torment saw the city that harboured her memories … and her shame. Or maybe it just felt higher because she couldn't fly?

'You wanna come back, lass?' Violet wheezed. 'This is gettin' heavy.'

The wind blew her hair and the wide sleeves of her shirt. Torment hoisted herself up the staff, groaning, her shoulders aching, while Violet pulled. How very impractical that her spirit had taken on a form that could not even survive entering her own mind palace. She would have shattered every bone – did spirits have bones? – and been left to rot with the wailing and accusing souls that languished down there.

'Heave ho,' huffed the old woman as she gave the last tug.

Laboriously, Torment raked her claw-like fingernails into moss and tufts of grass, pulling herself over the edge as clumps of damp earth tumbled to the depths below. Then Violet shut the door behind her and with a wave of her staff made it rot to dirt before her eyes.

'Why would you make it vanish?' Torment gasped, propped up on her elbows and still short of breath. 'I took so long to make it work.'

'Because your mind resistin' to expose its entrance is just sound instinct, really.' She leaned on the lump at the end of her staff again and smirked down at Torment. 'Other spirits could get in … or demons of yours out.'

'Demons?' Torment asked. 'Like Yonderdemons?'

'That's just an eejit name the children of Bastion made up for "scary spirit".'

'Children of what?'

'Ah, never mind. You've learned enough for a day.'

'No.' Torment picked herself up again. 'I still don't know how to return to my world. Or how to get to Phileander's mind palace. Do I create a door leading there too? And what do I have to do once I'm there?'

'What have you just learned about where you are?'

'I'm ...' Torment thought hard. This all made her head hurt. So she was in the dream wilds, which were in a way the nearest neighbourhood to the Hitherrealm in a world of many worlds. Before, she had probably been in a kind of alchemically created amalgam of her and Vlad's and Phileander's mind palaces. Torment was almost certain that the moment at which she had traversed into the dream wilds was the moment when she had walked out into the desert through that door in her mind's version of Castle Quelm. She had also just learned that she could make a door appear that—

'But of course,' she said, snapping her fingers. 'My Hall of the Conscious Mind is where my spirit resides when it's not out exploring my mind palace.' She pointed wildly to where the door had vanished, her mind racing. 'That blue sky was my Nexus of Association. When I just opened that door, it behaved exactly like the door through which I have to go to explore my mind palace proper. That means that here in the Yonderrealm, wherever I am – or rather, my spirit – acts, in a way, as my de facto Hall of the Conscious Mind. Back in the Hitherrealm, I spent most the time operating my body like a coachman does his carriage, and whenever I take a "step back", I basically just step away from the reins.' She spread out her arms. 'But here I don't have a body. Here I'm always just my spirit, roaming free. And my mind palace is always just ... a door away.'

Violet smiled and nodded. 'You truly are a fast learner. So to return home, what's your missing connection, you reckon?'

'My ... window. It's the connection between my spirit and my body. Could I manifest that as I did the door to my mind palace?'

'That door led to a place that belongs to your spirit. You carry it within you as we speak. Your body is something different altogether. It is a vessel that is not part of this world.'

'Then maybe ... what I need is a bypass through someone else's mind palace. Someone who is still connected to the Hitherrealm, and preferably close to my body?' Torment looked at the witch questioningly.

The crone shrugged. 'What are you lookin' at me for? Sounds solid, that. You're the expert.'

'No, I'm—'

'Yes,' Violet snapped, 'you are. That's the whole point. That's why the door worked. Because you knew it would, silly crow. And about that "palace" of yours' – another painful tap on the head – 'don't let anything get in that doesn't belong there. Or out, for that matter. There's a reason spirits don't tend to open their doors like that. Whatever slips in can haunt you somethin' wicked – turn you upside down. And whatever's already in there haunting you can escape and go on a rampage. All kinds of vermin can develop in your noggin. You'd do well to crop the weeds once in a while, so you would. Tend to your grove.'

With another wave of her staff, the forest and all its animals turned to sand, along with all the stones and bushes and branches. The night sky and the moon were blown away too, like a flimsy veil – a conjurer's trick giving way to the glaring reality of an eternal desert noon. All was dry and coarse again. Her feet sank into the sand.

'What did you do that for?' Torment complained.

'Enough talk for today,' replied Violet brusquely. 'Time to rest.'

She flicked her staff once more, and promptly a tent erected itself around her.

Baffled, Torment stood outside that cone of coarse beige canvas, once again in a barren, boundless nowhere feeling as tiny as an insect. This time, at least, a layer of clothes shielded her from the blazing sun.

She pushed aside the fabric in front of her and took a peek inside. Violet was currently fluffing a cushion on a bed of hay and burlap.

'What—' Torment began to whisper, soon realising there was little reason to be quiet. 'What am I supposed to do?'

'You're not supposed to do anything, lass.' Violet lay down on her side, facing away from Torment. 'But if you don't want to shrivel up like a prune, I recommend you find shelter from the sun. Remember what you learned. Good luck.'

And with those words, the drapes fell shut in front of Torment's face. No matter how hard she tugged, the cloth wouldn't move anymore. The tent might just as well have been made of metal.

～

AGITATED VOICES WOKE Torment from a most uncomfortable slumber, all through which those evil eyes had watched her from the shadows. The beast had kept urging her to flee, tugging at her basest instincts like marionette strings. Torment had resisted. Now the beast lay in wait, patient, poised to strike.

What had Violet said about 'cropping weeds'? Had she gotten wind of Torment's deception?

Her back ached. Sand was everywhere where it didn't belong. In her crow's body, she had needed little more than a stick to sit on, and her claws and muscle tension would keep her upright through a long, relaxing period of sleep. Then there was the annoying disadvantage that these human eyes appeared to require absolute darkness in order to allow her to come to rest, and the sun had remained stubbornly at its zenith.

'I should crush you like the worm you are,' boomed Violet's raspy voice, 'you spineless scoundrel.'

'You wouldn't scare me even if this wasn't a dream, you brittle-boned harpy.'

Torment had heard that other voice before.

'A dream?' yelled Violet. 'Dim-witted gob! Who gave you permission to stomp through the veil of worlds like a steam hammer and flatten everything you see just because you're too daft to realise you're *not dreaming?*'

Torment crept sleepily out of her hovel.

In front of Violet's tent, at the end of a winding trail of fading footsteps snaking across the dunes all the way to the horizon, stood a strange man. He was broadly built, dark-haired and scruffy, wearing ill-fitting leather trousers and a tattered vest. His body was covered in dried blood, and in one hand he held an equally blood-crusted lumberjack axe. With the other, he clutched a small bird that seemed only half conscious and badly battered.

Violet was confronting the man, who towered at least a head over her, with her robe as dishevelled as her matted hair.

'Torment?' growled the man irritably, glancing over at her and her makeshift bedstead.

'Vladimir?' replied Torment groggily, struggling to her feet.

Sure enough, the man had yellow eyes with slitted pupils and a feline pair of fangs. The long, deep cut across his face had scarred already. Torment found this curious. After the short time that had passed, there should have still been a scab where the giant cat had slashed him. Torment also noticed long, claw-like fingernails.

'Is this a trick, you crotchety old bat?' snarled Vladimir, lifting the axe blade to Violet's throat.

The witch remained unimpressed. 'Release Fringilla this instant and I might spare you from wiping your spirit from existence like the man-shaped smudge of dirt that you are.'

Vladimir eyed the witch intently and Torment heard his brain rattling from afar. 'I think,' he began slowly, 'I'll just chop you to pieces like those other phantoms before.'

'Don't,' said Torment, gradually coming to her senses.

He looked back and forth between the two women, irked and indecisive.

'Don't,' repeated Torment, raising her hands placatingly.

For a disconcerting stretch of time, Vladimir wavered … until he finally lowered his axe and let go of the bird.

The brambling dropped to the sand, its feeble flutter unable to keep it aloft. Violet picked the bird up gently, whispering soothing words, and let it slip away into her hair.

Torment approached this tense encounter cautiously, hands still up, as if that would keep anyone from killing each other. It wasn't much of a mystery who'd be killing who in this face-off. She didn't know what 'phantoms' he had chopped to pieces earlier, but they had certainly not been equals to the likes of Violet, creating whatever she felt like out of thin air.

Torment stepped between the two, one hand turned toward each of them.

'No chopping to pieces,' she said to one side, 'no wiping from existence' to the other.

'*Hrmph,*' replied Violet, grabbing the cloth of her tent, which abruptly folded in on itself, transforming into her twisted old staff in her hand and leaving no trace of a tent ever having stood there.

Vladimir said nothing, and Torment still imagined she could hear his brain ticking while his suspicious eyes examined her new body. Something bad had happened to him and it still lingered in his bones. She understood him well enough by now to see through his calloused facade, human-shaped or not.

'How splendid,' said Torment after a lapse of awkward silence. 'I'm sure we'll all be the best of cronies in no time.'

Vlad's bushy eyebrows lifted ever so slightly. 'It really is you, isn't it?'

'No, I'm an impostor. This was all a test; you failed.'

'What?'

'Of course it's me, you ape-headed vagrant,' snapped Torment, nudging him in the shoulder.

From that point on, things reluctantly went uphill. Vlad and Violet practised tolerating more than befriending each other, and it didn't help that Vladimir kept appending comments to his apologies, such as

'I just don't like little birdies bossing me around.' It wasn't until it became apparent that Vladimir was particularly partial to Violet's strong
amber beverage that the three of them came to a mutually satisfactory
arrangement. He allowed himself to be persuaded to take the whole
bottle and retreat to a steep-sided dune to wait for Torment, who in
turn assured him that she wouldn't be long and she had a solid grasp
on how they might proceed.

'You ought to be wary of that one, lass,' murmured Violet when
the two sat cross-legged opposite one another again.

'He's harmless,' said Torment, glancing at him over her shoulder.
'Well, except for whoever he took that axe to.' A shiver ran down her
spine as, unbidden, she recalled the bloody scene she had left in the
crowery. He must have had a similar experience. Or more of them.
Over on that dune, she saw a scared little cat in a very dark place, hiding behind the face of a scary man.

'Anyway,' said Violet, 'I see you've … managed.' The old witch
surveyed the crude shelter of hardened sand in which Torment had
holed up from the sun.

Torment thought back to her clumsy digging a few hours ago, accompanied by curses carried across the desert on heated air as thick
as molasses. Eventually, tears had flowed again, this time of despair.
She hadn't thought she would have enough moisture left in her. The
droplets had made the sand mouldable, much like the mortar she could
mix with her saliva to fix a nest. Not that she had ever had to build a
nest, having been a messenger crow living in a cage, but as with all her
kind, the knowledge of nest-building had been passed on to her by the
All-Mother even before she had hatched.

'This is not how wet sand normally behaves,' Torment noted, 'so I
do believe I managed to manifest my will somehow.' She reflected on
her state of mind during the sculpting of the structure. 'But I needed
some kind of rationalisation to make it work. Like the stepping-back
thing with the door. A bridge that allowed my mind to outsmart itself.

Tears to soak the sand.' Then, suddenly, a realisation surfaced in her. 'It's not all that different from our world, is it? Every nest, every wall, every tool created is a manifestation of some creature's will. The process of labour is just … less rigorously defined here.'

A satisfied smile crinkled the crone's face. 'Ah, sure, you're as sharp as a tack.'

Torment returned the smile proudly. But her pride was quickly overshadowed by an all too familiar reality. 'Phileander made me well.'

Violet gave her a wry look. 'Do you have your path from here figured out by now?'

'Not really.' Torment wrapped her arms around her knees and watched Vladimir. He had finished his bottle and was steadily growing impatient. 'But I know that I will. I understand now that you couldn't possibly explain it to me and that I must make my own solutions. I'll explain them to myself along the way … while I look out for a bridge to outsmart myself. And I'll look after him.' Torment felt Violet's concerned gaze on her. 'And after myself, don't worry.'

She turned back to the old woman and the two of them shared a confiding look. They bade each other farewell in silence. So many things she hadn't asked her, hadn't dared ask her. About homunculi and how they are controlled. About the weeds in her mind palace and how to not be afraid to go there. About vampires. Torment pushed aside a last pang of shame. Then, with a final squeeze of Violet's hands, she got to her feet and prepared to leave.

'One more thing before you go, Torment.'

Torment turned around again.

'You said you two were "souls remade",' said Violet. 'Souls aren't made.'

Puzzled, Torment stared back at her.

'Like plants,' said Violet. 'Someone may have planted seeds and soil, but souls grow of their own accord. And just like plants, they need both light and shadow to do so.'

'Why are you telling me this?'

'The question tormenting you is written all over you. Clear for all with eyes to see but hidden from yourself.'

'Can you ... read minds?' asked Torment anxiously.

The old woman laughed. 'Can I see when you're lying, you mean?'

Torment swallowed, unable to say anything.

'I can see the dark stowaway in you, aye. Even if it goes out of its way to hide from me. I went toe to toe with its kind once, a long, long time ago.' For a brief moment, Torment saw this woman for what she was – a spirit older than tree or earth or sea. 'We know each other well enough,' said the witch, 'it and I.'

Torment gathered the courage to speak. 'If you knew ... why did you agree to help me?'

'Light and shadow, Torment.' Violet's ancient eyes gazed into her, doubtless laying bare all that Torment had been trying so desperately to wrap her tortured head around. 'In just the right balance, a wonderful soul might grow from it.'

Torment felt her stomach tighten with self-loathing. 'A dishonest soul.'

A wink. 'A little dishonesty can be tolerated in a pinch.' Violet raised her staff and gently tapped Torment's forehead with it. 'But you didn't lie to me, Torment. You just misunderstood the question. You really do see those meadows when you close your eyes.'

That strange pressure welled up in Torment's eyes again. 'But I don't.'

Warmly, the old woman smiled. 'Try it.'

Torment closed her eyes, afraid of what lurked inside ...

And a sea of green unfolded before her mind's eye, swaying in a gentle breeze. Like her wonderful place above the clouds. For the third time, thick tears squeezed through her tight-shut eyelids, a warm and steady stream.

'Did—' It was hard to speak, as if there was a huge worm lodged in her throat. 'Did you do this?'

'No.' Torment heard the rustle of Violet's sleeve, as if the witch was gesturing. 'And neither did I do this.'

Torment opened her teary eyes. Around her feet, gentle grass was growing – a field of green that extended several paces out into the desert before breaking up into sparse individual bunches. She could not yet fully account for how she had suppressed the vampire's influence just then or how she had given form to the image in her mind. She knew it had something to do with confidence, with *attunement*, and that she had started along a path the rest of which she had to find by herself.

'You coming or what?' yelled Vlad from the edge of the field.

Torment wiped away her tears and gave the old woman a kiss on the forehead.

'H-how do I—' she began to ask, but the beast, sensing her intentions, still would not let her, even as it was exposed.

'Don't go asking me how to get rid of it,' Violet responded. 'It would be the wrong question, anyway.'

Torment's voice wavered. 'Will I be fine?'

'Fine? Probably not. But who is?' The old woman's eyes told her clearly that this conversation had come to an end. 'Now go, lass.' In an odd gesture, Violet tapped a finger on her forearm, right above the wrist. 'However slowly, clock's still a tickin'.'

Torment nodded. 'Wish Fringilla a speedy recovery from me.'

Then she stormed off to Vladimir, her meadow cushioning her feet like a bed of feathers.

'Did you see that?' she burst out excitedly.

'Your little gardening session?' Vladimir shouldered his axe and shrugged. 'Sure, birdie. Impressive.' Then he nodded back in the direction she'd come from. 'Your geriatric friend seems to have turned to dust. That normal?'

Torment looked back. She saw only her little meadow now, like a

splash of green paint that a giant might have dropped onto the desert.
'I suppose so.'

'Huh,' he replied. 'So, what now?'

'Now we break into Phileander's mind palace.'

Vlad nodded as if all this was quite obvious. When nothing was
normal anymore, Torment thought, then indeed anything was normal.
'Lead the way, then,' he said.

Torment set off in the direction that felt most promising. She
made sure every fibre of her spirit was focused on the sanctum of the
philosopher's mind as their destination.

Vladimir's hulking human shape caught up to trudge along beside
her.

'Wanna swap stories while we walk?' he asked.

'Sure – why not?'

ALTHOUGH HE HAD been the one to suggest sharing stories, Vladimir
had been quite reserved. While he had listened intently to Torment's
experience in the crowery, he had only tersely told her about a people
of bipedal, brown-furred animals with flat tails he had stumbled upon
living in a village society by a river on the forested edge of the desert.
In vague terms, he had told her that in his disorientation it seemed they
had suffered a fate much similar to that of her crow siblings. Torment
knew better than to judge or jump to conclusions. She was reminded
of how she had felt when she had awoken among her mutilated kin.
They had been memories, she assumed, of the members of her murder. Since she had entered the desert, when she tried to remember her
siblings from the crowery, she found she had forgotten many of them.

After many hours of walking, the desert slowly turned into steppe.
And just like the desert, the word for this kind of landscape, and a
basic understanding of it, derived from some buried knowledge whose

source she could not trace. She only knew that this knowledge came from somewhere far above the clouds of her mind palace, and she could feel that as she tapped into it, all this knowledge collected in places at the bottom. She would have to sort it into her nests some-day – collections of facts about plants or about how streams of water carved the earth. Torment and Vladimir passed the strangest grasses and shrubs, crossed dry riverbeds and scattered rocks. There was not a straight shape in sight. This, Torment realised, was nature at its pur-est – a gentle chaos of perfect symbiotic equilibrium. Undisturbed, this land might live on forever, whereas the One City, in its attempt to impose order upon the chaos of nature, seemed to teeter eternally on the edge of collapse.

Despite its alien nature, something about this place rang truer than the world she knew. For a moment, a notion crossed her mind that per-haps this was the *true* world, forgotten and empty, while all the spirits were off dreaming of the One City. Yet for all its emptiness, the steppe was brimming with subtle signs of life. On more than one occasion, Torment was tempted to satisfy her hunger on the myriad lizards and bugs, had not the indulgence of a hunting instinct risked unchaining her only recently reincarcerated vampire. Compared to this display of unbridled nature, the One City felt like a necropolis, filled with lifeless contraptions and lost souls wandering.

'Perhaps we could just live here,' Torment said after a few hours. 'Maybe that's why fate brought us here. To escape not only Phileander but that whole crowded place.'

'You mean reality,' grouched Vlad, kicking a rock as he walked, which tumbled down an incline, letting loose a little avalanche of red earth.

'But what makes this less real, Vlad?'

'I don't know, birdie; maybe the fact that we're' – he cut down a dry, thin thing, half bush, half tree, with a single stroke of his axe – 'bloody *dreaming* it?'

'Or maybe we've just woken up.'

'You've gone crazy. That old bat screwed you up in the head.'

'Look, crony—' She stopped, taking Vlad's hand, which thoroughly flustered the cat-man, who tensed and stopped in his tracks as though he was scared to trigger a trap or something if he moved a muscle. 'I've been learning a lot about the world at large lately. About the worlds out there. I think we've somehow crossed over into the Yonderrealm. The realm of spirits. We're spirits ourselves.'

'No, we're not. Even if this was something other than a dream, we're a cat and a crow. Not a normal cat and a normal crow, perhaps, but we're *real*. We're flesh and bone.'

'We used to be. But what do you think made our flesh and bone move?'

'Muscles and a brain. Maybe you want to start focusing again.'

'What do you mean?'

He pointed with a grim expression at the uninhabited expanse with its odd hills and bushes and pools of water, the scar on his face bending the lines into which it had creased.

'You told me you'd get us to that mind palace thing of Phileander's by *manifesting with your mind* or whatever. Now you tell me you're considering *living* here. In some barren-ass dream shithole. Maybe the reason we've been trudging through nothing for hours is because you're not "manifesting" hard enough.'

Torment scoffed, letting go of his hand and breaking eye contact to look out over the plains. 'Why don't you "manifest" along, then? And even if it's a foreign concept to you, I can hold two thoughts in my head at once, you lumbering oaf.'

A growl escaped him. 'What is that?'

'Well, my thoughts on Phileander, naturally, and on—'

'No, *that*.'

His large, coarse hands cupped her chin and drew her gaze to a figure standing a short distance away between a head-high rock and a shallow ravine. Upon looking more closely, Torment noticed that the figure was translucent, wavering like the heat above the desert sand.

'Is that Phileander?' Vlad whispered.

'Probably,' Torment said. 'Let's go and have a look.'

'Are you mad?' he hissed, clutching her arm.

'Look, don't worry. It's just him daydreaming. Dreams project spectres of our spirits into the dream wilds. I've seen him before in the desert. He can't see us.'

Vlad still looked sceptical.

'But perhaps we can find some clues,' added Torment, 'as to how far he might be on his way back to the tower.'

'On your head be it, birdie.' He gripped his axe firmly and released her arm.

They approached the figure cautiously and soon recognised that it was indeed Phileander. He looked frozen in time at first, but as soon as they were closer, they could see his mouth move very slowly. It appeared he was talking to someone, but where that someone would be, there was only the rock. When they were only ten paces away from him, Torment saw that, as with the apparition in the desert, he was not standing directly on the rocky ground but on a ghostly surface hovering above it, as translucent as he was himself. The surface was not even; it was a wide step of a set of marble stairs. The stairs appeared to be curved slightly.

'I'm not that familiar with anything going on on ground level in the city,' said Torment. 'Do you recognise those stairs?'

Vlad nodded. 'It's the stairs leading up to the Fountain of Fair Tidings, about an hour away from the tower for a human on foot.'

Torment went over the numbers in her head. Another hour, plus the stairs he would have to climb in the tower, meant they had at least two more days. Although Torment had to admit that counting days in a place where the sun never moved was a bit pointless.

'What I'm wondering,' said Vlad, as they walked another few steps around the rock to get closer to the Phileander mirage, 'is if him show-ing here means he's daydreaming … then why does it look like he's talking to someone?'

That was a very good question. And just as she made the next step, Torment saw the answer.

On that rock, on the far side of which she and Vlad had stood, sat a large brown-and-white hawk, almost the size of a human, and it was looking very attentively at Phileander's lips. It also looked very much as though Phileander was looking at the giant hawk.

The hawk was not translucent.

And just as Torment's crunching step froze on the scree, the bird's hooked beak twitched to the side and its disc-shaped eye turned to her. The yellow ring around its pupil widened as it focused on her and Vladimir.

'Shit,' spat Vlad, and the bird let out a screech that echoed in the ravine beside them, spreading its wings.

Just as the hawk cried out, the face of Phileander's spectre began, very slowly, to narrow its eyes and turn in their direction.

As fast as Torment could react, the hawk started lifting off. Some-thing whizzed past her, and with a meaty thud it met the hawk's chest and sent it whirling through the air to crash to the ground, where it twitched and squirmed, the axe blade buried in it up to the poll.

'What in—'

Vlad grabbed Torment by the hand and dragged her to the edge of the ravine, avoiding the turning gaze of Phileander.

'Apparently he can see more than you anticipated. And he has al-lies.'

'You don't know that,' answered Torment uncertainly.

But Vlad was already balancing on the edge of the ravine behind Phileander's back, and he dashed to the dying hawk. He yanked the axe out of its chest and hacked it sickeningly into its head for good mea-sure, stopping its writhing movements and feeble croaks, and wiped the blood off the steel on its white breast feathers.

Then he beckoned Torment over to him impatiently.

Still numbed and overwhelmed by the tumbling events, she followed mechanically, opening and closing her mouth in a futile attempt to comment on what had just happened.

Phileander had finished whirling around in slow motion, but they already stood behind him again. Next to them, the dead hawk emitted an odour of fresh, beguiling blood, and Torment felt a stirring inside her that set her feather-hair on edge.

'Let's go,' she muttered. 'Let's leave.'

Vlad dipped his finger into the hawk's blood and sniffed it, a hungry lustre in his eyes.

'Stop that,' said Torment. 'Come.'

She took his hand and dragged him along. He followed. When she looked back at him, the blood had been cleaned from his finger. She could not see if he had wiped it off somewhere on his trousers. They put the rock between themselves and Phileander's apparition, put distance between themselves and the carcass, spreading its seductive scent, and Torment led them into a canyon that sloped through the steppe, offering plenty of cover from eyes on the ground and in the air. 'The death of a spirit leaves a monster,' Violet had said. What did that mean for the spirit Vlad had just axed? Anyway, the thought of all the spirits Phileander might have in his employ to spy on them, to pursue them, to hunt them through the dream wilds, and the fact that he would surely know a way to drag them home by their spiritual heels to punish them, dispelled Torment's thoughts of retreating to this world for the time being.

She was focused on their destination. They had to bend their path through this world to lead into his mind palace and end this misadventure.

.

'The Wronged and Rotting dwell in deep, dark places, and it must be every guilty spirit's highest purpose to guide them to the light.'
—Ogden Flynt, *Spirits beyond Earth and Sky* (unfinished manuscript)

Chapter 10

SOMETHING QUITE UNEXPECTED INDEED

HAVING WALKED MORE hours, yet always sure to keep from spying eyes, steppe began to give way to marshland, and Torment's vampire roused at the sight of this new environment. Why it did she could not say. Perhaps, she thought, that thing had once been at home in a land like this. It was eerie enough. The swamp took the gentle chaos of nature and escalated it to a slippery, squelchy climax, squirming and rising and bubbling. Twisted giants, their roots like snakes entwined with the earth, stood like sentinels along the water's edge. The word 'mangrove' sprang to Torment's mind. A wet mist, the opposite of the desert's parched air, seeped through the luscious vines that grasped for the ferns below from the tangled canopy.

Leading to this nugget of knowledge, Torment imagined, was a swamp-scented current of air somewhere in her Nexus of Association. It would smell somewhat of rotten eggs.

In places, out of shadows and puddles, she glimpsed pairs of milky eyes watching them. Reproachful eyes. Hungry eyes. She just hoped none of them were spies for Phileander, because she would not know how to hide from them. Here and there, a branch sticking up from the mud looked strangely like a bone or some half-rotted limb. And sometimes Torment thought she could see them moving. Was this what the corpse-filled space beneath her mind palace might become when all the rest of her was gone? What a curious thought.

Heavy with moisture, Torment's shirt and feathers were pasted to her skin, damp air enveloping her like a blanket. It covered her mouth, her eyes, brushing against her face like a veil she couldn't shed. And it carried smells with it, wafting from the shadows like whispered secrets, sweet smells of decay and things below. Wherever they stepped, very carefully, deep impressions filled with brownish puddles, and all along their way, the sun still hadn't moved. But here the fog obscured its light, leaving them in perpetual gloom.

'Have we passed that puddle before?' asked Vladimir.

'Can't have,' Torment said. 'We've been following the sun all the time.' Which Torment was not certain meant all that much in this realm.

'Cos if we haven't,' Vlad said, 'who left those footprints?' He was pointing at impressions in the mud ahead in the shape of slim, elegant soles.

'Those are not the shape of my boots,' Torment murmured, crouching to examine them, 'and you're barefoot.'

These had been left by fine shoes, she gathered, with flat heels and a pointed design. Fashionable in the Three Baronies. How exactly she was able to make those deductions, Torment was not sure. A part of

Elisaveta in her, perhaps?

'It's a trail left by someone from the One City, and not far from where we live, judging by the fashion,' said Torment. 'This has been left by another spirit who is lost here.'

Vlad immediately went into a prowling stance. He took the lead, stalking with light steps, his axe at the ready.

'We're not hunting it,' whispered Torment. 'These are the footprints of a little girl or small woman dressed in modest Baronies finery.'

'Does this strike you as a place where all is as it seems?' asked Vlad dryly. 'Besides, what you just said all but screams that this is another agent of Phileander's.'

He had a point. But still, Torment would not want to let a chance pass to ask questions. She could use another traveller's insights on finding one's way through here. She had felt hopeful when she was leaving Violet, but since then every hour made her more anxious. How much time did they have left? And with her anxiety came doubts, and what little she understood about the way this world worked told her that as faith was what led you where you wanted to go, doubt was what led you astray. And she remembered those eyes watching from the bog. Who was to say the inhabitants of this swamp would not lay a trap like this, whether they were working for Phileander or not?

'Fine. Just don't axe anyone before we get to talk to them,' she said and waved him ahead.

Torment was no stranger to stealth and hunting – she had been leading them from hiding place to hiding place these past hours, after all – but her methods mostly required a bird's physiology.

They followed the tracks, and Torment was almost ashamed of how abysmally bad she was at sneaking. Human feet were about as light and elegant as boulders. But as she observed Vlad's flowing movements, the graceful motion of muscles under his furless skin, and tried to copy him, she got better. She stepped on rocks, which were insidiously slippery, or carpets of soft foliage, trying to avoid those smacking sounds. Yet it all felt pointless, as there were still those eyes watching them from the fog. It didn't feel as though they latched onto them by sound or sight or even scent. They saw what was in their hearts. They saw the doubt that ate at her.

Vlad lifted a hand to signal her to halt and ducked behind a large fern. Torment caught up with him, waddling past a big circular basin of bubbling brown water. In the dim light, with that wiry body, damp and muscular, and the squarish face with that wide scar down the middle, he looked quite like he belonged there. Not cat, not man, but a predator. And ruggedly handsome. A startling thought that she promptly pushed away.

He parted the tall leaves with his axe to reveal a view of a mangrove-lined clearing. And in the middle of the clearing, on a moss-overgrown tree stump, sat a sobbing girl with tousled blond braids. She was wearing a light-blue dress with lace hems and puffed sleeves – though soiled all over with black stains and discolouration – and high stockings with a striking blue, white and red chequered pattern on them. Her shoes were covered in muck, but the silver buckles flashing through the dirt matched the footwear Torment had surmised. The girl buried her face in her delicate hands and sniffled.

'So lost,' she said. 'So terribly, *terribly* lost.'

Torment listened inwardly to see which emotion currently prevailed: curiosity, compassion or suspicion. They seemed to balance each other out at the moment.

'Hello?' cried the girl, raising her head. She sat upright and mannerly, like a well-schooled little noblewoman, even in this uncivilised situation. 'Is there anyone out there? Please. I'm so woefully lost.'

Something about her pointy little face looked familiar. A resemblance.

'Maybe we should help her,' Torment whispered.

'No way,' replied Vlad. 'This smells fishy.'

'I don't think that's the—'

160

'Stick it, birdie.'

The girl made an exasperated gesture. 'Oh, I can't conceive however I fell into this deplorable circumstance!'

The bubbling behind them intensified. Torment turned around. Something rose from the water with an unsavoury sloshing sound – the head of a deer, bloated and missing an eye, munching on something.

'What the f—'

Torment put a hand over Vlad's mouth, keeping still and watching, repulsed as much as mesmerised.

'I must indeed be doomed,' the girl lamented, 'and now birds will surely gnaw my eyes!'

For the briefest of moments, Torment felt offended, but the sight of the rest of what emerged from the sludge, giving off the ripest reek of overdue corpse-rot, demanded all her attention. Instead of forelegs, the deer had human arms, holding the carcass of something that looked vaguely like it might have been a fish if not for its torso, to which clung remnants of decayed clothing. The deer-thing had been feeding on the carcass. Now it had desisted and was muttering.

'So hungry,' it rasped. 'Guilty, stuck a needle in it, does not deserve, no, not deserve, eat her.' It squelched forward from the mud, heaving its malformed body from the basin, pulling itself forth with a tangled mass of pale tentacles growing from where its hind legs ought to be.

'Hello?' The girl's voice rang through the clearing. 'Anyone?'

'Eat her, take her guilt, oh, how she wails, does not deserve, the rotting, so hungry …'

The thing ignored the two of them. It writhed past towards the clearing, dragging itself and muttering and leaving a stinky, slimy trail. It was all Torment could do not to retch, even with the hardened stomach of a scavenger. Although hers was now technically the timid stomach of a human.

It coiled across a bulging mangrove root and tossed the fish-man cadaver aside as it entered the clearing.

'Oh, immortals be thanked, finally someone hears my calls.' The girl sounded truthfully relieved. She definitely had to be able to smell that monster as well as see it. 'Can you help me find my friend?'

'Arrogant, guilty, ugly, food ...'

'I'm afraid I don't have food, good sir.'

'No, impaled, wronged, eat her, eat!' And the deer's head reared up, shrieking hideously into the mist.

'How awfully rude,' said the girl.

'We need to help her,' said Torment.

'Are you mad?' hissed Vlad, but Torment was already stomping out into the clearing with slurping steps.

'Hey,' yelled Torment, 'why don't you eat me? I'm guilty too.'

It had almost reached the girl, who was just standing there with her hands on her hips. The deer-thing turned around, spasming, fleshy tentacles squirming toward Torment.

'That's right,' said Torment, stumbling back a few steps. 'Lots of bodies in here.' She tapped her temples. 'Come on, you— oh, crikey.'

Its shrieking grew louder. It clawed for her with its human hands, and its tentacled lower part moved much faster than Torment had anticipated. It dawned on her that this might not have been the wisest course of action.

But then, with a sickening crunch, an axe dug into the thing's flank and spilled slippery guts over Torment's feet. She felt queasy from the stench and slipped, landing on her backside.

'Ugh, crap,' spat Vlad, making a gagging sound. Then, with another wet crunch, the deer's head came off. Or it almost came off, still dangling there, while the tentacles flailed and knocked Vlad off his feet.

'Oh, what an unpleasant affair,' exclaimed the girl, throwing her arms into the air.

Torment scrambled to her feet. A tentacle crushed a mangrove trunk next to her, rotten wood snapping and splintering. Vlad's axe lay in the mud two paces away. He was wrestling with a tentacle.

Bloodless, lifeless, filthy thing. No sustenance, but still … I could destroy it.

Torment ignored the voice. Slipping a few more times, she inched toward the axe, on all fours mostly, dodging tentacles and that wheezing, biting head that still dangled from a string of half-decayed muscle.

Vlad had ripped a tentacle off the thing's rear, yet still it wrestled with him, strangled him.

Weak little crow can't do it alone.

'I'm not,' she gasped. She reached for the axe, but one of the thing's hands gripped her wrist. From the corner of her eye, she saw the girl reaching out a hand to the monster.

'No,' yelped Torment, 'run, you stupid—'

Splat!

Giblets of rotten flesh rained onto the clearing. The hand around Torment's wrist was gone. Corpse slime covered her as well as Vlad, who had just finished tearing apart the tentacle and looked up in confusion, and the dress of the girl, who still stood there, one hand outstretched where she had touched the monster. She seemed not at all surprised it had exploded. In fact, she simply wiped her face and hands and curtsied.

'How tremendously gallant of you to rush to my aid, but I'm afraid it was wholly unneeded. Are you two all right?'

Vlad stared at her. 'Scratch my immortals-damned bloody arse, girl, that was …'

'Really close,' said Torment, dizzy from nausea.

'I was gonna say "amazing", but yeah, that too.'

'We're all right, I guess.' Torment wrung the stinking residue from her shirt and stooped to one side to spit bile. 'Thank you, Miss Adelaide.'

'Oh dear,' said the girl, 'you seem quite shaken. But …' Her eyes widened. 'You know my name. However do you know my name?'

Torment wanted to answer, but her stomach wouldn't let her. She put her hands up in apology and ran back to the water, next to which she vomited profusely and wherein she rinsed herself hastily.

Vlad followed her to do likewise, minus the vomiting, and the girl, too, did what she could to make herself more presentable. Judging by the stains on her dress, this was not the first time she had made something – or someone – explode, and she had been wandering this world without a change of wardrobe for quite some time.

Torment warily searched within herself for the vampire's presence. She was getting better at suppressing it, she thought.

When they had all finished cleaning themselves with brackish swamp water, she sat down on a rock next to the girl, while Vlad stood nearby, picking tentacle scraps from under his fingernails with the axe blade.

'I met your mother,' Torment said, 'or rather, I was there when she met with a man called Phileander. Do you know him?'

'No, I don't think so. How is my mother?'

'Worried about you, I think. Hard to tell through the theatrics.' Torment mimed that thing noblewomen did where they put their hands to their foreheads and feigned fainting.

'Oh, yes, I suppose old people can be a bit hard to read.' Adelaide looked disappointed. 'I had hoped you might know my friend. We were supposed to meet days ago. I told no one else in this place my real name.'

Torment shrugged. 'Maybe I do. Is it a witch called Violet?'

'No, he's a magician called Zephyrus Thistlewhisk. He promised to take me back home when I had finished, and we had an appointment.' She slapped her hands on her knees. 'But he is always so terribly late. One of his many unfortunate vices.'

'Finished with what?'

'Why, defeating the Black-Eyed Mushroom Queen, of course. Wasn't everyone looking forward to being rid of her?'

164

Vlad cleared his throat. 'Look, girl, we're just passing through. We don't really care about that mushroom deal or any of that other weird crap going on around here.' He pointed at her with the axe. 'But that exploding trick, that seems handy. How do you do it?'

She shifted uncomfortably on her seat. 'I fear I swore an oath not to—'

'Scratch that. Spit it out, girl.'

'Vlad,' Torment chided, 'stop pressuring her. She's lost. And ... she can make people explode.'

Vladimir glowered for another second or two. Then he lowered his axe and grudgingly returned to his claw care.

'But maybe we can help each other, Miss Adelaide,' Torment said. 'You could come with us. We want to return to the One City as well, and I already have an idea how we might get back into our bodies. And you ...' Torment counted on her fingers for a moment. 'You must have been in here for almost half a year. I bet my beak you know a thing or two you're actually allowed to talk about.'

Adelaide beamed at her. 'Why, Lady Feather-Hair, a bit of company would be most appreciated. What things would you be most curious about?'

'Right. Call me Torment. What do you know about homunculi?'

'Oh. What a curious word. Nothing at all, I must admit.'

'And ... vampires?'

'Oh dear, oh dear. Only that they are the most dreadful creatures, destroyers of worlds, and that they are all gone thanks to the Lords and Ladies of the Courtly Beacon.'

'So, nothing about, I don't know ... eating their brains? And what it does to you?'

Adelaide looked most exasperated. 'Why ever would you propose such a ghastly, ludicrous thing, Lady Torment?'

'Ah, well, forget it.' Torment jumped up and stretched herself. 'Maybe I'll think of some less ghastly questions to ask along the way.'

And maybe she ought to be more cautious with the ones she decided to speak out loud, Torment admonished herself.

'Let's go, then,' said Torment, taking Adelaide's hand. 'Always follow the sun.'

∾

TORMENT FOUND ADELAIDE quite a pleasure to converse with. She was polite and clever and of good cheer. And she seemed to have quite the adventure under her belt as well. She confirmed that much of this world appeared to be deserted and that what few beings lived here were very curious beings indeed.

'One thing the old witch told me,' Torment said, 'and which I seem to have begun to learn as well, is to *make things happen* in the dream wilds. By believing them very strongly.' Her voice, like most sounds in this swamp, barely carried a few paces. 'Have you had that experience as well?'

Adelaide gave her a circumspect look as she sauntered ahead in the fog with her hands clasped behind her back.

'I have. But now it frightens me dismally, and I am very keen indeed to keep to the local customs and beliefs.'

'Why?'

Adelaide put on a grave expression and didn't answer right away.

'I was taken in by a village some months ago,' she said after a while. 'A wonderful little people. Their children liked to listen to fanciful tales I told them – tales I had read back home. And once … once I told them a scary one. And, oh, my dear Torment, what a woeful thing … do you know what storytellers do when they tell a ghost story? When they want to give their audience a jolly good fright?'

'What?'

Adelaide stopped and turned around. She held out her hand. Torment took it, and young Adelaide squeezed it hard with a tear in her eye.

'Oh, woe is me, Torment. They do all they can to make their tale seem real. They affirm twice and a hundred times that everything is as true as they say, and that if you listen very closely, you can hear the howling outside, the scratching on the walls, the snarling in your neck, the rattling of the bones.' The girl threw her arms around Torment's neck. She had to stand on tiptoe. 'Oh, Torment. Dear, dear Torment. Don't force me to tell you what happened next.'

Torment did not need to ask. She had a rough idea. What she was more concerned with, presently, was the feeling of being hugged for the first time in her life. She had never hatched chicks. Yet now she felt a peculiar desire to care for this girl, even though Adelaide could undoubtedly look after herself perfectly well.

Torment returned the embrace.

'Vladimir here,' she whispered, 'has had a similar experience, I believe. Maybe you two can—'

'Leave me out of your little cuddle session, birdie.'

'But—'

Vladimir flicked the axe blade with his claw, making it ring. 'I said no. A bunch of dream creatures bit the dust. Not real, not relevant. I don't care.'

Adelaide detached herself from Torment and shrank back a few steps. Torment scowled at Vlad.

'They were spirits, true as you or me or Adelaide.'

'Yes, Vladimir. Just imagine,' Adelaide suggested shyly, 'even if this is the land of our dreams … imagine if our Hitherrealm were just a dream in the head of a giant. Would that old giant have any right to stomp on our houses and squash us?'

Vlad scoffed. 'I know I'd have a right to gut that stupid giant and reclaim my home. Now cut your dogshit and leave me alone.'

He trudged on and Adelaide followed, eyes downcast. The next mile passed a little less convivially.

Torment had not seen those eerie eyes for a while now, and they appeared to be steering towards less unbecoming parts of the marsh-land. The air was less rotten, the dampness sultry but fresher than before.

'We should rest,' declared Torment after a stretch of silence. 'See if we can find something dry for a fire.'

'What for?' moaned Vladimir, trailing off into a gaping yawn that betrayed his fatigue. 'We're asleep already, and if that time difference thing pans out, it's been barely over an hour since we passed out.'

Torment was growing increasingly frustrated with Vladimir's pig-headed ignorance. 'Again, we're not simply dreaming. We're separated from our original bodies entirely.' She dug her fingertip into his hairy chest. '*This* is your body now. The form of your spirit.' Then her finger drew circles over their heads. 'And this is the world we're in. Some part of the Yonderrealm. It takes its toll on this body, just as our world takes its toll on your four-legged, furry one. Or maybe not just the same way, but in some way, surely, even if it's only because we *believe* we have to grow tired and hungry because that's what life in the Hith-errealm taught us.'

His face still exuded utter denial. It had been that way since they had left Violet. Torment could imagine his reasoning all too well: to accept the true nature of this strange world was to accept that he had committed terrible murders.

'Vladimir,' Torment said, taking his hand, 'these people, these …'

'Beaver folk.' Vlad finished her sentence, withdrawing his hand.

'Yes, them. Wash their blood off your hands in this marsh.' She pointed to a stream beside them. 'You were not in your right mind. You're not to blame.'

Vladimir glowered at Torment, and she noted a faint reddish glow in his eyes. 'You think that's what's bothering me?' Without warning, he drove his axe into the nearest mangrove trunk with a loud thud, and Adelaide gave a startled cry. Then he pointed to his clothes. 'I was in my right mind enough to take from their bodies what I needed.'

She stood her ground in his staring contest.

'I'm a cat, Torment,' he spat, raising a claw that would have served to slit her throat no less easily than the crow master's knife. 'I will have you know that I've sliced open more than one helpless crow for no better reason than being bored.'

Adelaide gasped, and Torment saw her slowly begin to stretch out her hand towards Vladimir, but Torment shook her head ever so slightly.

'I will not turn against you,' she said gently, 'or doubt your friendship, no matter how vile you are to me. You want someone to call you a monster, to punish you? Do it yourself.'

He took a step towards Torment and drew his face close to hers, his breath hot on her cheeks. His thoughts and feelings seemed as clear to her as if they were her own. She saw Vladimir caught in the same vicious circle she had found herself in as he reflected upon his nature as a predator with a reshaped mind now capable of self-loathing. It was a wonder, she thought, that it had taken this long for him to snap. She had twice his wits and willpower and still it took her all to restrain that shame or even start to reason with it.

'I will not blame you,' she said.

'I'm not to blame,' he snarled, 'because there's nothing to blame me for. The weak die. The strong live. That's the way it works.'

She'd seen Vladimir use his head to butt things far more often than to think about them carefully, so she wasn't surprised that denial won the day once more.

After a while, Vlad was the first to avert his eyes. 'If we rest here,' he growled, gazing at the murky sky, 'will I have to listen to any more of this presumptuous birdbrain dogshit?'

She nudged his shoulder. 'No more dogshit, crony,' she assured him, trying to keep a cheerful tone to her voice. 'I swear it on the All-Mother's tail feathers.'

Torment winked at Adelaide, who still seemed distrustful of Vlad but calm. Since she had met Violet, a kind of faith had taken root in Torment, a growing trust in the way her spirit interacted with the weave of fate around them, the empathic, living fabric of this strange world. It was this faith that would carry them to Phileander's mind palace like leaves on the wind. She could not let this sourpuss snuff it out if they were to reach their destination swiftly.

Torment was quick to do the groundwork for their camp. She had grown more accustomed to her new body and scurried through the surrounding vegetation, gathering branches and plucking a worm from the soggy soil here and there. Adelaide was keen to assist her in every way possible. Vladimir, on the other hand, seemed content to curl up on a moss-covered rock and watch Torment with his chin resting on his fist, unaffected by her scolding looks.

Every once in a while, a growl or purr would sound from that rock, making her wonder whether he might have changed back into a cat, but it turned out to be only his stomach rumbling. After a while, he got up with an indistinct grunt, which Torment chose to interpret as 'see you in a bit'. Then he pulled his axe from the trunk and headed off into the underbrush.

A while later, when they heard the smacking footsteps of his return, Torment and Adelaide were still lamenting the state of their gathered wood, which was altogether too damp to burn.

Torment looked up at him from her crouch and saw that he was carrying the body of an animal over his shoulder. Torment had never seen its like. It probably weighed twice as much as Vlad himself, elongated and serpentine, covered in iridescent, mirror-like scales that must have made it nearly invisible as it slithered through the shallow waters.

Adelaide clapped her hands with a look of wonder. 'What a terrifyingly beautiful beast you have felled, Vladimir.'

He dropped it in front of them, its massive triangular head flopping to the ground with a squelch. It grinned at them lifelessly, its cavernous mouth lined with rows of serrated teeth that could have shredded either of them to pieces. Four stocky limbs ended in long webbed claws. It made Torment uneasy to think Vlad had killed this thing alone and with apparent ease. But then, Adelaide would have had an even easier time, albeit with less of it left to eat.

'You'd better get that fire going,' he said. 'I've a feeling our human guts won't react as kindly to this here fella's raw meat as we're used to.'

Adelaide looked puzzled. 'Why would you be used to any other kind of digestive organs? And why would you point out they are human?'

Torment grimaced. 'Long story. Anyway, the wood is too wet.' She felt her faith falter. 'I ... I've never made a fire,' she murmured, as if it had just occurred to her. 'By the immortals, I didn't even have *hands* until a day and a half ago.' Torment looked at Adelaide. 'Do you know what to do?'

'Why, of course I do. It's quite obvious, isn't it? You have to dry the wood.'

'But how?'

Adelaide crossed her arms in front of her chest. 'How did *you* not have hands?'

Torment frowned. 'What has that got to do with—'

'You can do it, birdie.' Vladimir slumped back onto his rock and yawned. 'You reunited us with miles and miles of deadly wasteland between us, and I saw you make grass grow in the desert with your mind.' He clasped his hands behind his head and closed his eyes. 'You can light a few twigs.'

What was it, she reckoned, with people going to sleep and expecting her to work miracles in the meantime? But then again ... it had worked the last time. And also Torment could not accept the notoriously nihilistic Vladimir managing to muster more faith than her.

She grabbed a bundle of branches and began to strain her imagination. Faith. Self-manifestation. The wood was too dry. Whatever she came up with, she would need to wholeheartedly believe it.

'Any more words of encouragement?' she muttered.

'I believe in you!' declared Adelaide, clapping her hands again.

'There's a mountain a few miles ahead,' replied Vlad, eyes still closed, 'with a huge black building on top with something golden at the centre that looks like the Tower of Undreamed Truths.'

That was it. A smile crept over Torment's face. She knew it had to be Phileander's mind palace. She didn't hope or assume – she *knew*.

'Whatever you've been doing to get us there, birdie' – he yawned – 'guess it's working.'

It was working. Of course it was. They were leaves in the wind, and the wind was her will, and these branches …

Without further ado, Torment took the wood in both hands and wrung it out. Water oozed from it like from a wet towel. Slowly but surely, her sapling of hope grew again, rivalling those mangroves. She dried the whole batch of wood that way and stacked it neatly. Then she was seized with confidence, and by merely rubbing her fingers together, she sent sparks flying, setting the pile ablaze in the twinkling of an eye.

Adelaide gave an enthusiastic gasp. 'That is exactly how I would have done it.'

Torment admired her work and grinned. As a bonus, the fire also served to dissipate the stench of decaying fish. She had found it not an unpleasant smell initially, permeating the air all around. But since the unfortunate interlude with that grotesque decayed thing from the swamp, it had begun to offend her less carrion-accustomed human nose. The carcass of that amphibian monster in their camp, however fresh, reminded her unpleasantly of it. Torment wondered regretfully whether she would ever enjoy a scavenger's feast as much as she had before.

At least when it came to carving his game, Vladimir participated diligently, apparently having taken a liking to that new axe of his. Then they roasted the meat and shared a meal in silence, Vlad more keen to seek wisdom in the flames than in conversation. Young Adelaide seemed to sense something that kept her from speaking up. Vlad's yellow eyes shone brightly in the twilight, a cat's eyes, baring an inner conflict Torment could only relate to oh so bitterly. And in silence he took that conflict to bed, or in his case, the rock.

Adelaide lay down close to Torment on their nest of moss and twigs, and Torment welcomed the closeness. She remembered how, as a crow, she had liked to huddle together to sleep and found this desire unchanged.

'You keep talking of mind palaces,' whispered the girl.

Torment hummed affirmatively.

'I've heard talk of such things. Places that crop up in the dream wilds now and then, like lost humans, but not often. Say, is "Phileander" the man's true name?'

'How do you mean?'

'If it was, you might have an easier time finding your way to the home of his spirit.'

'I ...' Torment pondered. Being with Phileander, she had heard about the power of true names, of course, but she had never stopped to think if his was truly *Phileander*. Or hers *Torment*. 'I don't know.'

'He is a philosopher from the Tower of Undreamed Truths.' Adelaide turned around to look at Torment. 'And my mother commissioned him to bring me back, didn't she? Is that why he sent you? To bring me back?'

Torment froze. It felt strange how she was afraid to tell the girl the truth, that Phileander cared nothing for her, experimented on her sleeping body even. Torment had not known the need to withhold a truth out of compassion before. It still felt like cowardice. But Torment also felt all the more connected to this young human. They had both fallen prey to Phileander's lust for power.

'No, he is ... a dangerous man who needs to be stopped,' Torment whispered back, stroking Adelaide's arm. 'But you are right that I will bring you back.'

'Perhaps you will,' she groaned drowsily, 'or perhaps we are lost forever and doomed to never-ending madness.'

And with those disconcerting words, she fell asleep. What should she be most afraid of, Torment wondered; her maker, the dangers of the Yonderrealm, or maybe herself?

Lying awake with no stars to gaze at through the fog, Torment observed her fingers, which were longer and more bony than a typical human's, the nails more pointed. Then she looked over at Vlad's hybrid features, his teeth, his claws, his hair.

'I can't help but think,' she whispered over to him, 'that our half-arsed metamorphosis might be self-imposed, stemming from an identity struggle that, despite your simpler disposition—'

'My what?' he hissed.

'—you share with me,' Torment concluded.

'What did we say about presumptuous dogshit?'

'Well, we didn't define exactly what *counts* as dogshit—'

Without moving the rest of his body, he cut her off with his hand. 'You said we should rest. So rest.'

And that was that. Eventually, Torment dozed off, and strangely enough, she dreamed. Before she could contemplate the confusing metaphysics of dreaming in the dream wilds, she had already slipped through the cracks of this reality into another. In it, a radiant Elisaveta in silver armour was standing guard over an iron cage containing a giant sabre-toothed serpent flashing evil eyes. It was a comforting dream, in a way. There was a flurry of other scenes, other places, other hopes. Torment was gathering black feathers from the city's gutters and fashioning them into the likeness of a crow. But it fell apart and she was sad.

But when she opened her eyes again, back in that rotten-egg-smelling mire, she immediately forgot most of it. The dozen or so spearheads aimed at her from all directions, hovering a mere feather's breadth from her nose, seemed rather the more pressing issue.

'The mortality of others affects a spirit just as much as its own. Especially if it carries the guilt of having helped it along once or twice. And yet there are kinds of spirits for whom killing, even torture, is commonplace. Take cats, for example – for as much as I adore them, I shudder to imagine the contents of their minds.'
　　—Ogden Flynt, *Spirits between Earth and Sky*, Vol. 2

Chapter 11

A MORSEL OF GUILT

THEY HAD BEEN walking for perhaps half an hour when the first dwellings emerged from the swamp. There were a few huts, makeshift constructions of branches tied together with braided vines. Wary eyes peered from their shadows out at the little posse marching through.

Two lines of guards armed with spears flanked Adelaide, Torment and Vlad in lockstep. Their tabards and shields bore a red toadstool on a green field. But the crest was by no means their most peculiar feature, for the heads poking through their jutting white ruffs, defying their otherwise anthropoid appearance, were those of *fish*. The sheer incompatibility of their head shape with the basic physiology of upright-walking apes led to the downright ludicrous effect that their flat fish faces gawked perpetually skyward, as if to catch the rain with inanely gaping mouths. Mouths apparently incapable of speech, seeing as the only member of this party who had exchanged words with them thus far was their non-fish-headed leader marching ahead of them. His glossy green and equally confounding head was that of a broad-mouthed frog.

'You,' he called to one of the huts, and a shy little girl with a sala-mander's head stepped forth from behind a fern leaf curtain. Her dirty rags stood out next to the frog-man's spotless doublet. 'Run to the palace. Tell them to fetch Lord Heron and to notify the scribe. I am bringing three defendants from Bastion.' The salamander girl nodded hastily and ran off.

Vlad leaned in from behind Torment and whispered, 'Should've split up guard duty.'

'That would have been prudent, wouldn't it?' Torment sighed.

'Prudent indeed,' added Adelaide, quite cheerful for someone tak-en captive.

A gargling sound came from the fish soldier walking behind them, carrying Vlad's axe. She couldn't tell whether the sound amounted to as much as speech, but it was easy enough to interpret as 'shut up and keep moving'.

'It would have indeed,' said the frog-man over his puff-sleeved shoulder, his tone proud but friendly, 'to protect yourself from the wild. As for us' – he raised his hand from his sword hilt, indicating his troops with a wave – 'you would only have delayed your inevitable capture.'

Vladimir scoffed. 'You saw the remains of the monster we killed.'

'Ah, yes.' Frog-man laughed, each ribbity chortle expanding his white-spotted throat into a bubble as big as his head. 'Congratulations, mighty warrior, on managing to fell a baby gigafin.'

Vlad stayed silent behind her.

Torment cleared her throat. '*Baby*, you said?'

'Indeed, my lady. Be glad its mother wasn't around.'

With a smirk, she turned around to Vladimir, who rolled his eyes and mockingly mimed the words 'indeed, my lady'.

'Well, they haven't seen the remains of that *other* monster,' said Torment, 'that this little girl here disposed of.'

'But I'd be so terribly embarrassed to flaunt that,' whispered Adelaide, 'and never dare use that frightful trick on someone as perfectly polite as Mister Frog here, who surely has his reasons for detaining us.'

'Enough of this chitchat, ladies,' insisted Mister Frog over his shoulder.

Vlad seemed intrigued by Adelaide's power but not at all intimidated. He had been carrying himself in a manner that all but told of his confidence that neither their new companion nor these captors posed even the slightest threat to him – as if only out of mercy, indifference or laziness he had not yet cut them down with his axe. Torment wasn't so sure. There was something about how the frog-man moved that told her he was dangerous with that sword at his belt. But fear of defeat was not the reason she had opted against violence when they awoke at spearpoint. At least, not fear of their captors. There was a parasite in her that urged for bloodshed and she would not indulge it. At any rate, her curiosity outweighed any ill will towards these people.

Their escort led them along a winding footpath skirting the ponds and dwellings that dotted the area. The huts they passed grew larger, sturdier and denser. Above the porches dangled lanterns made from a sort of plant capsule, hollowed out so orange candlelight could filter through its honeycombed seed cavities. In the air hung muted chatter and herbal scents from simmering kettles. It was a proper settlement they entered, inhabited by industrious humanoids bearing the heads of various aquatic, reptilian or amphibian creatures.

Adelaide kept uttering sounds of delight and wonder, each time hushed by their captors.

Among the houses – many built on poles directly over the water – strange overgrown structures protruded from the depths. They looked ancient, often more like giant debris strewn across the marsh than the ruins of buildings, and for untold ages the swamp seemed to have tried its best to swallow them. Now the inhabitants of this settlement were unearthing these relics and repurposing them for shelter. Many were made of a curious kind of rock that seemed to have been moulded into angular shapes rather than cut, others of unreasonably large pieces of steel or even glass – rare and precious materials no one in the One City would be megalomaniac enough to try and construct an entire building out of.

'Halt!' shouted the frog-man, fist raised.

The entire troupe came to a stop like a finely tuned machine. They waited for a stooped newt-headed woman to tug a snail the size of a mule across the path. The animal's impressive spiral shell was draped with ropes and bags. A large metal hook stuck out of one of the pouches, along with various tools for building and digging, and several vials of differently coloured liquid hung from another. Torment made a mental note of this as they stepped over the wide whitish trail of mucus.

Shortly thereafter, they moved on to a large group of particularly majestic mangroves, the roots of which reached well overhead before joining to form trunks that stretched towards the sky. The path entered a portal wrought from the roots, with creepers climbing up them. It reminded Torment of the rose-covered garden bowers of the Upper Silk Quarter back in the One City. Two fish soldiers stood guard at this entrance, saluting the frog-man as he passed and led them into a gnarled colonnade of roots filled with thick and sultry air.

∾

AT THE FAR end of the colonnade, the mangrove interior opened up into a great circular courtyard surrounded by galleries and balconies of roots and with a giant toadstool growing in the centre. On the broad, bulging cap of this toadstool – like a pun made flesh – sat a colossal toad. Notwithstanding its size, it was really just a toad – ancient, warty and with a golden crown on its head. Dozens of fish guardsmen lined the courtyard, sturdier ones than their escort, with gold-lined tabards and heavy halberds instead of spears.

Torment flinched as a fish-man a few feet beside them began blowing a resounding fanfare into a long silver trumpet.

'You know,' Vlad whispered again, 'we could've just killed them all and went on our way … back when it wasn't an entire army.'

'Perhaps,' said Torment, 'but at what cost? We're doing this right.'

Adelaide gave a huff of exasperation. 'You're quite the brute, Vladimir.'

'Suit yourse—'

'Silence!' bellowed the frog-man, motioning reverently to the toad. 'You stand in the presence of His Most Merciful Majesty, High Justice of the Court of the Mellow Marshes and King of the Wronged and Rotting, Tröllapadda the First.'

The frog-headed man stepped aside and, together with their fish soldier escort, formed a lane to the toadstool throne. The soldier behind them gargled again, prodding them with the shaft of Vlad's axe.

As they stepped forward, two figures came into view on either side of the giant toadstool. To the left stood a man-sized stilt-legged bird with an elegant curved neck and a long straight bill. Its plumage was grey and white except for its head, on which two black stripes ran from wide, alert eyes to the back of its head, where they merged into a small wisp that looked almost like a coiffure. To the toad-king's right, there stood a man.

'You have a human at your court,' Torment blurted out.

Vlad shook his head. '*That's* what you find weird about it?'

Then Adelaide, Vlad and Torment flinched alike as a thunderous rumble echoed through the courtyard. Tröllapadda the First had spoken. His rutted neck shrank back to its normal huge size.

The lanky bird stretched its neck and launched into a full-throated declamation. 'His Grace Tröllapadda the First acknowledges with the utmost pity that the three of you are cursed with the same grotesque deformity as ails our poor court jester.' It gestured with its wing to the full-bearded man on the right of the throne, clad in red and green velvet, who took the opportunity to make a courteous bow. His bonnet had two tips that hung down on either side of his head. 'His Exalted Justice shall graciously consider letting thee serve your sentences as fools at this court too, shouldst the weight of your crimes prove light enough to warrant such generosity.'

Vlad looked down at his human body with an expression that didn't seem like he disagreed much with calling it a deformity.

Adelaide gave the jester a friendly burst of applause.

'Excuse me, from bird to bird' – Torment pushed forward with a raised index finger – 'seeing as the only crimes you could possibly charge us with would be poaching and trespassing, I would like to point out that the borders of His Majesty's kingdom are poorly, if not at all, signposted.'

'Silence!' yelled the frog-man from behind them again.

''Tis good now, Sir Felix,' said the bird. 'These foreigners shall be granted some leniency.' Then it craned its long neck toward Torment, eying her intently with the large discs of his eyes. 'I, Lord Heron of the Three Fates and herald to His Most Merciful Majesty, welcome thee at the Court of the Mellow Marshes. Not all is as it seems, Lady Torment from the realm of Bastion. You do not look like a bird, for instance, and the crimes you named art not the ones you stand accused of.'

Vlad frowned. 'Realm of what?'

'What crimes are they, then?' Torment asked.

A servant hurried into the courtyard from somewhere beyond the

ring of guardsmen, his shiny face that of an amphibian animal Torment couldn't quite pinpoint. He knelt panting before Lord Heron and
presented three heavy-looking rolls of parchment.

'The scribe,' the servant wheezed, 'has prepared the scrolls of malfeasance, m'lord.'

'Why, Lady Torment, tis all the crimes.' The bird's neck retract-
ed and he turned his piercing gaze on the scrolls. 'Every single one
brought against thee by His Majesty's wronged and rotting subjects.'

The man in red and green velvet applauded and giggled manically.
'All of them!' He began a little dance in front of the toadstool, singing,
'All the crimes of these fine folks, shall decide their weighty yokes. All
the souls they wronged to rot' – he bowed to her, grinning – 'shall cast
on them their righteous lot.'

Adelaide seemed to have lost the urge to clap and glanced over at
Torment, worry wrinkling her forehead.

Vlad looked at Torment, claws out, visibly at the end of his patience. Torment gave him a barely perceptible headshake, whispering,
'It's you who brought us here, after all.'

'What? Me? How would—'

She turned to the bird. 'We'll stand trial, then, Lord Heron.'

Vlad snorted. 'You gotta be kidding me.'

'I'm afraid we might not have a choice either way,' said Adelaide.
She took a deep breath. 'I'm going first.'

'Now?' asked Lord Heron. 'Or do you wish to deliberate?'

'Without further ado, my dear Lord Heron of the Three Fates.'

Adelaide stepped in front of the toadstool and curtsied. She
straightened her dress, though it did little to make it look less tattered
and there still clung a corpse smell to it.

The bird beckoned a servant with a wave of his wing. 'Bring the
fates!'

Another newt-head brought a corked glass jar with a green and a
blue light buzzing around in it and placed it before the toad-king. They

looked like coloured fireflies.

'Well, then' – he unrolled one of the scrolls – 'these art the charges brought against thee by the Wronged and Rotting, as recorded by His Majesty's humble scribe.' He cleared his throat. 'Thou art named Lady Adelaide Lidelle of Bastion, unrepentant and unjudged, is that correct?'

'It is, with the exception that I am dreadfully repentant.'

'His Majesty shall be the judge of that. Tis but the one crime, actually.'

'And I know it well, Lord Heron. It haunts me every day what happened to that woeful village – how I brought their doom upon them by poisoning the dreams of their children.'

Lord Heron seemed uncomfortable. 'What are you talking about?'

Adelaide clasped her hands in a pleading gesture. 'My crime. Making those poor children believe—'

'Break thee off, you foolish girl,' cried Lord Heron.

Some of the fish soldiers started muttering in their gurgling voices, and Sir Felix nervously cleared his throat.

Young Adelaide raised her hands in frustration. 'But by making them believe, I made it all come—'

'La la la la la!' screamed the jester, putting his fingers in his ears. Some of the fish-men gave off panicked noises.

'Silence!' shouted Sir Felix.

'You made nothing befall any village!' cried Lord Heron. 'Whatever happened did so because it has happened and you have nothing to do with it, certainly not by making anyone *believe* anything.'

The bird fidgeted anxiously on its long legs.

Sir Felix had his hands clasped around the hilt of his sword, and Torment thought she could smell the fear in the courtyard.

'Spout such dangerous heresy again, my lady,' the frog knight choked out, 'and I'll have to strike you down where you stand.'

'I … apologise,' muttered Adelaide.

They were afraid, Torment noted, to be made to think about the fact that their beliefs shaped their environment. A realisation formed in her of how utterly terrifying it must be to live in such a world.

'Good,' said Lord Heron, regaining his composure. 'Most valorous indeed. To commence with reading your crime, then.' He raised his leg to hold the scroll in front of him again. 'So, tis writ here that one night, when you were but six years old, you impaled with a sewing needle an unsuspecting and utterly innocent moth, who did nothing to you but rest upon your chamber wall, and thus administered to it a most painful and uncalled-for demise.' The bird looked up again. 'What say you in your defence?'

'This is so stupid,' whispered Vlad.

'Huh.' Adelaide straightened up. 'That is my crime? My one and only crime?'

'As brought against thee by the Wronged and Rotting,' confirmed Lord Heron.

'So I didn't ... *wrong* the Black-Eyed Mushroom Queen when I made her explode so gruesomely into a thousand slimy pieces?'

'I assume you were ordered to do so by that raggedy rabbit, were thee not?'

Adelaide put her hands on her hips. 'If by *raggedy rabbit* you mean my dear friend Doctor Thistlewhisk, then yes.'

The bird stretched forth its head until its beak almost touched Adelaide's nose. 'You can hardly be held accountable, then, can you?'

The jester hopped around the frog. 'Why, Sir Felix should be tried, for every single foe who died.' He started doing pirouettes along with the singing. 'A thousand blows, a thousand foes, accused him in their dying throes.' Then he stopped in front of Adelaide, wiggling his hands. 'They decompose, they feed the crows, so I suppose' – he leaned in with a conspiratorial whisper – 'if killing on orders was a crime, oh golly, would this frog do time.'

'Thank you very much, Sir Jester,' said Adelaide, greatly embarrassed, and gently pushed the man away. 'I think I understand. I will bring forth my defence for that sordid affair with the moth, then.' She addressed the toad directly now, gesturing up to it as she spoke. 'You see, Your Majesty, O most fair of all judges, I was but an oblivious little brat. I hardly knew here nor there nor anything of the world. That poor moth had sat there for so long on the same spot on the wall, unmoving, it had even caught dust. I thought surely it must have already been dead.' The girl started pacing, gripping her chest. 'I was just so enamoured with bugs and butterflies, and I wanted to conserve this beautiful moth behind glass, just like the ones in my father's room, so I stuck a needle in it. And, oh, woe is me' – Adelaide fell to her knees before the toadstool – 'it squirmed and liquid oozed from it as it was skewered and I saw its pain and I was so terribly, *terribly* upset. So distraught was I, I did not sleep well for many nights and cried often.'

'Is this all of thy defence?' said Lord Heron, unmoved.

'Uhm …' Adelaide shifted on her knees. 'Yes, my lord. I regretted it most dreadfully, but it was long ago, and surely such a crime weighs not so heavy. I was a child, and it was only a moth, after all.'

The toad's body inflated to a big balloon and a rumbling croak shook the courtyard.

A newt-headed servant hurried to uncork the glass jar, and both fireflies sped out, flitting upward to escape.

Tröllapadda the First's long tongue darted forth and caught the blue speck of light. The green one escaped to the mangrove canopy above the court and out of sight.

'The blue fate!' screamed Lord Heron. 'His Majesty hath judged thee, Adelaide of Bastion!'

Adelaide had defended herself well, Torment found. She was not very familiar with legal proceedings beyond what vague knowledge she had been imbued with upon her transformation, but a sensible judgement would surely be forthcoming.

'What a waste of time,' muttered Vlad.

'And ... what now?' said Adelaide.

'Now we welcome our new subject to the Mellow Marshes.'

A sigh of relief escaped her. 'Oh, how very kind that you would take me in,' said Adelaide, still kneeling, 'but, you see, my mother worries about me and I— *ahck*—'

Shaken by a sudden convulsion, Adelaide clutched her head with both hands. Something fell out of the front pocket of her dress – a black stone.

'Adelaide?' gasped Torment as cold realisation squeezed her heart.

The girl threw her head back and let out a wheezing moan, arms cramped and twisted, and then her head burst open. Bones cracking, the whole of her body was ripped apart and six black, twig-like legs stretched out of it. Two blood-smeared antennae unfurled. Torment looked on in numb bewilderment. This shuddering bloody mess wrapped in a torn light-blue dress had been her friend. Now it was but a cocoon. And it was being shed.

When it was done, what little was left of Adelaide Lidelle was stuffed into sacks by newt-headed servants. In her stead, a man-sized moth was crawling away from the toadstool toward the exit. It still dripped with the girl's blood and with a pungent, greenish liquid that oozed from a hole that went from its back to its belly.

Sir Felix and Lord Heron watched the giant insect with joyous satisfaction, and the jester clapped and cheered – though in the human's eyes, Torment thought she saw a sliver of the horror she herself felt in her very core.

Vlad seemed less stricken by what he had just witnessed, but he looked concerned and focused and surveyed the courtyard in a way that looked very much like battle preparation.

Sir Felix motioned for them to step forward. 'Who is next?'

Torment took her anguish, wrapped it in a bundle and filed it away. 'We, uhm ...' She looked at Vlad.

'We wish to deliberate,' said Vlad.

'Yes,' muttered Torment, 'deliberate.'

'Very well, then,' cried Lord Heron. 'Sir Felix, show them to a chamber.'

The frog-man nodded, and Torment scuffled in the direction he indicated.

A shiny black stone or glass ball on the floor caught Torment's eye. It was the item that had fallen out of Adelaide's dress pocket. She picked it up and put it into her belt pouch. A memento of a short-lived friendship.

'Do not try to reason with spirits yonder. Theirs is a different kind of reason. This goes double if you find yourself in their domain. However, if all else fails, I have found two approaches to dealing with spirits that seem almost universally applicable: Running away, and hitting them really hard.'

—Ogden Flynt, *Spirits beyond Earth and Sky* (unfinished manuscript)

Chapter 12

A TWINGE OF CONSCIENCE

SIR FELIX HAD left them in a small private room, or rather a room-shaped knot of roots and flowers, and told them to prepare for their trials. Torment knew – on a very theoretical level – how judicial proceedings worked in the Barony of Quelm, the Tower of Undreamed Truths and other neighbouring districts of the One City. But this was a different kind of trial altogether – a trial of spirits. She sensed important clues to the shape of her higher purpose shimmering through a thin layer of earth, barely a beak's scrape away from being uncovered.

'You can't possibly intend to go through with this dogshit,' said Vlad.

'What else would you have us do?'

'Escape. Fight.'

Torment would have been lying if she'd said it hadn't crossed her mind. Adelaide's crimes appeared minuscule compared to hers. To Vlad's as well, probably. There were so many she had wronged who had rotted, so her chance of mercy – of survival – seemed slim. But then again … she had been following the orders of the crow master and the baroness. It didn't exempt her from her own judgement but apparently it might from this court's. And she had made some helpful observations.

'I know what happened back there was all kinds of wrong,' said Torment, 'but I don't know, Vlad. I have a feeling this trial is important.'

'Phileander is coming for us,' he groaned incredulously, 'and maybe time flows differently here or whatever, and maybe we still have a day or two, but we don't know what awaits us in that tower.'

'You're right. We don't.' Torment shrugged. 'But perhaps this trial will prepare us for it.'

Vlad grimaced sarcastically, wrinkling his wide scar. 'That new en-lightened shtick of yours rather smells like blind faith. Being screwed with by some stuck-up swamp vulture and a dancing buffoon while something eats you from the inside is step one in overcoming Philean-der? Really?' He crossed his arms. 'And what was that about me bring-ing us here? I brought us to this world, granted, but not this toad-king circus. This is the opposite of what I want or … believe or whatever. I think I've been clear enough about wanting to grab what we need and get the fuck out of here.'

'Is that really all you want?' Torment asked. 'Are there no sins you seek to wash yourself clean of? To get punished for – subconsciously, perhaps? Because that's the thing about this world.' She tapped him on the nose. 'It listens to the truth within you, however repressed it may be, and renders it real.'

'And you think I have a repressed desire to be pushed around by weird fish people? Or have insects crawling out of me?'

'No. Those absurdities strike me as … bizarre beyond the scope of your limited imagination.' She glanced through the entrance at the tapestries adorning the hallway, lavishly embroidered with the strangest histories. Then she thought of the ancient structures throughout the settlement, relics of a long-forgotten past. 'This place and its people have existed long before us, and we're certainly not the first spirits to be tried at this court. But the geography of the dream wilds seems unfixed … responsive.' Turning back to Vladimir, she saw him clench his jaw, wrestling something bottled up inside. 'I believe that when you consider yourself on a "path", headed for some kind of "fate", this world can take that quite literally.'

He scowled. 'Then I guess your "path" got sidetracked by an obsessive desire to fix me. Which I never asked for, by the way, thank you very much.'

Torment nodded thoughtfully. 'A legitimate proposition.' She peered inside herself, carefully so as not to disturb the beast, and found a glimmer of truth in what Vladimir had said. There was a desire to help him deal with his own darkness, and it did cloud her focus. Had *she* brought them here? And killed Adelaide in the process?

No. Adelaide had acted of her own free will, and she had known the dream wilds and their risks as well as her. This didn't change anything. Sending her will out into the world to become the wind that carried them went both ways. It meant Torment had to trust that wind to carry her where they needed to be. And this place felt right. Even after what it had done to Adelaide. Maybe because of it. And when push came to shove, Torment knew a few tricks, like letting her Wronged and Rotting out through the door of her mind, for example, rather than having them rip her open.

In the end, they both needed to better understand what their spirits were made of, especially in this world where spirits shaped reality around them, before they went and cast them into the lion's den that was Phileander's mind palace.

'So?' asked Vlad.

'You're welcome,' said Torment as she turned toward the entrance.

'For what?'

'My efforts to fix you. Fix us.'

'Wait,' said Vlad. 'What's your plan?'

Torment looked over her shoulder and took a deep breath. 'Winging it.'

She could physically feel Vlad's annoyance as she stepped out into the hallway.

And so she submitted herself to the wind of fate, headed to have her soul judged, and announced, 'I am ready to stand trial now.'

Sir Felix and a few guards led them back to the toadstool courtyard, where a group of courtiers had now arrived in addition to the many fish-headed halberdiers. The courtiers consisted of yet more anthropomorphic amphibians, mostly frogs, with the men wearing either ruffles or stiffened cravats with puffy ties, while the women wore flowing gowns with mud-stained hems. Most of the males were carrying slender swords on their belts.

Whatever whispered gossip these people had been engaged in fell silent as the two defendants were brought before the king. Some nodded to Sir Felix in greeting.

Lord Heron still stood to the toad-king's left, while on the opposite side, the jester was busy braiding his beard. Under one wing, Lord Heron had tucked away the two remaining 'scrolls of malfeasance', and next to him stood two new corked glass jars, each containing two fireflies circling one another, one glowing green, the other blue. 'Who shall go first?' he asked, neck tilting.

Torment stepped forward, nervous. 'That would be me.'

Two halberdiers stepped out of the ring surrounding them and positioned themselves on either side of Torment.

'Very well.' Lord Heron lifted a tall, twiggy leg and grasped one of the scrolls with his talons. 'Hear, hear. These art the charges brought against thee by the Wronged and Rotting, as recorded by His Majesty's humble scribe.' He held up the scroll and unfurled it, revealing it to be a length of parchment as tall as Torment herself. Longer than Adelaide's, certainly. 'Thou art one Lady Torment of Bastion, formerly nameless crow, unrepentant and unjudged, is that correct?'

'I don't really know what "Bastion" is supposed to be and I've had my share of repentance now and again, so—'

'This is a formality, not an inquiry,' said Lord Heron, glancing sternly over the edge of the parchment. 'You need not understand, merely confirm.'

'How can I confirm if I don't know whether it's true?'

'The scribe is infallible. Prithee, just confirm so we may continue.'

Torment slowly began to sympathise with Phileander's frequent tirades against bureaucrats that she'd had to listen to when he had sat at his correspondence.

'Well, if I must,' she said blankly. 'Under the condition that this scribe is truly infallible, I confirm that their information must be correct.'

The bird squinted his eyes. 'Well, that has to suffice … for all tis worth.' He turned back to the scroll. 'I hereby raise the first charge against you, brought by His Majesty's subject, formerly a nameless magpie, who you have doomed to expire at a ruefully young age.'

The jester drew in his arms, bent forward and began to hop around in front of the courtiers in ridiculous imitation of a bird. 'Oh, so ruefully young a magpie was I,' he wailed. Then he pretended to peck at something on the ground.

The frog-faced crowd did not laugh. They regarded Torment plaintively. Vladimir just looked deeply uncomfortable, eyeing the man like a particularly revolting boil that it was impossible to look away from.

'It stands writ here,' Lord Heron continued, 'that as the both of you approached a ripe rat carcass in the street, in an area commonly known as the Lower Lamp Quarter, the aggrieved wast pecked by thee so viciously, it didst not survive the following winter for its injuries. What say you in your defence?'

She remembered it now. It had not been a thing that weighed as heavily on her conscience as many other sins. Perhaps wrongly so. Torment wondered briefly how that scribe did it – how they knew deeds from her past she hardly remembered herself. This world, whose very fabric was sensitive to secrets of one's soul hidden even from oneself, did that scribe tap into that? Could she learn it too?

'Lady Torment?'

'Ah, sorry, yes.' Before she went into her defence, Torment needed to confirm a few things.

'Is there' – she pointed to the scroll – 'is there nothing in there about … about my fellow crows? Or about dignitaries and agents from the Three Baronies, perhaps, who were murdered on the orders of the Baroness of Quelm? Or about a … certain … something inside me?'

'What the fuck are you doing?' hissed Vlad behind her, shortly followed by Sir Felix chastising him.

Lord Heron's looks over the edge of the parchment grew more and more irritated.

'Are the charges on offer,' he huffed, 'not grave enough for your discerning taste?'

'Oh, never mind, my feathered fellow. The charge is … perfectly grave enough.'

She might just have this trial in the bag. All the death she had wrought on the orders of the baroness did not count at this court.

Neither did the killing of her kin in that dream of her old crowery. Torment took this as evidence she had truly been at least partly within her mind palace then. Those crows were not wronged spirits, because they were but part of Torment's own spirit. Her memories.

'Are you stalling?' squawked Lord Heron.

'No, it's me thinking, bicker-beak,' snapped Torment. 'Is this a court or just a fast-track soul disposal? I'm allowed to plan my defence, right?'

'Do you intend to question every single step of these proceedings?' he asked. 'Because it *will* prolong them needlessly.'

'No,' answered Torment, slowly beginning to get her thoughts in order. 'In fact … In fact, I intend to shorten the proceedings' – she rubbed her chin between two fingers while her brain was spinning – 'by framing my defence in such a way that it applies to the entirety of my charges. Hey, are they all about squabbles over food on the streets?'

Lord Heron sighed and quickly skimmed the parchment. 'Aye.' He looked at her bemusedly. 'More or less.'

'Perfect.' Torment immediately lapsed into lecturing with a raised forefinger. 'Because food, as you might be aware, is a necessity for survival. But of course you will want to object that my survival was never in jeopardy, presumably in contrast to that of my victims, since I could always rely on being fed by humans. However' – Torment lowered her forefinger to point it at Lord Heron – 'survival is an instinct, and as such, acting on it is not subject to rational or ethical consideration. Therefore the crimes brought against me all amount to acts that nature compelled me to do. And being compelled is just about the same as being *ordered*, is it not?'

Once more, a rumbling roar ran through the courtyard. Trölla-padda the First had spoken again, with regally inflated croaking sac. Otherwise he appeared wholly impassive.

'His Majesty,' declared Lord Heron loudly, 'is most displeased with your impertinence, for clearly you possess the faculty of reason and are thus culpable for all your acts in full.'

'I do now, I agree, but I didn't then. I was an animal, driven by un-fettered instinct. Only later was I changed to be able to understand the consequences of my actions in full.'

'This is your defence? You believe a want of understanding washes you clean from all responsibility?'

'I ...' Torment thought for a moment. 'I am only able to regret it now. Back then, I was but a crow. Have you ever heard of the Crow All-Mother?'

'Do you intend to lecture me?'

'Only about things you might not be aware of.'

Lord Heron grumbled and ground his beak. 'We know tis a figure of devotion for much of crowkind.'

'*All* of crowkind,' corrected Torment. 'She is an ancient spirit con-nected to all my kin. She teaches us to hunt, to fight, to play, to do everything that crows do.' Hardly even a lie. If it was one, most crows would believe otherwise. Torment herself had only recognised it as superstition after her transformation. 'We do it all in her name. She whispers it to us.'

'Are you ...' Lord Heron shook his head in evident frustration. 'Are you declaring crows are wholly incapable of committing crimes?'

'I'm not.' Torment shrugged. 'You are. If you say following orders is fair game. Unless you say the ancient All-Mother's orders weigh less than, say' – she pointed at the frog knight – 'Sir Felix's orders from his king.'

Another ear-shattering croak shook the earth.

Lord Heron bowed his head obediently. 'His Majesty is ready to decide your fate.'

He pushed one of the corked jars in front of the toadstool with an outstretched wing. A newt-headed servant rushed to remove the cork, and the green and the blue firefly both soared towards freedom along erratic, sinuous trajectories.

Torment's heart raced. She believed she had played this right, had used the power of make-believe against these superstitious people whose survival relied on denying it. It left a sour aftertaste, though, and she couldn't get that pesky magpie out of her mind now.

Tröllapadda's tongue shot forth and caught the green specimen.

The blue dot of light – the one Adelaide had fallen prey to – escaped into the tangled mangrove tops above.

'The green fate!' shrieked Lord Heron. 'His Majesty hath judged thee, Torment of Bastion!'

The courtiers murmured. Whether they were murmurs of shock or relief, Torment could not tell. It was not inconceivable that *both* options ultimately led to death.

'And that means … what?'

Cartwheeling, the jester jumped in front of her, startling her. 'You're free to go, you silly crow.' He gave her a wide grin.

'I am?' She smiled and punched the jester on the shoulder, sending him reeling. 'Peck me, that's splendid!'

Then she turned around to hug Vladimir, who stiffened and grumbled. Inwardly, Torment brooded, more uncertain of herself than before. What had this trial shown but how good she was at rationalising atrocities? Just like her maker and master …

Sir Felix peeled the two apart and pushed Vlad forward, past the jester, who was still rubbing his shoulder.

'Your turn now,' he said, 'monster slayer.'

Vlad's growl had Torment worried the time had come and he'd just pounce on the frog knight now. But he didn't. He looked over his shoulder to give Torment an eyerolling nod, then straightened up and looked Lord Heron in the eye.

'Let's get this over with, Stilty Legs.'

'One more impudent than the other,' muttered the bird, unfolding the second scroll. It was significantly longer than the first. 'Hear once again. These art the charges brought against thee by the Wronged and

Rotting, as recorded by—'

'Yeah, yeah, I know the drill.' Vlad made a dismissive gesture. 'Chased mice and killed them to play with their corpses, little birdies too, all that cat stuff. My defence is the same as Torment's. Phileander changed me, yadda yadda, now I'm reformed. You can feed your king the green bug now.'

Lord Heron's beak didn't really allow him to grin, but the scorn in his eyes made up for that. 'Are you certain, Mister Vladimir, that your case is the same as your companion's?'

'That's what I just said, chum. The great cat boogaloo in the sky made me do it.'

The scroll flew through Lord Heron's scrawny claws as he skimmed over its contents. 'Well, well,' he muttered, 'what have we here?' The scroll's lower end dragged across the ground. 'My, my. Poor Beaver folk. And this? Oh. This is most peculiar. And we believed you were …' He looked up gravely. 'What say you in your defence against—'

'I confess.'

'You do?' said Lord Heron, astonished.

Vlad took a step toward him and two halberdier fish-men flanked him immediately.

'I confess I was a fool for thinking this would work out any other way.'

And he swung a claw for the left fish-man's throat – or where a throat ought to be – and snatched its halberd. Then, with a single stroke, he hacked Lord Heron's head off.

The court fell silent. Except for the fish soldier, who was writhing next to Vlad, clutching his wound, making weird gulping noises as he bled out. Lord Heron's neck stump coiled in the air for a few seconds like a dazed serpent, spraying rhythmic spurts of blood at those gathered. Then he too collapsed, bleeding onto the scroll, and lay still.

'Murder!' cried Sir Felix. The toad-king let out a thunderous croak, and the court erupted in mayhem.

Torment lost sight of Vladimir, who was being swarmed by fish soldiers. Sir Felix stood directly before her, shouting orders, swinging his sword around.

She snatched the frog knight's dagger from his belt and ducked among the agitated courtiers. Most of them only made squawking and ribbitting animal noises, and everything was drowned out by the omnipresent gargling of dozens of fish soldiers.

'Kill him,' cried Sir Felix. 'Kill him, and that treacherous crow too!'

Yes. Kill. Kill them. Kill them all.

Torment crammed the beast back in its cage. She continued to scuttle through the raucous crowd, trying to skirt the courtyard and find an opening to help Vlad. Fortunately, all those frilly frog people merely flailed around haphazardly and – contrary to Sir Felix – seemed barely any smarter than actual frogs.

Another croak from the giant toad resounded, but it was cut short by a wet-sounding smack, then an outcry of gargling lamentations. It appeared the Wronged and Rotting found themselves in want of a king.

And there it was – an opening.

The frog-men were forming a path for Vladimir, who scrambled backward. He had the jester, the human with the colourful clothes, in a stranglehold and was holding a short sword to his throat.

'Back,' Sir Felix urged his soldiers, 'or he kills the king. Again.'

Tröllapadda the First lay behind the knight, a squishy-looking mound of warty flesh dangling limply from the toadstool's head with a halberd jutting out of it. Around Sir Felix, several injured fish soldiers lay scattered, some unmoving. Vlad seemed injured too, slashes on his arms and legs. There was a lot of blood. Torment could smell it. She could smell it so much more clearly than she had any right to. She almost tasted it on her tongue. Hearty and warm and sweet and …

Just a lick. Just a drop. Trickle, trickle, little crow. Now!

It reared up inside her, nearly caught her by surprise. She had to be ever wary. Every second of every minute she had to be wary.

Weak. Pathetic. Afraid of it. So sweet and bright red, oh, we shall have it, swim in blood in darkness in pain, sweet pain, drink it all up. Let me …

When Torment opened her eyes again, she had a soldier in her grasp, feeling its frills opening and closing frantically under her palms. It was panicking, fish mouth trembling, and she had lifted it off the ground as though it weighed nothing despite all the chainmail underneath its tabard.

Stricken with disgust, Torment dropped him and he crumpled to the ground and crawled away from her, gulping and gasping.

Vladimir had reached her now, still with the jester – or the new king, apparently – in a chokehold. 'Would you stop messing around,' he hissed at Torment, 'so we can leave already?'

Torment nodded wordlessly, her mind still occupied with putting locks on a door in her head. Whatever barrier kept the vampire at bay now seemed more precarious than it had before her trial. Where faith was sturdy, shame was brittle.

'Alright, Frog Face,' snarled Vladimir, 'nobody follows us or I carve King Asswipe here a new windpipe. See how he rhymes then.'

'Oh no, oh no, please let me go,' the bearded man wailed.

'Can't get worse than that,' muttered Vlad.

'I'd love to plead in better verse, but for this case' – he struggled for words – 'I did not … rehearse.'

'You do not want to kill him,' Sir Felix shouted after them as they retreated through the colonnade of roots. 'Believe me. You don't want the Wronged and Rotting to go unruled.'

Torment tagged along, hardly listening. Long ago she had pecked at that magpie and it had suffered and it had died. It had been a bird like her. The things she had done as a mere crow … it had not occurred to Torment to revisit them. She had caused suffering when it had not been needful. Was that not more despicable even than the deeds of Phileander, who only ever caused suffering for 'the greater good'? But the toad-king had eaten the green firefly. She was acquitted. Forgiven. For lies …

It will never end, little crow, this moral quandary of yours.

The beast whispered through the door, the brittle shame-thing, rattling its chains, sneering.

This squirming over whether your newfound soul is already lost, whether you're deserving, whether you're good.

'Shut up. You don't know what I feel.'

Your goodness is nothing you will ever prove to yourself. Keeping up this charade is nothing but … torment.

'What? I didn't say anything,' murmured Vlad.

They were out of the mangrove palace now, back in the village in the swamp. The soldiers hadn't followed. So many of them were dead or injured. They weren't figments of a dream, she understood. They just happened to live where dreams came from. They were beings with spirits and bodies that could hurt and die and cause their bereaved to mourn.

'Hey, birdie, snap out of it. Keep that vampire in check.'

He knew of the vampire. He had one too, of course. He hardly ever held back with violence, yet he appeared so … in control. He had not turned into a monster when he had killed Lord Heron. He had just been Vladimir, a cat, fed up with being played with. His spirit was simple and robust, an immovable log. Perhaps that made him stronger against his vampire.

'Are you done staring at me now?'

'Right,' she said. 'Yes. Sorry, Vlad. Focus. Phileander's mind palace.'

Torment tapped her temples, just like Phileander did when he had to push through a mental block or particularly tricky puzzle.

'Should I dispatch this clown?' asked Vlad, moving his blade closer to the jester's neck.

'No,' Torment burst out, grabbing Vladimir's arm. The jester whimpered. 'We take him with us. Maybe he knows something helpful.'

Also, Torment did not feel prepared to handle the sight and smell of a throat being slit in her presence. The new king of the Wronged and Rotting nodded eagerly.

'Listen, jester,' she said, 'I mean, Your Majesty. We saw a newt-headed woman with a huge snail when we arrived. Do you know where she lives?'

'Old Miss Squibba? Yes, I do. To rhyme it, though ...' He grimaced. 'Phew.'

Vlad knocked him on the head with the pommel. 'Then say it bloody normal, Your Majesty.'

'Ow. Yes. Sure. Uhm ... not to rhyme ... haven't done that in some ...' He looked almost pained. 'Years.' His eyes widened and he smiled. 'Wow. That felt weird. But not as hard as I had feared.'

Torment snapped her fingers in front of his face and glanced nervously at the palace entrance. 'Snail lady. Where? Chop chop.'

'Of course. Uhm ... that third house to the right' – he pointed – 'where the lantern shines so bright – oh golly – anyway, cross that bridge, then through the thicket and you'll find her cave.'

'Thank you,' said Torment with a smile.

He looked tense and a little flushed. Torment wondered what it might be that he was dying to add right now. 'And in it a cricket' would have worked, or 'you might want to lick it'. Both clumsy, though. Either way, if he was to be of any use, a strict rhyming detox might be in order.

'Ogden Flynt was a delusional, boastful bastard churning out these unreadably self-indulgent tomes of drivel. They still keep plastering belligerent, denunciatory posters of him on the walls, all menacing with his raven-beaked plague doctor's mask. Yet Flynt was never really a mass murderer. He was simply a woesome fool.'

—Acingetorix Jonathan Gesian, *On the Commonplace of Calamity* (annotated edition)

Chapter 13

A SHUDDER OF SHAME

THE SWAMP HAD given way once more to a new environment, and they were wandering through a dense, dark forest of evergreens and frosty winds. The two of them had backpacks now, and they made the former jester-turned-monarch walk between them so they could keep an eye on him.

Old Miss Squibba had willingly parted with everything Torment had asked for as a tithe to the Court of the Mellow Marshes – several yards of rope, metal hooks, bags, some strips of poached gigafin and a couple of vials of various powders and liquids. Torment had not asked what they were for. She had decided to simply have faith these alchemical agents would do exactly what was needed whenever it came to it.

Now and then, between the pointed treetops, the mountain would come into view. Grey mists hung on its slopes like a great wispy amoeba, trees and jagged rocks sticking out here and there. And crowning the mountain's peak was Phileander's mind palace – a twisted castle, a cobbled-together monstrosity of a building surrounded by high walls with spiked battlements. It did not surprise her that Phileander's mind was a fortress. At its centre lay a grandiose reinterpretation of the Tower of Undreamed Truths, the observatory atop it much larger and gleaming gold instead of brass.

The closer they got, the darker the forest grew, the thornier its undergrowth and the colder its air. A smell of mildew wafted in the fog, and indefinable critters crawled away wherever they stepped.

'Why, trees that have needles – how very odd,' murmured the jester. 'And they carry their seedles in a prickly pod.' He picked up a pinecone and turned it in his hand as he walked. 'Haven't left the palace for ages. But the more things I notice, I think "I should know this" and remember to have seen it on pages.'

'Would you shut up?' grumbled Vladimir.

'Never mind that sourpuss,' said Torment. 'How come *you* were the next in line? You don't really seem related to that toad.'

'No. I was just his adviser. But no one was older or wiser. I may seem like a fool, not the first choice to rule, but honestly, a toad doesn't either.' He smiled sadly at the pinecone. 'Ah, the knowledge once in my possession, before my mind underwent this … regression.' He tossed the pinecone over his shoulder and turned to Torment, whispering, 'But in all discretion, if you want my confession, I have nary a clue of the rules of succession.'

She had soon given up trying to wean him off rhyming. At any rate, when he wasn't distracted by a sword to his neck, he was astonishingly easy to converse with. It gave Torment a pang to think of the last companion she had so enjoyed chatting with. But this man was very different from Adelaide. It was clear he had been lost in the dream wilds far longer than her. So long, his body in the waking world was certain to be long deceased. And there was a sadness in him. A strange, hidden sadness, the reason for which he appeared to have all but forgotten.

Vlad was casting the jester-turned-king curious glances from time to time. He was probably asking himself why this man would so readily come along with them when the circumstances of their joint departure could hardly be described as harmonious. Torment asked herself the same question. She wondered whether he had been a sort of prisoner there, and if so, how it then made sense that he would also be king.

Something moved in the treetops. Torment saw a shape, spotted white feathers and huge, circular eyes. A bird, and a big one, fluttering away out of sight on eye contact. An owl perhaps? Was it one of Phileander's spirits, spying on them?

'We should get a move on,' said Torment. 'And avoid contact with spirits from here on out.'

Vlad paused, gripping his backpack straps, and sniffed the air. 'Do you smell that?'

The jester sniffed too. 'More pinecones.'

'Bittersweet nightshade,' Torment noted. She would recognise the scent anywhere, even with a human's nose. It was one of her favourite snacks. Maybe *the* favourite now that blood and dead meat had been spoiled for her.

'That's not what I'm smelling,' said Vlad grimly.

'From over there?' Torment pointed some way to the right, where there was a steep embankment leading down. Vlad nodded.

'That's bittersweet nightshade, no doubt about it, crony.'

Torment hurried off until she remembered that those berries were poisonous to humans. She slowed her walk and sighed. What pleasures were there left for her? But Vlad walked past her and picked something off the ground that had been nestled in the soft carpet of pine needles.

'What is it?'

Vlad turned it in his hand. 'Some kind of pastille.'

'Not a berry?'

He took it in his mouth and chewed on it. 'Definitely not a berry.'

The jester strode past her and picked up another pastille not far from where Vladimir was standing.

'Liquorice,' he said with a smile and ate it.

Those clearly smelled of nightshade. Both of them were going to have serious problems later.

'All right.' Torment clapped her hands. 'Let's get back on track. These sweets are a distraction.'

But Vlad was already three pieces of liquorice ahead, flicking them into his mouth. 'Didn't you just go on about "following a path" or something?'

'Yes,' Torment said, 'and you about how much of a waste of time that was. We're almost there.'

Vlad picked up another pastille and cast a smug grin at Torment. 'And here is a road leading in our direction that will make us go twice as fast.'

'Oh.' Torment jogged over to him. 'I was right about that path thing, then, wasn't I?' She smirked at him.

There was truly a road here, or at least a trodden path, and the trees lining it had little holes in them that glowed with a yellow light. Curious. Along the path those liquorice pastilles lay scattered. Vlad seemed positively ravenous for them, leading their way by some distance, backpack slung leisurely over one shoulder, picking up sweets.

'What does it even mean?' Torment asked, walking beside the jester. 'Being King of the Wronged and Rotting?'

'Oh, it … means to have death breathing down your neck and to keep your rotting subjects in check. I think.'

Torment patted him on the shoulder, making the tails of his cap wobble. 'Hey. You're managing to add more and more little words that don't rhyme.'

'I know.' He gave a sad smile. 'I was good with words once, I believe. I have a whole lost "me" for which to grieve.' He stared into
space as he walked as if he was searching strenuously for a thread of
thought. 'I felt something when the dominion of the Wronged and
Rotting passed over to me. A terrible guilt for a terrible deed, and I
remember not what it could be.' He seized Torment's hand and regarded her forlornly. 'I think I must bear the guilt of all the crimes that
all the wronged dead begrudge. And I don't think I am ready for this
responsibility.'

When dealing with humans who were lost in strange places, a lot
of handholding seemed to be required.

Torment spotted something odd on a branch. Or someone.

'Is that mouse wearing a waistcoat?' she asked.

The King of the Wronged and Rotting looked in the direction she
pointed and waved absently. The mouse waved back. Then it ran off
and into one of the glowing holes in the tree.

'Oh,' Torment realised. 'They're doors and windows.'

A few steps ahead of them stood a giant and particularly perfo-
rated tree that shone brilliantly. Vlad stood in front of it, munching
on liquorice and having an argument with a mouse that was carrying
a basket of nuts along a branch. So much for avoiding further contact
with spirits.

'I can bring a sword wherever I want,' he growled.

'By what right?' the mouse squeaked.

'By right of being able to squash you with my pinkie.'

There was a door at the foot of that tree that was much larger than
the mouse-sized ones. Not quite their size, but they could fit if they
made themselves really small. Torment smelled scents that reminded
her of both the One City and Violet's grove in a way. There were baked
goods and ale but also nuts and bark and lots of animals. Mice, mostly,
but there was probably also a badger inside that tree.

Torment turned to a mouse sitting on a bench upon a branch at face level, who was feeding aphids with some tiny crumbs from a small pouch. 'Excuse me, mouse. What's in that tree?'

The mouse winced. 'No need to shout. It's the best tavern in all the forest. Now, away with your big old face. You're scaring the little beauties.'

Grabbing the jester by the sleeve, Torment went over to Vladimir. 'You finished eating those? I want to go in the tavern.'

'Why?' He pointed past the big tree. 'That mountain with the castle is only an hour away – two, tops. Time is almost up. And you just told us to *get a move on*.'

'I know. We don't need to dawdle. But it's the last opportunity to ask around.' She whispered the rest: 'Perhaps these spirits here know Phileander. That castle doesn't look like it appeared yesterday.'

The jester nodded. 'And I'd like some ale, if it's not stale.'

Vlad shrugged. 'Maybe they have some of that strong stuff your witch friend gave me.' Torment smiled, gave him a peck on the cheek and crouched down to open the little door.

THEY HAD TO crawl through. Inside they could only kneel, and still they almost touched the ceiling. All the furniture was carved directly into the wood. By all rights, the tree should be dead, hollowed out as it was. But Torment tried not to think about that too hard. Clearly this tree stood by the grace of the staunch belief of all these mice alone. It wouldn't do them much good to balance that out with her own disbelief only to have this room collapse around them. She put her backpack down at the entrance. There were a couple of tables for larger animals, which meant the two badgers sitting at the rear, and one larger bar, in front of which sat a white rabbit wearing a top hat and a black velvet cloak. The rest was little spiralling galleries along the walls, filled with mice at mouse-sized tables.

'Huh,' said Torment. 'I think I might have an idea who that rabbit person is.'

Vlad was clearly not too happy about his humiliating position. To move around, they had to crawl or slide on their knees.

'Great, birdie. That relates to our issue how?'

'He's a *magician*,' she whispered. 'He pulled Adelaide *into* the dream wilds somehow. He knows things.'

The jester tapped her on the shoulder. 'Drinks?' Apparently it was easier for him not to rhyme if he stuck to single words.

Torment nodded and crawled up to the bar, immediately smelling a strong fragrance of fermented beverage emanating from the rabbit. He was anthropomorphic, like so many beings in the dream wilds. He swayed on his seat, and his eyes were bloodshot.

'Whaddarya … one of my g-girls?' he slurred at Torment. 'Pe-nolope. No … *Polenope*. Ah, fuck.' He took a sip of ale. 'You're too big to b-be one o' my girls, anyway.'

'You're not how I imagined you,' Torment said, 'Doctor Zephyrus.'

'That's Thistlewhisk to you.' The rabbit puckered his whisker pads and puffed up in front of her. He made an effort to get his voice a little more under control. 'Or better yet, the Great Doctor Zephyrus Thistlewhisk, Master of Mirages, Illustrious Illusionist, Shadewalker from the Murky Lands and Albino Arcanist galore.' He crossed his eyes for a moment and twitched the floppy rabbit ears poking out from under his top hat. 'Wassadall titles? Probly. Dunno.'

The jester pushed a drink over to her from the side. The jug was a little too small for her current size, but she could pinch it between her fingers. A chubby mouse in a smock was wiping the sweat from its forehead after having carried three jugs as big as itself up to the counter.

The mouse looked up at them. 'Any of you seen any Beaver folk lately?' it squeaked. 'I'm missing some regulars.'

Vlad coughed and ushered the jester to a table at the back. He slid across the floor so hastily, he hit his head on a beam and cursed.

'I'm sorry,' replied Torment. 'I've heard rumours they ... might not come by again.'

'Pity,' squeaked the bar mouse and scurried behind the counter.

'Ya seen where all my liquorice went?' asked Thistlewhisk, shaking an empty bag under his triangular little nose.

'You spilled it on your way here.'

'Fuck.' He tossed the bag aside. 'Whaddiya want again?'

'I wanted to ask you some things. About mind palaces or what a homunculus is or how to defeat a vampire.'

'The fuck?' He tugged at his whiskers and looked at her glassily. 'Why would I know all that shit?'

This was by far the rudest encounter Torment had ever had. 'Because you're a magician.'

'Not that kind of magician, crow lady.'

'Then how do you know I'm actually a crow?'

'Tiny bit of mentalism.'

'Is that all you can do?'

He let out a loud belch and took off his top hat. Then he reached into it and pulled out what appeared to be a living human baby, crying and squalling.

Torment backed away, bewildered. 'Is that a human young?'

'Duh, numbnut,' huffed Thistlewhisk. 'What else would it be?'

'I don't know.' Torment thought back to the illusionists she had seen on the streets of the Merrymen's Quarter. That squealing baby in the rabbit's hand was quite distracting. 'A pigeon, perhaps?'

'A what?' He gave a snorting laugh. 'Here ya go.'

Dramatically, Thistlewhisk lifted his cloak and hid the chubby child behind it. Then, a second later, he revealed it again, and now the poor thing had sprouted white-feathered wings from its back.

He tossed it into the air and it squalled and fluttered, tumbling through the taproom, throwing up on a clamouring mouse waiter and bumping against the door frame before it flew outside.

'Pigeon … stupid. Where's my fuckin' beer? Did I fuckin' vanish it again?'

'No, you spilled it.'

'Ah, fuck.'

Torment lost her patience and dragged the drunk up to her face by the collar of his cloak.

'What, by all the immortals, is wrong with you, Thistlewhisk?' she snapped.

Momentarily sobered, he stared at her. His breath smelled of ale and puke. His whiskers twitched.

'You wanna know what the fuck is wrong with me?' He knocked her arm aside. 'Let me tell ya. I've been abducting little girls for a fuckin' millenium to make them fight a giant evil mushroom that grows back every ten years. That make any sense to you?' He reached behind the counter and refilled his ale from the tap. 'Cos it sure ain't to me.' A pocket watch slipped from his coat. 'Fuck, I missed my appointment.' He squinted at the watch. 'Little Penelope. No, that ain't right … Clementine?'

'Adelaide.'

'That's the one.' He grinned, relieved. 'Ya seen her?' His glazed red beady eyes were wet and desperate.

None of this was going even remotely how Torment had hoped it would. No reason to prolong this needlessly.

'She died. Just a few hours from here, in the Mellow Marshes.'

Something extinguished in his eyes. His muzzle trembled, then he turned away and spoke quietly. 'They always die on me. I'm a fuck-up.'

'I don't really know about that thing with the Mushroom Queen, but I wish I could contradict you on that.'

He downed his little jug of beer. 'I always skullfuck the shit out of this clusterfuck and then it's all fucked, and now I have to go look for that fuckin' eye again.'

'Eye?'

'Queen's eye. Black little thingy. Dangerous in the wrong hands.'

Torment reached into her belt pouch and placed the black glass ball in front of him.

'Thank me when you're sober. I'll be long gone by then, though.'

He gawked at the thing with a blank face. Then Doctor Zephyrus Thistlewhisk began to cry. With a whimper at first, but soon big tears rolled down his scrunched-up face. He collapsed onto the counter, sobbing heart-wrenchingly and muttering things Torment could not possibly understand through all the snot and wailing.

Torment placed a hand on his back, feeling a mixture of pity and disgust.

'I—' The rabbit looked up at her from his misery. 'I— I don't want this anymore,' he rasped in between sobs. 'I don't want to f-feel like this anymore. Please.'

'I wish I could take your sorrows in return for that eye,' said Torment gently.

'Y-you … you think you could?'

Torment raised an eyebrow. 'It was a figure of speech.' But as she thought it through … she probably could. These were the dream wilds, after all, connected to all spirits' mind palaces, and his sorrows would surely take on some concrete form within his. He could probably retch out his *heart of sorrows* or whatever right here and now if someone only believed in it enough.

Thistlewhisk's eyes widened and he winced at a sudden choking spell.

'Oh,' Torment noted. 'Crikey.'

He craned his neck down and squeezed his eyes shut, pushing a bloody pink lump out of his throat. It landed with a splat.

'What,' he panted, wiping his muzzle, 'what the fuck?'

Torment looked at the thing on the counter lying in a little red puddle. It certainly looked like a heart.

'I feel …' The rabbit clutched his chest. 'I feel so much lighter now.'

Torment took a deep breath.

'Thank you, crow lady. What is your na—'

'Don't mention it,' Torment groaned. She picked up the slippery little heart and began crawling over to Vlad and the jester to fetch them and get out of this mad place as fast as possible.

Trickle, trickle …

That feeling in her hand reminded her of something. Of a little crow heart in her mouth, delicious and stringy. Sweet blood. Her hand was wet with it. That tiny thing was filled to the brim with it. Why had she even picked it up? Torment panicked. But she was already losing control. The coppery scent was overwhelming.

Sleep now, little crow.

The last thing she saw was Vlad questioning the jester intently. Odd. Then the heart in her hand, in her mouth – she chewed and the taste filled her up and then red was all she saw.

She was falling. *It* was falling. A little crow. A teeny tiny frightened crow, unable to move its wings or close its eyes. All was dark except for the swamp below, a blood swamp, a vast field of glistening red. The crow hit the surface of a red lake, but it was silent; there was only blood sticking to its feathers and the taste of iron in its beak. There stood a figure at the edge of the lake, glowing a faint white, so very far away. The crow remembered it briefly. It was a woman who had helped it once in a similar situation. She couldn't help the crow now. Soon it was submerged, claw, beak and feather, and it felt a pulse below. The crow pushed with its wings through liquid thick as resin, exhausting itself, trying to get to it. The pulse was life.

It opened its eyes and there was a great heart in front of it, much bigger than the crow itself, floating, pumping. Waves came from the heart. Waves of unbearable pain. But pain was life. Pain was an anchor and pain was an armour. It made the crow remember. It had a name. Torment. With a forceful drag of her wings, Torment pushed her way inside through an open artery.

In the darkness, she felt the pain of all the deeds not done that had been needful, of all the suffering inflicted out of weakness, cowardice or ignorance. A young girl, red-haired, sitting alone and whimpering, then another, blond braids and a cheerful temper, crying out in pain. Torment remembered her. She had wanted to care for her. Then she had killed her – led her to the butcher's block. A magpie huddled in a corner. It glared accusingly out of hollow sockets. Only a frozen skeleton was left of it. It was too painful to look at.

'Give in to true remorse,' said a muffled voice.

Torment turned around. There stood a man with a funny cap with two protruding tips. But he also had the beak of a bird on his face, of a crow or raven. And bespectacled eyes. No, the beak and the spectacles were fused together … a mask of some kind.

'You're fighting a vampire, Torment,' said the man in the mask. 'I remember about vampires now. And I remember about my guilt, just a little of it. Please, Torment. Remorse leads to self-acceptance. It can defeat it. Please. Don't kill me.'

'I'm not killing you,' said Torment. She didn't want to kill anyone. Not him, anyway.

'Yes. Yes, you are.'

The mask slid off his face. She knew that face. It was the jester. The King of the Wronged and Rotting. And she was clutching his throat with her hand.

'Please,' he wheezed, 'don't kill me.'

His face was blood-smeared. It wasn't the jester's blood, she noticed. It was the blood from her hands. The blood of dozens of torn-apart mice and at least one of the badgers. She spat out something that had been stuck between her teeth. It was a tiny boot.

Torment let go of the jester. She was still very dizzy, cold sweat all over her skin. Vlad didn't seem to have intervened. He probably couldn't have without endangering himself. He pulled her outside, helped her to her feet and pushed her along the road, and the jester followed.

Why did that man still follow them after what she had nearly done to him?

Why would anyone want to follow her, to be with her, to endure her? Had she ever done anything but harm?

'The dead are angry. I can hear them scratching at the walls of Bastion. They are out there and they are legion and they are angry. This is why I must dream.'

—Ogden Flynt, incoherent ramblings found post-mortem in his home

Chapter 14

A Hint of Forgiveness

THE DIZZINESS SUBSIDED after a while, and Torment washed the blood off in a stream. The only thing that remained was the shame and the guilt, and it felt so much heavier than before. It made every step, every breath, every thought of going on an agony. Her backpack straps dug into her shoulders.

'It'll get better,' said the jester.

'How do you know?' asked Torment. 'Have you had a vampire in you too?'

'Oh, no. I would not have had the strength to withstand it even a second.' He smiled. 'But I have caused as much grief as one, most likely.'

'Do you know your name by now?'

'No. It has been … too long.'

Torment could see in his eyes how it shamed him. So much so, he even forgot to rhyme altogether.

'Your name's Ogden Flynt,' said Vlad offhandedly.

Torment stared at him. She almost walked into a tree.

'Ogden Flynt,' whispered the jester, feeling the words with his tongue. 'Ogden … Flynt. Yes. Yes, that feels right. I think I' – he mimed the stroke of a quill – 'I think I once used to write.'

He seemed excited, eyes widening, following a long-lost trail of memory.

'How would you know that, Vlad?' asked Torment.

Vladimir gripped his backpack straps and sighed. 'Recognised his style. Fella wrote a few bad poems in his day. Phileander prides himself on his collection of Flynt's works. I read a biography once.' He regarded the unkempt man. 'Trim away the bush and he matches the portrait on the cover.'

'What else do you know about me?' Ogden pleaded. 'Tell me, Vladimir of Bastion.'

'You wrote all kinds of stuff about animals and plants and history and all that. Then you went nuts – kept meditating yourself into the "realm of spirits" until one day you just didn't wake up.' Vlad shrugged. 'Then you died. That was, like … eighty years ago.'

'Eighty years in our world. That means' – Torment multiplied in her head, counting fingers – 'you've been lost for about two thousand dream wilds years.'

Ogden stopped in his tracks. He stood there for a moment and shivered. Then he dropped to his knees.

Vlad let out a frustrated breath. 'We're kind of in a hurry. Don't want to follow in your footsteps, you know.'

The long-dead scholar did not react. He just sat there and stared at the forest floor littered with rotting needles. His mouth moved silently.

'Give him a moment.' Torment leaned against the nearest tree trunk and pulled out a pouch of gigafin jerky. 'We're almost there, anyway.' She pointed in the direction of the mountain, where the forest appeared to be thinning out already. Then she chewed on her meat, squinting at her companion. 'You surprise me, crony.'

'What? You think when I made the Somniatrinus potion was the first time I ever read a book? I had lots of time to kill in the tower.'

'It's just … you don't strike me as a connoisseur of culture, Vladimir.'

Torment saw that reddish glint in his eyes again. 'Well, if it please Your Crowness, high queen of sophistication, this humble cat could also prance around like fucking Phileander, bragging about how well-read he is.'

'He doesn't do that.'

'No, he's just a humble old chap, isn't he? You and him could have a laugh at simpleton Vlad together. Why' – he stepped closer, pressing a clawed finger against her chest – 'you could marry him. Already look like his ex-wife, after all.' He slit open the shirt Violet had put on her. 'Just make sure he doesn't disembowel you.'

Ogden muttered, 'I remember things. Such a terrible thing.'

She had endured it once, for Vladimir's sake, but Torment was getting tired of it. She didn't deserve this treatment.

'Why are you so mean since we were reunited?'

'Mean, am I?' He laughed without humour. 'You never respected me. You and your fucking holier-than-thou attitude, like a moralising, even more obnoxious version of the old philosopher. Even when you're drenched in the blood of your prey.' He took her jaw in his hand, almost frightening Torment for the first time since she had met him, before her transformation, a leering cat on the ledge above the fireplace. 'When all I've done was for you.'

223

SILAS A. BISCHOFF

The sky blackened, which only served to emphasise the fire in Vlad's eyes, and heavy raindrops pattered through the crooked, pointed treetops.

'So dark,' mumbled Ogden, 'the forest ... the thing in the forest. Mine. I remember it.'

A flash of lightning made Torment flinch, and Vlad still gripped her, pinned against the trunk.

'Phileander never threatened to kill me, you know,' he snarled. 'I never owed you anything. In fact, he saved my life, and it has never been as comfortable and safe as it was in the tower. I did this for you, you ungrateful crow. To give you a chance at life.'

Thunder rolled over them. Their eyes were fixed, and hers teared up as she realised he was right. Torment had not known who she was, she still didn't, but the parts she had been made of had come with confusing baggage. There was a voice that told her she was a traitor to her kin, a monster, an abomination, a murderer and worse, yet the voice that spoke through her beak – or lips – was ever right, ever wiser than her counterpart, ever the victim of wrongful circumstances. Outwardly superior, inwardly ashamed. Why was that so? It was a crude fault that felt so pitifully ... human.

Pitiful. Weak.

The beast spotted an opening, claw in the door, her resolve crumbling under a wave of shame.

Swallow your guilt, drink it all up. Rip him apart.

They were soaking wet, Vlad's hair plastered flat to his head, and another ray of lightning split the sky, cast the world in black and white.

And in the whiteness of this flash there gleamed a set of many eyes in between black trees. Strange eyes, disgusting eyes, a cluster of them moving in sickening synchrony.

'Vladimir ...' croaked Torment. Thus strangled, she almost sounded like herself again.

He gave her a fanged, lopsided grin. 'Is this the point where you know better than I what really drives me?'

The cluster of eyes shimmered pale in the dark. Long shadows moved like many legs akin to ghastly, bone-like twigs.

'No … Vladimir … monster.'

'What?' he snapped. 'Am I a monster? Or a misguided, depressed loser? Get your damn story straight, birdie.'

'Spirits,' muttered Ogden, still kneeling, 'of the dead, the many dead, the wronged, the rotting, beyond the earth and sky … vengeful things …'

Oh, there will be blood, there will be battle. Hail the night.

The monster stalked nearer, looming over Vladimir.

'No,' she croaked, 'behind you … monster.'

Finally he saw it in her eyes, let go and whirled around.

In the pouring rain, as thunder roared, the next bolt of lightning cracked through the storm as the pines bent near bursting and the vile thing was revealed in all its monstrous glory. A mass of cadavers, fused, intertwined like the roots of the trees, supported by stilt-like legs, some eight or more, thin and bony and tapering, skin bulging like beech bark. The eyes … all shapes and sizes in so many shrivelled heads of robins and rats, pigeons and goats and dogs, of deer and the children of humans, all maggot-eaten and haggard and grown together.

'What the absolute scratchin' fuck?' sputtered Vlad, pulling the sword from his belt.

Drool dribbled on him from numerous gaping mouths and he threw himself to the side.

A limb dug into the very ground he had just stood upon. Mere inches and Torment would have been impaled. A magpie's tiny skull poked from a joint of it, turning to look at her from empty sockets.

'Beyond the earth and sky,' babbled Ogden, gaping at the monster, 'spirits of the dead, I found them. Defiled and vengeful. Hide, oh, immortals, I had to hide …'

I know this thing. Maggots eating away at the carcass of a world. I know it, filth, unworthy!

Not even the oh-so-ancient beast inside her managed to make sense to Torment. A bundle of fused heads hunched down and screeched at her, spewing foetid slobber, breath of decay, a piece of rotten gut dangling from the thing's belly above her.

Torment spun along the pine trunk, putting it between her and the thing right before an impact shook it.

It sent her reeling, stumbling over a pitted piece of fungus-eaten wood.

'Over here,' yelled Vlad, 'you ugly fucker!'

She heard a sickening thud as Vlad started swinging. Then a chorus of breathy, rattling, accusing voices.

'We rot. We rot,' they chanted. 'You can hurt us no more.'

One of its limbs pinned Torment to the ground, its point of tiny human finger bones pricking her skin.

We could destroy it. Let me out. Give in. It could not harm us and we could break its legs, crunch its little skulls, scatter it on the forest floor.

'Shut up,' shrieked Torment, fumbling for the dagger in her belt. 'It doesn't even bleed.'

Somewhere in the darkness, she heard Vlad grunt in pain as he was flung around, skidding through the bushes.

Her hand found the hilt and started hacking at the barky, slimy thing atop her, piercing corpse skin and woven bone. It did not budge.

Ogden still muttered, 'What have I done? Forgotten. Must never forget. Wrong. All wrong.'

The magpie's skull was just a hand's breadth from Torment's face. 'Pecking at us, always pecking.' A whisper-voice came from the tiny beak. 'Make it good. Make all go away. Join us. Be free.'

'Perished by the thousands,' sung the heads on the other end of the thing's body, 'for your arrogance, wise man. For your word, plague doctor, scholar, adviser, king, we rot. Rot with us. Rot!'

Torment heard Flynt wail. The leg on top of her bent and the body lowered itself, rotting arms reaching forth from it, many human arms of different sizes.

'You belong with us,' whispered several half-decayed human faces on the underside of the monster's belly. 'You wronged us, you have been wronged, you shall rot.'

'I did nothing,' Torment screamed, still hacking. 'I don't even know who you are!'

The many hands grasped her, began tugging at her legs, her feet, her face. 'You brought the letters to kill us. Come now.'

'I didn't know!' Torment sobbed.

Ogden's laments, louder now: 'Oh, immortals. It will swallow us, the world, everything. What have I done?'

'It is time,' whispered the magpie, and the thing raised Torment's body up. She couldn't move as she neared a maw that opened in its belly, made from a thousand jaws and teeth and tongues, slobbering and reeking of death so terribly, it felt as though it ate at her mind, gnawed at her from the inside.

You will cost us dearly, cost us blood, cost me this precious vessel – give in now!

'No,' sobbed Torment. 'I would never recover. You'd consume me. I— I don't trust me. No ...'

She tried to kick at the soft parts of its maw, but a set of over-long canines snapped shut around her calves, piercing leather and skin and muscle, sending a dizzying pain through her that erupted into a scream. It was all she could do to let her body go limp and surrender. She could not enter her mind palace, but she could feel the beast pulling relentlessly at its chains inside her. It seemed that Torment's denial was enough to keep the chains in place.

'No, please,' cried Ogden. 'Oh, you revenant, you vile thing, let—' His cry ended in a lengthy wheeze or a sigh, almost relieved-sounding.

Then Torment fell back onto the moss and needles and twigs. The stench subsided. She was so dazed, she hadn't seen what had become of the monster. Had it devoured her and she had once again crossed into a new realm, another layer to this cosmic play of folly? But no … the pain was still there, throbbing and burning in her ruined leg. The chill wind was still there, the dampness from the rain, the scent of mushrooms and earthworms in sodden soil. The scent of old trees. The scent of dream stuff and blood and shame and of Vladimir, the man-cat, the brother, the victim, the only friend and companion. She heard him panting somewhere near.

You are weakness through and through. Unworthy. Don't call for my aid, little crow, not ever again. I shall bide my time as night eternal nears, and once your guard is down … oh, sweet blood shall rinse your rotten worlds. All of them. Bastion most of all. Diseased with shame and fanciful dreams of vermin rotting in their guilt and desperation. Such sweet hunting grounds, such sweet gravity of death, true consequence, true thrill. Red blood. Despicable meat. Prey, the lot of you.

And then …

… the beast rattled its chains no more. It went silent, uncannily so, and Torment shivered. Ever so slowly, she raised herself on her elbows and looked around. Pain lurked beyond the edges of her consciousness, in waiting for a wrong move.

The little magpie's skull lay on her chest. The rest of the thing was gone. Maggots littered the ground, squirming, burrowing, as if fallen from the flesh when it had disappeared around them. The grey of the world lightened again, ever so slightly, and the rain clouds mostly cleared.

Never had the weight of guilt in Torment's heart been greater. She could not even say what she felt guilty about. It was the essence of guilt. She felt as though she must carry the weight of every fault ever committed, every drop of blood shed, every child lost and every heart broken. Adelaide's grim fate was her doing. Torment had taken her under her wing and led her to her doom. She had sown terror in that tavern, ravaged the peaceful, defenceless spirits there. Even the one friend she had, she could offer nothing but hurt and sorrow. She felt tears on her face.

Vlad sat on the ground next to a motionless Ogden Flynt, who lay face down in a dark puddle. Blood wetted Vladimir's blade.

'You stabbed him,' whispered Torment.

'That damn thing came from his screwed-up mind. What was I supposed to do?' He averted his eyes. 'You wanna say your bit? Your sermon of pity and contempt?'

Torment had no bit to say. Nothing that would manage to pass the lump in her throat. What was it with her human body and its tendency to shed water from the eyes whenever her emotions got tangled up? And tangled up they were, all in a painful knot.

'I'm sorry,' were the first words that eventually made it out. 'I'm sorry for how I … how I am. I'm not right. He made us … made *me* wrong. I'm all wrong, Vlad.'

'Oh, shut up. No one's made wrong.' He stood up and licked his blade clean. 'We're just us. Cat, crow, something else, what's it matter?'

'There's no … there's no wind of fate guiding us. It's all just chaos, and everything's made up. This place, it … I thought it might lead me to my purpose, Vlad, but all it shows me is that it's … it's all made up.'

Ogden's doom was her fault, too. She was only death. Her very essence was the murder of Elisaveta and her baby. So much suffering. If the death of a spirit truly left a monster, what did they leave in their wake? The beaver folk, Adelaide, the soldiers at the toad-king's court, those mice, Ogden …

'You're overthinking this, birdie. Our purpose is what it always was – to take what we want when we can. When opportunities are rare, we toughen up and wait, ready to jump.' Vlad walked over and held out his hand to her. 'Good we're finally at eye level, though. Now let's get out of here.'

'I …' She looked at her leg, which was a bloody mess. Her trouser leg was all shredded. Torment even thought she saw white bone through the red. 'I don't think I'm going anywhere.'

He looked at her leg long and thoughtfully. 'You're suppressing your vampire entirely, aren't you?'

Torment nodded. 'I'm … not as strong as you. I can't trust myself to use its powers.'

Vlad shrugged. 'You probably are wiser than me, after all. Just don't go on about it. Other ideas?'

Torment thought for a moment. He was right – she was clever, she knew that. She just had to pull herself together. 'The potions.' Torment pointed to the tree, where her backpack had fallen and spilled its contents. 'The flasks we bought or, uhm … extorted from the newt lady.'

It didn't matter what the substances were made to do. It mattered what they were believed to do and how strongly. Torment had done it before – willed a thing, manifested a belief. She had forced her will on the desert sand, the wood in the swamp, had even sparked fire from thin air. This whole unfortunate affair, Ogden's rekindled memories spawning this … thing – it was all still further evidence of how the fabric of the dream wilds worked. And Vlad had been well aware of it, had listened to everything she and Violet had said with keen attention. Of course he had. Why would she have thought him too daft to do so? He had gotten Phileander's face and she his personality. Quite the better deal on his part, really.

Vladimir squatted next to her bag and rummaged through it. He brought out two vials and a small sealed bowl, which Torment knew to contain a greasy paste.

'Didn't know which one would work best for you.' He held up a globular vial of crimson liquid. 'This one looks like it heals, no?'

The image of a silver syringe shot through Torment's mind, with a small recess in the metal through which a dark red mass could be seen sloshing around behind thin glass.

'Oh no, that's not the one. Give me the yellow stuff.'

'Really? Looks like sickness to me, but suit yourself.'

'Not helping, crony.'

230

'Right, sorry.' He uncorked it and brought it to her mouth.

'Wait,' Torment blurted out.

She was uncertain. Red or yellow? Had she made the right choice? Did the choice even matter? Torment knew the one thing she must not do in order for this to work was *doubt*. But there she was, doubting, so it obviously couldn't work. Hence it wasn't doubt, it was certainty. It was a vicious circle, a checkmate, a deadlock in supernatural impotence.

What a conundrum. How could anyone believe in the face of doubt?

Stupid crow. By making a leap of faith, of course.

A mind imbued with above-average human genius and she used it to run in circles like some earthbound chicken chasing seeds. Obviously it *could* heal her, because she only had to believe it did.

'I think I'm ready,' she said. 'Up the beak with the stuff.'

And so Vlad tipped the vial. A sour juice ran over Torment's lips and down her throat. It was a disgusting sourness, like gastric juice. Sickly.

Sickness. Had Vlad been right about the yellow one?

And as it occurred to Torment how terribly ill-timed a doubtful thought this was, the doubt turned into a certainty of having just ingested poison.

Vlad's eyes widened. 'What's wrong?'

His worried expression only fuelled Torment's conviction. The poison intensified, no longer merely sickening her but burning, making her heart flutter. She was dying. Torment couldn't even scream, only convulse and squeeze out a pitiful moan as a tightness constricted her chest and she broke into a cold sweat.

Hastily, Vlad turned her on her side and jammed a finger down her throat.

Torment retched, emptying her whole stomach onto the pine needles.

'I'm saving you, you understand?' He told her. 'You just get it all out, birdie. You'll be fine, I know it.'

She wanted it to be true; she wanted to trust him. All Torment wanted at that moment was a friend to trust, a friend to tell her all would be well. Her word was not enough. She did not believe she would be well – not on her own.

Her heart calmed. The burning sensation faded. The bileful stuff she had spit out sizzled on the earth, green steam rising from it that bit the eyes.

'You don't trust yourself with the vampire' – Vlad scowled down at her – 'or the potions. What's up with your spirited crow self, cawing in the face of fear?'

Torment didn't know. She was only beginning to understand her faults, bit by bit. She understood the vampire wasn't one of them, not really. She was beginning to make out her personality, a blurred image of her, the parts she had been made of, and she didn't like herself. She didn't even like what she had been as a crow. Was that her purpose, perhaps? To eventually become someone it was worth being?

Vlad took Torment's hand, which was clenched into a fist, and pried open her fingers. The magpie's skull rested in her palm.

'You up against your conscience, birdie?'

Torment shook her head, shrugged, nodded ... then shrugged again. Human gestures for a human weakness. Self-doubt was not for crows and cats. It was all very tiresome indeed.

'But ... you're all right, Torment. Insufferable sometimes, but all right. Toad-king certified all right, even. If that's what this is.' He gave her a wry grin. 'Come on. Bag your morals and pull out that sharp beak again. My claws, your wits, working in tune ... we'll crack open Phileander's mind in no time and be back to haunt him by supper.'

She refrained from informing him that it was already past suppertime back home. It was reassuring to have him on her side again. Enough to give her some of her strength back. But would it be enough to make the potion work? The fact this question crossed her mind alone proved it was not.

'Neither wits nor beak will help me walk.' She sighed. 'And even among those two things, I have but one together … and barely.'

'That leaves my claws. And my stubbornness.' He uncorked the crimson potion. 'I'd say that's plenty.'

He lifted the bottle to drink, but in a moment of insight he put it down again and began to take off his trousers. It was his only piece of clothing.

'Uhm … what are you doing?' For all her newfound humanness, Torment had not yet embraced the human trait of ascribing a mystical interpersonal significance to the sight of another's sexual organs. Still, Vlad's undressing in this situation struck her as odd.

Naked, he gulped down half the red liquid. And not long before the thin mouth of the vial had left his lips, he began to change. His hair grew to a thick and shiny black fur, covering his brawny body from the neck down. He grew thinner around the waist, his thighs grew larger, and he bent over. Vlad laughed, looking down at himself, over his shoulders at the wriggling tail that grew out of his rump. He had kept his mostly human head, albeit with larger, more pointed ears covered in a fine black fuzz.

'You made yourself a *sphynx* again,' cheered Torment, still weak and dizzy, 'and you're large enough to carry me.'

'Could have carried you either way, but it's way more convenient like this.'

He trotted off with a bounding, four-legged gait, picked up his things with his mouth and brought them back to Torment. The way he was used to.

He also looked more at ease with himself, less tense. Maybe he had gotten a glimpse of himself earlier, a reflection in a puddle, and seeing how similar he looked to a younger Phileander was what had made him so cranky? It made sense it would upset him more than it did her. Vladimir seemed so much surer of who he was than Torment. But hadn't she concluded that their transformations had to be rooted somewhere in their subconscious? Torment, on her part, knew there was a disgusting fragment of herself that longed to be both Phileander's daughter and his wife. To be loved by him. Yet she hated him more than anything. What did Vlad feel or think? Why did she ever presume to know?

'Look, Torment, you just cut off that trouser leg, smear the paste on it and bandage your leg.'

'What if it's—'

'It's just a herbal remedy to keep the wound clean.'

'How would you know—'

'Torment, I'm telling you. I understand you're all jittery with your hurt feelings turning everything sour and whatnot. But I'm telling you, I'm sure what this paste will do to you. Just roll with it.' He lay down on his stomach next to her and licked his paws. It was sort of odd, a grown human male licking his paws. 'Hop on when you're ready. Or … crawl on, I suppose.'

Torment did as he had told her – cut a bandage with her dagger, used the paste and tied it tightly around her leg. She also used one of the trouser laces to thread the magpie's skull onto it like a charm and hung it around her neck. Then she put on both their backpacks and crawled onto his back, and the two of them rode on speedily through the forest to the edge of it and up the mountain. Vladimir jumped from rock to rock, up and up the incline.

It got darker, and the sun seemed to descend another inch with every foot of slope they scaled.

Until they arrived at a starry night over the dark castle where Phileander's mind held court.

Chapter 15

A SIP OF FAITH

THE WALL WAS dark and slick and very high. As a crow, Torment would never have given it a second thought. A wall, an obstacle … how ludicrous that a stack of bricks should shut her out. A well-tiled roof, perhaps, or shuttered windows. But a wall? Nonsense. Downright insulting.

'Stop scratching at it,' Torment snapped. 'You won't scratch a hole in it any time soon.'

'No, but it feels good,' nagged Vlad. Although, begrudgingly, he stopped and sat on his backside like a proud statue, letting his tail swish.

Torment stood next to him, braced against the wall to keep from falling over. 'There really wasn't a door?' she asked, rubbing her chin. They'd paced all around it.

'No. Why would there be? He'll hardly have to enter his mind palace from the outside, will he?'

Torment wasn't so sure she was enjoying clever Vladimir. *She* liked to be the one pointing things out like this. But she wasn't doing that anymore. Shoo. Out with it. Bad thoughts, bad attitude. Vlad was a friend – more than that, actually – and he had every right to be a smart-ass.

'We need to scale the wall, then,' she decided. 'It has these evil-looking pointy things on top. Perfect for hooking the … hook there.'

Hooking the hook. Had she lost all eloquence along with her self-confidence? Anyway, she started tying their rope to one of the metal contraptions. It was a steel rod with a ring on one end and three hooks sprouting from the other like a flower.

'The crenellations, you mean,' murmured Vlad, inspecting his claws.

He was testing her patience, surely. She would let him. Torment swung the metal thing in a circle, then let it loose to hurl it up the wall. It made it about halfway, clanked against the stone and plunged back down, making Torment scream and topple over.

Vlad gave a purring laugh.

'My leg's half bitten off,' snapped Torment. 'It's not funny.'

'Oh no.' Vlad scrunched up his face. 'Must be … *torment*, what you're going through.'

Torment pulled herself onto one leg by the wall and hobbled over to the hook, muttering curses along the way. Let him tease her for a bit. He had earned it and perhaps she deserved it.

Vlad tilted his head. 'Anyone ever told you how melodramatic that name is, by the way?'

'Well, you may come to understand it better if you go on like that.'

Torment set to work again, looking intently and critically up the wall that towered over her four times her height.

'There's a way, you know,' he purred, raising a paw, presenting his cat features, *'birdie.'*

'Can't do it,' muttered Torment, swirling the hook.

'You don't even have to convince yourself the potion does what it does. I already did it.' He made that gesture where he let his fangs snap along a claw that gave her goosebumps. Like cracking joints. 'It'll give you wings.'

'No, it …' The red stuff would wake her vampire. She didn't know how she knew it, or rather, it didn't matter why she imagined it – the imagination alone would put her soul at risk. Red and sweet and … oh, she could already hear it in her head. She didn't want to conjure the damn thing up. 'I just can't, Vlad.'

She tried another time. And another. Every time the metal hook fell back down uselessly. How was a crow to know how to do these things? Why couldn't she just fly? Why couldn't she just believe in herself?

'Oh, All-Mother peck my eyes, give me that potion,' Torment snapped, casting the rope aside.

Vlad looked down at the backpacks. 'You're the one with the opposable thumbs.'

She crouched and pulled the vial from the pack. It was still half filled with the crimson liquid. She eyed it sceptically. Back in their world, Phileander practised the science of alchemy. Clear-cut rules determined his results. Here, this liquid was but an idea to be filled by make-believe. Torment pondered how the nature of this world gave power to the self-assured yet took it away from the wavering, the faint-hearted. From her. In the waking world, Torment would never have second-guessed that this potion must do to her exactly what Vladimir had demonstrated. Common sense. But now she feared what her mind would make it do. Common nonsense.

The nature of this world was both a blessing and a curse. No wonder the dream wilds were so deserted. All but the insane must surely have perished long ago, for the insane must have been like gods over the rest. And the insane must soon thereafter have drowned in the terror of their own delusions. What few inhabitants were left, like the swamp people, surely survived only by virtue of their staunch adherence to simple beliefs, rendering their environment *just* predictable enough.

'Am I insane, Vladimir? Or am I a swamp person?' She removed the cork, swirled the glass and sniffed. No smell of blood. More like maple. 'Or am I, perhaps, a mad god?'

Vlad grimaced in bewilderment. 'It's a manic up and down with you. You're a freakin' crow, Torment.'

'A crow. Hold that thought,' she said. 'Here flies nothing.' She closed her eyes and drained it in one gulp. It didn't taste like blood, luckily.

But nothing happened. Torment opened her eyes and sighed. 'I can't get it to work, Vlad.'

He shook his head. 'But you don't have to. I already did it. Look …' He strode over to the edge of a steep cliff that went all the way down to the foot of the mountain. 'Come. I wanna show you something.'

Torment walked up to the edge and peered down.

'What?' It was just a long drop down to pines that looked like mere blades of grass. 'Oh no, you—'

Vladimir shoved her.

'Treachery!'

But she was already hurtling downward at breakneck speed and Vladimir couldn't hear her.

And then she felt the wind. She felt it like she hadn't felt it in a long time – since she had first entered the realm of dreams and flown again, in fact, and before that every day in her life as a crow … when she had been as free as she had ever been.

And she spread her wings, caught the wind, made it hers. The wind had always been hers, for she was a crow and crows could fly. Oh, and how she flew. She had always been proud of it, even before she had known what pride was. It was the All-Mother's gift to her. Torment laughed.

She brushed the tops of the pines with her hands as she rushed by. With her hands. Yes, she had hands on the tips of her wings. And she had human legs and a human torso, and around her eyes she felt her feathery hair whipping across her human face. The sleeves of her white shirt had ripped to reveal her stately black wings, spanning wider than her arms had before, probably reaching almost to the ground as soon as she landed on those human feet again.

Which she did, after a whirl-around and a rise-and-dive and another turn. She winced at the twinge of pain in her injured leg as it touched the earth.

'I don't know,' she said, a little out of breath, while the dust settled around her feet, 'if I want to kiss you or kill you.'

Vlad groaned and scratched himself with a hind leg. 'I knew it would work, birdie, so it worked. Perk of being in this together. You don't always have to be the one believing in yourself.'

Torment held an arm up against the night sky. She admired its broad sheet of feathers that reflected the stars and merged with the blackness in between. Gratitude filled her, and relief, and an unexpected new emotion. She took Vlad's face in her hands, feathers touching fur, and kissed him on the lips.

He froze. In a non-weirded-out, pleasantly surprised way, Torment hoped.

She felt pleasantly surprised herself, as her heart made a leap and a rush went through her and she was suddenly convinced the two of them together could accomplish anything.

Her lips parted from his, and she smiled, gauging his eyes.

'What a ... disturbingly human thing to do,' he muttered.

Torment thought she could see a hunger in him, repressed with great effort ... which excited and frightened her in equal measure. The human experience held instincts and urges that compared to nothing she had known as a crow. She longed to glimpse Vladimir's heart and see all that was in it, but at the same time she was bitterly afraid of it. A strange craving for affection gripped her.

'Right,' she said, brushing that impractical emotion aside, and went to pick up the rope. 'See you in a flap, crony.'

And she took off, soaring upwards on swift wings – one, two, three beats – and landed on the ramparts.

The immensity of the castle sprawled before her – thin, pointed spires atop black stone walls with buttresses jutting out, creating many spaces of shadow and dividing the grounds in complex patterns. Here and there black things fluttered from the roofs – other corvids, bats, winged things of the night. A mist rose from the castle, carrying smells of alchemical brews and vapours, of ink and wine and heavy dust. The overblown copy of the Tower of Undreamed Truths lay behind a twisted keep, several watchtowers and something resembling a cathedral with looming stained glass windows. From her position, she could see no entrance to the tower. But it had to be Phileander's sanctum containing his Hall of the Conscious Mind ... and his spirit. There were footbridges spanning from the ramparts to the inner buildings, hundreds of them, like a web. And on some Torment saw hulking figures patrolling, glinting in the starlight.

'Guards?' she whispered to herself. *Her* mind palace had no guards. Could she make it have guards? She rested a hand on the hilt of the short sword just to reassure herself. Not that she actually knew how to wield it. Little puffs of steam rose from the figures' heads. Were they machines? From afar, Torment thought she could make out metal parts and bundles of tubes on them. Shiny. Curious. At any rate, better not to fly over the compound and let them spot her.

Quickly she tied the rope around one of the merlons, made doubly sure the hook held fast and descended back to Vladimir.

'It's large,' she said. 'Much larger than mine, I think.'

'Your what?'

'My mind palace. Never saw it from the outside.' Torment rubbed her chin in thought. 'Not even sure it has an outside. I'd have to manifest it in the dream wilds for that.'

Vlad clawed a forepaw on to the dangling rope and gave it a testing tug. 'And make yourself vulnerable? Why is Phileander doing it, anyway?'

'I don't think he is. I think we're doing it. We're pulling it in.'

He gave a grunt and turned back to the rope. 'You'll have to tie it around my chest and pull me up.'

'Me?' Torment presented her long spindly arms that stretched along the upper edge of her wings. 'No way I'm pulling your poundage, my well-built compadre.'

He bowed his head down to his rucksack and fetched out a small bottle of milky liquid with his mouth. 'Shtrengf Pofiom.'

Torment took it, held it against the light and put on an anxious face. 'Strength? You sure it won't just turn my brain to pudding or something?'

'I swear, you crabby, crotchety corvid, with the utmost respect, I will rip your—'

'Oh, caw down, crony. Just kidding.' Then she winked and took a sip.

Sure enough, she felt a pulsing strength surge through her muscles. Her uncertainties might not always allow her to trust herself, but she knew she could trust Vladimir.

Torment fastened the rope around his sinewy feline torso. So beautifully the muscles moved underneath his slick, black fur. Then she soared back onto the ramparts, and indeed her arms proved strong enough to pull her companion up. Bracing her good foot against the battlement, she pulled – heave ho – each yank a pace up the wall, until a large paw grasped an embrasure. Leaving scratch marks in the stone, he drew himself up and leapt onto the battlement.

'Where to now?'

'Good question,' said Torment, freeing him of the rope. 'Let's see. What do we need?'

'Knowledge,' said Vlad, 'to break the bonds the bastard has on us. And today's memories would be great, so we can destroy some of it. If he wants to punish us, back there we won't have … powers.'

Torment nodded. 'And we need a way back. Violet told me I'd need a connection to my body.' She looked at the golden dome atop the tower. 'In all of the dream wilds, this would be the most likely place to find one.'

'Let's just start looking for his knowledge about homunculi.'

Torment looked out over the castle. 'It'll be hidden in one of the less conspicuous buildings, I suspect.'

Her gaze wandered to an unassuming half-timbered house, some-what crooked, seemingly no more than an insignificant outbuilding. It wasn't high; no bridges led to it. They would need to get down to the ground. The rope could—

'Torment,' hissed Vlad, 'something's coming our way.'

One of the big machine figures was hoisting itself up a stair to the ramparts not far from them.

Torment cut the rope with her dagger and threw it over the battle-ments, along with the hook. She would leave no traces for the guards to warn Phileander of their coming. They had left their backpacks below, so now they only had themselves, the dagger and the sword. It would have to suffice.

'Let's go,' she whispered and darted off along the ramparts, away from the approaching machine. She made sure to dodge the gaze of the guards, head always pulled in. Vlad was close on her heels.

One of the things climbed another set of stairs to the ramparts just up ahead, its silvery head turning with a creak as it surveyed the outer bailey.

Torment hopped off the ramparts onto a footbridge protruding from the wall at about mid-height and stretching over part of the bailey. It ended in a door to a free-standing watchtower about a dozen feet above ground.

Vlad followed with a mighty bound. They were swift and silent and invisible, two children of the night in their very element. It felt glorious.

The watchtower abutted directly onto the crooked timber-framed house. In all likelihood there was a connecting door at ground level.

Vlad sped past her and pressed himself against the wall beside the door. Head lowered, shoulders hunched as stalking felines tend to do, he peered round the edge. Torment dashed to the other side of the door.

'We should get inside as soon as possible,' whispered Vlad. 'Too exposed out here.'

'There's one of them inside,' said Torment. She could see it clearly now, stomping along the circular walls from loophole to loophole. It was a bulky thing like living armour, with gears and rods and tubing to move it. A clockwork knight with a silver mask depicting a deadpan Phileander. Its arms contained particularly complex machinery, with straps and blades and something that looked like a crossbow. An interesting part shone in its chest where a heart ought to be, catching the light of the wall-mounted torches. A glass case holding something golden.

There was another door at the far side, leading out onto a balcony, and a trapdoor in the centre of the room.

'We need to get down,' said Torment, 'onto the castle grounds and to that little outbuilding.'

She peered down the bridge. Several more of those steaming knights walked their rounds down there, some holding lanterns.

'Will Phileander notice us when one of those things does?' asked

Vlad.

'Not sure. Don't think so.' Whatever went on in her mind palace when she wasn't there, thought Torment, affected her subconsciously at best. 'He can't have his attention so divided. They'll have to alarm each other and report to his consciousness.'

She examined the room again. The clockwork knight was too big to just rush to the trapdoor when it wasn't looking. It was bound to get in their way.

'Let's take it out, then,' said Vlad. 'We can manage one, right?'

They had to. She couldn't see another way. 'Then down the trap-door and into the house?'

Vlad nodded. 'On three?'

'Wait …' They knew so little about these things, except they were obviously fighting machines. Torment knew fighting of a kind. Crows fought over food. Sometimes she had fought prey that had under-standably objected to being eaten. Neither of those situations had been fights to the death between equal opponents. Her heart pounded. 'We need some tactical advantage, right?'

'We'll surprise it,' said Vlad, who seemed utterly at ease. She saw it in his eyes. Fighting for his life against stronger enemies was not new to him.

Torment remembered those oversized street cats they had faced in a back alley right after escaping Phileander's and Vladimir's shared memory. Right before she had tumbled into her nightmare of the crowery … and the crow master. Those cats had been Vladimir's night-mare, she realised – his demons from the past. He'd been on the streets as a kitten, bullied half to death by his own kin. It made sense.

'More tactical advantage, I mean,' whispered Torment with a quiv-er in her voice.

Of course, there was one fight to the death against a superior op-ponent she had won … the crow master, wearing Phileander's face. The advantage she had used then was out of the question. Even if she managed to lock the vampire up again, who was to say she wouldn't wake to see her fangs digging into Vladimir's heart?

'Let's pincer it, then,' whispered Vlad. 'You come in through the opposite door.'

Right, she had wings. She couldn't fly across the castle courtyard without being spotted, but certainly once around this tower.

She took a deep breath. 'Got it. Bird's gotta do what a bird's gotta do.'

Then she ran towards the edge, took off and turned sideways in the air, wings pushing her along the tower wall, which almost scraped her back as she cut a tight arc.

Seconds later, Torment's feet connected with the parapet of the tower's balcony, halting her flight and sending a pain up her ruined leg that drew a stifled cry.

She crumpled to her knees on the balcony floor, and when she looked up, the clockwork knight was facing her, pumping steam from his nostrils and extending a blade from his arm with a vibrating *zing*.

'Oh, crikey.'

Stomp, stomp, stomp, it came at her, raising the other arm, and a *snap* rang out.

She splayed a wing before her face, and a piercing pain bit through the feathers. The tip of a metal bolt rested just before her eyes. By all rights, it should have shot right through. But she had *willed* her wing to stop it. Maybe she was getting the hang of this after all.

When she lowered her wing, the colossus had reached the door and lashed out with its blade.

Torment stumbled sideways as she awkwardly wrenched the short sword from her belt. There was a clank and flying sparks where she'd been kneeling.

It turned its head with a rusty creak. Its blade loomed over her, and Torment knew she didn't believe in it enough for her raised sword to be able to stop it.

A black blur caught the knight's head – Vlad's paw – and pulled it, staggering, back into the tower. Steam hissed, steel protesting, keeping it on its massive feet.

Forward. She limped, wings wrapped around her, reeling into that hunk of metal.

It fell.

Vlad was on it, pounding and scratching, pinning it down as best he could.

'Kill it,' he growled.

'How?'

'Damned if I know.' The thing rammed its blade into Vlad's side and he gasped, 'Fucking kill it!'

She had to stop crowing about and think, All-Mother damn it. There – that glint again. The glass case in its chest. Torment leaned over it, caught a knee in her guts like a cannonball, stealing her breath, and jammed the sword into it.

Missed by inches, stuck it fast in a gap between armour plates. Wait, was it bleeding? No, that was Vlad's blood.

The dagger, then.

'Kill it!' Vlad jerked up, hit by something.

There was an opening right under the glass thing. She slid the blade in and levered against it.

The knight seemed to panic – spasming, steaming, emitting a smouldering smell.

That strength potion! Surely it still had some residual effect? Yes, yes, of course it did!

Crack – the case came loose.

She pried it out … and the thing gave off a last waning whistle before it sagged into a pile of scrap metal.

The two of them leaned on the pile for a while, breathing heavily. The scent of the metal was intense, coppery … oddly enticing. Sweet.

'You're bleeding,' Torment remembered.

'You don't say,' Vlad wheezed. The way he was stretched out on the armour, he almost looked like dear old Vladimir making himself comfortable on the mantelpiece. But the blade was buried in him to the base, right behind his right foreleg, and he was spilling something bright red in the torchlight. And sweet. There was power in his blood, she could smell it. No, not she. It. She thought she heard it chuckle in its prison in her mind. She had to be wary, ever wary.

'You think we could … y'know' – Vlad tilted his head – 'do something about it?'

'Right.' Torment still stood there, staring, dagger in hand and clutching the glass case to her chest. 'Against the bleeding …' That herbal paste would have come in handy now. But they didn't have their bags and she had used up all of it anyway.

Torment snapped and raised her finger in a flash of wit. 'I've used up that herbal remedy.'

'Yeah.' Vlad frowned. 'I know.'

'That means, my skewered friend, I have it *on* me.'

'Oh.' His eyes widened. 'Right. Bit unhygienic, though. And don't you still need it?'

With all that adrenaline, Torment had nearly forgotten about the pain in her leg. Indeed, she didn't feel any pain now. Why, it was only reasonable to conclude that adrenaline had nary a thing to do with it. That herbal paste had miraculous healing properties, no doubt about it. Torment grinned. She would be a fool not to believe it still had enough punch in it to fix up her friend.

Contentedly, she unknotted the scrap of leather around her leg and unwound it. The skin underneath was scarred, caked with dried blood, but otherwise fine.

'I see,' said Vladimir. 'I underestimated that paste, didn't I?'

But it had dried out by now. Of course it had dried out after so many hours. How could it still work if it had dried out? Oh dear … she had ruined it now.

'What?' said Vlad.

'I … I think I messed it up by having too much common sense.'

'Torment,' said Vladimir sternly, 'I forbid you to think another thought, and now please just slap the damn thing on my wound.'

Torment put down the glass case. It was tubular, sealed with silver lids, and appeared to contain a hovering golden disc the size of her hand. She strained to block out the sullen voice in her head, which kept repeating how it was all for naught and she was to blame, and slowly pulled the blade from Vlad's flesh. Blood oozed plentifully.

'Put it on,' gasped Vladimir anxiously. 'Quick, quick, now.'

He could die here. Her chest tightened and a whimper escaped her as she hastily pressed the encrusted rag to his side. He could die and his body back home would stay unconscious forever until its heart gave out.

Vlad let out a drawn-out, alleviated sigh. He closed his eyes and smiled.

'Are you—' There was a lump in Torment's throat and she could feel that tears were on their way again. 'Are you just playing this so I believe it worked? Oh crikey, why did I ask that? I have to … I have to believe it worked. I—' Torment sobbed. She didn't believe it. All she believed was that she had killed her only friend because a teensy-tiny misstep had thrown her into a vicious tailspin of guilty thoughts.

'No, I'm fine,' said Vlad conversationally. 'Really. You can take it off now.'

He winked, got up and shook himself so the rag flew away and she was sprinkled with little spatters of blood.

'But— but …' Torment had grown certain the paste wouldn't work anymore, but she had never believed it would work this quickly to begin with. His fur was still wet with blood, but he no longer appeared to be losing any. As he took the lightest of strides to the trapdoor and sat down, tail waving, his movements were as graceful as ever. It was proof it had worked. Whatever slight chance there still was that he was putting on an act, she had to disregard it, because, trick or no, she *needed* to believe. That Vlad might just be too tenacious to die, that was a belief she could settle on. Torment sighed. A questioning mind such as hers made utilising the dream wilds' thought-manifesting properties quite exhausting.

'You coming or what?' He pawed the ring-shaped handle of the trapdoor. 'We'll need those opposable thumbs of yours again.'

'Coming.'

Torment tucked the dagger into her belt, picked up the glass tube and headed into the depths of Phileander's mind.

'Over the years I have become a figure of both fame and infamy. Admittedly, the latter has far outweighed the former of late. So chances are you, dear reader, wish me dead, in which case I can assure you that we are in complete agreement. But there is something I have yet to do, and as prone as I am to making disastrous mistakes, I am not one to shy away from my responsibilities.'

— Ogden Flynt, *Spirits beyond Earth and Sky* (unfinished manuscript)

Chapter 16

A Sense of Foreboding

There hadn't been a connecting door to that crooked house, not directly. What there had been were plenty of stairs leading down and then a wine cellar. It was not Torment's place to judge human architecture – she hadn't even partaken in what little architecture crows usually dabbled with in nest-building, what with her having been domesticated and all that. Yet a wine cellar below a watchtower seemed unusual. But knowing Phileander, it might just be that all cellars around here were wine cellars. In fact, any other things Torment could think of that Phileander might store in deep, dark places in his mind she was quite glad not to stumble upon just now. She would prefer to ease into his mind palace. Quite certainly, ghastly encounters lay ahead.

The air was cool and damp but not musty. There were no cobwebs, as far as she could see in the dark grey, and all was in good order, sorted by vintage. She brushed along the shelves as she explored the aisles. The only imperfection was a thin layer of dust upon the bottles, and Torment could hear inside her how Phileander had once said, 'To swipe the dust off the label before uncorking, revelling in the fine vintage, dear Torment, is integral to the refined ritual of decanting a Timzani red.'

'What did you say?' asked Vlad, glancing around nervously.

'Nothing.'

That memory … it had positively echoed off the walls. Torment gulped.

'We might want to be careful with conjuring up Phileander's presence in our minds while we're here.'

Vlad nodded without asking further.

'It's too dark for human eyes,' Torment nagged. 'We should have taken one of those torches off the walls.'

'Don't tell *me* that.'

'Why?'

'Thumbs.'

'Ah. Yes.'

Despite that inconvenience, it was good he now wore this shape. Otherwise he probably wouldn't have been chunky enough to pin down that clockwork death machine. And he might just still be as irritable as he had been before.

A sweet smell rose to Torment's nose, one that reminded her of … dead things. She felt something soft under her boot and heard a squelch and a snap. Bone and rotted meat. She could barely see it in the gloom, but there was a faint rectangular green glow on the floor. Torment remembered the bodies in her own basement. They had already been many. What would Phileander's counterpart hold?

Torment gulped.

'What are you doing?' asked Vlad. 'Found something?'

'Perhaps,' said Torment cautiously.

She drew her hand closer to the thing she had stepped on. It recoiled at first. Then it crept closer. Like a timid animal.

'Knock it off!' came a gravelly voice from the depths.

Torment froze.

'Who was that?' whispered Vlad.

'I have very good hearing, you two pests,' screeched the voice.

It came from below the glowing rectangle. That was a trapdoor leading further down. Something was rustling down there, scuffling, like a great swarm of rats.

'Stop it! Whatever you're doing.'

'But … we're not doing anything,' said Torment, bending down to the trapdoor.

The lid slammed open, almost into Torment's face, and she stumbled backwards.

A figure stuck its head up from the trapdoor, illuminated by a green light from below, looking left and right, its gaze finally locking onto Torment.

'You!'

Dozens of arms and legs and torsos, mostly too decayed to still be attached to each other, wriggled out of the trapdoor and across the floor like worms. The stench of death long since past was overbearing, oozing from the opening with an almost palpable thickness. The irritated figure was humanoid, but with a slumped, bent-forward posture and a furry, almost canine-like face. Its ears were long and pointed, and it wore a fashionable suit jacket over a shirt with a stiffened collar and a gore-soaked cravat.

It pointed a long-clawed finger at Torment. 'Stop making them do that.'

'I'm not making anyone do anything.'

It gestured in annoyance at the corpse parts teeming around. 'This. They're not supposed to do this. I'm a ghoul for a reason.' He glowered at her. 'I don't like to have to run after my food.'

From the edge of the green glow, Torment saw Vlad prowling closer.

Torment inhaled deeply – which she regretted immediately – and whispered, 'Don't attack it.'

Vlad paused.

'*It?*' crackled the ghoul. 'Very flattering.'

'Relax,' whispered Torment. 'Easy now …'

'I'm not moving,' hissed Vlad. 'Should I stop breathing too?'

The ghoul turned around in his hole in the ground and gave Vlad a whack on the head. 'She's not talking to you, meathead.'

Vlad's retaliatory strike came in a flash, but the ghoul intercepted the paw undeterred, at the same time twisting it so that Vladimir crumpled to the ground. He grunted and squirmed, and each time he tried to rise, the ghoul would just twist a little on the paw he was pinning to the ground and Vlad would drop back down with a yelp.

'Be a nice kitty,' it scolded.

At the same time, the autonomous pieces of corpses settled down a little. Torment didn't know exactly how, but she had an effect on this rotten meat. She tried to get it to move back into the green pit, but it didn't work that precisely after all.

The ghoul seemed satisfied nonetheless. It let go of Vlad, who retreated and glowered at the green-lit corpse-eater from a safe distance. Then it started leaning out of its hole and dragging the strewn delicacies back into its home. It held one up that was so far gone, the flesh had nearly taken on the consistency of a paste upon the bones.

'Ah' – it took a deep whiff of it – 'the ripe ones, like Roquefort or Gorgonzola, positively dripping off the bone, and with the most succulent green mould.'

Torment tasted bile in her throat.

The last decomposing thigh disappeared into the hole.

'Wonderful,' said the ghoul. 'All back in order. And you' – he scowled at her again – 'you mark my words, corpse meddler. This is not a body dump for your perverted necromantic convenience; this is the kitchen of Richard L'Homme de Pioche. And it is defended. Now scram.'

And he ducked down again, slamming the trapdoor shut after him.

Apparently, Phileander had acquired a solution to the issue of the bodies in the basement. Whether it was intentional or just the kind of vermin bound to move in to such a place, she couldn't say.

They explored the rest of the cellar, steering clear of the trapdoor.

'I think there's a pull-down ladder on the ceiling,' said Vlad. 'And another trapdoor. Leading up.'

Torment hardly saw a thing, but reaching up where he stood, she could palpate planks of rough wood on the cold stone. She pulled it down with a clatter and went ahead, pushing a wing up against the trapdoor above her.

She opened it just a crack at first. The smell of hay hung in the muggy air, along with that of tea leaves, goats and something freshly baked. On well-trodden floorboards Torment glimpsed sunspots in between the feet of a table and chairs, but no feet of people or giant steam-powered knights.

With a flourish, she opened it all the way and swung herself up. It was a quaint room. There were beams supporting the low ceiling and whitewashed walls hung with painted pottery, as well as windows out onto a tiled roof under a midday sun, even though it had clearly been night outside. This discrepancy barely made her sweat after all she had seen.

The small boy sitting cross-legged on one of the chairs, however, gawking at her, made Torment start.

Snarling, Vlad leapt out of the trapdoor behind her, ready to jump whatever foe she faced, and the boy fell backwards off his chair, spilling tea onto his crumpet, and scrambled backwards to the wall.

'Miss!' he screamed. 'Miss Baba! There're monsters in your basement!'

'Hush,' said Torment, raising an open hand, but the boy just stared at her unfolded wing-arm. It did look majestic in the sunlight.

'Miss Baba!' Even louder now.

'Quit that,' hissed Vlad, stalking past her, 'or I'll bite your head off.'

That worked. The boy left his mouth open for a moment, then closed it and wrapped his hands around his arms.

'Look,' said Torment, 'he doesn't mean that. Or ...' She looked at Vlad, tail swishing, claws out. Even level-headed as he was, he had probably meant that. 'Well, he can't bite it *off*, can he? With that tiny human mouth. Gnaw at it at best.'

Vlad growled. The boy trembled.

Perhaps this was not how you calmed a frightened child. This was a terribly unusual interpersonal situation for Torment, although she had a hunch most humans would consider it far more normal than what Torment had grown accustomed to by now – like long-dead scholars, drunken rabbit magicians, toad-kings or, not least of all, sociopathic philosophers. Meeting young Adelaide had come close, but she had already vanquished an evil mushroom queen by then. This one really seemed to be just a normal boy.

'We're not monsters,' Torment said.

From the chained door inside her mind, she could feel the beast's amusement at the lie. Next to her, unhelpfully, Vlad made a 'not too sure about that' face.

'I don't think you wanna know what's *really* in the basement, boy,' he said, sniggering.

'You wouldn't be the first monsters I've met,' mumbled the boy. 'Just the first who so blatantly look like it.'

Vlad scoffed. 'Might just be one yourself, actually, judging by where we are.'

'You better believe I am,' the boy said defiantly. 'And what do you mean, "where you are"? Miss Baba is nice. This is a no-monster house.'

Vladimir was right, of course. This was clearly a memory, a childhood one, and there was only one person it could be from.

'Phileander, is it?' asked Torment gently.

The boy looked nothing like the monstrous man she knew – the one she so strangely feared and admired at once. He was such a small and gangly thing, underfed, scruffy haired.

'Phileander …' The not-yet-philosopher let this name sink in. 'I don't actually have a name, but did you know Phileander was the name of one of the One City's founding spire builders?' He relaxed somewhat and rested his hands on his knees. 'I think I will like this name. No one would dare bully a man so powerful, he can light up the sun.'

Vladimir prowled around the table, sniffing the tea-soaked pastry with a grimace, and seemed altogether unconvinced that he should not bite off this boy's head after all. Or gnaw on it.

'Bullied, were you?' he snarled. 'Monkey see, monkey do, I suppose.'

'I never bullied anyone. I wish I could bully them back.' Child Phileander scowled. 'But I'm a clever boy on streets that are for strong-armed ones. Or ones with powerful parents if the streets are higher up.'

Torment pulled the glass case out from under her wing and put it on the table. She squatted before the boy.

'But your parents must have some power.' She remembered Phileander going on about the order's stain of nepotism.

'I don't have any parents at all.' He glanced over at Vlad, who had lain down on the table, making it creak and bend under his weight. 'Where did you get that?' His tone was accusing.

'He's not a *that*,' said Torment.

'I'm not *hers*,' said Vlad.

'I meant the mirror.'

'What mirror?' Torment's gaze fell on the case and the golden disc hovering inside. 'The knight's heart?'

'Knight's heart?' The boy furrowed his brow. 'Are you daft, bird-woman? It's Miss Baba's hand mirror, plain and clear. You stole it.'

'Uhm …' It seemed unlikely he would understand if she told him she'd cut the thing out of a piece of living armour that his future self had created in order to protect his mind from intruders. 'I didn't know what it was.'

'It's Miss Baba's mirror she gave me to trade in for coin, so I can buy food and maybe a bed for a few nights.'

Torment walked over to the table and removed the upper lid. Carefully, she plucked the disc from the tube.

She regarded the boy with a tilted head. 'Can't you stay and eat at Miss Baba's? Isn't she your master?'

Young Phileander rose, irritated. 'Firstly, it would be "mistress", and secondly, why would anyone be my master?' He reached for the disc. 'She took me in for a night and I'm to be gone before her husband comes home, or he will be very cross.'

Vlad jumped off the table and the boy stumbled back.

'So bad? I thought this was a no-monster house,' he purred. 'This aimless banter, heart-wrenching as it may be, has gone on long enough.' Vlad stopped with his face so close to the boy's, their noses nearly touched. 'You'll end up being the greatest bully of them all. Now tell us what you know about homun—'

'Vlad!' Torment pushed the cat-man's face away from the boy's. 'Careful. Break the pattern of the memory too much and we might draw attention …'

'What are you two crazy beasts talking about?' Phileander grasped for the trinket in Torment's hand. 'Give me back my property.'

'Don't give him anything,' Vlad growled. 'Who knows what he can do with it? It's clearly some source of power.'

260

Torment examined the boy's expression as he looked at the golden thing. She knew this look – a desperate gratitude and a hunger for care and affection.

'It's a source of trust,' she said as she figured it out. 'A part of his … kinder side. His innocence. That's what he locked away in those knights to guard his subconscious.' She smiled wryly. 'Clever, really. This way he's rid of it and doesn't need to guard his mind palace consciously.'

'You speak nonsense,' cried the boy. 'I have no trust! You said you're no monsters, yet you rob me.' He was still grasping for it, too short for Torment's long feathered arms. 'No one will protect me, not Miss Baba, not anyone!'

He kicked Torment's shin, but he was so pitifully weak, it didn't hurt even a little bit.

'I'll have to fend for myself. Slay you if I must.'

Vlad smirked toothily. 'He's not wrong.'

Oh, stupid cat. But wait – Torment had sworn not to view him so arrogantly anymore. He was just wired differently.

She handed Phileander the golden thing. He took it reverently, and at once his demeanour changed dramatically. The boy's features softened.

Putting a hand on Vlad's flank, Torment whispered, 'Where would I be, after all, if I hadn't trusted you?'

'Dead in the forest. Or your cage.' He shrugged. 'Confusing circumstances lately. But you might still end up dead if I betray you.'

'Which you won't, because we're friends. Fatebound, even.'

The boy had unfolded the mirror, smiling at his likeness, and Torment cupped his hands in hers, closing it again.

'You hold on to that. You know how to fend for yourself and find shelter. This is a symbol of something far more precious.'

He looked up and gave Torment a reconciliatory smile. 'Thanks, bird lady.'

She smiled back and nodded and tugged at Vlad's fur. 'Come. We must go further along his memory.'

Torment headed for the front door.

'Wait,' said Vlad, hurrying after her. 'Won't that just lead out into the castle grounds?'

'No. It's where he'll go next, so it leads to future memories.'

Vladimir hadn't explored his mind palace as she had hers. He didn't know the rules of the place.

And just as she had expected, the door led out into a hallway. These were Phileander's Halls of Memory, and the rooms were connected by pathways of association. It made sense that they would take the shape of corridors, seeing as he had spent most of his life in the complex of interconnected castles in which the Tower of Undreamed Truths was nestled. Most of these hallways were elegantly furnished, wood-panelled and hung with eerie oil paintings. Vlad only glowered at them suspiciously, at sinister scenes of dirty streets where grim faces leered from the gutters. He could relate to them – had ones to match in his own mind palace, perhaps. On these walls, they were where Phileander's associations with the past had been memorised. He and Vlad had both been street urchins, as they had just found out, alone in a world where beast and kin were the same.

Yet Vlad was right to be suspicious. In some of these paintings, Phileander appeared to be depicted himself, and Torment couldn't shed the feeling that in them his eyes moved to follow their every step.

'We'd better avoid his gaze,' whispered Torment.

Vlad nodded.

Stomp.

'What was that?' he hissed.

Stomp.

She knew that sound.

Creak, stomp. Hissing steam. Just a turn behind them.

'Run,' Torment said and started down the hall in bounds, away from the deadly clockwork knight.

She took turns, left, right, Vladimir soon overtaking her. Afoot – or paw – he was at a significant advantage.

'Where to?' he asked, whirling around at a junction.

She ran too fast to study the paintings. They were the clues to follow. Anywhere – just somewhere to hide.

There – a glint, a shimmer. When in doubt, follow a shiny thing.

'To the right!'

They sped down the hall.

Stomp.

How was that bulky thing keeping up?

Stomp.

The hallway opened up into a room full of mirrors, tall standing ones mostly, of many shapes and sizes. A few were draped with dusty sheets.

Vlad groaned. 'How are we gonna hide in here?'

It was almost a labyrinth, winding passages of zigzagging light from the chandeliers hanging from the ceiling.

A pain, a shatter. She had run into one of the blasted things. A pile of shards showed her a fractured face, feathers of black and a mask – silver, dead-eyed, Phileander's sharp features.

Stomp.

'Torment!'

Vladimir, nervous, somewhere and everywhere.

Clues – she needed clues. Glass crunched under the soles of her boots.

Torment jumped at the sight of Phileander in an oval framed with gilded stucco.

Had it been silver? Or him in the flesh, pale, with a doublet the colour of berries? In the background, she thought, she had seen the great entrance hall of the Tower of Undreamed Truths in all its black-marbled glory.

Stomp.

This room was a gallery of some sort ... or a trap, perhaps. She just had to find the trails of association.

'Shatter them,' she cried. 'Push them over, clear the way!'

Vlad did not have to be called twice to the hitting of things hard with his paws. It crashed and clattered and clinked, and streaks of spectral light flashed upon stone.

There were doorways in the walls being gradually revealed, leading to adjacent rooms – more galleries. They were labelled with bronze plaques atop artfully carved frames.

Architecture.

Stomp.

Plants.

Bestiary.

'There!' Torment yelled, darting across a sea of shards, grabbing Vlad's fur along the way.

They spilled, reeling, into a ballroom of grotesqueries frozen in time. An ape-like thing with lobster claws, a six-foot centipede and next to it three dogs with swan necks and bills. Some of them glistened like wax, others were utterly lifelike – taxidermied beasts from strange dreams or alchemical experiments.

'Find a spot and freeze,' said Torment.

'What? That's your plan?'

'Improvisation, crony.'

He did as she bid, and Torment searched for a spot of her own. In between an oversized sparrow and a rat with reptilian scales, she posed as all the statues did, transfixed in the midst of movement, pretending to be taking off to fly.

Vlad just stood there stiffly and glowered straight ahead. She hoped it would be enough.

The steaming hulk stepped through the door, metal plates reflecting the lantern light. It had different weaponry than the one outside, shorter blades and syringes and nozzles on the ends of glass capsules filled with acrid-smelling liquids. They burned in Torment's nose, or maybe that was just the reagents used to preserve these unsettling exhibits. It took all her resolve to remain still as it passed her, trudging with a weight that sent vibrations through the stone and up her legs.

It passed so close, Torment could see the glass tube embedded in its chest close up, almost touching it. She had to fight down an urge to peck at the glass, even though she had no beak anyway. The case contained a single dahlia flower with dark petals, hovering as if on display. The lanterns, positioned strategically to illuminate the bestiary's inhabitants to maximum dramatic effect, heated up Torment's face and drew trickles of sweat she hoped dearly this automaton was too simple to draw conclusions from.

With a nerve-racking screech, it turned its silver head, and its blank eyes rested on her for a disconcerting stretch of time. She held her breath and thought about how they had hardly bested the first one.

But before her bated breath broke out in gasps, it stomped on and out of the room.

Torment collapsed and panted and took deep breaths. The guard's resounding steps were far away enough now.

'That was close, birdie.'

Absently, still watching the way the knight had gone, Vlad scratched himself where that stab wound had been. The blood had dried, matting his fur, which must really have been itching by now. Torment hated nothing more than sticky feathers. Or at least, had hated nothing more before Phileander came and raised that bar a thousandfold.

'Well. The more we dawdle, the more close calls we'll get.'

She took up her search for clues again. They needed to follow associations that would lead to memories or knowledge concerning esoteric rituals, 'ill-researched phenomena' … magic. Torment took a peek into all the outgoing hallways. Many were hung with still lifes of things that interested Phileander, like various foods or historic sites within the One City. Others had windows, showing various shadowy views of the intricate, three-dimensional mazes of buildings that were the city's lower districts. Things lurked in the deep there, malformed and hungry things bred in even lower layers of the city that had once been its surface before more buildings had been built on top of them. One corridor was hung entirely with clocks. Phileander's mind palace was a place of well-sorted, utterly bewildering curiosities and a youth that was shrouded in terror. It seemed much larger than hers, more elaborate … more intentionally crafted.

'What exactly is it we're looking for?' asked Vlad.

'Paintings depicting motifs of alchemy, shelves with esoteric oddities, that sort of stuff.'

'You seem to have a knack for this mind exploring thing.'

When they had fled that guard, they had strayed somewhat off the path of Phileander's life's recollections and into an area of the storage of knowledge, it seemed. It would be much harder to navigate without knowing the philosopher's mental filing methods. If his patterns were anything like as complex as the ones he used to sort his books and records and weird artefacts, Torment would never be able to decipher them in time. They had better follow his memories again.

'Here,' Vlad called to her, his voice echoing from an upward staircase. 'Look at this.'

Torment fluttered across the room and ran up the stairs two at a time. At the top, Vladimir was gazing out of a bright window.

'Notice something?'

Red-shingled roofs, luxurious stone structures, arched bridges and the dazzling mountain flank of ever more intricate architecture escalated to the peak of the One City in the distance. It was a sunny day, and for once the sun was as Torment had known it to be all her life – its light fed from the sunthread arching proudly across a blue field. And at its end, that dreadful storm circling the innermost spires. A vortex of black clouds and purple lightning. Her death sentence.

266

'I know that view,' Torment muttered.

Vlad nodded grimly. 'It's from the Tower of Undreamed Truths.'

This had to be the path leading to his memories in the tower. They were back on track.

She took Vlad in a fraternal headlock and kissed him on the cheek, much to his discomfort.

'Splendid. Steady on then, crony.'

'I have to believe that I will be dead by the time anyone reads this. In the unlikely event that you are one of the few souls saddened by this circumstance, do understand that I have learnt quite a few things about death. It is not at all what you think. So do not be sad for me. Be afraid for yourself. I am most likely better off.'
—Ogden Flynt, *Spirits beyond Earth and Sky* (unfinished manuscript)

Chapter 17

A GLIMPSE OF CORRUPTION

FROM THERE ON out, the halls looked very much as Torment remembered them, albeit slightly grander. It was a sign they were still in a time when it had all been new to Phileander, having more of a shine to it. A fresh breeze came in through the windows, but it did not carry the scent of the One City as Torment remembered it. Rather, it was an amalgam of smells a human would be more inclined to notice – cooked food and spices and latrines and smoke from countless hearths.

After another set of winding stairs leading up, lit by wall-mounted candle holders and decorated with reliefs of strange patterns and symbols, they reached an unassuming redwood door. Around it, the stone was carved with octagrams and pentagrams and concentric assortments of glyphs from long-forgotten scripts.

Torment knocked on the door.

'What are you doing?' Vlad's ears twitched nervously.

'Behaving in a manner that is congruous to this memory, my jumpy compadre.'

'In!' called a muffled voice from inside.

Torment grasped the door and opened it.

Beyond lay a study, a similar room to the one her cage stood in but smaller. And it held not nearly as large a collection of morbid curiosities yet, and the smell was more that of the den of a human youth drenched in the musk of puberty. One who hadn't left his desk in a while.

And there he sat, back to the door, hunched over a book, surrounded by more books – no, positively besieged by them. He wore a midnight blue robe, like the young acolytes she had seen in the tower, and there was still a mop of tangled hair above his lanky neck.

'What is it, Gustav?'

The voice was like the present Phileander's, but it did not have that edge to it yet, that over-accentuation of words that lent them a biting sense of disdain.

Torment stepped aside and waved Vladimir in. 'What?' the cat whispered.

'It's a boy's name, I think. Go and be Gustav.'

More honestly, Torment found herself momentarily distracted by the fact that she found teenage Phileander's scent strangely … alluring.

Grudgingly, Vlad plodded into the room. Young Phileander turned his head and his eyes widened. He had that characteristic long nose of his now, though covered in reddish pimples.

'What, by all the immortals, are you?' he breathed.

Vlad cleared his throat, shuffled his paws. 'Uhm … Gustav?'

Phileander rose and lifted a book like a weapon, and it looked heavy enough to actually do damage. 'You're not even human!'

'Human enough for my taste,' growled Vlad.

Torment rushed in, hands outstretched in appeasement. 'Claws in, books down, everyone.'

Phileander's jaw dropped at the sight of her, though his focus was on her face, not her feathers.

'You're … the spitting image of her,' he mumbled, 'just older. And winged?' He shivered. 'What are you?'

'Well, I'm not that old – I'm in my prime, actually – but we're … spirits,' she intoned. 'You called us.'

He narrowed his eyes. 'I did?' His gaze trailed off as he pondered. 'I … did read that Talmaaran invocation out loud yesterday.'

Torment pointed a finger right between his eyes and nodded. 'Yes. Talmaaran. That's the language I heard.'

'But it's supposed to open communications with the Sisters of Eternal Night …'

'Yep,' said Torment. 'That's us.'

'But there's supposed to be seven of you, and he's not even—'

'Poppycock.' She waved her hand dismissively, shedding feathers over his stacks of dusty tomes. 'There's six of us and you should be glad even one took the time.' She gestured to Vlad. 'He's my body-guard.'

She could almost feel Vlad's vexation physically.

Phileander set his book aside and clasped his hands, curiosity apparently outweighing suspicion. 'Which one are you?'

Torment rolled her eyes. 'The crow one, obviously. Now, enough of me. Tell me about your … woes. We have places to be.'

Phileander rubbed his chin and hummed. 'You're not how I imagined, but I guess that is to be expected from a spirit of old. There should be no harm in accepting your aid and counsel in my current predicament.' Nervously, he glanced past the two through the open door. 'Can anyone else see you? I read you're to appear in a dream, not knock—'

'Consider this a daydream. Only you can see us. Now spill the beans, human. Chop chop.'

'Right. Apologies, Your Nocturnality. My woes …' He wrung his hands in thought. 'Where to start? Ah. Yes. So … there is this mission to which I consider myself called, wise spirit. To adjust the ways of the world such that no child must ever suffer a fate of neglect and abuse.'

Vlad scoffed. 'No *human* child, you mean.'

'Why … yes? I'm human.'

'Never mind him,' said Torment. 'It's a noble cause.' She scratched the back of her head. 'Nobler than I anticipated. Go on.'

He slumped back into his chair. 'Right … So, here I am, pursuing the power to better the world, and now I meet this girl.' He gestured to Torment with a wistful glance. 'The one you look so much like. Gustav encourages me to court her, but she is so high above my standing' – he ruffled his hair in frustration – 'I'll make a fool of myself.' Young Phileander sighed. 'I fear I already did by sending her that dahlia – alchemically altered to bloom for the next couple of centuries or so – and her father's men brought it back to the tower in person, along with a warning. And also, if I keep thinking about her immortals-damned beautiful face all the time' – he kicked over a pile of books, stirring a plume of dust – 'how am I to focus on my learning? Being in love is bloody distracting.'

He looked distraught. From a rational point of view, Torment found he had hardly described a 'problem' at all, let alone a 'predicament'. Indeed, his love contradicting both his own and his beloved's family's interests should make his choice rather trivial. Yet a part of her, one that was itself tormented by irrational bouts of yearning for Phileander's or Vladimir's affection, could relate to his despair quite viscerally.

'So?' Vlad blurted out. 'What's my *mistress* to aid you in? Sulking?'

'I don't think that's helpful, Vladimir.'

Phileander grimaced. 'Vladimir? Not a very Talmaaran-sounding name.'

'No,' Torment rushed to say. 'He's a … slave.'

'Of course I am,' Vlad hissed, '*Your Nocturnality*. And you know what would be helpful? Cutting this whiny, lovesick dogshit and getting to the point of him talking about that ritual.'

'What ritual?' asked Phileander, perking up.

'All in due time, human,' Torment replied, 'and you shush, slave.'

She might be pushing it too far again. In waves, she sensed Vlad's painstaking efforts not to pounce on her there and then. Anyway, this version of Phileander did not look like he had already glimpsed the same dark secrets that marred his present self. But he seemed close.

'My companion is right, though, human. How should I help you? Make you forget about her?'

'No!' cried Phileander, agonised. 'Yes. Perhaps … I don't know.'

Vlad gave a resigned growl. 'You're aware you just gave every conceivable answer to that question, right?'

'I know,' Phileander lamented, throwing up his arms. 'It's the greatest dilemma of my life, and I once had to survive a winter in the Lower Scraps, with nothing but frozen rats to eat that I had befriended a month before.'

'Now, now,' said Torment gently. 'I'm sure it's not that bad.'

Tears welled up in Phileander's dark-ringed eyes. 'We will never be together, will we? Oh, Elisaveta. I meant to keep that dahlia, but I can't seem to find it anymore.'

'There, there,' muttered Torment awkwardly, patting his head. 'Now, to understand this fully' – it was time to probe, ever so carefully, for what they needed to know – 'what powers *exactly* do you pursue to better the world?'

His teary eyes lit up with a fire she knew all too well. Yet she knew it burning cold and bright, whereas his still burnt ... warmer, more softly.

'I am certain the answer lies in the Everstorm and the Courtly Beacon it enshrouds. We speak of its creators as if they still ruled the One City, but they don't.' He gazed out of the window of his study which faced the centre of the city. 'Up there lies all their power, unclaimed. My will would be law. The kind that requires no enforcers but myself.'

His gaze twitched to her wings, greed flashing in his eyes.

'You couldn't just fly me there right now, could you, spirit?'

A shiver ran down Torment's spine. She felt smaller all of a sudden, seeing the shadow of *her* Phileander in him and the bars of her cage in the corner of her eye.

'No,' she said. 'As I said, just a daydream. And even if ...' She gulped. 'We'd most probably die in there.'

'I feared as much.' He turned to his books again. 'And I fear I might have called on you in vain, great spirit, for if I were to forget Elisaveta, my heart must surely wither or turn to lead.'

Vladimir groaned from the corner where he'd lain down.

Torment felt as though *her* heart had turned to lead, knowing the fate for which this love was headed.

'Look, human,' she forced herself to say with a steady voice, 'you will be granted to call on my counsel whenever the need arises. Just keep a lookout for us.'

And so they left him to that memory and continued up the Tower of Undreamed Truths, or rather Phileander's memory of it through the years. Occasionally, they thought they glimpsed his spectre climbing the steps alongside them. As with the phantom Torment had seen in the desert so long ago, his pace was crawling, as time for him progressed more slowly than for them. But considerably less so than it had in the desert. Add to that the fact he had apparently reached the tower already and you had a recipe for failure. Or a really close call.

Torment kept looking in on his memories here and there, saw him outgrowing the robes of an acolyte and moving to a bigger study – the one she knew. This man called Gustav was constantly at his side, curly-haired, freckled and always grinning. Had he known what Phileander would become? Would he have remained his friend if he had? Tried to set him on the right path? Could Phileander still be saved? And if not, was it really just her life that was at stake, or perhaps the fate of so many more who might suffer at the hands of a deranged narcissist wielding the power of the gods?

'These symbols, Torment,' said Vlad, pointing out a mural on a corridor wall. 'I know them.'

They were primitive-looking signs composed of wedges and carved lines like claw marks, each different and aligned in circles. Torment felt like she knew them, or at least a part of her did. The same way she knew what meadows looked like. A memory older than herself.

'It's near the Forbidden Library. Brother Bartosz is Keeper of Forbidden Lore there, although he keeps nothing from Phileander. He seems to have some leverage over the guy.'

'Who doesn't he?' Torment murmured. 'But he told me there was nothing about the ritual in any book in the tower.'

'In the present, perhaps,' said Vlad, 'but there must be a memory somewhere around here of him getting into that library the first time.' He turned to her, eager. 'That's where we need to go, birdie.'

A sound suggestion, she found. 'Lead the way, then.' And she beckoned him onwards with an outstretched wing.

ON THEIR WAY to the Forbidden Library, they soon spotted a young Phileander sneaking along the corridor ahead of them and followed him silently at a distance. He looked about the same age as in the last memory Torment had peeked into, or only slightly older. His clothes were uncharacteristically simple: trousers of black-dyed wool and a lace-up shirt. The Phileander who had captured her wore silks and fine leather and coats embroidered with gold or silver brocade. He was immensely rich, Torment realised, which he had not yet been when he was sneaking down this corridor one night many years ago.

They were nearing the end of the corridor, at which a black double door awaited. It had silver inlays in the shape of a pentagram surrounded by a circle of glyphs, glinting in the red light of the coals that smouldered in the two braziers flanking the door.

Five paces before the door, Phileander stopped and glanced over his shoulder.

Torment inhaled sharply and Vladimir tensed. But memory-Phileander didn't seem to see them. Apparently, if they chose not to interact and simply kept their distance, the memories just played out as Phileander remembered them.

He reached into the air in front of him as if grasping for something invisible. When he appeared to have found what he was reaching for, he kept his hands still, mumbling something under his breath. Then he went on. He stopped several times again, once to feel out something on the wall while mumbling again and once to very carefully select the stones he trod upon while counting down the seconds his soles remained on each.

'What if we trigger something nasty?' whispered Vlad.

Torment thought for a moment. 'I don't think that's possible. He doesn't know we're here and we don't know how any of these mechanisms work, after all.'

Phileander had just reached the door and was tracing the silver lines of the pentagram with his fingers. When he had finished, he put the palms of his hands against both wings of the door and pushed. It rattled, but the door remained shut.

'Cursed thing,' murmured Phileander, pushing again, but ceiling-high jets of flame shot from the braziers and made him fall back, cursing. Torment could feel the heat on her face where she stood.

276

Then Phileander whirled around and ran back from whence he had come, straight at Torment and Vladimir, but shortly before he ran into them, he startled and stopped, almost toppling over.

'What?' He could see them now. 'But you're ... you're those spirits!'

Torment noticed she had put her hands in front of her face and lowered them again. 'Uhm.' She glanced over at Vlad, who just shrugged his cat shoulders. 'Yes, well ... greetings, human.'

But before this awkward conversation could continue, the walls and the ceiling and the door to the library blew apart into whirling dust. Torment had seen this once before, shortly after she and Vlad had entered the realm of dreams and intruded upon a memory Vlad shared with their master – the memory of Phileander in his reading room, revealing what he had done to acquire the elixir that could create a homunculus.

Memory-Phileander's eyes turned hazy and absent and he turned away from them, while the dream dust solidified to form a room. It was Phileander's study again, much more modestly furnished and much emptier than Torment knew it. As soon as all the motes of dust that formed the window frame had settled, she could even see her usual nightly view of the One City through it.

'I know why you chose this room,' said an old man's voice, and Torment drew back into a shadow, Vlad's warm breath close beside her. 'Quite the view. Most men would not care for it. It makes them uneasy ... this tempestuous heart of our world.'

The old man sat on a chair next to Phileander's desk, with a chalice of wine in his hand. His white hair was wispy, his eyes set deep into his face. His smile had a cruelty to it, similar to the older Phileander's. The younger Phileander standing in front of this man, however, wore a pained expression – the kind of inward-looking gaze of one lost in the maze of contemplating their own shame.

'I remember every book you requested, Phileander. I know why you can't take your eyes off it.'

SILAS A. BISCHOFF

'What is it you want from me, Keeper Gaurm?'

'The brother who confessed to that failed attempt at breaking into my library, he is your friend, is he not?'

A twitch in Phileander's face. 'Which is why I was called to testify. You know this. Get to the point.'

The old man gave a throaty laugh. 'Ah, yes. You're no man of idle words. Many, sometimes, but not idle. You're a man of conviction and ambition. So much of it, in fact, you would let your friend take the fall for you.'

Phileander glared at him. 'What are you insinuating?'

'Oh, relax. I have no interest in harming your career. I like you, young man. You could have a bright future here.' The old man's smile widened, revealing yellowed teeth. 'In fact, I would like you to even further incriminate Brother Gustav. Surely you must know some dark secret of his, or how to fabricate one that is believable, at least. You two are so close, after all.'

'Why would you want me to do that?' snapped Phileander. 'And most importantly, why would I?'

'I shall be frank. Young Gustav has become quite popular with the younger philosophers. So much so, in fact, that he threatens some carefully prepared elections for important offices within the order – like the one for Keeper of Forbidden Lore, for instance.' He raised his chalice to Phileander. 'Why, you could soon benefit yourself from such … *preparations*. But to give your plans' – he nodded in the direction of the Everstorm, flashing in the night outside – 'a bit more of an immediate forward momentum, how about half an hour in the Forbidden Library without supervision?'

Phileander snorted resentfully. 'You expect me to betray a friend for so little?'

'So little?' the Keeper of Forbidden Lore repeated with a chuckle. 'Well, well … betraying a friend is worth a higher price, you say?'

Phileander remained silent, clenching his jaw.

278

'Ah, I knew I had judged you correctly. You'll be a great man one day, Phileander, a great man.' Then he rose, drank up his wine and set the chalice on the desk. 'A full hour, then. No supervision.'

And with those words he turned and left the study. And Phileander was left to brood on the darkness behind his eyes.

Vlad and Torment remained in their shadow and watched him as he paced, sat down, clasped his hands and glowered into the night, then stood and paced again. They waited for what felt like hours. Torment hoped it wasn't as long as it felt, because the actual Phileander would be nearly upon their actual bodies in his actual study by now.

Vlad scratched at the floor tiles impatiently. 'When's he going to betray his friend so we can follow him to that stupid library already?' he whispered.

Torment had asked herself the same question. Even younger Phileander would not have spent so much time dawdling and brooding over a decision he had all the information to make. That was something he despised in others and prided himself on never having indulged in.

'I think it might be too painful a memory for his mind to go there,' she suggested.

'Humans,' hissed Vlad. 'Hypocrites and cowards.'

'Hello?' said Phileander, perking up and peering into the shadows. 'Who's there?'

That had been a whisper too many, it appeared. Torment stepped forward into the candlelight and spread her feathered arms. 'It is I, human. Sister of Eternal Night.' Vlad followed with a sigh of annoyance.

Phileander examined them sceptically. 'You? I thought you were nothing but a weird dream my lovesick adolescent brain cooked up.'

'Nope,' said Torment. 'Actual spirits. Still owe you a favour, too. I sensed your … inner turmoil, human, so I decided to check on you. What's the trouble this time?'

He still frowned at them distrustfully. Torment remembered another detail about the first time they had entered one of Phileander's memories, in the reading room. Phileander had recognised them in the end and cast them out. Torment cursed herself for having betrayed Vladimir's name and her being a crow when they had spoken to his teenage self earlier. It was paramount they kept their interactions with the memory-Phileanders to a minimum.

'I face yet another dilemma,' Phileander said then, watching the Everstorm. 'To own up to a crime I committed – or tried to commit – and prevent a friend from being punished for it or to let him be punished instead. Or, as has just been added to my plate of one bite more distasteful than the other, to let him be punished even worse and make considerable progress in my mission to reshape the world.'

She almost sympathised with him. Everything in Torment wanted to tell him that what he was considering was a mistake – that the guilt and the shame he would lay on his heart would crush it, and he would emerge a man without a heart at all. That his noble cause hinged on him still being a good man when he came to power and that the path he chose would snuff out any chance of that. But it would serve no purpose. He had already done it. All it would do was close up that memory for them for good. But how to open it? What would ease Phileander's mind to allow itself to tread there?

'Mistress?' hissed Vlad. 'Are you just going to stand there rubbing your chin, or will you give this man some advice?'

'I'm pondering his dilemma, so ... patience, please.'

She had to defend his actions before himself. Torment remembered her trial in the court of the toad-king. Where there were exemptions of judgement in one's principles, there were loopholes ... and twisting those cleverly could ultimately rationalise every atrocity. That was what she had learned.

'I think the case is clear,' Torment said to Phileander. 'If your career in the Tower of Undreamed Truths is ended or stalled, your failure would allow so many more people to suffer, so many children to be left out on the streets, than just this one friend getting a scolding. And letting him be punished will be painful for you too, so is it not really *sacrifice* rather than betrayal?'

Phileander looked up at her, nodding and taking a deep breath. 'Perhaps, yes. It is not like I'd go unpunished. Shame would be my burden to humble me for my time as a ruler. But … I don't know if I have it in me to lie to make things worse for Gustav.' He turned back to his desk, propping himself on his elbows and massaging his eyes so hard, it must have hurt. 'He did so much for me. It would be too shameful a deed.'

Torment's heart hurt with what she had to say to him. The words tasted bitter in her mouth. 'Oh, but your greatest shame would be to let him suffer the consequences in vain, without you making the absolute most of this opportunity, would it not, human? Think of the children of the future. Of an eternity of wealth and security. Who are you to deny them that for your own petty conscience?'

Phileander paused for a moment. Then he straightened up and looked at her with intense eyes. The contortions of pain on his face straightened, giving way to cold, iron determination.

'Why, you're absolutely right,' he said. 'What am I even doing here? I'm not some snivelling defeatist. I have a greater purpose, and this … this agonising over loyalty and friendship, it's just holding me back.'

The walls dissolved again.

'Finally.' Vlad sighed.

When the dust converged to form new walls again, they were further away. It was a larger room, probably on a lower level of the tower, near the black marble entrance hall. It had lavish woodcarvings upon the panelling and the two columns in the centre. At the far end, a tribunal of older philosophers sat behind a row of tables, and the dream dust whirled around Vlad and Torment to shape many more figures gathered to witness the proceedings. Torment could see Brother Gustav's mop of copper curls. He stood facing the tribunal.

'On the case of an attempted break-in to the Forbidden Library,' announced an elderly woman at the rightmost table, 'we will now hear the testimony of our esteemed brother Phileander.'

Torment felt oddly complicit in what was about to happen. And it felt wrong to listen in on whatever Phileander was about to reveal to smear this Brother Gustav's memory. What right had they to be voyeurs on this poor man's most miserable moment?

'Come,' said Torment, tugging at Vlad's fur. 'We don't need to watch this.' Then she hurried toward the room's only door at the back of the crowd.

'Wait,' said Vlad. 'Don't we need to stay until he—'

'We can move futureward through his memories,' said Torment. 'No reason to linger in the less important ones.'

'If you say so.' He trotted along. 'You're the mind palace expert.'

Torment opened the door and a wave of light and fresh air washed over her. They stepped out onto a balcony on the side of the tower and the wind whipped through her feathers. The balcony was large, one of the kind that had connections to some of the footbridges leading to the various districts and castles and convoluted tumbles of stone structures surrounding the Tower of Undreamed Truths. There was another gathering of philosophers, and she could make out Phileander in the first row, his face hard and his eyes blank.

'I think you'll wanna skip this one too,' said Vlad next to her.

'What? Why?'

But as she turned around, she saw why. From a brass flagpole jutting out of the tower wall hung a rope that was tied into a noose, which was hung around Brother Gustav's neck, who in turn stood on a wooden stand. The sun turned his curls to gold, dancing in the breeze, and for some reason he was still smiling, even if it was a sad smile. Next to him, a man in a black cloak was preparing to read something off a scroll, but Torment was already trudging back to the door.

'Now I wonder what he said to them,' said Vlad, catching up, 'that they went and offed the guy.'

She could already see the open door leading to a murkier place. A dusty smell greeted them – one of old wood, leather, ink and paper. A smell that was prevalent in Phileander's study as Torment knew it. Books – lots of them. It appeared they would finally enter a memory of the Forbidden Library. And with it being directly adjacent to Gustav's execution, Phileander evidently hadn't wasted any time claiming his reward from the old Keeper of Forbidden Lore.

After all the fuss about it, Torment found the library somewhat anticlimactic. The room wasn't even as big as the one Gustav's hearing had taken place in, and everything in it was old and seemingly in ill repair. It had creaking termite-eaten floorboards, cobwebs between the cramped aisles of overflowing bookshelves, and a single desk at the opposite end, with a many-armed candelabra and just enough space for one of the bulkier tomes.

They found Phileander sifting through the rows of books three aisles to the right. He looked focused, murmuring to himself as he inspected the spines, only occasionally pulling forth a volume to glance briefly at the cover and put it back again. He appeared to be looking for a specific item and to know exactly what it looked like.

Torment crept closer until she was crouching beside Phileander. He noticed her.

'Ah, spirit.' He smirked. 'Come to join me in my moment of triumph?'

Out of all the past Phileanders they had met so far, this one felt most like the one she knew.

'What knowledge are you looking for?' asked Torment.

'All of it.'

'In one hour?'

'Oh, I will have all the hours I need.' He chuckled.

She took a step back to let him continue searching for whatever book he sought. He took a while, once and again cursing about the sorting pattern, and when over half an hour had passed, he slowly but surely became nervous.

Vlad grumbled beside her. 'I'll be so pissed off if we find out he just wasted his hour and didn't get into the library for another ten years or something.'

But sure enough, as Vlad finished speaking, Phileander gave a satisfied 'ah, yes' and pulled out an almost unassuming but very old-looking book. It appeared to be bound in a peculiar pale leather unsettlingly similar to human skin, and the single symbol adorning its cover seemed to be depicted in the form of scarring. Whatever being's skin this volume was bound in, it must have had this symbol cut into it when it was still alive. The symbol reminded Torment of the ones on the mural lining the way to the library – a brutal sign invented in harsher times, long ago, for cutting into stone – or skin, for that matter – rather than painting with ink.

Vlad and Torment followed Phileander to the desk, where he put down the book, opened it and leafed through the pages quickly without even looking at a single one of them. When he stopped, the page he was smiling down at was empty.

'What?' whispered Vlad. 'That's no book of rituals.'

Pst,' chided Torment as Phileander perked up briefly in irritation. 'His consciousness must not get wind of us closing in on it.'

Then the young philosopher pulled a flask of red ink and a quill from his coat pocket and began writing on the empty page. Torment leaned forward cautiously to get a glimpse, but the words were written in a strange language she didn't know how to read. When Phileander had finished, placing the final stroke of his quill with a self-satisfied flick, they heard a door open and urgent footsteps approaching.

The gaunt Keeper of Forbidden Lore stepped up behind Phileander, his thin white wisps wafting. He gave no sign of being able to see them, just like all the bystanders in the other memories. It was probably a good thing she had pointed out to teenage Phileander that only he could see them.

'The first time I grant you a favour and already you're defacing the inventory?' Gaurm snarled.

'Oh, Brother,' said Phileander, playing the innocent, 'is my hour up already?'

'Unsupervised does not mean unwatched.'

'Oh, actually, it kind of does mean that, Brother. But I don't mind. You see, I didn't deface just any old book. This here is the Book of Death.'

'Nonsense,' snapped the old man, pushing past Phileander to look at the tome. 'Superstition. Old wives' tale. It's one of the unidentifiable ones.'

'I might not have had access to this library, but there is plenty of secondary literature to be found elsewhere on the topic of this little beauty.' Phileander smiled. 'Say, Brother, why is it that you yourself have brought a piece of parchment and ink with you?'

'What? I didn't.' But just as the old man said it, he was taking said items out of his coat, and Phileander quickly lifted the book off the desk to make space for him to arrange them. 'What?' asked Gaurm incredulously, looking down at his own hands smoothing out the parchment and beginning to write on it. 'Why am I ... what have you done?'

'Ah, Brother, as I have just laid out in the record of your tragic passing, it so happens you wrote a guilt-ridden confession and bequest mere hours before you took your own life.'

The old man's eyes widened in horror as he recognised the words he was putting down.

'You see, the crafty old Keeper of Forbidden Lore was actually an accomplice to Gustav's treachery and had weaselled himself out of being held accountable by extorting one poor Brother Phileander. Thus, plagued by the shame of his misdeed, it was only fitting that Keeper Gaurm would hang himself from the side of the tower and declare Phileander his successor, don't you think?' He patted the old man on the back; he didn't appear to be able to answer any longer and only stared at the letter he was writing, white-faced and shivering. 'I'll leave you to it, then.'

Phileander carefully sorted the book back into the shelf where he had found it while Keeper Gaurm was rolling up his parchment. He dripped wax on it with trembling hands to seal it with a silver ring, then walked out of the library to conclude his ghastly business.

Phileander watched him go, and his mouth was curled into a smile that his eyes did not share.

'Well,' whispered Vlad, sitting next to Torment and swishing curly lines into the dust with his tail, 'stage set, enter Phileander, I suppose.'

Torment could only nod, as her chest felt painfully tight. A feeling of grief struck her, as though she had just witnessed a part of herself being sacrificed on the altar of Phileander's rise to villainy.

'I know there are those out there who think I have overstayed my welcome, who tell me "this is not your story anymore, old man" and continue to slate me left and right. Yes, I see you, Gesian. But in the journeys of my dreams, I have seen things that I cannot keep to myself, that I must not keep to myself. The One City is more than a home, a nation, a world — it is an experiment. It is a maze for hundreds of millions of little human-shaped rats. But to understand that, one must first understand its origins. So I have compiled the most comprehensive account of the Lighting of the Beacon and the Age of Dawn yet written.'

—Ogden Flynt, *Monuments of Yesteryear*, Author's note

Chapter 18

A GRAIN OF TRUTH

THEY LOOKED ON from the shadows of the Forbidden Library as Phileander, the newly appointed Keeper of Forbidden Lore, spent hour after hour studying its ominous contents. Torment avoided coming into contact with him again, which was made easy by his obsessive research that rendered him practically blind to anything but the latest ancient grimoire upon his desk. There were so many powerful secrets to explore by staying and glancing over his shoulder, but they had no time to waste.

The entrance to the library, Torment found, led yet again into another night of Phileander's sleep-deprived reading and frantic note-taking. So Torment and Vladimir kept walking through that door and up to the desk, taking a peek at whatever new spell, recipe or ritual Phileander was currently reading and turning back as soon as they had confirmed it was unrelated to the creation or binding of homunculi.

He read essays on the most terrible poisons that would eat away at one's happiness or cause pain whenever a certain word was uttered; descriptions of horrifying places within the bowels of the One City, where things of great power lay hidden, guarded by beings of deathly depravity; spells wrought with the anguished cries of the dying that could make a person succumb to desperate love for the spellwright or the deepest hatred of one whose hair was burnt on brimstone cinders. Once, they were alerted to take a second look when they saw him reading a text on an old ritual that required the blood of a vampire. But it didn't mention homunculi. It seemed to be merely a method of preserving a human's severed head so that it can later be roused again and asked a question about the deceased's secrets.

'Torment,' whispered Vlad on what felt like the hundredth night, leaning in so close to a new book Phileander was studying, forepaws upon the tabletop, that he almost touched the mumbling philosopher.

Torment hurried to join him – and there it was. *On the Binding of Blood and Spirit*, a transcript of a text far older, as was written in its fore-word, devised during the dark ages before the Lighting of the Beacon. The chapter on the creation of a homunculus, in either its vampiric or its 'sparkbound' form, was one of the first. Torment almost forgot to breathe as she watched the pages being turned and regarded the grue-some illustrations – diagrams depicting the exact method of cutting open the womb and the bloodletting of one's progeny, and old copper-plate prints of vampires in their primeval form, hosts of them under a black sun, some on pale, leathery wings, warring over a sea of blood.

The candle soot in the air made Torment's eyes water, and she dared not blink for fear of missing even a single detail. A sour smell of red wine rose from Phileander's mouth into her nose, both revolting and stirring a disturbing desire in her. Now and then, her gaze darted to her master's lips, which silently read along.

Vlad let out a quiet gasp. It was but a footnote. A clause on the binding of a blood slave. Not only must the master have conceived the unborn baby, from whose blood the elixir is obtained, in honest love – the binding of a homunculus will only hold so long as its master does not feel remorse for killing his beloved and child.

That was it. That was the key to their salvation. Before Phileander could turn the page again, Torment grabbed it and ripped it out.

Phileander cried out and jumped, toppling his chair with a clatter.

'What, by all the immortals …'

Torment backed away from the desk, and so did Vlad. She clutched the page to her chest. The feathers on her right wing were singed where they had brushed against the candle flame.

'You …' Phileander wanted to go after them, but he stumbled, grasping his head and gasping.

Torment seized the opportunity to unceremoniously crumple the page, put it into her mouth and swallow it with a scraping pain.

Phileander fell to his knees, moaning in an apparent bout of head-ache, and the whole library tilted.

Torment tumbled into a bookshelf and Vlad instinctively dug his claws into the brittle floorboards. Books and scrolls cascaded onto the floor with a great commotion; everything creaked and shelves tipped over. The candelabra slid off the desk and its flames extinguished, leaving them in murky chaos as Phileander screamed in agony and outrage.

'I think' – Torment fluttered up to try and escape the sliding books and furniture, hitting her head on the sloping ceiling – 'we damaged the memory. It's – ouch – it's falling apart.'

'Ah, dammit, birdie.' She only saw the dark grey silhouette of a cat dodging and leaping and clawing. 'Where's the door?'

Torment couldn't see it. She landed on an empty spot of the upper side of the twisting room that all the furniture appeared to have already slid away from.

'Follow my voice,' she called. 'I'll make us a door.'

Then she stuck her long talon-fingers into the cracks between the boards and tore with all her might. The wood was rotten enough to break. Bright blue light broke through and a whiff of clean air. Vlad pushed himself off a fallen shelf and landed next to her, helping viciously to enlarge the hole in the floor.

'Is that ... the city from above?'

'It's my mind palace,' Torment yelled, leaping through the hole and into the blue sky.

She beat her wings and sought out an air current on which she could glide to hover on the spot. Above her hung a hole in the air, frayed by splinters, from whose shadow Vlad was looking down on her.

'You could do this all the time?' he yelled.

'In a pinch,' Torment replied. 'Jump.'

'I can't fly,' protested Vlad, holding on to the edge as the room he was in appeared to tilt further.

'I'll catch you.'

'But—'

'Just do it!'

Vlad jumped – a man-headed cat tumbling earthward, rotating in the air, helplessly pawing at it.

'Torment!'

She was already swooping down with folded wings and wrapped her legs around his body. Fluttering and straining, she tried to slow their fall, but he was too heavy.

'We're still falling!' he shouted.

'I'm aware,' she snapped, exhausted, a headwind tearing at her feathers. If only she could command servants in her mind palace like Phileander – preferably ones that could fly. The grip of her legs around

Vlad's chest loosened.

'Don't you dare drop me,' he hissed.

A slim white shape shot up from below. Just as Vlad slipped through Torment's legs and fell away from her, the white shape spread out wide wings of thin bone underneath him, and Vlad held on to the shape with clenched paws.

Torment lowered herself to fall in line next to the giant magpie, who somehow soared through the air even though there was not an inch of skin on its bones.

'It's a … damned skeleton,' Vlad yelped. 'You've got some weird crap in your mind palace, you know that?'

'Oh, you don't know the half of it, crony.'

Vlad was visibly displeased with his vulnerable circumstance. 'So, what … we're out now? Returning to our bodies?'

'No. If it were that easy, I could have gotten us back a while ago.' She began to rise again towards the hole leading to Phileander's mind palace. The skeletal magpie followed. 'My mind palace is disconnected from my body at the moment. And it's risky to keep a door open into the dream wilds, and definitely into Phileander's mind. We're only sitting out the … renovations we triggered.'

She turned to the magpie's skull, a larger version of exactly the one she wore around her neck. 'Look, I don't really know why you're helping us or what your whole deal is, my bony friend, but … thanks.'

The magpie didn't reply. It simply followed, silent and obedient. Torment still felt the weight of guilt dragging at her when she looked at this reminder of sins past. But it didn't feel so *haunting* anymore. There was something going on here, Torment sensed — something to do with how those corpses had reacted to her back in the ghoul's basement.

They were drawing circles around the hole in the sky, and Torment held on to her feeling of being present in Phileander's mind palace. She could feel that it was still connected to hers through that rift, and she held on to that with all her will. If she started feeling lost, Torment understood, any pathway they left her mind palace by would only drop them in the middle of that dreaded desert again, or some other desolate corner of the dream wilds where spirits roamed in despair. But they had made their arduous way to where they were, to Phileander's mind, and Torment held on to that dearly. After a few laps around that hovering hole, its edge began to rearrange itself – with the sound of cracking wood – into the rectangle of a door frame.

'Now,' called Torment and shot through the opening.

The magpie skeleton followed close behind.

~

THEY WOUND UP in one of the many corridors of Phileander's Nexus of Association. Vlad rolled off the magpie's back. There were paintings on the wall, sombre paintings of crows and cats and bowls filled with blood. And there was a stomping noise and a hissing of steam and Phileander's voice echoing from across the hallway.

'You meddlesome pests! You have made a grave mistake.'

A silvery giant stepped around a corner and loomed over them as they clambered to their feet and paws and bony talons.

The spiked head of a hammer sped down at them, attached to the clockwork knight's arm, and it was all Torment could do to cower and raise her hand.

She heard a rattling and a cracking impact.

The giant magpie had jumped in front of her, and the hammer had gotten stuck in its ribcage. The knight yanked and its steam engines ran hot.

'Oh, Torment!' seethed Phileander's voice, ever closer. 'Vladimir!'

Dragging the clockwork knight along with it, the magpie dragged itself to the still-open door they had just flown through, leading out into the clouds. The guard's metal feet protested, digging deep furrows in the floor.

Then the skeleton and the knight fell through it and the door slammed shut and Vlad and Torment were left in the gloomy corridor – but not alone.

They heard the all too familiar sound of Phileander's boots echoing through the halls. Not some past version of him but the resolute gait of *their* Phileander – their angered master.

Without a single word between them, the two ran off, away from Phileander's footsteps and his voice calling them and into the shadowy halls of his memories.

This seemed a more recent section of his life. This, and the disruption they had caused, explained Phileander's awareness of their presence in his mind. His Hall of the Conscious Mind would be close. The associations in these halls were not far from his knowledge of who Torment and Vladimir were, so hiding in plain sight would no longer work.

'Where to now?' Vlad panted next to her. 'How do we get out of here?'

She led them around a corner at a junction, utterly at random, while she contemplated their next move.

'We have to destroy his memory of today, and we have to get as close to our bodies as we can.' The solution was obvious. 'We have to enter his Hall of the Conscious Mind.'

'Simplified version, please, and no snide asides.'

'We need to follow his memories to the future – to the present day.'

'We're running the wrong way, then, birdie.'

'What?'

Vlad came to a halt, and so did Torment. She couldn't hear any more footsteps. Not yet, at least. Phileander's spirit couldn't be far away, and he was certainly still looking for them. At least that would slow him on his way to his study – or so she hoped. Torment remembered the philosopher often sitting perfectly still at his desk, gazing into himself. She had just thought he was brooding. He had been wandering his mind palace then, she now understood, and he hadn't looked as though he would be able to do a lot of walking around in that state.

Vlad pointed a paw at one of the paintings in their current corridor, gold-framed portraits between wall-mounted candle holders in the shape of dahlia blossoms. They were all portraits of Elisaveta.

'Weren't we just in a corridor dedicated to ours truly? Last I heard, this gal's been dead for a while.'

'True,' murmured Torment. 'Well ... which way smells more like murder?'

They peered into the darkness in both directions and sniffed the air. It smelled of flowers and wine. The faint sobs of a crying woman carried along the hall. Torment made out the direction the sobbing came from, and she noted a subtle difference in the smell ... more wine, less flowers.

'That's the way,' she said and started to walk.

Now and then, they passed doors that stood ajar. These were memories from before their time at the tower, but too recent and connected to them for Torment to dare take a closer look. In passing glances she saw deals made, pacts sealed, throats slit in dark alleys, reassurances whispered that no life outweighed the greater good.

Yet there were also doors leading to fairer places. One showed a dining room, beautifully furnished, panelled in polished rosewood and hung with a gold chandelier. There was an alabaster bust on the mantlepiece depicting the face of Elisaveta, smirking a charming little smirk, masterfully carved. Torment remembered this room. She had seen herself in it once in a dream, facing Phileander. Echoes of sweet conversations wafted through the air. 'Isn't it a bit vain, my love, dining in a room with a sculpture of oneself?' 'Perhaps, but I needed that cheeky smile to persist for eternity, my dear, didn't I?' 'Oh, kiss me, you silly man.'

Then there were doors leading into a bedroom, always the same one. Those doors had a pull on Torment that was hard to resist. There were Elisaveta and Phileander sitting on an enormous bed with dishevelled wine-coloured silk sheets, feeding each other grapes from a silver tray and laughing. And Phileander lacing a cup of wine with something before he handed it to her, breathing tender affirmations of affection. Elisaveta in a white nightgown, pacing, crying for Phileander to come to her, to hold her, punching the wall until her knuckles bled.

Then a storeroom with a brass plaque numbering it 154 and Phileander in it, cursing. 'No, hide the thing away. No one shall ever see that smile again. Put the bust in the darkest corner and forget this room ever existed.'

Then the bedroom again.

'Why are we stopping?' whispered Vlad.

'Just another look,' said Torment. She hadn't even noticed how she had drawn closer and closer to one of the doors, absorbed in a view that squeezed her heart, twisted her stomach and spread a chill to her forehead and limbs.

Elisaveta was pregnant in this memory. 'Don't leave again, my love; don't go,' she wailed, grasping Phileander's coat.

'I have to work, dear,' he said in irritation, brushing her hands aside.

A mad desire burned in Elisaveta's eyes. 'Each moment without you hurts, my love.' Her face was contorted and wet with tears. Torment felt a tear on her own cheek as she watched.

'Have you drunk your tea yet?' asked Phileander sternly, glancing over at a breakfast tray. 'It will soothe your nerves, dear. It is important you drink it all up.'

'Of course,' she sobbed. 'You told me and I did it. I do all you tell me. I will stay with you, my love, forevermore.'

Phileander stiffened. He turned to leave. There were tears on his face as well. How very odd to see him cry. Torment had not thought it possible.

'Forevermore, my love,' she wailed. 'Forevermore!'

But Phileander was on his way to the door … the door through which Torment spied. He was just inches away now, eyes narrowing—

Torment stumbled away from the crack.

'Torment!' the voice boomed through the door. 'Oh, you pesky crow, I have you now!'

'Damn you, mawkish bird,' Vlad exclaimed. He grabbed her by the collar of her shirt with his mouth and pulled her along.

Still disorientated and with her vision blurred by tears, Torment struggled to her feet. Phileander was chasing them again, his voice now seeming to come from every direction, and more than once they had to take a turn when their master appeared in a corridor up ahead.

'Wait,' muttered Torment. 'Are we running in the right direction?'

Vlad was taking the lead now, making decisions more quickly than Torment could follow. But she was coming to her senses again. The philosopher did not seem to chase them around his mind palace by running after them but by emerging suddenly in hallways in ways that puzzled Torment. He not only had the advantage of this being his own mind but also of being far more skilled in manoeuvring in mind palaces than Torment had imagined possible. Every experience she had had in her own mind palace had been full of unpleasant surprises. Phileander, on the other hand, had made the iron control of his mind – as well as those of others, for that matter – a science, and he had mastered it.

An open door caught her eye, showing her the reading room with the burgundy armchair in front of a fireplace. Torment paused briefly to look into it. It was as it had been back then, frozen in time, with Phileander's bald head peeking out over the headrest. There was the sideboard with the orrery she had landed upon.

'Birdie!' shouted Vlad, and at the same time, that memory-Phileander stirred in his seat – no doubt taken over by their master's spirit.

Torment cursed her curiosity and ran on, flying for a stretch to catch up with Vlad. They had already been in his mind palace. They'd been here long ago, right after they had taken that potion and fallen asleep. Had Torment only understood the nature of this place sooner ... it would have spared them much trouble. But thinking in the subjunctive was pointless, indeed downright dangerous. Torment's spirit was only where it was, and she only was who she was, down the path that lay behind her.

As she was distracted by her thoughts, something tripped Torment, and she toppled over and skidded across the rough stone floor, cursing.

A small figure had run into her and caught her feet. It was too dim to make it out for certain, but the way it moved – hopping strangely and wobbling around erratically – confused her, and she made to leap to her feet and catch up with Vlad.

But after two paces she got tangled up in strange strings hanging from the ceiling, halting her. Up ahead, in the dark red glow of some memory door left open, Torment saw Vladimir pawing at his own pair of wonky little figures. She saw the silhouettes of yet more strings around Vlad connecting those figures to the blackness above. It was as though the little things only moved by the grace of those strings being tugged and connected to their limbs. Marionettes.

'Stay,' croaked a voice at her feet. 'The master bids it.'

Torment looked down to see the outline of a crow, somewhat crude looking and with odd gaps where the joints were.

'Give yourself up,' called Phileander's voice, 'and I will consider leniency.'

Torment stomped on the reconstruction of herself and heard wood crack underneath her boot. She ripped the threads and ran on, Phileander's steps close behind her.

Vlad had disposed of his puppets as well and their pursuit continued, her legs burning and her sides aching and her breath growing shorter. At least they were now in parts that could only be weeks old at most. His Hall of the Conscious Mind was close.

Out of the corner of her eye, she saw two more Torment puppets and a Vladimir puppet, who carried a limp body between them
towards a dimly lit landing from which a staircase went deeper down.

'Oh crap,' muttered Vlad.

Phileander stood some twenty paces ahead of them, and there appeared to be no further junctions before him. At the same time, they
heard him calling and stepping behind them. A pungent-sweet smell
of corpse-rot hung in the air. There were shapes bustling around Phileander's legs up ahead.

'That's just one of the memory ones,' said Torment and continued
down the hall.

The Phileander they were running towards wore a red nightshirt
and matching pointed cap and looked somewhat sleepy and confused.
In front of him, a pile of corpses was spilling out of what appeared to
be the door of one of the tower's privy chambers. A number of little
wooden Torments and Vladimirs, dangling from dancing strings, toiled
to get the overripe and, moreover, shit-smeared bodies out of the way.

Stepping on the spot, as he apparently had a call of nature, the
memory-Phileander glanced at them groggily. A suspicious scowl began to spread across his face, and Torment skipped the rest of the way
to him, bouncing from one foot to the other while her head and hands
bobbed about uncontrollably, mimicking the puppets.

'Join in,' she whispered to Vlad.

He looked as though he would much rather give that memory of
Phileander the relief it sought by cutting it down, but he played along.
The suspicion on night-robe-Phileander's face gave way to even deeper
furrows of confusion, which Torment filed as a success.

As they wobbled and tugged at the corpses, they peered into the
shadows up ahead. The hallway ended in a door, a bulky-looking metal
one.

'I recognise it,' whispered Vlad. 'It leads into the topmost level of
the—'

'Got you,' snarled Phileander. He must have emerged behind them, just like that, and now he had his hands held up as though strings were attached to his fingertips, and it appeared that Vlad – eyes wide and unable to speak – was at the other end of those strings.

Vlad's paw slammed Torment onto her back with the strength of a bull, knocking the wind out of her and cracking her ribs.

'Careful, Vladimir,' crooned Phileander, 'or you will crush the poor bird.'

Everything spun around her, and only dimly did she make out the philosopher approaching with his hands twisted and wriggling as Vlad pinned her to the floor. Dead things lay all around her, and the foetid fumes of their decay corroded Torment's wits. Dead things, rotting things … wronged things. Spillage from his basement.

'What in— Stop that!'

Phileander was briefly distracted, and Vlad ripped loose from his grip. Torment sucked in a lungful of air. It burned in her chest and tingled in her fingers. For a moment she thought about how bothersome it was that even in worlds of thought she was dependent on oxygen, and whether there was anything to be done about that, but there were more important things to focus on.

When she was back on her feet, still staggering, she saw that Vlad had knocked Phileander – the newly arrived spirit-Phileander – to the ground, where all those corpses were now crawling over him. She heard his muffled cursing and screaming under the writhing heap. This wouldn't stop him for long, she feared. Torment spurred her rotting little friends on in her thoughts, and one of them, wearing a very tattered dress, lost her shrunken head to an enthusiastic tug on her legless body. It detached with a strange popping sound and rolled across the floor. At least half a dozen Torment and Vladimir marionettes were busy dragging the corpses away, and Torment couldn't hear Phileander anymore. Perhaps he had used that displacement thing he could do.

'Torment,' hissed Vlad beside her, 'we need to get through that door.'

She whirled around, still stumbling from dizziness and suddenly aware of the pain in her bruised chest.

'Yes – door.' She shook her head to clear her senses.

Nightshirt-Phileander was still standing there, his look of confusion replaced by the kind of resignation a person might adopt upon concluding they must be having a particularly unhinged dream. Torment started stumbling towards the door in the shadows ahead.

'It has a combination lock,' said Vlad. 'One with those knobs you have to turn.'

Torment turned around. She had to pull her wits together. The door was likely to lead them closer to the Hall of the Conscious Mind. Phileander's memory-self from whatever night he belonged to surely knew the combination to the lock.

'Has he ever opened it in your presence?' she asked.

'A few times, but I didn't get a good look at—'

'Was one of those times at night?'

He looked at her in puzzlement. Then it occurred to him. 'Oooh. Right.' He looked down at himself. 'I don't really look the part anymore, though. Too big as well.'

This was all taking too long. Torment scurried a few steps back and, with her taloned fingers, promptly severed the ropes of one of the Vladimir puppets, which sagged over the mouldy arm it had been tugging on. Then she picked up the strings with both hands, each grabbing a bundle of them in a way that allowed her to cause the marionette to make at least halfway cat-like motions.

'Just describe to me what you did on one of those nights,' she whispered to Vlad as the two of them met before sleepy Phileander.

'I don't know what all this ruckus is about,' he mumbled, 'but I would really like to use the facilities now. And what's with this smell?'

'Don't know,' whispered Vlad. 'Just cat stuff. Probably rubbed my head against his leg. Yes, I think I did that – the right one.'

Torment proceeded to brush the puppet against Phileander's nightshirt, feeling a little silly.

'What are you doing?' muttered memory-Phileander.

'More elegantly,' whispered Vlad, 'and with the tail up.'

'You enjoy rubbing against that vile bucket of—'

'I can't help it,' he hissed. 'I'm a freakin' cat, all right?'

Torment did her best to follow Vlad's direction and nodded to sleepy Phileander, encouraging him to look down. And indeed, as though hypnotised, he turned and walked beside the Vladimir puppet, which Torment made bob up and down in her best improvised performance of the Vladimir strut, and he started mumbling at it.

'Oh, Vladimir. If you knew what an honour it is to enter the observatory. In fact, every philosopher who wanted to go up would have to go through me.'

Then he started turning the little numbered knob on the large steel door, making it click.

'And I haven't granted anyone entry in years.'

Urgent footsteps in the hall again, or above them, perhaps, or around them, it was hard to tell.

As soon as the door swung open, Vlad knocked nightshirt-Phileander's head against the wall so hard, he fell unconscious instantly. Then both of them rushed through the door and Torment pulled it shut behind them with a resounding *clang*.

'There is only one good thing that has ever come from trying to control an immortal, or trying to tear the veil of worlds, or trying to harness the power of the Courtly Beacon. Yes, some have tried. All of them fools. Some of them dangerous fools. That one good thing is, of course, the culling of the dangerous fools.'

—Acingetorix Jonathan Gesian, *On the Commonplace of Calamity* (annotated edition)

Chapter 19

A Rift of Souls

This was not the observatory. It was but another maze of hallways, narrower now, unfurnished and bare, with only cold, rough-hewn stone surrounding them. And it was even darker. The halls were curved where their walls followed the outer edge of the tower, which tapered towards the top, and Torment heard the wind howling beyond. There was a sky smell on the air, a rain smell, one of damp dust and minerals washed out from old, unrendered masonry. But there was another scent as well, hidden underneath. Red wine, with a hint of something that made Torment uneasy. As did the echoes of their footsteps. They mixed with the echoes of the steps pursuing them, making it even harder to avoid running right into Phileander's spirit.

'We should hide,' whispered Torment. 'He'll always find us if we keep stumbling around in here, making noise.'

'Where?' Vlad replied. 'It's all just corridors. There's not even any doors.'

'Shadows. That alcove over there. It's as good as any.'

'I don't know.' Vladimir peeked around a corner nervously.

'Any better ideas, crony?'

He cast a last glance over his shoulder and strained to listen to the echoes of approaching boots. Then he grumbled and slipped quietly into the alcove. Torment squeezed in beside him, wrapping her black-feathered arms around them both to shroud them deeper in darkness.

She felt his fur against her skin where her trouser leg had been torn off, where her shirt was ripped, felt his warmth. The steady heaving of his breath, the firmness of his flanks and his smell … Even though his feline scent was one she had feared as a crow, it now reassured her immensely.

'Oh, Torment,' rang out Phileander's voice, 'was this your idea? You have learned to enter your mind palace. Impressive. But dangerous, my dear … foolish.'

His steps were close now, perhaps right there in the hallway in front of them. Torment kept her wings folded around them, pressing Vladimir against her. She tapped into her inner fledgling, convinced the beast couldn't see her as long as she couldn't see it. Vlad stiffened beside her. He sniffed at her, tense. His heartbeat quickened.

'You're lost, aren't you?' their master sneered. 'Don't worry, dears. I'm home now, but a few steps away. I can pull you back into your bodies. But don't blame yourselves.' Phileander paused and appeared to knock against the stone, turn around and listen. He was so close, she could hear his cloak rustle. 'It was a misjudgement on my part to treat you so laxly. You poor, ignorant critters only jeopardise yourselves with such antics. But you are cherished *assets* to me. I promise you, my dears, that in the future you shall experience the rigour and discipline you deserve.'

The coldness of those last words, sharp as the scalpel he so eagerly wielded, cut right to Torment's marrow. But a gust of billowing fabric betrayed the brisk swirl with which he headed for the corridor and strode away on determined heels.

Torment allowed herself to peek through her feathers and around the corner out of the alcove. The philosopher was withdrawing into the blackness. She saw him stop momentarily, in apparent irritation, and lean against the wall. He seemed to put his ear to it, as if to eavesdrop. Then he recoiled and marched on, muttering angrily, until he was gone.

'Did you see that?' whispered Torment.

'What? Your wings in my face?' Vlad spat demonstratively, as though he had a mouthful of feathers.

'Something distracted him over there. Something in the walls.'

'A trap, most likely,' said Vlad. 'We should follow him. He'll be returning to his body now. Doesn't that mean he'll be leading us to that consciousness hall you've mentioned?'

With careful steps, Torment left the alcove and started sneaking down the corridor. 'It's on the way, anyway.'

Vladimir followed.

As they neared that spot on the wall, Torment thought the smell of wine intensified. As did the unsettling feeling it carried. There was a noise … faint, almost inaudible – strange bubbling, gurgling wails.

'Don't stop again,' Vlad hissed. 'Damn, you're easily distracted, birdie. There's no time.'

'You go ahead,' she murmured, pressing her ear to the wall. 'I'll be right behind you.'

He snarled in frustration and prowled on down the corridor.

Torment was not unaware of the urgency of their situation. She did not intend to linger. But anything that could disquiet Phileander in his own mind palace was potentially useful. Whatever this was, this wailing thing, it was close to his conscious mind, yet it was … walled in. *Repressed*, perhaps? But how to get at it? Torment felt along the edges of the jagged bricks, scraping her claws through the crevices, scratching and prodding. The wall was as solid as any other. She needed a pick or something similar. A pick … to *peck*. She was a bird, wasn't she? She *should* have a beak. At her current size it would be formidable too. If only she had more of that crimson potion. Time was running out and Vlad was already far ahead.

But why should she need a potion to be a bird? It really bugged her. If part of her spirit was human and part of it was crow … it all just hinged on what she *felt* she was. Torment looked at her wings, so black in this murky twilight that they almost vanished, her feathers slivers of the night itself. They were beautiful.

A movement under her skin, her jawbone elongating and her nose too – Torment felt her lips curl back and recede to make place for coal-black bone tips growing from her mouth. It was a weird but satisfying and utterly painless experience. Cross-eyeing downward, she saw the contours of the stately instrument of pecking and burrowing her face had sprouted. Torment couldn't repress the caw that urged itself from her throat, a call of excitement and confidence. A warning to Phileander, if he was listening. She hoped he wasn't, though.

It would have made no difference, anyway, for pecking and levering out the heavy bricks of the wall was louder than her caw by far. Clangourous strikes rang out along the corridor, sparks flying, chippings scattering, bricks cracking. Stone after stone clattered to the ground. And the smell of wine intensified, as did the wails, occasionally drowned out by the bubbling noises. Torment identified the unsettling undertones of the scent as the familiar aromas of blood and mildly decomposed human flesh.

A pale light shone from the opening Torment had created. She paused to listen for any sign of Phileander's return. The different speeds at which time passed, even over short distances within the mind palace compared to one's Hall of the Conscious Mind, should suffice to delay any reaction from Phileander to the noise she had made. Vlad's utter helplessness against their master's control, however, was an unpredictability.

Torment stuck her head through the opening, which required some manoeuvring. Admittedly, this proved a rare instance of a foot-long spur of bone sticking out of one's head being somewhat disadvantageous. In the dark, cavernous space between this wall and the next, in the midst of cobwebs and a latent odour of mould, stood an open barrel. The pallid light emanated from something that was floating in it.

A slightly bloated human infant, white as ivory and blue-lipped, was floating, bawling, in a full cask of wine. Now and again its weak, choppy kicks would cause it to submerge, and its lamentations would be smothered by the wine. It sounded distant, strangely as though it was not there at all but only the memory of a child echoing in Torment's head.

There was a slit across the infant's throat. It had bled out into the wine, and it smelled so rich, so full-bodied, so sweet. A dessert wine to indulge in and wash away all sorrows – yet laced with tragedy. Even the vampire inside her seemed to have noticed this; it roused momentarily but hesitated and then desisted. Waiting. Something else was roused in Torment more strongly than the vampire. It could not desist. A more rational part of her thought the pale glow of the baby might be practical in these dark halls. Also she sensed that her peculiar commanding effect on the dead extended to this wee thing as well. But that was not why she reached into the wine and took it out.

A motherly instinct compelled her. Torment even hummed a little lullaby, even though she should not be able to hum with her beak at all. The humming rose from somewhere deep inside her. She had heard it before – and the baby reacted to it. Writhing in Torment's arms, it groped for her beak … no, it groped for the sound that came from it, the humming. It fed on it, grasped the sound as though it was a mother's breast, gobbling it up until all fell silent around them. It ate the sound of Torment's boots as she stepped back from the hole in the wall. It ate the howling of the wind outside, the odd echoes of drops of water or settling wood or scurrying things on the ground.

She started walking down the corridor, hoping to find Vlad again. It had not escaped Torment's notice that at this moment she was connected to whatever dwelled in her of the spirit of the late Elisaveta. It was she who sung from her beak, who hugged that baby tightly and who kept the vampire at bay. Torment sensed an anguish in her, so dark and deafening and chilling a despair that it almost broke her. Chained in death as in life, lied to and manipulated, forced to care and love senselessly and boundlessly, burning her up from the inside. But she had to allow Elisaveta's spirit to come to the surface, at least for a little bit. After all … she was the most dangerous weapon to wield against Phileander.

Torment's steps carried her swiftly around corners and along halls, the baby's glow lighting her path. Still she hummed, the little thing at her shoulder, her shiny black beak nestled against it. Still it sucked in all sounds. There was an odd little black-and-red thing on the ground, slimy and chewed up. Torment briefly took a whiff of it. Her beak came with the perk of a crow's heightened olfactory sense. It was a piece of liquorice, the kind Thistlewhisk had lost in the forest, with a subtle coppery smell to it. Vlad had left her a trail, apparently.

But she didn't even think she needed a trail. It was not only she who was humming that lullaby. It came from somewhere else as well, faint, reverberating … like a song trapped in a bottle. It was a beckoning call to her, or at least to the part of her that was connected to Elisaveta and the baby. The dead thing squirmed in Torment's grip, reaching for the wisps of song wafting through the halls with its stiff, anaemic, stubby fingers.

310

And soon Torment stepped around a corner to see her destination. It was a corridor that ended in a winding staircase leading up. Torment remembered it vaguely, just flashes of it as seen in her mesmerised state, Phileander's fingers wrapped around her tiny, trembling body in which raced a tiny, trembling heart. These were the stairs to the observatory beneath the tower's brass-domed roof. Fitting that this would be his Hall of the Conscious Mind. It was from here that he peered out at everything that mattered to him in the waking world.

She passed the last piece of spat-out, chewed liquorice, her steps all but silent. The only sound to be heard, ever so softly, was Elisaveta's lullaby trickling down the stairs.

Climbing up and up the steps, she cloaked the baby's light underneath her wings and entered the inner sanctum of her master's mind.

TORMENT LET HER gaze wander to get a brief sense of the lie of the land, then hurried over to Vlad, who was crouching behind a massive desk laden with piles of books. It was larger than her Hall of the Conscious Mind and certainly larger than the interior of the actual observatory. The vast dome of cold metal overhead had something solemn and daunting about it despite its rich golden hue.

Vlad turned to her, looking alarmed, moving his mouth. But Torment could not hear a word. Still, that lullaby was the only audible sound, muffled, emanating from a figure hunched over a telescope at the far end of the room – Phileander.

The telescope must be his window to the waking world.

Torment gave Vlad a reassuring nod. He still wore a wary expression and kept tapping his ears with his paws, but he nodded back. His gaze lingered curiously on her beak.

A more thorough look from the safety of their cover revealed to Torment a chaos of numerous desks and shelves, with a tumult of

Torment and Vladimir puppets, whose dancing threads faded to nothing somewhere midway up the dome. The marionettes were collecting documents from the desks, apparently to haul them away later. It all had the look of a place that was usually well maintained but had been momentarily thrown into disarray due to recent frantic activity.

With a sudden turn, Phileander left his position at the telescope – a far more adept movement than Torment's slow and meditative *step back* – in order to frequent one of the many desks with the unfurled scrolls and notes and open books on them. Recent memories, no doubt. Halfway, the philosopher paused, frowning, looking around suspiciously. The way he tilted his head told Torment he too was experiencing the baby's deafening effect.

Torment hoped dearly that Vladimir would be quick-witted enough to play along voicelessly, because there was absolutely no margin for error now.

She rose and ran toward Phileander, who started and raised his hands, but before he could do whatever he had been about to do, Torment placed the baby in his arms.

His face contorted in the corpse-child's glow, confused at first, then shocked, then twitching in an indecipherable torrent of emotions.

Behind him Vladimir paced slowly in a circle, poised to pounce.

Torment whirled around and dashed over to the telescope.

She tilted her beak sideways, put her eye against the ocular and—

Her hand was clasping the knob of the door to Phileander's study. A strange hand ... on a strange body, stiff and draped in heavy fabrics. Torment looked over her shoulder – *his* shoulder. At the end of the corridor she saw Sister Catalina approaching, a little out of breath. Then a painful tug right behind her eyes, and—

She was yanked back into Phileander's Hall of the Conscious Mind with such force that a fistful of feathers was ripped out and she fell, skidding across the floor. A familiar menacing stomping and hissing sounded from behind her.

'Pestering, impudent vermin,' Phileander seethed. He loomed over her, hands raised once more in his puppeteer's stance.

There still lay a residual silencing pressure on the room, but it was slowly receding. There … two of the marionettes were dragging the dead baby down the stairs.

An invisible force turned Torment's head back to face her master. Then it pulled her to her feet.

'You have overstepped so many lines, you meddlesome little mite.'

Torment's reply came out in an unintelligible croak. She was not yet reaccustomed to speaking with a crow's vocal apparatus, not to mention that onrushing dread for her life. She felt as though in free fall.

We could kill him now, little crow. Rip him apart. Take him over.

Now was not the time to lose control.

But he is powerful. Yes, we could bathe in blood, drink our fill. Let—

No. This was her fight, for her life and her freedom.

As he was pulling her closer, Torment's eyes flitted left and right, over Phileander's face and embroidered coat, searching for any weakness to exploit, any opening.

On a desk, piles of hastily scribbled notes—

'What are they up to?'

'I forgot something. What was it? Did they do this?'

'Disengage. To the study, quickly.'

There was a table, set for two and left in a hurry. From the inn he had been at, perhaps?

She had never seen him this angry. Around his neck was a pendant – a silver locket engraved with dahlia blossoms. The humming … it originated from that. She couldn't move a single muscle of her own accord.

Vladimir grunted behind her. The silencing effect was lifted, and Torment heard the noise of a struggle – creaking metal and heavy stomps and hissing steam.

Phileander's hand closed firmly around her neck, merciless eyes following the length of her beak, meeting her gaze. They sucked the life from her, the hope ... nothing of young Phileander's pain was left in them. It was all locked away somewhere.

Two puppet crows began tying her feet.

A beastly roar, a cracking noise – then a thing of glass flew past the philosopher's head and shattered.

Among the shards was a lock of black hair.

Behind her something crashed to the ground, something heavy, and the hissing stopped.

Phileander was distracted, for only but a second before he reached out to seize control of Vlad.

Torment got her beak under the chain of the locket and tore at it with a jerk of her head. It came off, clattering to the floor and flicking open.

For a second, all was still again.

Phileander stared at the thing in utter horror.

And Torment stumbled back as her invisible strings came loose. Over her shoulder, she glimpsed Vlad atop the fallen clockwork knight, tearing it apart in a snarling frenzy.

Up the stairs marched three more of them, wielding swords, cross-bows, spikes and needles dripping with acrid-smelling liquid. Echoing up the stairway, reverberating under the dome, could be heard the steady march of an army.

'Forevermore, my love!' A woeful shriek resounded, piercing Torment's ears, curdling her blood. Turning, she saw Elisaveta floating above the locket, her nightgown radiating. It was blindingly white. 'Look at me,' she screamed. 'See me! Yours, all yours, forevermore!'

Phileander covered his ears, his eyes squeezed shut, muttering, though Torment couldn't hear what.

'My love!'

Clockwork knights swarmed the dome, cordoning them in.

'The memories!' Torment cawed over Elisaveta's screeching wails.

Vlad got off his fallen prey, noticed the preponderance of enemies closing in.

'His memories,' she yelled, 'from today!' She pointed at the various candles burning on the desks.

Vladimir nodded to her, leapt over to one of the desks and tried picking up pieces of parchment with his mouth, but he couldn't get hold of them, and then the knights were upon him. A spiked metal club hit him on the side, sending him crashing into another metal colossus with a terrible crunch.

Torment kicked the puppet crows aside and tore at the rope with her beak. She couldn't see, but she heard Vlad taking punishment, cursing, gasping in agony, but also another knight falling, shaking the ground.

The rope came off.

Torment caught a glimpse of a most uneven battle. Vlad was bleeding profusely yet still on his paws, standing his ground. A warrior.

She could deal with those memories now – burn them before Phileander had finished dealing with Elisaveta. But Vlad might not make it. Torment had left him to fend for himself once before, in that alley. Not again. She was not so helpless now.

Torment ran to the edge of the dome, gripped one of the brass segments by its edge and pulled. For some reason she had thought they would all be movable, like the one covering the opening for the telescope. But they were bolted fast together. It didn't matter. A friend was in peril. It matched a hundred strength potions. And also she wasn't just pulling at it from the inside.

Clang!

A dent in the brass. Something pounding it from beyond. Already, Torment could smell them.

Clang! Clang!

More dents. Bolts loosened. The scent of crows and the dreadful musk of a man from her past. Torment tore and pulled and screamed in pain as her tendons strained near rupturing.

She reeled as part of the segment detached and bent inwards.

A broad-shouldered giant pulled himself through, clad in black leather, chains wrapped around his fists. Following him came a thunder of caws and a storm of black feathers – crows in their hundreds flooded in through the opening. The crow master's gaze turned to Torment.

'You've gone rogue, little bugger. Need to be put in your place.'

Torment reared up before him, thrusting out her beak and squawking loudly in his face. 'You're *my* nightmare.' She pointed at the knights, who now all but obscured Vlad from sight. One of them was trudging towards Torment, but a whirlwind of screaming crows slowed its advance. 'You want to stay in my head? Defend it.'

She had not been sure it would work, but she had really, really hoped it would. And hoping something very desperately was pretty much the same thing as believing it.

The crow master's attention turned to the knights, and with a deep growl he tightened the chain and started walking. And the crows did their part, standing by Vladimir. At least, Torment hoped so.

Near the telescope, Phileander was tying a rope tightly around this haunting memory of Elisaveta with the help of his marionettes. His face was a mask of pain, and she still lamented loudly.

It was all thunder and screaming and stamping and pecking – utter bedlam. Torment barely knew which way to stagger. She went to a desk and started holding all the notes and scrolls over the candle flames. Repeatedly, the flutter of a crow would whirl up the parchments until one extinguished the candle and Torment had to go over to another desk, but a clockwork knight was hurled into it and it shattered, nearly burying Torment underneath it. The crow master's chain was wrapped around the arm that had held a double-bladed axe, which was now stuck in what was left of the desk.

She cawed in frustration, grabbed a still-burning candle with her beak and took off, soaring around the dome in a circle. Here and there she descended to set fire to what memories she could find. But soon that candle was extinguished too, and Torment stumbled through the fray in search of another.

She bumped into Vlad. It was a wonder he could still walk. His fur was in tatters, blood-soaked.

'Scratch the memories, birdie,' he shouted. 'They're all in a shambles now anyway. Let's get out.'

Perhaps he was right. Some of the notes were burning, others being ripped apart by angry crows or torn-off parts of shattered clockwork knights. At the very least, they were in a terrible mess, and most of the marionettes to sort them where they needed to go were destroyed and scattered.

Torment looked over at the telescope. Somehow, Phileander had returned Elisaveta to the locket. She just saw him close it, shutting in that radiant light, and shove it into a pocket of his waistcoat. Then he turned around to the telescope. His movements were erratic, twitchy, painstaking. This havoc wreaked on his conscious mind had not left him unaffected. But he would enter the study, if he had not already. Timing was of the essence.

'We need to look through that telescope right when he lays eyes on our bodies,' yelled Torment, 'but before he— Watch out!'

By a hair's breadth, they dodged the crow master as he was slammed into the ground by a knight with a great mace for a hand.

Vlad needed no further explanation. They made their way to Phileander. He was looking through the ocular now. When she had been looking, he'd had his hand already around the doorknob.

'Now,' she shouted.

Incredibly agile for his battered state, Vlad jumped, vaulting off a massive desk and hurling himself against Phileander. The two of them tumbled, entangled, across the floor.

And Torment ran.

She was at the telescope, bending down, getting that beak out of the way—

A blurry view of the study swayed before her, and she felt a terrible headache. Her perspective was odd, more from the height of a human child than a man of Phileander's size. She rubbed her eyes.

There was the book on the floor, the one with the recipe for the dream potion, and next to it the pestle and mortar, still filled with that sludge. And behind it stood the desk, atop it a lump of black fur and a cage. And in the cage sat a crow, huddled at the bottom, and she could *feel* that crow. She opened its eyes.

Strange, causing herself to move while watching from the outside. But those black little beads. Torment saw them, and she saw behind them through her window – the connection that had been lost.

Her head hurt. She was so dizzy. She lurched backwards, away from …

She shook her head. Torment sat in a cage, a large one, which hung in another one, and that in another, and so on … but it was furnished, and before her there was a window, and through it she saw the bars of yet another cage, one that stood in a room, upon a desk, before a cat whose eyes were twitching …

Torment fluttered onto the windowsill and—

Pain. Weakness and nausea and pain. A high-pitched whine in her head eclipsed all other sounds. She had the headache of her life, but the head which throbbed was that of a crow. The body being weighed down by the burden of a corporeal world was that of a feeble, trembling bird. There was no mistaking the feeling of inhabiting this body. It had been fitted to her spirit by nature's finest tailors, at least until her spirit had been tampered with. Funny how she had never come to appreciate the wonder of her body before she had been forced to spend a while without it. When she had first returned to the waking world from her mind palace, an eternity ago in her mind, the difference had felt subtle. It did not feel subtle now. With all the clarity of a gut punch, this was a different world – an *in*different world – governed by rigid rules with no regard for purpose, hope or despair. A reliable world. The metal bars around her were made of the harsh, immutable stuff of reality. Stuff that wouldn't suddenly blow apart into wisps of dust and reshape into some swamp monster or nightmare king or any other outlandish, nasty surprise. And the smell that filled her nose was that of Phileander's study, complex yet familiar, and of a pungent, slimy potion that still tainted the bottom of her cage.

At long last, though it had in fact been hardly more than two hours, Torment was back.

Chapter 20

A Shred of Compassion

V LADIMIR'S EYES FLICKERED open and his body tensed under the impact of waking reality. His head had been resting pressed against the bars of the cage, which had probably left painful impressions. There was a scar across his face, pink and furless, leaving a cleft in his muzzle. He had not had it before, and it reminded Torment of the cut he had received when that giant cat had attacked him in their shared nightmares.

'Torment?' A human voice came from somewhere else.

She turned her head and the world turned along with her, vertigo making her flap her wings in fear of falling. The ringing in her head ebbed away, gradually letting through the soundscape of Phileander's study. Someone was gagging or coughing, thrashing about on the floor. She heard a muffled meow, hoarse and pitiable.

'Torment,' came the voice again. It was Catalina's. 'What is happening here?'

The plump philosopher in her blue robe knelt next to Phileander, who was holding his head and shaking uncontrollably. He let out half-articulated moans, some of which sounded much like Torment's name.

'Wrahk ...' Torment shook her head again, trying to remember how to talk. 'The book ...'

Catalina appeared to be tending to the philosopher. She had laid him on his side in a way that minimised the risk of him hurting himself during his seizure. Now she looked at the open tome on the floor. She inclined her head as she read.

'Somniatrinus? A potion to share dreams?'

'Yes,' said Torment, 'and if you're extra lucky, it even throws your spirit into a different dimension that it's really difficult to get out of. Close it and put it back on the shelf up there.' She pointed with her beak. 'Into that gap.'

'You have the recipe, so you can order me around,' said the woman dryly. 'Got it.'

'Look, Sister, I'm really sorry about how I behaved. You'll get the recipe right away, and all the answers you desire, but right now we need to hurry.' Torment looked at Phileander. His condition was unchanged. She thought she heard his mumbling echo in her head in a way that it shouldn't. 'Before he comes to. And please could you clean up that mess Vlad left preparing the potion?'

'What have you done?' Catalina asked, but she rose and began covering their tracks as Torment had asked.

Vladimir was standing now, looking around, meowing in a way that sounded as though he had not yet realised he could not talk anymore.

'A lot,' croaked Torment. 'Phileander … might not be the same after this. Hopefully.'

'What's that around your neck?' Catalina had come up to the desk, looking for something with which to wipe the mortar clean.

'What?' Torment unfolded her wings, drawing her beak through her feathers. There was something there, hung around her neck on a thin leather strap. It was the magpie's skull. Torment let out a thoughtful caw. How could she have brought it back with her? Or Vladimir his scar? Torment also noticed scars on her right leg. It was hard to make out the resemblance to the injury her human limb had suffered in the dream wilds, with her crow feet looking so different, but it was there. 'Curiouser and curiouser,' Torment crowed to herself.

Vlad, meanwhile, had withdrawn onto the mantlepiece. He had curled up, but his eyes remained wary. They followed Catalina as she put away the last little vials of the ingredients Vladimir had used.

'Thanks,' said Torment. 'So, listen up. Hair of newborn, plucked with malice. Three. Heartstrings of rabid dog, acquired any which way—'

'Wait.' Catalina frowned and waved her hands. 'What's this now?'

'Your recipe. For the elixir.'

'First you make me jump through hoops for it, now you just give it to me?'

'Look, I know I've been a jerk to you just yesterday, but …' Torment averted her eyes for a second. 'I've had a few formative experiences since then.'

Catalina nodded slowly, still frowning, glancing over to the book she had just put back where it belonged. She was adding one and one together behind her eyes.

'Very well, then.' She grabbed a piece of parchment and a quill. 'Three hair of newborn, next was heartstrings of rabid dog – how many?'

322

Catalina noted down the ingredients and amounts Torment gave her.

'Good,' said Torment after they were done, with an anxious glance at Phileander, who writhed on the floor and whose voice still resounded somewhere in the back of her head. 'Now that you have the recipe ... couldn't you just kill him? He's defenceless right now.'

The woman cast a long look at Phileander, as though she was considering it. 'No. My pact with him forbids it. And even if I could—'

'Just break the pact, woman.'

'It's not that kind of pact.'

'Well' – Torment took a deep breath – 'pity. Just heave him onto the chair, then, and get out of here before he wakes up. We can talk more later.'

Catalina nodded and did as Torment had asked. She was stronger than she looked and draped the philosopher onto his seat with casual ease. Then she laid his head in his arms upon the tabletop as though he had simply fallen asleep.

When Catalina had gone, Torment closed her eyes and sought out her memories of the crowery at Castle Quelm. As she had suspected, those memories were presently not too easy to recall. They felt like distant echoes, hard to grasp, like a tale told by someone else very long ago. But Torment forced herself to remember the crow master's face. She pictured him in her mind's eye as he made his rounds from cage to cage, prodding at crows who misbehaved, selecting the next one to receive a task – and a reward afterwards. Torment could feel the memories return to her, flooding in one by one, distinct scents of different members of her murder cropping up in her imagination. The crow master and his servants were returning to her mind palace where they belonged.

'What?' rasped her master's voice. 'Where ...'

Torment opened her eyes. Phileander stirred, raising his head.

'I don't ... I ...' The philosopher blinked around in disorientation.

'What happened?'

'Are you unwell, master?' Torment fluttered onto the perch in her cage. 'You were sleeping. And an hour before that, you stumbled in here drunk beyond your wits.'

'Drunk?'

'Shamefully so. One too many, perhaps, or a sip from a bad batch during your meeting in the Thrice-Woven Curse. How did that go, by the way?'

'I …' Phileander furrowed his brow and pressed two fingers against his temples. 'I can't remember. I don't remember any … What time is it?' He opened the shutters and looked out into the night. 'I will have to inquire via crow how that meeting went.'

'That bad?' croaked Torment. 'Did you meet with someone dubious who might have spiked your drink? An unexpected enemy?'

'No, Torment.' He sounded annoyed, and still he pressed his fingers to his temples in what she hoped would closely resemble an excruciating hangover. 'I have to brew myself an infusion to sober up. Excuse me.'

He stormed off, darkly brooding, and left the two of them alone in the study.

Vlad perked up and blinked at Torment, but it was not the right time to chat with him just yet. There was still a loose end to tie up.

Torment closed her eyes and took a step back into her Hall of the Conscious Mind.

THIS WAS A routine visit, and Torment did not want to arouse unnecessary suspicion by allowing Phileander to catch her entranced again – she certainly did not want him to drag her out of here by a chain. She stepped away from the window, opened the cage door and soared out into the blue sky beyond.

Tangled threads of scent greeted her, branching out and downward. Associations to guide her. But what she sought was not a regular part of her mind palace. She looked for an irregularity – a rift.

There were old scents, like that of the crowery, of the Lemon Gardens in the Lesser Silks, of the bird baths on Baron Bothyra's balconies. But new ones too. Torment made out the rotten egg smell of the Mellow Marshes, the smells of pinecone and mildew from the forest bordering on them … there was also a stream of arid desert wind. Circling high above, Torment could even make out parts of the city below where the endless buildings were interrupted by patches of landscape like when she had roamed it in the dream wilds.

Torment saw what she was looking for. There was a single black cloud among the white ones, smaller and elongated, shaped like a waving pennant. No scented wind current led there, but as she drew nearer with mighty wing beats, Torment noticed a smell of scorched wood and paper. As she had assumed, it was a plume of smoke originating from a spot in the sky where the air felt … sensitive. Like the soft pink tissue over a freshly healed wound. A scar in the fabric of her mind.

She circled the spot, but she could not make out any remaining tears leading into Phileander's Hall of the Conscious Mind. The rift must have closed by itself. Without a spirit deliberately keeping a foot in the door, pathways between mind palaces seemed to be unstable – or between mind palaces and the dream wilds, for that matter. Torment found that thought tremendously reassuring. But not unexpected. Were it otherwise, many such rifts would have existed, and entering or leaving the dream wilds would not be as difficult as it was.

Resolutely, she made her way down, letting herself fall with folded wings, spreading them again as she crossed the air current flowing towards Castle Quelm. The crow master's sweaty odour was strong in it, but she needed to be sure and really see him. Also, Torment found her fear of that man was not what it once used to be. Not since she'd awoken from her first dance with her vampire amid his scattered entrails. Torment wondered how he was even still alive in her mind palace. Had the vampire only killed her fear of him?

In a swerving dive, Torment landed on the edge of the skylight from which the crows took off on their messenger flights. Sticking her head in, she peered into the shade and found the swaying cages alive with birds aflutter, cawing, some of them sleeping. By a work table, the crow master was busy chopping up meat into bite-sized cubes for his servant's feeding. Before he could look up and spot her, Torment flew off again.

So all their tracks were covered as well as they could be. How thoroughly Phileander's memory had been wiped remained to be seen. So far, Torment was feeling optimistic, given Phileander's reaction when he had woken up back in his study.

Torment caught a whiff of the dusty smell of the Forbidden Library, of deteriorating paper and old ink.

She turned to follow it to a crow's nest crowning a bay window of an unremarkable house in a nondescript neighbourhood somewhere among banal memories of winding bridges and streets and lengthy flights over the city. It was one of her little collections of curious knowledge. This one held exactly one item.

Nestled in a shaggy shell of sprigs and bits of wood lay a crumpled page of yellowed parchment. It was the page she had ripped out of that old book, containing the clause on the binding of a homunculus – to never feel remorse for the murders committed to create it. She had ripped that memory from his mind and taken it into hers. Torment had seen how his memory had been damaged. She was quite certain he would not remember it. And by his own admission, he had nowhere to read up on it again. But was it truly safe here?

Torment remembered how she had heard Phileander's voice in here as his binding had taken control of her, had dragged her spirit through her own mind palace by a chain. Some part of him was in her. It was not inconceivable that this part could find the memory and snatch it away again. After all, even with what she had learned, Torment's knowledge of the twisted complexity that was the workings of spirits and dreams was still wildly incomplete.

Phileander had installed an army of guards within his mind palace. It had probably taken him years of research and practice to achieve that. But then again, so had entering his mind palace in the first place, in all likelihood, and Torment had mastered that in a second. So … how had he made them, those clockwork knights? They were driven by the mementos in those glass cases in their chests: the hand mirror, the dahlia, the lock of hair … things he felt strongly about. Pieces of himself, in a way.

Torment ran her beak through her breast feathers. Even in here, she wore it – the magpie's skull. It had served her before, even if she had not understood how and why. Had she already done it? Created a sentinel for her mind palace by accident? She tore off the pendant and dropped the skull into the nest.

'Guard it,' she crowed. 'I would say with your life, but … ah, never mind.' Torment hopped back to the edge of the nest. 'Tad inappropriate, coming from me. Noticed it myself, Bigbones. Hope you don't find that name offensive.'

Torment waited for another moment, feeling a bit awkward. But the skull did not grow into a giant skeleton before her. And even if it had, she doubted it would have had anything to say. But Torment knew it had heard her. She felt it in her bones, so to speak. It made her think of one last thing she wanted to do before she returned to wakefulness.

She plunged into the shadowy depths between the buildings, descending along half-timbered walls. A stench of decay wafted up from below. Like a dense cushion of corpse-rot gases, it blanketed the cobblestones upon the footbridges and the crevices leading to the undercroft beneath her memories. When she spread her wings to land, the deathly fumes were blown apart, revealing a patch of rusty grating.

SILAS A. BISCHOFF

Through it, accusing glances greeted her from milky eyes.

It was not just accusation they met her with. There was also respect. They did not grope for her as they had before. Neither did they call out, curse her, or in fact do anything but stare.

As she hopped along the grated gutter and looked down at them, Torment noted that the buildings were not quite crow-sized anymore. The scale of it all appeared to have increased to about half human-sized. Many of the faces below she recognised. Humans from the baronies, mostly nobles, some servants.

'Open this for me, would you?' Torment asked a sturdier, less-rotted man staring up at her.

Without hesitation, the man grasped the bars and lifted the rectangular cast-iron grate. He had worked in Baron Dormengard's kitchens, and the baroness had once suspected him of poisoning her soup after a formal dinner. It was interesting how many details Torment realised now about events she had understood so little about when they had happened. The part of her that thought like a human found it astonishing that she would even have memorised noises that had been all but unintelligible to her then or images of scripts she had not been able to read. But the part of her that had been a crow knew it had indeed been normal for her to memorise peculiar sequences of sounds or visual patterns with perfect accuracy.

She fluttered through the opening into the dank, dark space below. It was a sewer, the kind that ran under the cobblestones inside the bridges, carrying the sewage of the surface dwellers down through shafts in the bridge piers into an intricate network. Among the feet of the rotting human corpses, Torment found other animals whose untimely deaths she had helped along. Birds and small rodents. Quite possibly many of the insects here were dead as well. They would have been hard to tell apart from the live ones who ate away at the corpses.

'I'm ... sorry you're dead, you know?' Torment croaked.

The man did not answer. But he tilted his head and stared at her

328

slightly differently. Perhaps it was gratitude, or forgiveness, or scorn.

'Right.' Torment hopped on to the next one. It was little more than a vaguely humanoid lump of maggots. 'And you, you're a little far along the way, so I don't recognise you, but I regret your death too.' She rose onto one of their shoulders. 'To all of you,' she cawed, 'I regret your deaths. There might be grounds to justify my part in them, but I really don't feel like invoking them. I take my part of the responsibility for your losses and I regret them.'

Many-mouthed moans answered her, mostly incomprehensible. 'Thank you,' breathed one fresher specimen near her. 'Much appreciated, Your Highness.'

Torment was taken aback by the title. But this was her mind palace, after all. People with palaces were usually addressed with titles, particularly within their palaces. Most of all, though, there was a freeing sense of relief. She felt as though she had just taken a huge leap towards that peace of mind Catalina had mentioned once.

'Look, my rotting fellows, you don't have to waste away down here.' She pointed upward with her beak. 'Feel at home in my memories if you want. Use this place as you please. I only ask in return that you keep a lookout for any strangers sniffing around. Particularly those of the bald, long-nosed, well-dressed variety.' Torment cawed loudly so all could hear. 'Do we have a deal?'

More moans wheezed from decayed throats. She thought they sounded somewhat cheerful. Movement came to the undead masses, and indeed the bodies – large and small, human and animal – began to rise from the gutter.

Torment watched them swarm towards the exit, towards the light, and as the corpse smell steadily receded, she caught a whiff of blood again. Always the beckoning smell of blood, reminding her of the enemy she had not yet found a way to rid herself of. She even thought she heard the distant echo of a heartbeat making its way up from somewhere deep and dark. Torment winced at every *ba-bump* sending subtle vibrations through the wet sewer walls. She had found the shaft leading to the depths of her despair – and the vampire's prison – within her Hall of Reverence, above the clouds of her mind palace. Surely descending further down from here, well below the surface of her mind, would lead her there as well. But the vampire was dormant now. She just had to ignore him.

The last rotting critters scurried through the open gutter overhead, and Torment's tidying up of her mind palace was complete. Satisfied with the results, Torment took off and ascended back out into the light, over streets now populated with the rotting, and skyward. The magpie would guard her most precious stolen memory, and the liberated bodies from her basement would provide a measure of counterespionage. Slowly but steadily, she was seizing control of her mind palace.

On swift wings, Torment swept up and through the open portal into her Hall of the Conscious Mind, and from there without further ado onto the sill of the window, through which the crumpled face of a cat glared at her grumpily.

'What is it, crony?' she croaked, impressed by the effortlessness with which she could now return to full consciousness.

He meowed babblingly, still not used to his inability to speak. Then he started pointing at the communication parchment, positively punching it in irritation and impatience: 'Aghast you return to mad place so soon.'

'Understandable. I don't intend to make a habit of it, rest assured.' Torment hopped to the edge of her cage and leaned toward Vlad with her beak turned sideways. 'And now,' she croaked quietly, 'let's hatch a plan to make Phileander repent.'

~

WITH EVERY DAY that went by, Torment saw more clearly the changes in her master's behaviour. It was as though his edges had been smoothed

A CROW NAMED TORMENT

out since their return from the dream wilds. But there were also cracks and nicks left behind. He was more often kind and thoughtful, but also broody and irritable. In a way, Torment found, this made him even scarier. In his prior coldness, he had been more … predictable.

Vlad was out hunting small game. It was a golden morning, Phileander's hour of dealing with correspondence. Torment found the rustling of paper and the scratching of the quill, accompanied by wafts of sweet-smelling steam from freshly baked pastries, quite comforting and homely. She realised now that this was the Elisaveta part of her. In the end, little had been left of that woman besides an agonising desire to be with her lover. Like Torment, she had been bound by a cruel curse courtesy of Phileander.

The philosopher was still in his morning robes. Before, he would never have been that slack. He had been one to scold every sleepy-looking brother and sister he saw in the hall in the dreadfully early morning hours for their shameful laziness. Now he himself craved the simple comforts he had once so despised. He held the quill still, ink dripping heedlessly onto the parchment, and his absent eyes gazed out over the glowing shingle roofs into a sky of orange and lavender streaked with rosy clouds.

'What troubles you, master?' Torment crowed.

'What?' He roused himself from his daydream. 'I … It's nothing.' Anger creased his brow again. Anger at himself, most likely.

'You're only human, master, despite what you may think. There's no shame in being plagued by sorrows.'

'What do you know, stupid crow?' Phileander snapped. Then he took a deep, sighing breath. 'I'm sorry, my dear.' He gave her a weak smile. 'You … do know sorrows, don't you?'

'And I know *you*, master. Better than most. It's how you made me. You also made me to be wholly at your mercy.' Torment tilted her head. 'So who better to share your sorrows with? After all, I am to be your assistant, am I not? The more I understand you, the more helpful

331

I can be.'

'Why would you even want to be helpful? I am your captor and soon to be your killer.'

'You're also the man who gifted me with this rich mind so full of insight. Would a long life as a messenger crow have been fuller than the few weeks you are giving me? With this wonderful sense of being more than just my flesh and feathers?' Torment squawked with a flutter. 'I don't know. Perhaps we're even. Perhaps I should be grateful.'

It was only half a lie. She did feel gratitude, admiration, contempt, rage, love … terror. For all her love, Torment knew that if she could, she would still kill him where he stood. And it would not be the cold dispatch of an enemy or the desperate killing of prey. It would be a cruel and bloody affair of the heart, painful as only love can be.

Phileander smiled. 'It is good to hear you think like that.'

Most people seemed to think that love and hate were opposites. Torment realised then how sorely mistaken they were. Hate does not contradict love – it necessitates it. Hate is what *becomes* of love.

He looked into space for a moment and chuckled. 'I have poured out my heart to Vladimir from time to time, when enough wine had run its course. But he is a rather poor conversationalist.' Then he nodded. 'I shall take you up on your offer, then, little friend.'

'So, what was on your mind just now, when you were looking out the window?'

'A childhood memory. One of the few … pleasant ones, actually. I hadn't thought of it for many years, but lately … I can't help it.'

'If it's a pleasant memory, then why do you look so sad?'

'Well, because it's a pleasant memory, I suppose. All good things become sad things when they're over.' Irritation found its way back onto his face. 'I understood that long ago, actually, and I took measures to prevent becoming an embittered old man who does naught but wallow in his misery.' His hand went to his chin. 'What has changed?'

'Tell me of the memory.' Torment interrupted these dangerous thoughts. 'Is it about a place? A person?'

'Oh, both, in fact. I don't remember if I ever told you that I grew up on the streets. I'm not highborn or sent here by a rich family like most philosophers. I was taken in as a youth for my promising prowess of intellect.' His pride seemed to have remained unscathed, Torment noted. 'And when I was, oh … probably no more than eight years old, there was a kind woman who took me in for a day and a night. And a morning with the most scrumptious freshly baked crumpets and a cup of tea that warmed you from the chest to the fingertips.' A brief flicker of confusion crept across his face. 'And there was something odd in the basement—'

'Who was the woman?' Torment cut him short again. 'What was her name?'

'It was … Miss Baba, I think.' He blinked quizzically at her interjections. 'I even think I … yes …'

Phileander stood up and walked over to an old chest in a corner of the study. He opened it and rummaged through its contents, muttering to himself.

'Ah' – he produced a palm-sized disc of discoloured gold – 'her hand mirror.' He flicked it open and held it in a ray of sunlight, deflecting it into Torment's eye.

'Hey!' she squawked.

Phileander gave a laugh that for once was playful and not sardonic. But it trailed off into a sigh, and when he gazed upon his face in the stained old looking glass, his grin turned sour.

'Why, after all these years, do I feel so sentimental about it?' he murmured. 'I was to trade it in for food and lodging. I could have spent a whole winter well-fed in a warm room for this. Why didn't I?' He regarded it with a gloomy frown. 'It was stupid to keep it. I never needed it.'

Torment remembered her role in this, remembered what she had told his little memory self. She was treading on a knife's edge, she realised.

'Something you're that attached to,' Torment crowed, 'must be a powerful ingredient for magic rituals.'

'How often do I have to tell you, there is no such thing as magic? There is only an infinity of possibilities swirling underneath a thin sheet of ice we call the *natural order*.' His thin grin returned. 'An order the likes of us do not bow to, do we, Torment? Why, you must be right. That must be why I kept it.'

His face hardening, Phileander regained much of his old dead-eyed composure. He snapped the mirror shut with a sharp click.

'Which reminds me, Torment dear,' he said in that familiar, unsettlingly calm way of his, 'I have some training in mind for you.'

'Training?' Her confidence deflated frustratingly fast.

'The experiment is due soon, and in the short time you will survive inside the Everstorm, your usefulness will hinge on things you still have to learn. You wanted to be helpful, didn't you?'

Torment trembled. 'Yes, master.'

SHE WAS ENGAGED in a tug-of-war with Phileander's emotions and suspicions. It was always two steps forward, one step back. The net result was a step forward, of course, but it went slower than she had hoped. And the fatal experiment was to take place in but a week.

In dreams – even just daydreams or innocent, unconnected reminiscences – Torment often thought of the men and women and many animals whose deaths she had helped to bring about. They would crop up in a memory of the crowery or wave to her when, as so often, she dreamed of flying. They were peaceful, almost comforting reminders, which was strange because when she had been repressing it all, it had seemed to weigh so much heavier on her. Yet still no day went by that she was not plagued by irrational regrets, while Phileander remained infuriatingly unrepentant. It was not fair.

The training Phileander subjected her to was in basic autosomatic thaumaturgy, mainly to do with the redirection of lightning energy through such pathways in her body as would least endanger her life. To that end, the philosopher had commissioned a device from Sister Evelyn, who was most adept in applied mechanics and who had looked upon the plans he had handed her with utter bewilderment. The device consisted of a roll of coiled copper wire, a crank and two extending threads with weaved-in copper fibres, at the ends of which were small hook-shaped needles that could be lodged in the skin under Torment's feathers. The needles pricked uncomfortably, but most of the pain this training inflicted on her came whenever the philosopher began turning the crank. Torment's skin and muscles would tense and a strange vibrating sensation would clench her innards tight, petrify her, make her feathers prick up and crackle. According to Phileander, this was but a fraction of the energy one of the Everstorm's lightning rays would send through her body. Torment's task was to try and change the path the flow took as it coursed from one hooked needle to the other.

Torment was not very fond of this kind of education, and she thought back wistfully to her mind palace sessions with Catalina. In fact, she had not been able to organise another meeting with her, since Phileander liked to conduct her training in the evening hours he would usually have spent in his reading room. And that was particularly unfortunate, seeing as the woman had a significant part to play in their plan. Another part of it was to deepen Torment's relationship with Phileander, but the man's obsession with his experiment made it hard to get through to him.

'I don't think I will get much better at this,' croaked Torment one night after a lengthy session of diverting energy along the surface of her chest that would otherwise have coursed through her heart and stopped it. 'Is there nothing else you have to teach me, master?'

She was gasping for breath; her whole body tingled and her feet were numb. He had cranked the device particularly hard, and a sharp, offensive odour permeated the air, similar to the smell of scorched metal.

'Perhaps,' said Phileander, raising his head from behind the device, where he had noted down Torment's latest results. 'But this skill will be the most important in prolonging your life.'

'For a few *minutes*,' she cawed, 'when I have days yet ahead of me and would greatly appreciate it if I could spend at least one of them without being tortured.'

'Tortured?' His eyes widened. 'I don't intend to torture you, my dear,' he swore, raising his hands. 'The path to greater good is paved with sacrifices, and a bit of your comfort is surely the least of them.'

'I'm already sacrificing my *life*.'

'No, Torment,' he snapped, '*I* am sacrificing your life. And it is neither my first, my last, nor my greatest sacrifice.'

'Do you hate me so much that you would not grant me at least one evening of peace before I die?'

'I ...'

'Please, my love.'

He flinched. 'What did you just say?'

'I said "please".'

'No, I meant ...' The philosopher closed his eyes and took a deep breath. His face softened. 'I'm sorry, Torment. You're right. In fact, it may be better for my own peace of mind as well if we spent your last evenings in a more ... considerate manner.'

Torment stretched her wings. 'I haven't flown in days. Flying through a storm is no easy feat if you're weakened and your wings are stiff.'

'Oh.' Phileander nodded with a slightly surprised expression, as though this had never occurred to him. 'You're absolutely right. And we both know you can't possibly disobey me, which I am certain is not an enjoyable sensation even outside your cage.' He gave her a sympathetic smile and started to fiddle with the cage door. 'Please understand that I am not happy about your sacrifice. Not at all.'

She understood that. She understood perfectly well how even this new, gentler Phileander was ultimately more interested in his own absolution than in her wellbeing. Yet Torment could not help but feel the most profound appreciation for this feeble gesture. It was instilled in her very essence and it disgusted her.

As soon he had opened it, Torment hopped out of the cage, fluttered around once in a circle and then flew onto one of the upper shelves, raising a dust cloud.

Phileander put down his quill and regarded her thoughtfully. Worry etched his brow. 'The ritual that forces you to obey me,' he murmured, 'I ... I would never forget a detail about it.' His gaze trailed off and he muttered, more to himself than to her, 'Not about something this important.'

He stood there for another few seconds. Then he stormed out of his study without another word. Vladimir darted into the room and onto the desk just before the door slammed shut behind the philosopher.

For a moment, the cat stared perplexed at the empty cage. Then his gaze flicked to Torment, who fluttered down onto the desk, where there was still an open ink pot and some blank sheets of parchment.

'It'll be a close call again,' she squawked, 'but the plan, my crony, is *on*. I'll write a note for you to deliver to Catalina.'

Then she took the quill in her beak and began to write, deciding that three days hence, the last night she would have on this Earth, should Phileander get his will, would be the night they broke him.

'Wonder not where spirits come from or what they are made of. They invent themselves from nothing. They are themselves the dreams of the living universe about what it means to be alive.'

—Ogden Flynt, *Spirits beyond Earth and Sky* (unfinished manuscript)

Chapter 21

A Dash of Remorse

PHILEANDER HAD DINNER with Torment every night after he concluded her training. They had it in the great dining room one floor down that Torment had seen in the memory in his mind palace and before that in a dream. It was she who had suggested it. He would sit at one end of the long table and she upon the tabletop at the other, directly in front of her plate. A lavish candle holder would always be lit between them, and a soft, cosy ember would crackle in the fireplace. He even had one of the tower's cooks prepare delicate meals based on her preferences: raw and blood-drained meats, elderberries, lightly cooked eggs that were soft at the centre, braised slugs and live worms, peas and sprinklings of seeds.

The first night had been a bit awkward and there hadn't been much in the way of conversation. The second night had been better – warmer and more jovial between them. Phileander had arranged a bouquet of roses and lilacs, scenting the room like Torment's favourite gardens in the upper districts. She had mentioned this fondness only once, and it astonished her that he had remembered. He had opened up a little that evening. Torment found it rather telling that he would fill these last nights he had devoted to her by relieving himself of his own worries. But she swallowed her offence, for it fit nicely into her plan. Apparently young Adelaide had died two nights prior. It stung to be reminded of her. Phileander had already deduced from his examinations that her spirit had departed, for she had stopped murmuring in her sleep and her eyes had ceased to move. What troubled Phileander most, however, was how the girl's death affected him. He found himself ashamed and unable to charge Lady Lidelle the fee he was entitled to. Once again, Torment had to change the subject when he began to talk himself into a rage, mad at himself. It never ceased to amaze her how this cold, unflappable man, this epitome of ruthless self-control, could be rattled by the admission of even the merest emotion.

And thus came night number three – their last dinner before he would send her off to perish in his pursuit of unlimited power. They had reached the main course, and when they lifted the silver dishes covering their plates – hers smaller and with a ring on it that made it easier to grab with her beak – it revealed bowls of deliciously steaming goulash with a potato dumpling in the middle and garnished with parsley. It smelled of roast beef, greasy fumes, peppers and onions, hearty and herbal.

'A simple meal,' Phileander crooned, 'but one of my old favourites. It recalls my youth, when I used to dine with the other acolytes in the refectory. What a hopeful, heady time that was.' He sighed and breathed in the vapours with his eyes closed. 'I wanted you to share that with me on this special night.'

'How … thoughtful,' Torment crowed. Spicy and heated foods did not agree well with her corvid stomach. She glanced at the alabaster bust on the mantlepiece, half in shadow. It had not been there the night before. Catalina had brought it here just as Torment had instructed her.

'I've had strange dreams about that time,' Phileander mused, tasting a bite of the red-dripping meat. 'Visitations of spirits, half beast, half human.' He chuckled. 'What do you make of that?'

'I've had strange dreams too,' deflected Torment nervously, 'of … this very room.'

The philosopher smiled. 'That is only natural, my dear. These last two nights must have been overwhelming compared to your simple prior life.'

'But I've had those dreams before.'

His forehead creased. 'How do you mean?'

'I … I knew this room before I entered it for the first time, master.' Torment let the statement sink in a little and puffed herself up. He regarded her with a hint of uncertainty playing around his eyes and the corners of his mouth. 'In those dreams, I was human. And you sat where you sit now, only less wrinkled and' – she cocked her head – 'happier.'

Phileander was speechless – didn't even blink anymore. He had frozen with his wine cup half aloft.

'In them, you called me by a different name.' Torment kept the tension up, while Phileander grew paler and paler. This was a pivotal point, she realised. There was no telling how he would react. This was why she had chosen the very last night for this – there were no second chances either way, and she needed as much of his goodwill for this as she could get. *'Elisaveta.'*

First, he just stared at her, wide-eyed and trembling. 'Stop playing games!' he blurted out then, slamming his cup down on the table so hard it spilled. 'Did Vladimir put you up to this? I should never have told him that name.'

'No,' croaked Torment with a fright she hardly had to feign. 'It was a dream, my love, I swear. Please.'

'What?' His hands were clenched white-knuckled around the edge of the table and he was halfway to standing up. 'What did you say?'

'It was a dream!' She cawed and fluttered back onto the headrest of the chair on her side of the table.

She thought a vein must surely soon burst in his temple, so tense did he look. But the philosopher closed his eyes and began to take deep, slow breaths to calm himself. He settled back into his chair.

'Forgive me, Torment. I didn't mean to frighten you.' He opened his eyes again, and she saw that they were moist. 'It makes sense, in a way. The ritual may have …' It seemed Phileander dared not continue, his mouth agape. He just looked at her long and pensively, his hands clasped together, and then he began to drum absentmindedly with the fingers of one hand on the back of the other.

'What, master?'

'It … may have bestowed upon you traces of her … being.'

Very well. She had her beak in him. Now it was time to twist it. 'Tell me about her.'

He shuddered and looked down. 'No, I … I don't think that's a good idea. There is …' With a suddenly wary expression, he looked back up at Torment. 'There is something I forgot. This all has to do with something I—'

With a flourish of her wings, she leapt to the centre of the table. 'In those dreams,' she crowed, 'I sometimes hummed a song, although I never heard it before. Do you know it?'

Before the philosopher could reply, Torment began to echo the melody of Elisaveta's lullaby. She couldn't *hum*, of course, but she could come pretty close with deep and throaty crows. Slow, sultry, bittersweet tones. As she sang, she hopped closer to Phileander, keeping one of her eyes fixed on him.

This was it. Behind his eyes, she could see his defences crumbling. She sang those slow and mournful tones, the lullaby become a dirge, and were she human now, she knew that she would weep. She wanted him to hurt, her love, to suffer as she was hurting. He backed away, pushing his chair across the floor tiles with a piercing screech.

'Stop, stop!' The philosopher raised his hands.

Torment stopped singing. Not of her own will but Phileander's. The binding curse still held.

'I will tell you,' he gasped, 'if you don't sing that song again. Not ever.'

The philosopher struggled to compose himself, sweat glistening on his ashen pate in the flicker of the candles. With a shaking hand, he seized the wine bottle and emptied it into his cup, draining it in one gulp.

'Elisaveta used to sing it when she was … pregnant. In fact, you remind me of her sometimes.' Phileander looked at her miserably, slumped as if after an exhausting feat of strength. 'It makes it so much harder to do what I must—' His voice broke at the last word and tears filled his eyes. 'Excuse me.'

At that, he stood up, almost knocking over his chair, and hurried out of the room.

～

SHE WAS GETTING close, Torment could feel it. When he had forced her to stop singing, her obedience had felt *wonky* in a way. It had set in with a grind where before it had been swift and absolute. He would soon be back in the dining room. Perhaps she could …

Torment took a step back into her Hall of the Conscious Mind. Several quills were scribbling away at a tome of anxieties, a dozen notes of ideas and a sprawling diagram of her plan. She knew it well enough;

no need to go over it again. Instead Torment fluttered to the cage door, opened it and shot downward like an arrow. Down and down she dropped, the city at the bottom of her mind palace speeding towards her. She spread her wings at the last second to land on a lamppost on a bridge lined with stacked, haphazard dwellings between which clotheslines were strung. An older memory, and the buildings were still near human-sized. Two corpses were shuffling along the pavement nearby.

'Hey,' Torment cawed, 'you two.'

The corpses paused and turned towards her, waiting. In one, despite its sunken, sallow face, Torment recognised the Marchioness de Sato, wearing a pair of mould-ridden knickers. Torment remembered how the baroness had had her murdered by her lover in the bedchamber.

Torment flew over to them and alighted on a porch balustrade. 'Can you gather all your' – she considered for a moment what she should call them – 'rotting comrades?'

One of them moaned affirmatively, and the two of them shambled off in opposite directions – at an amazingly slow pace. She had no time. This wouldn't do at all.

Torment shot up into the air again and circled wide, searching the ground. There were some of them in narrow alleys, two seemed to be playing chess in a flower garden, and a lone legless torso was dragging itself across her memory of the dream wilds desert. They had really taken her offer to feel at home in her Halls of Memory to heart. But none of those would do. She needed a fresher specimen – one who could speak and spread her message quickly.

She spotted two of them skipping along a park path, hand in hand. Two girls. They looked lively enough.

Torment quickly lowered herself to a rose trellis and, crowing, commanded their attention.

The girls whirled around. 'Yes, Your Highness?' said the one with blond braids.

A searing stab of regret struck Torment as she recognised the face. 'Adelaide?'

The girl smiled, but her expression was quizzical. 'Why, how perfectly sweet that you know my name.'

'Of course I do. You're *my* memory of you.'

Adelaide tipped her head to one side and looked thoughtfully at the girl next to her. That one was smaller, red-haired, and she had red-ringed eyes from crying. Both were pale as porcelain, blue-lipped but otherwise unscathed. Adelaide wore not her light-blue dress but a nightdress, perfectly clean, and her body showed no mark whatsoever from her gruesome death by moth. Although, Torment realised, in a way that had not been her death at all. What she had witnessed in the dream wilds must rather have been the disintegration of Adelaide's spirit. Her body had only withered away afterwards.

'I do not believe we are your memories, queen crow,' said Adelaide then. And she had to be right, because Torment had no idea who that other girl was. 'Her name is Penelope,' Adelaide added, as though she had read Torment's mind. But of course, she was *in* Torment's mind. This stuff would never not be confusing to her.

'Penelope, splendid – no time for this,' croaked Torment. 'I need your help. I need you two to spread the message to all the ...' What, by the All-Mother, should she call this lot? They— oh, but of course. Torment realised then what the tenants in her mind palace were known as. 'To all the Wronged and Rotting. They are to keep a lookout for meddlesome figures sneaking about, probably sporting the sharp-featured face of a human male, long-nosed. They would be, uhm ... rattling chains, I suppose, manipulating things to alter my decisions.' Torment cawed in annoyance. 'Oh, honestly, I have no clue what's going on in here while I'm at the helm.'

'Oh, dear liege, we know perfectly well what you're talking about,' said Adelaide, scrunching up her face. 'Those dreadful pests overran the city the other day like a cackling, screaming swarm of locusts, going on about stopping that beautiful lullaby that had resounded over the streets for hours before they crawled from their holes. Then the song stopped.'

'The other day?' repeated Torment dumbly. 'For hours?' But of course, time flowed differently here. 'Yes. That would have been them.' Torment bent down to the girls. 'They are hiding now, but they must still be around. I am working to weaken them – hopefully wipe them out. But I need all of you to help eradicate this infestation from my palace, understood?'

'As you command,' replied the two girls in unison.

Then they turned on their heels and went to leave the park. Torment looked after them and could soon hear them calling out into the streets. 'Hear, hear,' they were shouting, 'a message from your sovereign!'

She had seen that other girl once before, she recalled, but very briefly, and she was not sure when and where. Had that been a hint of a blood smell on those girls? It must have been Torment's imagination, because if anything, those two had looked rather anaemic. And why had this unfounded sense of guilt gnawed at her while they had been close? As if Torment alone was to blame for the ruin of thousands, as if everything she touched must surely be doomed. Why did she have to bear this responsibility? She was unworthy, she—

Wait a minute. This wasn't her, this was— there, she heard it again. So faint. So far away.

Ba-bump. Ba-bump.

Then it came back to her. She knew whose memories the girls had been. Torment took off and followed the rhythm, the coppery scent, the guilt. There was a secret weapon in her mind palace that she had almost forgotten about. She swept along her Halls of Memory on wings of haste, under underpasses, around corners and down into the darker undercity. There were layers down there she had not seen before. With each visit to this place, Torment noted, it grew more intricate yet.

346

Ba-bump.

Walls rushed past her and the beating grew louder. Torment landed near the grating of a gutter. She knew this must be the same place where she had descended into the sewers of her mind palace earlier, though the surroundings were different now. It was shady and dank, and several levels of footbridges interleaved between here and the surface. There were no rotting vassals nearby – they were probably all heeding her rallying call further up – so Torment levered the grate open with her beak, pushing it aside just far enough to squeeze through the opening. Slowed down or not, time was precious.

She raced through the murky tunnels, the sound of the heartbeat mingling confusingly with the constant dripping of the sullage of her mind. Here, countless corroded bad ideas, false memories and outworn hurts would be flushed away to become fertiliser for fresher, more fruitful thoughts. But the intensifying smell of blood quickly overpowered all others. Strangely – suspiciously – the vampire did not speak up, did not even stir. Whatever Torment was doing here, working to break Phileander's bond, the beast was willingly leaving her to it. Not exactly a reassuring thought, but Torment had no time to dwell on it.

Ba-bump. Ba-bump.

She arrived, touching wet stone with a flutter. It was a bit anticlimactic. In front of her, glinting red in a pitiful ray of light from a tiny crack far above, beat a little heart in a puddle of blood. With each beat, red sludge oozed from a ruptured artery protruding from it, while another flap of blood vessel hanging in the puddle sucked up some of the blood. A perpetual recycling of stale, bloody misery, mixing steadily with her mental sewage. That unrelenting feeling of worthlessness, of irredeemable shame, of being nothing but a cancerous cyst in the fabric of the world, washed over her in waves with every pulse.

This was just what she needed. If Phileander's heart of shame had stopped beating, then why not kick it into life with the pulse of another? Thistlewhisk's heart. This bloody knot of muscle had certainly done a number on her. Could it possibly work, bringing it back? She was not in the dream wilds anymore but the Hitherrealm, hard and unbending to any spirit's will. On the other hand, she had brought that magpie's skull back with her. It had hung around her neck with all the weight of physical reality. She and Vlad had brought scars from that place as real as any.

Torment grabbed the rabbit's heart and sped back through the tunnels, leaving a trail of blood drops behind. She squeezed through the half-open grate and shot up on a spiralling flight path past the interleaving bridges and into the sky. Time was of the essence. This could only work if Phileander had not yet returned.

Fast as lightning, Torment tore through the hovering door and her window into the waking world.

She was back in the dining room – still alone, thankfully – and something was lodged in her throat. Torment hopped over to Phileander's plate, gurgling. She made it there just in time to choke a bloody lump into his goulash without leaving traces on the tablecloth.

Hastily, she mixed it in a little with her beak and made her way back to her end of the table.

～

PHILEANDER CAME BACK, wiping his eyes with a handkerchief, carrying a new bottle of wine. The bottle was old and dusty, its bulbous body wrapped in wicker.

'My last bottle of Monatillado,' he said, sitting down and examining the bottle fondly. 'A sweet, strong red like they don't make them anymore. We can drink to our farewells. Like the old days.'

'Whose old days?' Torment crowed.

'Leave it,' he snapped. 'Just … don't. I'm sorry. Let's lay this subject to rest for tonight.' He stood up, uncorked the bottle and walked over to Torment's end. Carelessly, he dumped the water still in Torment's drinking bowl onto the floor and refilled it with the rich, ruby drink smelling of overripe grapes. 'Better yet, let's lay it to rest forever.'

Phileander walked back to pour his own and sit down, leaving it unspoken that 'forever' and 'tonight' meant much the same to Torment.

He raised his cup. 'To you, Torment.'

'To us,' she replied, 'and the love that … binds us.'

Phileander inhaled sharply and averted his eyes, but he did not say anything to confirm he understood what she was referring to.

'Let's just eat,' he muttered after a while, sipped from his cup and ate.

Torment tasted her small serving of goulash as well. It was seasoned only lightly for her, and it was delicious and comforting. She wondered whether her liking of it was just a symptom of that fragment of Phileander within her. Beneath the shards of Elisaveta's shattered mind, the ancient monster lusting for blood, and the tainted touch of her master and creator, was there even anything that was *her*? Her spirit was held aloft above this maelstrom of doubt only by her sheer desire to break him, be rid of him and fly. She watched as he ate his own share down to the last morsel of meat, wiping up the final dollop of reddish-brown sauce with a bite of dumpling.

When he had finished his plate and laid down his knife and fork, he washed it all down with the rest of his wine. Torment stared at him. Nothing happened. Had she just imagined what had happened when she had returned from her mind palace? Had he really just eaten a rabbit's heart, filled with the essence of shame and self-loathing, or was she just going mad? A bit late to ask herself that now, Torment thought. Of course she was going mad.

Phileander cleared his throat. He looked down at his hands, confused at first, then back at her … but his eyes were misty and distant. His gaze lingered on something unfolding in his mind. His face was completely still, and he was no longer shaking, breathing heavily or clenching his fists. He seemed perfectly calm and eerily quiet.

Then a single tear ran down his cheek.

And another.

Behind his eyes, Phileander was screaming. Torment knew those eyes with the intimacy of one who had drowned in them. Those pupils held a darkness deep and cold as the black between the stars, a wounded soul trapped within. It had only just awoken. The pain that Torment had unchained in his mind echoed in her own, and she knew that a battle was taking place in it. But she could not join it now. Her battle was out here, with him.

Soft paw taps resounded in the silence. Through the half-open dining room door, Vladimir was entering the room. He had impeccable timing.

Slowly, Phileander turned his head. And when his gaze fell on the object that Vlad carried in his mouth, a whimpering moan escaped him. It was a dark-petalled dahlia. Not *the* dahlia, just one that Catalina had procured.

'Oh,' cawed Torment, 'look what the cat brought in.'

'Where did you get that?' breathed Phileander, clearly horrified.

'Never mind where he got that, my love.' Once more, she fluttered closer, landing in the middle of the table. 'It's more important what it comes with.'

His face turned back to her, bloodless and anguished, lips moving mutely.

'A warning,' she crowed.

'What— what is this farce?' he muttered.

With a leap, Vlad was on the table and laid the flower before him.

'What are you doing?'

'What are *we* doing?' Driven by the courage of one who has cornered their prey, she came as close as she could, taking the flower in her talons, and mustered her best Elisaveta voice. 'What have you done, my love?'

He rose to his feet. 'Stop it!'

She fluttered around his head, still holding the flower. 'What have you done?'

'Silence!'

'What have you done to our child?'

Torment had spoken. She had not remained silent. *She had disobeyed.* Victory drew a jubilant cry from her, and she dared to circle him even closer as he screamed and lashed out. Feeling the chains that had bound her burst, she crowed Elisaveta's lullaby, dodging his flailing arms as he stumbled backwards until he collapsed beneath her, wailing and sobbing piteously.

She was free. Torment felt her spirit soar inside her. She was so excited to explore her mind palace now, or perhaps hold a victory celebration in there. Oh, and the world outside. The starry sky beyond the windows and the wind it promised in her feathers. There was no point in putting it off any longer.

'I'm finished with you, old man.'

She flew to the nearest window, but an inch in front of her, the shutters slammed with a clatter, nearly crushing her beak. Torment swooped to the next, but its shutters slammed as well. She tried the door next, but it too slammed shut with a resounding finality – trapping her with the philosopher.

'Oh, Torment, you wondrous creature,' he said, calm and hoarse. 'I will never forget what you have done for me here. I will be sure to return the favour.'

Vlad was mewling and hissing as if in distress.

Torment landed on the ornamental carving atop the door frame, her heart now racing with equal parts triumph and dread. She looked down at Phileander kneeling on the dining room floor. He was holding Vladimir firmly by the scruff of the neck, pinning him down. The cat – so tiny in a human's grip – squirmed and yowled. His claws could reach nothing but smooth, hard tiles to scratch.

'Why,' she cawed in defiance, 'will you rekindle my dying flame of compassion as well? You're welcome, by the way.'

'No.'

He broke Vladimir's neck. It sounded much like snapping a twig. But never had the breaking of a twig resonated in her very marrow like this. Phileander dropped the body and the cat sagged limply to the ground, open-eyed.

'I will be sure to make you suffer before you die. You have caused me a great deal of pain, Torment. And senselessly so, as there is no merit in compassion for the dead.'

Torment did not allow herself to feel the pain of losing Vladimir. Nor the guilt she knew would tear her soul apart if she allowed it.

'You will find,' she said, trying to calm the tempest in her heart, 'that in this case there is some merit for me in the breaking of our bond.'

'Yes. The detail that I forgot, and by your doing, no doubt. Sealed with remorselessness. I still cannot recall it, but I can infer it from the hole in my memory.' He laughed grimly. 'You're far too clever for your own good, you immortals-damned fowl.'

'That's on you. You made me.'

'Do you also find merit in the breaking of Vladimir's neck? Because that's on *you*, Torment. You've rendered yourselves useless, and you had to be aware you know too much to be allowed to live.'

Phileander rose and kicked Vlad's body aside, his little head lolling at an unnatural angle. The philosopher's cold, wet eyes promised death as he stepped closer. There was still a sliver of his control left, Torment sensed, trying to hold her where she sat. His remorse hung on a thread. And Torment's neck would snap as easily in Phileander's hands as Vladimir's.

Right on cue, there sounded a tapping – Catalina. When it didn't open, she rattled and banged on the dining room door, kept shut by whatever sorcery Phileander had conjured up.

But he was distracted for a second, which was enough for Torment to launch herself and land on the bust that had recently been placed on the mantelpiece. Its white marble was cold to her touch. Had the damned woman arrived but a moment earlier, Vlad might still be alive. But it was Torment's fault, of course. This was all her plan, and Catalina acted entirely on her instructions, just as Vladimir had. Maybe she was about to get Catalina killed as well, along with herself.

Satisfied the door would hold, Phileander turned back to Torment. He grinned joylessly as he approached, his eyes screaming murder. But the grin was wiped from his face when he saw what she was perched upon.

'How did that get there?'

It was the bust of Elisaveta he had had made to immortalise the mischievous smile he so adored. Which he had banished to a storeroom for the remainder of eternity.

'It was always here,' said Torment, imitating Elisaveta's velvety contralto almost perfectly. 'It is I, my love. Don't you remember what I told you? I will stay with you forevermore!'

'No,' shrieked Phileander and struck out at her.

She dodged him, wings aflutter. His blows came slow and clumsy. He was just a man, after all, and she a crow.

'Forevermore!'

'Stop! Stop it!'

Phileander grabbed whatever his hands could find and threw it at her, while Torment switched from place to place in rapid swoops, landing on the backs of chairs, windowsills, the edges of vases, the chandelier, and always back to the bust of Elisaveta on the mantelpiece. His projectiles hit only loose black feathers floating where she had stood. Knives flew at her, the wine cup, the bottle, and the candelabra with candles still lit.

'Forevermore!' she kept crowing in Elisaveta's voice.

'Stop it, you pest! You vermin! Grim and ghastly thing!'

'Forevermore!'

'Demon!'

The banging on the door was now accompanied by the satisfying sound of cracking wood.

As she lifted from the bust, it shattered loudly underneath her, struck by a potted plant, and Torment was showered in damp earth.

'Forevermore, my love!'

Phileander howled in despair and ran over to the ruined sculpture. He clutched a splintered half of his wife's face in his hands, his eyes choking with grief.

'Torment,' cried he, 'thing of malice! Bird-devil!'

'Forevermore!'

'You, take your beak out of my heart and die. Just die already!' He reared up and tossed the chunk of marble at her with all his might.

Torment swerved out of the way. The piece of rock broke through the door with a great crash, leaving a jagged hole.

At once, a blue-robed leg kicked another section of wood out of the way and Catalina pushed herself into the room.

Phileander was flustered by the sudden choice of two targets. Catalina used the opportunity to grasp the candelabra from the floor, then ran over to one of the shutters, trying to pry it open with the branching metal in her hand. A ghostly force opposed her, pushing against the wooden flap.

'No,' bellowed Phileander. 'You wretched wench, we are pact-bound.'

'The— pact—' Catalina ground through clenched teeth, 'mentions— no *shutters*!' With the last word, she levered the window open and wedged the candelabra into it. 'Now, Torment!'

Torment was already sweeping towards the gap. In a twisting manoeuvre, she evaded a chair thrown by Phileander, swivelled past Catalina's ample hips, and—

She shot out into the blessed night.

Directly below her, a black figure flashed past her through the window, plunging into darkness.

Chapter 22

A SLIVER OF LIFE

TORMENT SAW THE figure tumble down along the tower wall in the shade of night, falling a great distance before it hit a roof and lay still. A little black bundle. Was that Vladimir? How? He could not have survived, could he? Had Phileander gone as far as to hurl his lifeless body after her?

A fresh night wind brushed through her feathers and she was as free as she had ever dreamed she would be. Night fires scented the air, and the distant muffled chatter of many humans behind stone walls wafted past her. Below, the city's jagged black shapes, dotted with orange lights from a million windows, flowed on and on forever. She circled widely around the silhouette of the Tower of Undreamed Truths. It clung to the flank of the One City, that Moloch heaping centrewards to pierce the sky. The storm she had spared herself from perishing in flashed purple against black. Torment could leave it all behind her now. She had but to fly.

But what if he still lived? What if that had indeed been Vladimir and he was now in pain? They were allies, friends, more than that, even … Torment loved him. She realised that only now as the simplest and most important of truths. Torment loved Vladimir. Like a brother and sometimes more than that. It was not the corrupted caricature of love she had inherited from Elisaveta. No, it was a love she had come to feel entirely by herself. It was her own, more meaningful than any affection she had been capable of as a crow. Torment longed to be able to shed tears now, for she had found a greater purpose. When survival was assured, what remained was to live. And that meant to love and be loved.

Torment propelled herself downwards with powerful thrusts of her wings, slicing through an updraught with a beak-first dive, shooting for the roof onto which the dark figure had fallen.

You have done well, little crow.

All-Mother damn it. Just what she needed. All she wanted was to know whether he lived.

So very well indeed. Now that you have broken our chains, why don't you just … take a step back?

'Leave me alone,' she croaked, still descending at breakneck speed.

Have it your way, little crow. Don't let me keep you from seeing to your friend. See for yourself.

Vicious, mocking laughter resounded in Torment's mind. A grim feeling of foreboding knotted her heart and stomach. She braced her wings against the headwind and slowed, landing right next to the black shape on the roof.

Oh, hail the night eternal.

It was indeed Vladimir. The scent of his blood was overwhelming … intoxicating. In the dream wilds, Torment had smelled this scent many times, and it had affected her. But that had only ever been the *idea* of a blood-scent, an abstract notion manifested in the wake of a spirit's memory and imagination. What she smelled now was something else. Its rich, metallic aroma, so salty, sweet and luscious. The crowning ingredient in the carnal trinity of debauchery and pain: flesh, bone and bright red blood. It beckoned her to feed. No, not her – the thing inside her. Torment shook her head, crowed into the night and fought back against it.

She couldn't. The beast was strong – so much stronger than it had ever been. It dawned on Torment that she had only ever glimpsed a shadow of it inside her. That seal she had broken, having driven Phileander to feel remorse, had bound not just her. *It* was free now too.

But the beast handed her back the reins … willingly.

As the haze lifted, Torment saw him. Lit only by the wan grey glow of the nightly sunthread – but a silvery filament strung from the Everstorm to the far horizon – Vladimir did not move. His neck was morbidly twisted and his skull cracked open. A rivulet ran beneath him, winding its way to the edge of the roof, shimmering black.

Trickle, trickle …

His eyes were open and bloodshot and still as marbles of yellow glass. His scar glistened in the starlight. Torment ran her beak gently through his fur. Should she hide his body? Prevent him from falling prey to scavengers? No. She was a crow; how dared she think this way? There was nothing shameful in becoming carrion. All living things were destined to feed the earth after their own feast had ended. There was a bitter beauty to be found in that. Maybe she should feed on him herself. To commemorate him.

Trickle, trickle, sings the blood.

No. This was not her. *It* was urging her, furtively, from the shadows of her mind palace. Torment understood then – the beast needed her to give in to temptation. It needed her consent. All it could do without it was make it harder to withstand. It was not out of courtesy it kept asking her.

Let me! You pathetic, weak and stupid thing. You must.

The beast was angry now. Torment had touched upon a truth it did not like. Let it do its worst, she thought. Willpower, or at least a hardened familiarity with suffering, she had acquired aplenty. She closed her eyes, beak buried in Vladimir's fur. His musk consoled her. Just one last whiff of it and she would fly. A last gentle stroke over the smooth skin underneath. Smooth and cold and … unscarred.

Why was he unscarred? Why, if he had suffered this scar on his face when the giant cat had clawed him, had he remained unmarked when that clockwork knight had impaled him? The scars on Torment's leg where Ogden's monstrosity of the vengeful dead had bitten her … what made those wounds any different from Vladimir's? And later, when he had fought so fiercely in Phileander's Hall of the Conscious Mind, Vlad had suffered so many cuts and bruises, he had been drenched in his own blood by the end of it. But those injuries, they seemed to have simply … vanished.

Do you get it now, you witless bird? Despicable, imbecilic meat-thing. Do it. Feed on him. Before he feeds on you – on us.

'No,' crowed Torment weakly. She felt Vladimir's cool body twitch under her beak. With a sickening grinding sound, bones shifted, spine twisted, skull fused. 'No …' A gasp tore from Vlad's throat, a coppery-sweet scent of meat-rot – carnivore, predator, beast-breath. 'No.' She was unable to move. Yet no curse bound her, neither a spell nor some spirit's work. It was but her own mortification. 'Come on … fight it, crony.'

You fool. Dig your beak into his neck, drink him dry – do it now.

Vlad's eyelids flickered, his chest heaved and an unnatural heat surged through him. Then his breath eased and his eyes fixed on her. Not yellow but smouldering red.

She flapped her wings to rise, cawing in fear, but found herself pressed to the bloodstained shingles faster than she could see what had happened. He was pinning her down, claws out. He was cutting into her chest, leaving a burning pain and a wetness.

Red eyes leered down at her. Nostrils flared and whiskers quivered at the scent of Torment's blood.

'Vladimir,' she choked out with what air she had left.

That cat is long gone, birdie,' rang a voice in her head. It was the distorted likeness of the voice Vlad had picked up in the dream wilds. Those red eyes above her smirked with a vile amusement. *'He had been fading ever since I first met you in the birthplace of my kind. Yonderrealm. Dream wilds. So many silly names you call it.'*

You need me, little crow. The two horrid voices tore at her sanity, ripping like talons across the tissues of her brain. The one in her and the one from Vlad like two maddening fragments of a greater whole colliding, interfering. *Let me take over and we shall gorge on him.*

She wanted to tell Vlad what she knew, that it needed his permission, that he could deny the vampire.

'The cat invited me in long ago,' mocked the red eyes. Those things were mind readers. Perfect predators. It ran a claw along Torment's neck, and she could feel the warmth of her life pour through her feathers. *'He gave himself up so readily, enamoured by my power. Understandable. It was I who led him to investigate the* Liber Somniorum, *paving the way for you to loosen our chains on your little … field trip.'*

Torment pecked at its paws, but the meagre wounds she inflicted healed faster than she could watch. Her struggle grew weaker with every slash of its claws, every lick of her blood it devoured.

'I swallowed them all.' Vlad's snarling echo in her head sounded more distant as it bit and bit and drained her. The world receded into darkness. *'Every sorry scrap of a soul I could find. Tiny, insignificant souls, hardly enough to sate me for even a day.'*

Oh, let me, little crow. Would you have it kill us without a fight? This thing is but a fragment of me, a sad copy of what we could be. Your spirit is a feast to my kind, so sweet and strong. I would rip this impostor apart, make its strength my own. Yes, sweet and strong.

'Yes, Torment,' added Vladimir's voice, *'let it. So I can drink it up along with you, merge with it, become great old Edimmu again.'* Another bite into her neck. Her skin and feathers would be in tatters by now, her body broken beyond healing. *'Oh, I shall scour the night again, wash Bastion clean with blood. It shall run over cobbles of this meat-huddle, all shall drown in it, and the sun shall blacken once again.'*

Yes, little crow. Let me. It doesn't know. It thinks us weak. It has not seen inside you. I *am old Edimmu. It* is *nothing.*

What was even left of her? Torment's memories dwindled; her spirit seeped away like sand through a sieve. To love and be loved. Had she loved this monster that stood atop her, fed on her, mocked her? Why? Why was it so dark, and why did the darkness tear at her so painfully? The little crow was confused.

Let me.

It had suffered enough injury to be doomed. That much the crow still understood. But there was another thing it remembered.

It took a step back.

THE LITTLE CROW tumbled into a storm. Darkness engulfed it, and a roaring noise, and it remembered it was once more than a crow. She was Torment, and this was her mind palace. Where was her Hall of the Conscious Mind? Or was this it? She was tossed about like a leaf, and all was chaos and violent winds.

There, above her, spinning with dizzying speed, was a circular patch of starry sky. Torment tore herself away from the elements and rose higher. Her wings ached, buffeted by the swirling currents, and she felt as if she were being beaten and plucked bare. But she persevered, teetering into the black expanse.

She had never seen night in her mind palace before. Exhausted, Torment glided away from the serpentine funnel cloud she had just emerged from. Above her, black rain clouds covered most of the stars, and it was pouring with a thunderous noise. The drops were thick and sticky on her plumage.

Blood.

It was coming down upon the city in a terrible torrent. Her Halls of Memory were flooded with it, and everything in them. No wonder she was forgetting so much. The blood rain threatened to drag her down with it. Up, up and past the clouds. Torment pushed desperately, pushed towards her Hall of Reverence. It must be there, the stowaway, the thing of terror – the vampire.

They hardly looked like clouds at all. More like an upturned wind-swept basin looming overhead, its surface undulating like billowing black silk. And Torment submerged in it. It was all blood, a thick veil of it enveloping her, pressing into her eyes, her nose, her beak. She was choking on it.

She emerged on the other side, spitting and gasping for air. The fields of grass below were wilted. Her meadows had become a waste of decay. Torment shook herself and blinked the blood from her eyes. When she looked up, she saw that it was not, in fact, night. The sun was where it had always been in the sky of her mind palace. But it was black. It was but a hole in the firmament, a bleak void where once a hot and blazing light shone down. Now the only light left was the twilight of the stars ... and two red glowing dots.

They were eyes but a short flight ahead of her, near where she had once found the shaft that led into the depths of her despair. The beast must have crawled out of it. She made out its outline – a slender, long-limbed humanoid.

Despite her terror, Torment flew closer. It was all that was left to do. There was nowhere else to go, no one else to turn to. Through the pervasive stench of blood, a primal scent pierced, awakening her deepest instincts … dormant, ancestral instincts. 'Flee,' those instincts urged her, 'fly and hide. Fire keeps it at bay. Fire and light.'

But there was no fire and no light and nowhere left to hide.

The vampire was hunched over something. It perked up at her approach, red eyes burning into her soul, drawing her closer. Long, pointed ears stood out from its elongated head. Its blood-smeared mouth grinned, clawed hands holding the shell of Elisaveta's shrunken spirit form. The woman's skeletal body seemed lost in those loose white robes. Torment felt it gone from her, the part that had been Elisaveta; her madness, her longing, her grief and her pain, all gone. Torment felt hollowed out. Vladimir was dead and she was dying and it was so hard to feel anything. Anything but numb dread.

She landed right next to it. The beast exuded hopelessness, like the antithesis of a warming flame in winter or a guiding light in the night. On its back sat large folded wings, white and leathery, with vicious claws protruding from the joints.

You know that we will both perish if I don't take over.

It did not move its mouth. Its voice rang out from the very air around her. A dread voice, cowing her, smothering her, pricking her like needles in the backs of her eyes.

I can defeat this cat for us and consume what it carries, and your body would heal. Just let me.

'What would become of me?'

Oh, little crow. The beast rose. It stood more like a giant vulture than a man, its arms almost long enough for its claws to rake the ground. *That is up to you. You just have to weigh a sliver of hope against none of it at all.*

Torment knew her decision already. She was too craven to condemn herself and take the beast down with her. She was too desperate for even the slimmest hope of life and freedom. And perhaps if she let it fight what had become of Vladimir, the two abominations would rend each other apart and rid the world of their miserable existence.

'Do it, then,' she crowed quietly. She bowed her head and resigned herself to ruin.

There was something about the absence of all hope that felt relieving. When there was nothing left to do and all that remained was fear, that fear turned into a cynical sort of bliss. Torment did not struggle when the beast's bony fingers closed around her neck and body and lifted her up. When it broke her wings, she was almost grateful for the pain, for it reminded her of being alive. And when it tossed her into the black shaft from whence it had crawled, Torment simply closed her eyes and surrendered to the shadow and the weightlessness. She was all alone now.

AND THERE SHE lay, in pain and darkness, and far above her she thought she could see flashes of battle on the rooftops of the One City streaking past an opening she could not reach. Soon she had forgotten her name again. The crow knew only that it needed to fly, but its wings were broken, and that it needed to be safe with kin or friends, but it had no one, and the only thing safe was the certainty of its eventual demise.

Who was the beast it saw through the crack in the blackness above? It was a cat – cats were dangerous. The crow should be afraid of it. But it was beyond fear. Instead it felt remorse and loss and a loneliness that was akin to vanishing altogether, like a drop of ink dissolving in a vast body of water. The cat appeared to be in pain. A beak struck it many times, in the chest, in the back, on the head. The cat was bleeding. The crow thought it recognised the cat. How strange. Why would a crow be acquainted with a cat? But 'acquainted' was too weak a word for what the crow felt, which was a painful but pointless emotion, and it pushed it aside as it watched and listened in vain. A howl and a hiss and a black beak buried in an eye. The crow caught a hint of the taste of eyeball fluid on its tongue, mixed with blood, fresh flesh and nerve tissue, sugar-sweet cerebral plasma and iron-rich brain. Something, somewhere, was rejoicing in a glorious, invigorating feast.

Blood trickled down onto the crow from the opening above. The crack revealed a beak, buried deep in the cat's skull through a shattered eye socket. Whose beak was that? The image confused the crow. The cat was struggling, lashing out with bloodied claws, but it grew weaker with each lunge. And the crack above receded further and further as blood still trickled from it, along with the odd bit of brain. Whatever hole the little crow had been thrown into to die was deepening. Soon, it thought, there would be nothing left around it but a black void in which it would languish eternally.

As the crow writhed on the cold floor of her prison, she felt a sharp object pressing against her chest. There was no light, so she could only feel it with her beak and her shattered wings, which sent a pain up her spine every time she moved them. There was something around the crow's neck – a hard, oblong object with a pointed end. A skull. She remembered this skull. It had once borne her shame, but now it gave her strength. The crow's name was Torment, it recalled, and the skull was a token of the first time she had brought death to a soul. It was the first of her Wronged and Rotting, and she had commanded it to guard something precious. A memory. Now it was precious no longer and it was lost, washed away by blood and pain. So the magpie had returned to its mistress.

'Help me,' Torment croaked, the wretched rattle of her voice haunting the silence.

A creaking and cracking, a twisting and rattling, a harking to Torment's command. The skull around her neck was moving and changing. But there was something else answering her as well. Through distant walls of grave earth she heard a many-voiced lament. It was them, her faithful dead, all still there somewhere. She had been mistaken. She was not weak, nor alone or lost. The magpie's skull burst from the band around her neck as it grew and grew. Even without light or warmth, Torment sensed the great skeleton of a bird unfolding before her, sensed its expectant, empty and obedient eyes.

'Oh, Bigbones,' Torment breathed as a great tension was released and the tiniest spark of warmth refilled her heart, 'please get me out of here.'

Dragging herself closer, her beak feeling the magpie's thin legs and up to its curved ribcage, Torment tried to grab hold of it somehow. But the giant simply grasped her in its great bony talons and took off. Torment heard the faint clicking of joints as bone wings flapped, the skinless blades of which should not, by any logic Torment knew, allow the thing to fly.

Torment felt a soft brush of air as they ascended. A dull light shone down upon her servant and saviour, drawing dark grey branches of bone against the blackness, stretching and twisting and moving as they would underneath the muscles, skin and feathers of a living bird. It turned its great head to meet Torment's grateful gaze. It was more than her servant or her subject. It was a part of her, a strength she had conquered for herself. The magpie skeleton evaded the steady stream of blood from the onrushing hole above them and spiralled right into it.

They launched through the opening into a clear and endless night of stars. The ground below was a featureless waste of dust, stretching into infinity in all directions, shooting away beneath them. There was only one destination. A relentless trickle of blood descended from somewhere above. And so they climbed higher, ever towards the blackened sun.

The vampire was feeding now. It would be enraptured in its gorging. Torment could feel it in the air, in the very fabric of what her mind palace had become. The time to strike was now.

Chapter 23

A FLIGHT OF
DEFIANCE

THE BLOOD POURED from a gash that seemed to have been slashed into the night itself. With clawed hands the vampire clung to its edges, his face buried in it, drinking and basking in blood. With languid beats of pallid wings it held itself aloft. The beast took no notice of the huge skeletal bird flying towards it, carrying Torment in its talons.

Briefly, she remembered when they had invaded Phileander's Hall of the Conscious Mind and the philosopher's spirit had appeared to them hunched over his telescope's ocular. The vampire was looking through the eyes of Torment's body out into the waking world, listening with her ears, feeling the wind in her feathers, tasting the blood with her beak. While it did so, the beast was blind to what was going on in here.

Torment let Bigbones circle the gash in the sky once, examining her adversary. Past the vampire's lustfully writhing form she could see a roof, its shingles reflecting the faint shimmer of the sunthread, and Vladimir's ravaged face and ripped ears. He was in the throes of death. No, not him – the vampire who had snuffed him out and taken his body.

It was hard to hold on to her memories, to keep them alive and focus on who she was and what she wanted. Had Vlad really been 'snuffed out'? Could she be sure that he was beyond recovery?

What a foolish thought. Torment wasn't even sure whether *she* was beyond recovery.

'I need to regain control of my body,' she said. 'Get that thing away from the window, ram it, pull it, anything, then toss me through.'

The magpie made another turn and remained silent. A quiet indecision seemed to emanate from it. Was it afraid?

'Don't worry, crony, you're hardly his type,' she crowed. 'You know, bit too lean and ... dry. No offence.'

Torment saw it tip its mighty skull over her.

'Come on, you can do it. What could he possibly do to you? I mean, I beat him to the peck. You're bone-dead already.'

Torment doubted it had been her powers of persuasion or her tactful reassurance. Perhaps it had just taken the magpie a little while to understand her instructions, or it had simply needed to manoeuvre itself into the best possible position for the swoop. Either way, the bird skeleton pushed forward now with a mighty sweep and, with Torment in its grasp, shot like an arrow at the white-winged fiend.

This was it. One last hurrah before her spirit would most probably be torn to shreds, leaving this beast as the sole possessor of her mortal coil.

She heard a sickening crunch and a screech that chilled her to the marrow, then the night was wheeling around her as she plunged through the—

Torment's beak was stuck deep in the cat's skull. She was sucking on a torn artery. The cat's heart still pumped hot blood through it. Nauseated, Torment pulled her beak out, and it produced a sucking sound that made her stomach turn. This was not just any dying creature … it was Vladimir.

No, it wasn't. Couldn't be. As if to prove her wrong, the cat's fatal wounds began to close before Torment's eyes. Its convulsions subsided. Torment was still dizzy from her harsh reawakening, but she was alert enough to hurry and stick her beak under the cat's body and hoist it over the edge into the depths of the city below.

She watched his four flailing limbs being swallowed up by the gloom. Torment would be safe for now. If Vladimir was still in there somewhere, he might just have a fighting chance. Or he would just shatter and die. No, that was unlikely. She had seen him recover in seconds from a broken neck and a cracked skull. Those things could heal, and they might be able to read minds, but they couldn't make a flightless body grow a pair of wings. Or if they did, then not very quickly. Or so Torment hoped.

She examined herself as she regained full control of her senses. She ran her beak through her feathers, stretched her wings, felt inside and under her skin. She was uninjured. The vampire had healed all her wounds. And she was no longer locked in a deadly struggle with Vlad. Torment did not need the beast inside anymore to save them. Could she revoke her consent, condemn it again to the depths of her despair? Torment had a gnawing fear that the chains that had bound it there had always been part of Phileander's binding spell – now broken.

It felt naive to believe this was over. As long as it was there inside her, she would never truly be free. She needed to find a safe place to rest. Torment was exhausted – too exhausted to further ponder her fate, make battle plans or mourn Vlad. She took off into the night. And after circling around the Tower of Undreamed Truths, she left it behind her, as she did the great spire mounting in the Everstorm. She left all of it behind and steered outward, heading for the edge of the city so many thousands of miles ahead. Things were said to be more peaceful further from the centre, more predictable. She longed to find a garden or a park and the company of other crows.

Torment staggered in the air. What was she fleeing from? Who had the cat been she had just thrown off a roof? *Torment.* Was that … her name? Why? Where did she come from; where was she heading? Why was she so unbearably sad, and why did her head—

A jerk, sudden and painful, and she was yanked back into her mind palace.

Slender fingers gripped her tightly. She was but a tiny bundle of trembling black feathers, and the beast squeezed her so hard, it felt as though she might burst like a grape at any moment. The vampire's face closed in on her, a protruding, snout-like mouth filled with serrated rows of teeth and curved canines, a delicately quivering nose somewhere between that of a man and a serpent, and its hairless, almost translucent skin contorted with irritation and wounded pride. But there was something else in the embers of its eyes – the sadistic gaze of a predator at its struggling prey, at a toy whose suffering might bring it pleasure.

You are not weak, little crow, I give you that. For the meat-thing that you are, for such a pathetic slave to a mortal shell and a tiny whimpering imagination, you are a resilient pest. I shall admire your perseverance as I squash your soul and devour it.

The crow tried desperately to remember where she was, and why, and who this horrid creature was that looked down on her, crushing her and sending a voice of screaming pain into her head.

Around them stretched an endless wasteland of grey dust and desolate cold. A giant bird's skull stuck beak down in the ground beside them. The crow knew this skull, but it was so hard to focus.

The winged beast raised a clawed finger and grinned ... then stuck it into her belly. It began to rummage in her guts, and the crow was in such terrible pain, she thought she must come apart entirely and die.

But this was not her true body, she remembered. This was her spirit form and she was in her mind palace. Or the blackened corpse of it.

Next to her, something was moving in the bird skull's eye sockets. She saw stars flitting past through them, spires in the distance. The waking world. In the Hitherrealm, she was still gliding through the air high above the One City.

The pain made it so hard to focus. And she was so much smaller than the fiend that tormented her. She had once been as tall as it was, she recalled.

A *vampire*, that was what it was. An ancient undying killer, a remnant from a dark age of the world. It pulled its claw out of her and licked off the blood. Then it lifted her towards its open mouth – a gaping black maw lined with a hundred knives.

She had been a woman once, many times the size of a crow. Part of her was still almost human. This beast could hardly swallow her whole if she ...

The crow grew. Most of its feathers contracted back into thickening skin. Her growing body pried open the beast's grip, and it growled as she fell to the dust, pressing her new hands to her bleeding belly to keep her entrails from spilling out.

I taught you that trick, remember?

The beast crouched down next to her, relishing the crow's agony. Her mouth was dry and full of dust.

Thunder – then a sudden quake of the earth, sending the vampire reeling.

It soared up on pale wings reflexively, snarling. Cracks appeared in the ground.

'I do, actually,' panted the woman. 'I even improved upon it.'

It had just been the flash of a memory and an idea as she had glimpsed the tip of a wing through the bird skull's eye socket a few paces to her left. The quake had made the skull topple over. She recalled a sip of a potion, the scaling of a castle wall. And she felt her arms elongate, bones reshape, the tickle of feathers growing, and she knew that it had worked.

You are only delaying the inevitable. Stop doing this to yourself and surrender.

As the vampire descended, she pushed off and beat her new wings as the ground shook once again with a deafening rumble and the searing pain in her stomach threatened to pull her down again. But she whirled around her enemy and flew over to the skull.

Something shiny poked out of the dust near it – the tip of a golden crown.

No time to look at it. The beast was closing in and she was growing weak and cold, and she bled profusely as she crawled to the skull.

She pressed her face into it as if it was a mask, looking through its eyeholes, and—

A throbbing pain in her corvid body. A concussive disorientation. She was lying on a roof again, a chill wind ruffling her feathers. While she had been struggling within her mind palace, her unconscious body must have run into a tower or chimney and fallen. That would explain the quakes.

It was so hard to remember, to focus – something was urgent, but … what? All she knew was that she had to fight. She had to get to safety. The crow fluttered dazedly under the eaves of a nearby dormer window and cowered there. Hopefully, it would shelter her from—

Yanked back inside, again in her humanoid form, she was dragged backwards by the feathers sprouting from her head. Her enemy had ripped the magpie's skull off her face and thrown it into the dirt.

This is futile toiling and wallowing, little meat-maggot. Flesh-slave. Your life, it trickles away. You inflict such senseless torment on yourself. Why would you not let this end?

Its claws dug into her scalp as it dragged her along. But her own hands had claws now too. Nails like a crow's talons. She struck wildly and blindly at its arms.

With an irritated growl, it spun her around and pulled her neck towards its bared teeth.

It was sheer instinct that made her grow a beak. It sprouted in seconds, a long and stately black appendage with which she pecked at the fiend's hideous face. Right in its eye, causing it to scream at an inhuman pitch that nearly burst her eardrums.

The eye began to grow right back, the beast howling in anger and then … intrigue. It released her. It began to circle her, growling and spreading its wings in menace.

Yes, you may have that dance, little crow. But forgive me for knowing only the waltz of ruin, the waltz of war and torment in the night to the steady trickle of your sweet, sweet blood.

It kept saying this word, rattling her. *Torment …*

The beast shot forth and she fluttered sideways, pecking at its lashing arms. She fought with the vicious abandon of a cornered animal. All the injuries she inflicted healed instantly, while every scratch she received left her body colder and weaker and wetter with blood. There was still a near-debilitating wound to her stomach, which she had suffered earlier in circumstances shrouded in violent confusion.

But this was only her spirit's form. She was in a mind palace. What did it even mean for a spirit to suffer injury? 'Harm come to your spirit,' she recalled a kind crone telling her, 'should trouble your more than cuts and bruises and broken bones. The death of a soul leaves not a corpse to feed the earth, it leaves a monster.'

She was so vulnerable. To be vulnerable felt as essential to her spirit as it seemed contradictory to her adversary's. It was a good thing, she thought. It was something worth defending.

It rushed at her like lightning, lunging, cutting deep. She hacked at it, but her beak did not connect and she staggered. The dust at her feet was spattered and soaked with her blood, shining black under a dark sun.

Torment. For the briefest moment, she saw herself reflected in the vampire's freshly regrown eye just before its red glow reignited and scorched away her mirror image. She beheld a bloodied, naked figure that could have sprung from a book of old myths, black-winged, with a beak protruding from a woman's face. It reminded her of something. A mask in the shape of a raven's beak – a plague doctor's mask. A jester's cap. A king's fool. A king himself.

So much came back to her, an onslaught of confusing fragments. She tried to sort her thoughts as she and the vampire continued to circle each other. The beast was toying with her. Its desire to see her suffer, its arrogant confidence in its own invincibility, its sheer pleasure in killing slowly, gave her precious time.

A glint of gold caught her eye. She remembered it, had seen it moments ago – a golden crown. She made a shaky, wing-flapping leap to the artefact and pulled it from the dirt. She had seen this crown before, adorning the head of a giant toad. It had become the jester-king's crown afterwards. And now …

You cling to foolish hopes. Your spirit is broken. You fought well and your misery was, oh … so sweet. But this is becoming undignified, so I shall end our sanguinary dance now. Thank you ever so kindly.

'My name is Torment,' she murmured, 'and this … this is my crown.'

Desperate delusions. Hold on to them as you enter the void, little crow.

The beast bent down for the kill, claws and teeth bared, promising there would be no more games or hesitation.

But its charge was cut short when something grabbed hold of its ankle.

A hand had emerged from the dust. The vampire growled, jerking its leg away. With an unsettling *snap*, the hand came off at the wrist, dangling from the fiend's slender shin like a tasteless ornament.

374

'This is one of my loyal subjects,' Torment observed. 'I am the Queen of the Wronged and Rotting, and they are heeding my call.' She said it more to herself than to her enemy as she realised it. 'They have been clawing their way up through the dust under which you have buried my memories.'

Another hand sprouted from the ground like a morbid, twisted flower of bone and tattered flesh, then another, groping for the vampire's feet and legs, clutching at its wings as it tried and tried in vain to take flight.

No, filth! Rotting, unworthy, bloodless filth!

Her legion's sweet smell of decay rose to Torment's nose. It smelled almost homely. A comfort. The ground had come alive, like an old carcass swarming with maggots. All the dead things were digging, crawling out of the dirt onto the starlit plains, converging on the beast.

Get this filth off me!

As its dread voice raked through Torment's mind, its mouth spewed haunting howls of fury.

Torment still held the golden crown in her hands, a trickle of blood running through the feathers on her arms, down her fingers and along the shining ring of metal spikes.

'I think it's all still there underneath these grey wastes, isn't it?'

The growing crowd of moaning, rotting cadavers held off the vampire for the moment, but they could not harm it. Her subjects fell, rent to ribbons, and it was only their sheer numbers that slowed the beast.

'My name is Torment, but … they don't torment me anymore, my Wronged and Rotting. I'm at peace with my guilt. Only you still torment me.'

I will more than torment you, you filthy vermin. Your spirit shall be kept lucid and in pain as I digest it, trapped and humiliated as I was, and you shall forever drown in blood and shame and misery!

It had nearly clawed its way through all the walking corpses that had risen from the ground, all the many hundreds of them. It scattered their shrivelled, putrid pieces in the wind as it inched towards Torment.

'I'm free of shame and misery.' Still she was talking more to herself. She had nothing to say to this parasite. She had everything to say to herself. 'I accept all that I am.'

A dam was broken. She was not just a being of flesh and bone and feather. She was not a homunculus. She was no creation of Phileander or the baroness or the crow master. No one else had named her. She was Torment, a crow's dream of being a woman, a spirit's dream of being alive and a dream of being the All-Mother up in the sky. She was a hope of once finding love without regret; she was queen of the discontented dead and mistress of this tiny, wondrous fraction of the universe that was her. And she was very fond of shiny things, so she appreciated this beautiful crown and put it on her head.

The vampire had severely decimated her forces, piling up rotting detritus all around and wading through putrescent sludge. Torment hated what was happening to her people, but this was their home, and they were defending it.

And they had bought her the time she needed to come into her own. For what was her mind if not a ship and she the helmswoman? The ground trembled and thunder rolled through her mind palace. It was her doing this time. Yes, she was a ship that could pierce the veil of worlds if she knew where to steer it. She had once created a door that led from the dream wilds into this place. Doing it the other way around wasn't really all that different.

An eternity of pain, fleshling. That's what you'll get for pestering me. You shall come to curse your very existence, you filth-thing, prey-thing, meat!

Twisted shapes broke through the surface of the ground, more branched, larger and stiffer than the limbs of corpses. Instead of the stench of life departed, they exuded the earthy and opulent stench of life in full swing. They were dense tangles of damp wood hung with pointed leaves, winding upwards. Rustling, creaking, crackling. Mangrove trees formed a ring around the battlefield. Finally, their arching roots burst forth, kicking up grey clouds of dust that resembled a leafless, upturned mirror of their canopy, and the trees settled down to rest.

At the centre of the cordon, the vampire tore apart the last three standing corpses in a spasmodic frenzy, adding them to the scattered piles of severed body parts. When it was done, it stood with its chest pumping, a winged god of violence enthroned on a mound of unbidden sacrifices. It looked not exactly out of breath but certainly agitated, its grimace an even more ferocious, deeply etched sculpture of hate.

You have displeased me. You have enraged me and spoiled even the sweet pleasure of torturing you. For over a thousand years have I not waged my wrath, you ill-made breed? You meat-filth. I shall not suffer you to defile this glorious night any further.

The ring of mangroves stemmed from her memory of the Mellow Marshes, of course, but the trees were more than that. A murky light shone through the curved, tapering gaps between their knotty roots, accompanied by a thick, fragrant mist wafting over the fallen dead. Pathways into the dream wilds, into her queendom of the wandering dead. Torment smiled. She sensed them. They were answering her summons.

The filth dares to smile! It roared and raked a claw through the detritus at its feet, spraying rotten entrails and shards of bone in a semicircle. *You have no right to be smug with me!*

It pushed itself off the ground and rose into a vicious dive, but a humming distracted it.

A large shadow shot through one of the root portals and crashed into the vampire, sending them both whirling through the air and into the top of a mangrove, snapping its branches and rustling its leaves. Intertwined in a writhing struggle, they fell to the ground.

The buzzing form was black as night, with vast, thin, vibrating wings. Crawling, jabbing, segmented legs jutted from its bulbous body, and it had huge shining orbs for eyes beneath delicate combed antennae. A moth. It dribbled a trail of viscous, pungent liquid from a hole in its chest as it fought.

But that was only the vanguard. Torment sensed the connection to her many subjects, a latent whisper hanging in the air, drifting in with the fog. She had bridged three worlds: the realm hither, the realm yonder, and in between, the realm of her own mind. She was at home in all of them. Perhaps she always had been; perhaps all spirits were.

Her hordes arrived to muster. Undead of all sizes and shapes shuffled into the cordon of trees, many of them bizarrely amalgamated, most not even remotely human except for parts like hands or faces sprouting from limbs or snaking tendrils of mouldering flesh. A groaning and gurgling echoed through her mind palace, a slurping and scuffling and wheezing. The mist that billowed around them was a cuttable blanket of putrescent fumes. It was glorious.

Torment picked up the magpie's skull again and peered through its eyeholes. In the Hitherrealm, above a rooftop of the One City, as seen through the eyes of a huddled crow, the night sky was turning rosier and the sunthread growing thicker by the minute. Her memory was returning, and she remembered very clearly the effect the sun had had on the vampire when she had allowed it to possess her in the desert.

With a thud and a spray of something pungent, the moth's head rolled to Torment's feet, its antennae stained and torn. She turned to see the body of the great insect, its shredded wings flapping and broken legs flailing as it crashed blindly into the mangroves and entangled itself.

The vampire flapped its wings, kicking at the tentacles that kept wrapping around its legs, dragging it back down. Over the incessant drone of her legions, its garish cries of outrage went almost unnoticed.

If the beast remained locked in battle in her mind palace until daybreak, all would be over. All Torment's army had to do was hold it until sunlight filtered through the bird skull's eyes. Then she would press it like a mask over its hideous face – if she could get close enough – and the vampire's gaze into the sun would burn it to ashes. Her body back in the waking world would surely burn with it, as would, in all likelihood, her mind palace. Perhaps Phileander had not been so far off in his vision of her greater purpose. She was to die after all, just not to the end he had envisioned. Torment found she was perfectly happy with that. It was a fair price to pay for ridding the world of this terror she watched ravage the ranks of her rotting subjects.

Torment closed her eyes, shutting out the din of this carnage. She had tried to meet her enemy with force and knew that she would be of no help to her faithful dead. But this was her mind they were all occupying. And in her hand she held the key to her consciousness. All she needed was for dawn to come. And to make time pass more quickly was a feat of the mind. Torment let the noise seep right through her. Her Wronged and Rotting would hold out, or they would not, and her life would end. Either way, she accepted her fate. And she felt a breeze dance across her bloodstained skin. The magpie's skull grew warmer in her hand.

How many spirits do you want me to slaughter in your stead just so you can slightly prolong your miserable existence?

'You're not slaughtering them, you powdered old bat,' she replied with a sad smile, keeping her eyes closed. 'They're past that. You are, however, putting them into an unfortunate state of disrepair, which I very much hope can be remedied.'

A pleasant warmth flowed from the skull that lay in Torment's lap, restoring some much-appreciated strength to the battered body of her spirit. She opened her eyes. The noise of the fray came back to her, but the scene had changed. The remains of her undead subjects had amassed into an impressive mound of obliterated bodies, filling the ring of mangroves so high that she could not see the treetops beyond. It was an almost homogenous mass of dead flesh, with bits of it twitching here and there. Atop it, the vampire was wrenching itself free from the grip of something half buried in the rotting rubble. And everything seemed brighter, dark grey giving way to browns and sickly yellows and even hints of healthy green on the trees.

Torment noticed that where she sat cross-legged, a wind had swept away the dust to reveal a floor of smooth gold, slightly curved. If this was her mind palace as she knew it, and she was now sitting on its highest point above her Hall of Reverence, then this must be her mind's representation of the sunthread as it arched above it – the golden band to follow and find the Crow All-Mother.

A ray of light from the skull on her lap was reflected off the golden surface, casting a cone of soft light.

She looked up to see the vampire circling over her like a vulture now, hesitant to descend. The light unnerved it. The tide was turning.

Torment grabbed the skull with both hands and held it out in front of her. A glaring beam of yellow light sliced through the mist before her. She rose to point it upwards, using it like a lantern or a blade of light to cut this beast from her sky.

Its scream carried through the void as it wound around the shaft of light, panicked, darting this way and that, degraded from hunter to hunted. Where the ray intersected with its wings, Torment thought she saw it leave blackened holes. And those holes seemed slow to heal.

She could harm it, perhaps kill it. Or maybe it would be enough now to simply don the skull and return to the waking world and just bask in the sun until this thing was burned out of her. But what if the beast only retreated into some dark corner to terrorise her again come nightfall?

No. Torment had to end it there and then.

The vampire picked up speed, flickering through the sky more than flying, appearing here and there as if from nowhere. It showed no signs of exhaustion. It was no longer playing with its prey; it was fighting a lethal foe. Meanwhile, Torment, spinning on her golden plinth that shone through the dirt, felt her arms grow heavier. Had she triumphed too soon? They could play this game until the sun went down in the waking world, or even a cloud passed before it, and the beast would fall upon her to complete its bloody work.

It found its opening much sooner, seizing a moment when Torment had lost sight of it and searched the skies, frantically waving the light around.

Got you.

Clawed hands grabbed her wrists from behind, bending her wing arms backwards. The bird's skull hung in her right hand, its light directed uselessly at the twisted tree trunks. Teeth touched her neck, a hundred ice-cold needlepoints.

But she instinctively transformed again. The magpie's skull fell, as did her golden crown, hitting the ground with a clatter, and Torment shrank back into crow form, aflutter while the vampire clutched at empty, foggy air.

She flew in a tight arc and landed by the skull. Long, clawed fingers nearly struck her as she turned it over with her beak.

With a hiss, the striking hand recoiled, scorched, and the beam grazed the vampire's face. It sliced off one of its pointed ears, melting its alabaster skin into a charred slurry.

Its wail of agony ripped through Torment like a saw blade. She squawked and floundered on the ground, colours flashing before her eyes.

Yet she caught sight of her enemy retreating like a wounded animal, shrieking and hissing. Its dazzling, disorientated speed whipped it this way and that, crashing into the towering pile of dismembered corpses, scattering them, then slamming into a tree, splintering its trunk. As Torment scrambled to her shaky feet, she watched the burnt beast tumble through the mangrove roots and out into the swamp.

The vampire had fled her mind palace.

And she was still alive.

Chapter 24

AN AIR OF RENEWAL

TORMENT HAD NOT yet found it within herself to close the portals or return to her body. She sat on the patch of gold and savoured feeling absolutely nothing for a while. That her enemy might not remain defeated for long, that it might heal somewhere and return to take revenge, only occurred to her after a long period of respite – a wonderful lull during which nothing occurred to her whatsoever.

The wind continued to dance around her, tickling her feathers, rustling the mangrove leaves and blowing away layer after layer of grey dust. She watched it unearth the golden band beneath her in slow motion. She appeared to be sitting on the very end of it upon a small platform, the perfect size to build a nest. There was indeed a magnificent crow to be found at the end of this thing after all. Torment chuckled. The mythical force she had once believed to be out there, that she had pined for, elusive and grander than she could ever be … it had never been about finding it. It had always been about finding she had had it all along. She was a part of everything. Ephemeral yet real. She was the dream of a city filled with memories of murder, of meadows on the clouds and of compassion for the lingering dead. She was the idea of being a bird named Torment who had learned to carry pain until it eased, to hurt and be hurt and to forgive either.

She was not, in fact, afraid of the monster coming back. Every further second she spent at peace with herself, she felt more powerful yet. Nothing would ever challenge her in her own mind palace again. And there …

The sun's rays from the magpie's skull had been shimmering through the wavering mist for what must have been hours. And the sky had turned from the colour of midnight to a deep, dark indigo. The sun was no longer a gaping black void in the sky but a rusty crimson orb. There were swirls on it, little eddies like a churning pond of liquid fire waking from a slumber. The light of the sun in the waking world slowly rekindled the one in her mind. Torment nipped at the skull a little, pushing it with her talons to direct the beam straight at the sun.

It wasn't long before it erupted into the white, blinding beacon it was meant to be, outshining all the stars with a sky of perfect blue and sending a wave of warmth across the grey wasteland. A gust of wind followed, revealing patches of dried stalks here and there, which immediately turned to lush green grass. Making grass grow in the desert was, after all, one of Torment's first tricks. If anything, the daylight only rendered the scene more unreal. Neither the scattered dead, nor those oddly shaped swamp trees, nor that dismal grey dust were meant to be observed in the absence of mist and shadow.

'This place could do with a wee bit of dusting, mind you.'

Torment recognised the grouchy voice at once. It was the sound of scratching on tree bark, with a hint of murmuring creek rapids. She turned to its source and saw the old witch coming towards her from among the twisted roots of one of the mangroves. This time she was wearing a different, more colourful and decorative robe. Violet wrinkled her nose and brushed the end of her gnarled staff over the blanket of grey dust that still filled Torment's mind palace.

'Good to see you too,' Torment crowed, sincere happiness filling her heart. 'How long have you been standing there? Have you been watching me fight this thing the whole time?'

'That wretched old leech whose trail I've just followed to your front porch? No, Torment.' She pointed her staff at the bizarre mountain of chopped-up corpses. 'And it looks more like these poor buggers did all the hard work, like.'

'I suppose they did.' Torment rose to her feet and fluttered over to the mound. She tugged at a protruding finger with her beak, triggering a small avalanche of body parts, which she quickly evaded. 'You don't happen to know how to patch them up again, do you?'

The old woman with the copper-coloured mane looked down at her sternly, leaning on her stick. 'As a matter of fact, I do. And' – she gave her a prod with the staff – 'you well and truly are a crow. Although – not *just* a crow.'

'Enough with the staff,' croaked Torment. 'You're a guest here. And yes. It's called a *homunculus*.'

'I understand that's what you were.' She studied Torment long and keenly. 'You're … something else now.'

'And what would that be?'

'Don't know. Something I never encountered before.'

'Well, you're a hermit living at the edge of the world, so …'

'Only for the last couple of centuries, you cocky little corvid. And for solid reasons. Reasons you will soon come to know.'

The crone gave a grave impression.

384

'So … I gather this is no social call.'

'No, Torment. You've let loose something vile upon the world. It's not at all in favour of Lilith's plans.'

'Lilith's plans,' Torment repeated. After all she had been through, this woman came in here and *chided* her? 'Look, I have the greatest gratitude and respect for you, Violet. That said' – Torment flew up to the knot at the top of Violet's staff and continued at eye level – 'I don't know this Lilith person, and believe me when I say that recent events have made me sceptical of powerful individuals with "plans". Besides, I was more than willing to sacrifice myself to destroy the vampire, but it was beak to beak and it escaped by a feather's breadth, and I'm not going to eat crow after giving it my all, you presumptuous old hag.'

Violet squinted and took a deep breath. 'Done?'

'Yes, I …' Torment averted her gaze and plucked at her feathers in mild embarrassment. 'I take back that last bit, though. I was crowing myself into a rage.'

The woman huffed and kept squinting at Torment. But then she winked. 'Ah, never mind. I gave up being easily offended millennia ago. Too tedious.' Violet gave her a wrinkly smirk. 'If you didn't have so many feathers on your ears, you might have noticed I didn't say anyone was blaming you.'

'I see. Seems I'm the presumptuous one, then.' Torment tilted her head. 'But if you're not here to punish me and you're not here to check in on a friend … that must mean that you *need* me.'

'Don't strain your ego, lass. But you're certainly … promising. And yes, I would like to offer you a partnership.'

'Partnership? Know that I've also grown sceptical of *binding relationships* with powerful individuals.'

'I wouldn't have it any other way.' She lifted a knobbly old finger and tapped it on Torment's beak. 'But we could start with *friendship*, couldn't we? Moreover, I think you'll like my little wood.'

That did sound tempting. Torment recalled the wonderful grove in the desert. And that must have just been a fraction of it.

'That must be a long flight.'

'True, but we could get better acquainted along the way.' She nodded to the mangroves from which she had come. 'You seem to have picked up new tricks quite quickly. I don't reckon you have anything to do with the untimely demise of the giant toad whose palace you currently occupy, have you?'

'Oh, that story has everything to do with the mess you see around us,' Torment crowed. 'And I'd like to tell it to you, truly.' She wrestled with herself for one more moment, but she was obviously too curious not to at least give it a peek. 'And I guess the good company can't hurt.'

TORMENT WAS OVERJOYED that she was not alone. She had a friend now, one that had not been forced upon her, and one she could see whenever she wanted. Violet had even helped her clean up her mind palace, which had been in a 'real feckin' hames', and Torment was very grateful. She had not yet held court in the Mellow Marshes, but she had once had an awkward run-in with Sir Felix, the frog-headed knight, who seemed none too happy with his new liege. A problem for another time. She was a spirit of both worlds, after all, and most of her subjects were still recovering anyway. And today was a clear and sunny day, with warm winds carrying her like a balmy cushion of air. The thick and tangible air of the waking world, and awake she was! More so than ever. Flying nearby, she spotted a messenger crow with a tiny capsule tied to its talons. Torment tilted slightly to the side to glide in its direction.

'Hey, crony. Those kind words you're carrying?' she cawed. 'A love letter, perhaps?'

It gave a sceptical flick of its head, as crows were wont to do, and understood not a word of what Torment was saying. Nor, of course, did it understand any of the words it carried. It was a perfectly normal crow, after all, and cared little for anything but the wind in its feathers. What a dreadfully dreary bliss that must be.

'Oh, never mind,' Torment crowed. 'You're probably looking forward to a juicy piece of meat and I'm just stressing you out. I'll leave you to it.'

And she strained her wings to lift herself a little higher. She would not make it as high as the clouds. Here in the waking world, there were no meadows to be found there anyway. But that didn't mean she shouldn't try. Torment watched the sunthread that stretched so evenly across the sky. It was her guiding light. 'Follow the sunthread after noon, heading for dusk,' Violet had said, 'and you'll be right on track, so you will. As the crow flies.' There was surely no Crow All-Mother to be found at the end of it either, but a friendly old witch to take her in seemed a good enough alternative.

The model of the sunthread in Torment's mind palace, the one of literal gold that arched over her Hall of Reverence, was even home to the little scurrying lizards she so liked to hunt. They didn't provide sustenance, what with them being only in her head and all, but they gave her delight. Torment had even moved her Hall of the Conscious Mind to the platform at the end of the golden band. It was perhaps a little pompous to lean so heavily on this idea that she herself had turned out to be the venerable crow she had always dreamed of being, but … that was precisely the way it was.

Below – so tiny, yet endless – the One City glided by. Only now she knew it was not, in fact, endless. Somewhere far away, there were fields and forests and even a strange big thing called 'the sea'. By Violet's calculations, Torment would reach the edge of the city before winter if she kept flying straight, the weather held out, and she kept finding enough food to keep her strength up. It had turned out that being more than a hundred times smarter than a common crow helped a lot in that regard. She didn't even need half her intellect to open windows and break into larders.

Convincing peasants that she was an evil spirit who could only be appeased by offerings of their finest cooking ... well, that was a different game altogether. Very rewarding, often with further benefits, but also a bit wicked. She didn't do it too often. Not when she could also be kind and exchange knowledge and services – like messenger flights – for hospitality. At least as long as fear and superstition didn't spoil the deal. Apparently, crows were widely regarded as bearers of ill omens, to which Torment took great affront, due to her personal history.

Otherwise, she enjoyed talking to people. Here and there she heard rumours of an epidemic of nightmares that had even left some people dead in their beds. Torment was all too familiar with the beast described by the afflicted. She knew better now than to judge this tragic circumstance her fault. But still, it was a wrong she wished quite dearly to right, and she could see more difficult times lying ahead, but with Violet by her side, that thought seemed almost comforting.

She was always careful to make a good impression on the humans, to dispel her kind's bad reputation. She may have dark wings, and she once had a dark purpose too, but whatever omens she bore, she made sure they'd be good.

She was a crow named Torment who always tried to be kind, and she held bright hopes and great ambitions.

ACKNOWLEDGMENTS

First of all, thank you to *you*! Yes, you, for reading this far. Thanks for sticking with it. (Assuming you didn't skip to the acknowledgments without finishing the novel – in which case, who does that?) I'm rather proud of myself for having written and published a book, but it would all have been pretty pointless without you. You're the star of this show. Books are for readers, and without you this would all have been an embarrassing waste of time, and I appreciate your time and your attention so much, you don't even know. I hope you enjoyed Torment's journey and will keep an eye out for what I'm putting out next, but either way … you're the best. No, take it. It's true. I love you. Thank you so much!

But further thanks are due to a number of wonderful beings:

To my loves, Sara and Ari. As with many books, this one has tested the patience and forbearance of those who have to live with an obsessive, often absent daydreamer.

To my parents, for the invaluable gift of reason, for nurturing my curiosity and creativity, for being role models of kindness and moral integrity, and for the many other privileges of having been raised by them, without which the creation of this book and all those to follow would have been far less likely.

To Hernán Conde de Boeck, who brought this story to life with the beautiful, eerie and whimsical art that graces not only the cover of this book and elevates it to a whole different level of style.

To my editor, Catherine Dunn, who understood exactly what I was going for and made it so that you can read this thing, *and* understand what's going on, *all while not* rolling your eyes at my attempts at sounding old-fashioned and gothic. In particular, I thank her for her patience and understanding of my glaring inexperience, not just in the writing department, but also in predicting word counts and meeting deadlines. As a young author self-publishing my dark fantasy debut, I couldn't have asked for a smoother editing experience.

To everyone who has read, discussed and hung out on the Author's Arcanum and Worldsmyths Discord Servers.

(Bear with me, I'm almost done!)

To Hannah, Chris and Deven, whose honest feedback, impeccable taste, stunning good looks and weekly writerly support are essential in my commitment to this madness of wanting to tell hundreds of thousands of words-long pretty lies for a living.

And finally – in some cases posthumously – I want to thank Lewis Carroll, Lyman Frank Baum, Edgar Allan Poe, Mary Shelley, Bram Stoker, Terry Pratchett, Michael Moorcock, Richard Bach, Otfried Preußler and Walter Moers (among others, but this section must end at some point) for having inspired this work.

And that's it. You stuck around until the credits finished rolling. You're one of those people, apparently. But this isn't a Marvel movie, so, alas, there isn't a post-credits scene. The book just ends here.

Milton Keynes UK
Ingram Content Group UK Ltd.
UKHW041849230924
448765UK00013B/246/J